DAMSELS IN DISTRESS

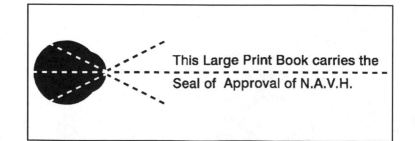

This Large Print Book carries the
Seal of Approval of N.A.V.H.

DAMSELS IN DISTRESS

JOAN HESS

WHEELER PUBLISHING

An imprint of Thomson Gale, a part of The Thomson Corporation

THOMSON

™

GALE

Detroit • New York • San Francisco • New Haven, Conn. • Waterville, Maine • London

THOMSON

GALE

LIBRARY OF CONGRESS CATALOGING-IN-PUBLICATION DATA

Hess, Joan.
    Damsels in distress / by Joan Hess.
      p. cm. — (A Claire Malloy mystery)
    ISBN-13: 978-1-59722-533-5 (alk. paper)
    ISBN-10: 1-59722-533-9 (alk. paper)
    1. Malloy, Claire (Fictitious character) — Fiction. 2. Women booksellers — Fiction. 3. Fairs — Fiction. 4. Arkansas — Fiction. 5. Large type books. I. Title.
PS3558.E79785D35 2007b
813'.54—dc22
                                       2007013735

Published in 2007 by arrangement with St. Martin's Press LLC.

Printed in the United States of America on permanent paper
10 9 8 7 6 5 4 3 2 1

For my new King family:
Janet, Reggie, Lauren, Jeremy,
and (of course) Becca

CHAPTER ONE

"Good morrow, Kate; for that is your name, I hear."

I blinked at the young man in the doorway. "Well have you heard, but something hard of hearing. They call me Claire Malloy that do talk of me."

"You lie, in faith; for you are call'd plain Kate, and bonny Kate, and sometimes Kate the curst; but Kate, the prettiest Kate in Farberville. Kate of Kate Hall, my super-dainty Kate, for dainties are all Kates, and therefore —"

"Mother," Caron said as she came out of my office, "who is This Person?"

"I have no idea," I admitted.

The peculiar man came into the bookstore and bowed, one arm across his waist and the other artfully posed above his head. He was dressed in a white shirt with billowy sleeves, a fringed leather tunic, purple tights, suede boots with curled toes, and a

7

diamond-patterned conical cap topped with a tiny bell. His brown hair dangled to his shoulders, rare among the traditionally minded Farber College students. "Perchance miladies will allow me to maketh known myself?"

"This milady thinks you ought to maketh known thyself to the local police," Caron said, edging toward me. "Start with the Sheriff of Nottingham."

He stood up and swept off his cap. "Pester the Jester, or Edward Cobbinwood, if it pleaseth you all the more."

"Not especially," I said. "Would you care to explain further?"

"Okay, I'm a grad student at the college and a member of ARSE. I was assigned to talk to all the merchants at the mall and on Thurber Street about the Renaissance Fair in two weeks. We'd like to put up fliers in the store windows and maybe some banners. Fiona is hoping you'll let us use the portico in front of your bookstore for a stage to publicize the event."

"A Renaissance Fair? I haven't heard anything about this." I noticed Caron's sharp intake of breath and glanced at her. "Have you?"

She nodded. "I was going to tell you about it when you got home this evening. The AP

8

history teacher sent a letter to everybody who's taking her course in the fall. We have to either participate in this fair thing or write a really ghastly midterm paper. I don't think she should be allowed to blackmail us like this. Inez and I are going to get up a petition and have everybody sign it, then take it to the school board. I mean, summer is supposed to be our vacation, not —"

"I get your point," I said.

"Look not so gloomy, my fair and freckled damsel," added Edward Cobbinwood. "It'll be fun. We put on a couple of Ren Fairs when I was in undergraduate school. It's like a big costume party, with all kinds of entertainment and food. ARSE will stage battles, and perhaps a gallant knight in shining armor will fight for your honor."

Caron glared at him. "I am perfectly capable of defending my honor without the help of some guy dressed in rusty hubcaps."

"What's ARSE?" I asked.

"The Association for Renaissance Scholarship and Enlightenment. It's not a bunch of academics who meet once a year to read dry papers and argue about royal lineage or the feudal system. Anybody can join. The country is divided into kingdoms, counties, and fiefdoms. The local group is Avalon. There are just a few members in town this

9

summer, but when the semester starts in September, Fiona says —"

"Fiona Thackery," Caron said with a sigh, not yet willing to allow me to dismiss her imminent martyrdom. "The AP history teacher. I'm thinking about taking shop instead. I've always wanted to get my hands on a nail gun. Or if I take auto mechanics, I'll learn to change tires and . . . tighten bolts and stuff like that. That way, when your car falls into a gazillion bits, I'll know how to put it back together. That's a lot more useful than memorizing the kings of England or the dates of the Napoleonic Wars."

"You're taking AP history," I said. "If you want to work at a garage on the weekends, that's fine with me."

She gave me a petulant look. "Then you can write the midterm paper: 'Compare and contrast the concepts of Hellenism and Hebraism in *The Divine Comedy* and *The Canterbury Tales*. Cite examples and footnote all source material. Five-thousand-word minimum. Any attempt at plagiarism from the Internet or elsewhere will result in a shaved head and six weeks in the stocks.' "

I cupped my hand to my ear. "Do I hear the lilting melody of 'Greensleeves' in the distance?"

"The only recorder I'm playing," Caron said sourly, "will have a tape in it."

Edward seemed to be enjoying the exchange, but fluttered his fingers and strolled out of the Book Depot to bewilder and beguile other merchants along the street. He must have had a recorder tucked in his pocket, because we could hear tootling as he headed up the hill. It may have been "Greensleeves," but it was hard to be sure. I hoped he wasn't a music major.

"Goodness gracious," said Inez Thornton as she came into the bookstore. Her eyes were round behind her thick lenses. "Did you see that weirdo in the purple tights?"

Inez has always been Caron's best friend through thick and thin (aka high crimes and misdemeanors). Caron, red-haired and obstinate, faster than a speeding bullet except when her alarm clock goes off in the morning, able to leap over logic in a single bound, is the dominant force. Meek, myopic Inez is but a pale understudy in Caron's pageant, but equally devious. Encroaching maturity tempers them at times. There are, of course, many other times.

"Tell me more about the letter from your history teacher," I said.

Caron grimaced. "This Renaissance Fair sounds so juvenile. Everybody has to dress

11

up as something and go around pretending to be a minstrel or a damsel or a pirate or something silly like that. There's a meeting tomorrow afternoon at the high school so we can get our committee assignments. It's like Miss Thackery thinks we're already in her class. She shouldn't be allowed to get away with this. It's — it's unconstitutional!"

"That's right," said Inez, nodding emphatically. "Aren't we guaranteed life, liberty, and the pursuit of happiness?"

"I'm not sure reading Chaucer and Dante will make you all that happy, but you never know," I said. "You'll find copies on the back shelf. Help yourselves."

Rather than take me up on my generous offer, they left. I would have felt a twinge of maternal sympathy had they not been muttering for more than a month about how bored they were. I'd never been to a Renaissance Fair, but I supposed it was similar to a carnival show, with tents, booths, and entertainment — not to mention men clad in armor made of aluminum foil, bashing each other with padded sticks.

Pester the Jester did not reappear, to my relief. I've always been leery of men in tights, especially purple ones (tights, not men). The few customers who drifted in were dressed in standard summer wear and more interested in paperback thrillers and travel books than in Shakespeare. Business is sluggish in the summer, when most of the college students have gone home and their professors are either wandering through cavernous cathedrals in Europe or sifting sand at archeological digs. The academic community as a whole comprises nearly a quarter of Farberville's population of twenty-five thousand semiliterate souls. Their civilian counterparts tend to do their shopping at the air-conditioned mall at the edge of town when the temperature begins to climb.

At six I locked the doors and went across the street to the beer garden to meet Luanne Bradshaw, who owns a vintage clothing shop on Thurber Street. It could have been a hobby, not a livelihood, since she not only comes from a wealthy family on the East Coast but also divorced a successful doctor and left him barefoot in the park — or, at least, penniless in the penthouse. However, she chose to rid herself of most of her ill-gotten gains via trusts and foundations, dumped her offspring on the doorsteps of prestigious prep schools, and headed for the hinterlands. Farberville definitely falls into that category. Despite being in the throes of a midlife crisis that may well continue until she's ninety, she's disarmingly astute.

She was seated at a picnic table beneath a wisteria-entwined lattice that provided shade and a pleasant redolence. Her long, tanned legs were clearly visible in scandalously short shorts, and her black hair was tucked under a baseball cap. As I joined her, she filled a plastic cup with beer from a pitcher and set it down in front of me.

"You didn't mention Peter when you called earlier," she said by way of greeting. "Are you having prenuptial jitters? It's unbecoming in a woman of your age."

"My age is damn close to yours," I said, "and I'm not the one who scrambled all over the Andes with a bunch of virile young Australian men for six weeks."

"I kept claiming I needed to rest just so I could watch their darling butts wiggle as they hiked past me. So what's going on with Peter?"

"The captain sent him to FBI summer camp so he can learn how to protect our fair town if the terrorists attempt to create havoc by jamming the parking meters. It's a real threat, you know. The mayor will have to flee to his four-bedroom bunker out by the lake. The Kiwanis Club won't be able to have its weekly luncheon meetings at the diner behind the courthouse. The community theater won't be able to stage its endearingly inept production of *Our Town* for the first time in nineteen years. All hell could break loose."

Luanne failed to look properly terrified. "How long will he be gone?"

"Two weeks at Quantico, and then a week at his mother's."

"Oh," she murmured.

I took a long swallow of beer. "It's not like that. She's resigned to the idea that Peter and I are getting married, or so he keeps telling me."

"But she's not coming to the wedding."

"No, she's not," I said. "She always goes to Aspen in September to avoid the hurricane season."

"Rhode Island is hardly a magnet for hurricanes, but neither is Farberville," Luanne said as she refilled her cup and mine.

"It's a tradition. She goes with a big group of her widowed friends. They take over a very posh condo complex and party all day and night. Besides, it's not as if this is Peter's first marriage — or mine. I'd look pretty silly in a flouncy white dress and veil, with my teenaged daughter as maid of honor. There's no reason why she should disrupt her long-standing plans for a simple

15

little civil ceremony in a backyard."

"She's probably afraid she'll have to eat ribs," said Luanne, "and toast the happy couple with moonshine in a jelly jar. Have you spoken to her on the phone, or received a warm letter on her discreetly mono- grammed stationery?"

The topic was not amusing me. "Not yet. Peter thinks we ought to give her some time to get used to the idea, and then go for a visit. Will you loan me a pair of jodhpurs?"

"Yes, but they'll make your thighs look fat."

I brooded for a moment, then said, "Did you happen to encounter Pester the Jester this afternoon?"

"Oh, my, yes. I couldn't take my eyes off his codpiece."

I told her about the letters Caron and Inez had received from the history teacher. "They're appalled, of course, and were rambling about their constitutional right to spend the summer sulking. I didn't have the heart to remind them that they'd already had their fifteen minutes of fame a month ago, when they were interviewed by the media after that unfortunate business with the disappearing corpse."

"Fame is fleeting," Luanne said.

We pondered this philosophical twaddle

while we emptied our cups. The remaining beer in the pitcher was getting warm, and a group of noisy college kids arrived to take possession of a nearby picnic table. I told Luanne I'd call her later in the week, then walked the few blocks to my apartment on the second floor of a duplex across the street from the campus lawn. A note on the kitchen table informed me that Caron and Inez had gone out for burgers with a few of their friends. It was just as well, since my culinary interests were limited to boiling water for tea and nuking frozen entrées. In the mood for neither, I settled down on the sofa to read. I hoped Peter would call, but as it grew dark outside I gave up and consoled myself with images of him on the firing range, learning how to take down grannies with radioactive dentures and toddlers with teddy bears packed with explosives. Or librarians and booksellers who refused to turn in their patrons' reading preferences to cloak-and-dagger government agencies.

What I did not want to think about was the wedding, scheduled for early September. Not because I was having second thoughts, mind you. I was confident that I loved Peter and that we would do quite nicely when we rode off into the sunset of domestic bliss, which would include not only more opportunities for adult behavior of a most delectable sort, but also lazy Sunday mornings with coffee, muffins, and *The New York Times,* and occasional squabbles over the relative merits of endive versus romaine. He'd been suggesting matrimonial entanglement for several years, and I'd given it serious consideration. But after my first husband's untimely and very unseemly death, I'd struggled to regain my self-esteem and establish my independence. I hadn't done too well on the material aspects, as Caron pointed out on a regular basis. However, the Book Depot was still in business, and we lived on the agreeable side of genteel poverty.

A distressingly close call with mortality had led me to reassess my situation. The emotional barrier I'd constructed to protect myself collapsed during a convoluted moment when a hit man had impolitely threatened to blow my brains out (not in those exact words, but that was the gist of the message). If commitment meant sharing a closet, then so be it.

The problem lay in my inclinations to meddle in what Lieutenant Peter Rosen felt was official police business. It wasn't simply a compulsion to outsleuth Miss Marple. In

all the situations I'd found myself questioning witnesses and snooping around crime
scenes, I'd never once done so for my
personal satisfaction — or to make fools of
the local constabulary. It just happened. Peter, with his molasses-brown eyes, curly
hair, perfect teeth, and undeniable charm,
never quite saw it that way. He'd lectured
me, had my car impounded twice, threatened me with a jail cell, and attempted to
keep me under house arrest. One had to
admire his optimism.

I was going to have to sacrifice my pursuit
of justice in order to maintain domestic
tranquility, I thought with a sigh. Somewhere buried within the male psyche is a
genetic disposition to drag home the carcass
of a woolly mammoth to display to the tribe.
Women, quite clearly, are above that sort of
thing. We only desire to tidy things up.

I tried to return to my novel, but the
specter of the wedding still loomed. The
ceremony itself would be low-key and
aesthetically appropriate. Jorgeson, Peter's
partner, had offered us the use of his
garden. Luanne had insisted on handling
the reception food and drink. I would, when
I had the wherewithal, purchase a modest
dress at the mall. Peter would no doubt
wear one of his Armani suits. Caron was

the designated maid of honor. She'd been unenthusiastic about the upcoming event, ambivalent at best, but a few weeks earlier she and Peter had gone off for a long lunch, and she'd come home in a suspiciously elated mood. Neither of them would elaborate on the negotiations.

It wasn't as though we were going to be married in a church amid all the pomp and piety, but I have an aversion to any kind of formal ceremony, especially one that obliges me to wear panty hose. I'd barely survived Caron's kindergarten graduation. Carlton and I had eloped, and ended up being married in a leaky chapel during a thunderstorm. The justice of the peace's wife had served chocolate chip cookies and flat ginger ale afterward. I remember the cookies better than I do the actual exchange of vows. Carlton must have, too, which would explain why he'd been in the company of a buxom college girl when his car collided with a chicken truck on a slippery mountain road. The college administration had done its best to hush up this particular detail, since liaisons between instructors and students were a big no-no. When a local writer threatened to expose the tawdry business, along with several other skeletons in the faculty lounge closet, she'd been conveniently silenced. I'd been high on Detective Rosen's list of suspects, which had not made for an auspicious inaugural relationship, although in retrospect, it had been flattering.

I resolved to stop fretting about the wedding, at least for the rest of the evening, and gave my attention to Lady Cashmere's stolen jewels and the mysterious light in the chapel.

The following morning I was perusing the fall reading lists from the area junior highs and high schools. Nothing was remotely controversial, indicating the religious right had cinched in the good ol' Bible Belt another notch or two. Intellectual constipation was not too far in the future. I'd gone into my tiny office to hunt up some catalogs and start calculating orders when the bell above the door jangled.

I went back into the front room, my fingers crossed that Pester the Jester was not coming back to further annoy me. A couple were waiting for me. The woman had short dark hair, a flawless complexion, and large, wide-set eyes that were already appraising me. The tiny wrinkle between her eyebrows suggested that she was less than impressed. Although she appeared to be no more than thirty years old, her white blouse and gray skirt gave her the serious demeanor of an executive assistant or a bureaucrat. That, and the briefcase she was carrying.

"Mrs. Malloy?" she said, daring me to deny it.

I chose not to be intimidated despite the mess on the counter and the cobwebs dangling from the rafters. The original structure of the Book Depot dated back to the days when passenger and freight trains had been vital to a burgeoning rural town. I still relied on an antiquated boiler for what heat I could coax out of it. Many of the cockroaches I encountered daily were likely to be nonagenarians, and some of the mice had gray whiskers. "May I help you?"

"I'm Fiona Thackery, the history teacher at the high school. I believe your daughter is taking my AP class in the fall." I nodded warily. "I'm sure she'll do fine," the woman continued. "I'm here to talk to you about the Renaissance Fair in two weeks. I realize this is short notice, but the idea came to me while I was on vacation after the semester ended. I attended one, and thought it would be a wonderful project. My students will have the opportunity to make history come alive, not only for themselves but also for all the children and the community. Profits will go to Safe Haven, the battered-women's shelter. I do hope you'll add your support."

"I'm pretty busy these days," I said, unmoved by her slick sales pitch.

Her consort cleared his throat. He was perhaps a bit older than she, but two inches shorter and significantly less polished. His face, pudgy and pale, was marred by the remnants of acne, and his hair looked as though he'd cut it himself — in the dark. He was wearing wrinkled slacks, a short-sleeved white dress shirt, and a bow tie. He reminded me of a suburban missionary. "I'm . . . ah, Julius Valens. I teach in the drama department at the college. Well, I don't teach acting or anything like that. My area is set construction, lights, technical stuff."

"Thank you, Julius," said Fiona. "I'm sure Mrs. Malloy appreciates knowing your field of expertise." She took a file out of her briefcase and handed it to me. "This is the schedule of events during the fair. I've included a copy of the information I'll be handing out to the students this afternoon, which will explain in more detail the various booths, concessions, and staged presentations over the two days. Members of ARSE will participate. Are you familiar with the organization?"

"Oh, yes," I said, "purple tights and all."

She frowned. "Not all of us are fools, Mrs. Malloy. I've only been a member for a year, but I've encountered very few court jesters. Most of the men prefer to wear the garb of knights and royalty. Our fiefdom is honored to be under the leadership of the Duke and Duchess of Glenbarrens. They've offered their farm for the fair. I'd planned on holding it at the high school or even on the college campus, but we can generate more profits with the sale of ales and mead. Please let me assure you that none of the students will have anything to do with the alcoholic beverages, and any of them caught indulging will be punished."

"Were thumbscrews in use during the Renaissance?" I asked.

"I'll look into it," she said with her first attempt at a smile. It softened her face and gave her a faint glow. I realized she was quite pretty, if not a classic beauty. Julius seemed to agree with me; he was gazing at her with unabashed adoration. Ignoring him, she added, "Now what we'd like to do is stage a few short events in front of your store in order to create curiosity and start selling advance tickets. It won't be the least bit inconvenient for you. Julius will hang a few banners and set up the sound equipment. There will be sword fights, musical presentations, and crafts demonstrations. I was thinking we could do this tomorrow and Friday this week, and Monday and Wednesday next week, for no more than an hour at a time."

I considered her proposal. "I don't want access to the store blocked. I'm certainly in favor of raising money for Safe Haven, but I can't risk losing sales."

Julius nodded. "We understand that, Mrs. Malloy. It'll take no more than half an hour to set up, and about the same when it's over. So two hours, altogether."

"And," Fiona said, "it will draw a huge crowd. You can feature books on the Renaissance in your window displays."

"Erasmus is always a bestseller in the summer."

"I'm sure he is. Julius, check for outlets for the sound equipment. I'll do some measuring outside so we'll be prepared to hang the flags and banners. Thank you for your cooperation, Mrs. Malloy. We'll see you tomorrow afternoon." She was taking a tape measure from her briefcase as she went out the door.

"I don't remember agreeing to this," I said to Julius as he began to crawl along the baseboard under the front windows.

"Fiona can be forceful, but she's usually right. Last year she had to go in front of the school board to get their approval to revamp the AP reading lists. This spring almost every student who took the test scored high enough to receive college credit."

"How long has she been teaching at the high school?" I asked.

Julius plopped down on his bottom and looked up at me. "Just three years. A year ago the AP teacher retired for what was euphemistically called 'personal reasons.' According to the gossip in the teachers' lounge, she was spiking her coffee with brandy every morning and nodding off during classes. Fiona anticipated the likelihood that the woman would be fired and began campaigning for the position. She's a fighter. She made it through college on academic scholarships, while working at the campus library and tutoring on the side. She has no patience with slackers."

"Is that so?" I said, beginning to wonder how Caron would fare in the history class. Her grades were always fine, but I'd been called in for more than my fair share of teacher-parent conferences over the years. She had her own file in the principal's office, and even the custodians greeted me by name. I realized Julius was waiting for me to say something. I opted to change the subject. "Are you a member of ARSE?"

"No, I mean not yet, but I'm going to join. I've been busy with the college productions all year, and I moonlight at several community theaters in the area. My assistants this year were more trouble than help; I couldn't trust them to do anything right. And Fiona can be demanding. She bought a little house as an investment, and I'm helping her fix it up whenever I have free time. We're engaged, but it's not official until I can save up enough for a ring. I'll be up for assistant professor soon, and I'm hoping to get a decent raise. Fiona enjoys teaching, but she'd really like to stay home and have children. She says she can put all her excess energy into volunteer work."

I had no hope of finding a subject that would not lead back to Fiona Thackery. "Well, good luck," I said lamely, then picked up the catalogs I'd dropped on the counter. "I'll be in my office if you have any questions."

Julius stood up and brushed off his dusty knees. "These outlets should be adequate, although the wiring is worn. I'll bring extra fuses, just in case."

"And I'll review my fire insurance policy, just in case," I said as I headed for my cramped office.

I held my breath until I heard him leave, then settled back with the reading lists, catalogs, and order forms to try to predict how many students would prefer to buy their books (and handy yellow study guides) from the Book Depot rather than the brightly lit, sanitized chain bookstores at the mall. If I understocked, I'd lose sales, but if I overstocked, I'd be forced to return unsold copies and lose favor with my distributors. The bookseller's version of Russian roulette.

Although I knew it was unreasonable to hope that Peter might have a moment to climb out of his hazmat suit and call me, I kept glancing at the telephone. It remained aloof. I ate a sandwich and a handful of limp carrot sticks, sold a gardening book to an elderly woman clutching an evil cat, and helped a newlywed find a cookbook for her first formal dinner party. At least I would never have to sweat over the consistency of hollandaise sauce or the presentation of raspberry mousse parfaits. Should the highly improbable specter of a dinner party loom, Peter understood the concept of caterers, having never seen his mother do more than pour tea. Other than that, any entertaining we did would involve a barbecue grill — and I would not be waving the tongs.

Late in the afternoon Caron and Inez came into the store. Their fatigued and slightly glazed looks suggested the meeting at the high school had not been brief. This time I did feel some sympathy for them, since I loathe meetings on principle. They exemplify the only legitimate reason for carrying concealed weapons.

"That bad?" I said.

Caron sat down on the stool. "Three hours' worth of 'That Bad,' " she said. "Rhonda Maguire would not shut up. She acted like her entire grade depended on convincing everybody how fascinated she was by this dumb fair. Even Miss Thackery was getting pissed off by Rhonda's incessant questions and comments. Half the class was dozing, the other half squirming like they needed to pee."

"Rhonda's knowledge of the Middle Ages is limited to Disney movies," added Inez. "King Arthur and the Seven Dwarfs meet Robin Hood and the Little Mermaid Marian. It was too pathetic."

"So what did you find out about your duties at the festivities?" I asked.

"We're on the concessions committee," Caron said, "but it's not as bad as it sounds.

Some woman from ARSE, Lanya or something, is in charge. We're going out to her farm to meet her tomorrow. Supposedly she's done this before and knows how to get all the food and drinks donated. We have to round up volunteers to work at the booths, but Miss Thackery said we can recruit from her other classes. If we can pull it off, we may not have to take a shift."

Inez nodded. "Yeah, but we have to make our own costumes. Peasant blouses and long skirts. Miss Thackery has a bunch of catalogs we can look through for ideas."

"That should be interesting," I said. "What about your classmates?"

"Carrie and Emily are in charge of the pony rides," Caron said, snickering. "They get to hold the ponies' leads and walk them in a circle. Around and around and around, all day long, trying not to step in piles of pony poop. Maybe we'll take them some lemonade in the middle of the afternoon."

"Louis Wilderberry and some of the other football players are going to be pirates," Inez contributed. "First they have to set up all the tents, stages, tables, and that sort of thing, but then they can spend the rest of the day promenading around, waving their cardboard cutlasses and singing sea chanties. Some of the kids who take band are going to learn to play lutes and recorders so they can be strolling minstrels."

"And Rhonda?" I said delicately.

"This is way funny," said Caron. "She and the other cheerleaders are going to be fairies. They have to wear green leotards, flimsy little skirts, pointy ears, glittery wings, and green makeup on their faces. You know, she looked a little green when Miss Thackery told her. They have to dance on one of the stages every hour, and spend the rest of the time painting kids' faces. Another woman from ARSE volunteered to be their dance instructor, so they have to go to her house to learn how to flutter. I can hardly wait."

"It doesn't sound that bad," I said.

Inez stared at me. "Would you like to dress up like a fairy in front of all your friends? She'll look like an escapee from a preschool production of *Peter Pan.*"

"Even Louis was snorting under his breath," added Caron. "C'mon, Inez. We'd better start calling potential concession workers. I for one am not going to peddle turkey legs and ice cream bars all day."

I watched them leave, then opened the file that Fiona Thackery had left on the counter. The Renaissance Fair would open at ten o'clock on a Saturday morning. Food and drink available included the aforementioned turkey legs, ice cream bars, and fresh lemonade, along with ale, mead, rum drinks (in honor of the pirates, I assumed), and sweets. Areas would be roped off for sword fighting and mud wrestling. At a safe distance, would-be Robin Hoods could test their skill at archery. Stage performances with dancers, magicians, musicians, and one-act plays would occur throughout the day.

On Saturday evening there would be a grand banquet presided over by the Duke and Duchess of Glenbarrens, with a feast and entertainment. Separate tickets required, limited seating, advance reservations suggested.

All in all, it seemed harmless.

CHAPTER TWO

The previous evening had passed uneventfully. Peter did not call, but his chances of getting through were negligible, since Caron and Inez had sequestered themselves in her bedroom with the telephone, bullying their fellow students into working at the Renaissance Fair. When they appeared periodically to make sandwiches and grab sodas, they'd seemed rather smug. I hadn't bothered asking for a progress report.

I spent the morning with paperwork, wondering why I'd ever thought that owning a bookstore meant reading books. The only ones I dealt with these days were ledgers, and my forays into fiction usually involved catalog copy and petty-spirited reviews. I sorted invoices by degrees of urgency, wrote enough checks to appease the wolves howling at the door, sent in my orders online (I hoped), then dumped the catalogs in a corner next to the boiler. Filing is not my forte.

Edward Cobbinwood ambled in while I was eating a late lunch and dashing off the crossword puzzle in the newspaper. He was dressed as he had been the day before, but was carrying a bulging backpack and a unicycle. "Good morrow, Mistress Malloy."

"Skip it," I said. "I gather Fiona has spoken to you?"

"It's really nice of you to let us use the portico." He looked around the store, which was sadly lacking in customers at that moment. "I guess things are better during the school year. This is a great little bookstore. I did my undergraduate work in Berkeley, and I always enjoyed hanging around stores like this."

"Like this?" I said. "Meaning what?"

His eyes flickered nervously while he struggled to come up with a tactful response. "Oh, I mean friendly, cozy, that sort of thing. Do you have events like poetry readings and signings?"

"The only authors who want to sign here sell their books from the trunks of their cars. The poetry crowd prefers to meet in places that sell beer and wine. I can sympathize with that." Since he showed no signs of leaving, I put down my pen and said, "Why did you decide to come here for grad work?"

"After twenty years, I was getting sick of the California frenzy and fruitcakes. That, and I was offered a full assistantship. I'm an art major, so I'll still be unemployable no matter where my degrees are from. What about you?"

"I made it halfway to a Ph.D. in English," I said. "The statute of limitations ran out on my dissertation before I ever got around to finishing it. No great loss to future generations of scholars of justly obscure British novelists."

Edward began to browse between the racks, but I could see the tip of his cap as it bobbled along like a primitive puppet. "I actually came here for another reason," he said so quietly I barely heard his voice. "It's kind of personal."

I winced. "Then I can understand why you wouldn't want to talk about it with a stranger. Are you looking for any book in particular?"

The cap bobbled back to the end of the rack and he came into view. "I don't consider you a stranger, Mrs. Malloy. You've been very kind to me."

"I'm sure I haven't, Edward," I said hastily. "I make every effort to be polite to customers, and I don't mind helping a good cause, but at heart I'm a cold-blooded, money-grubbing mercenary —"

"It's about my father."

I must admit that I was disconcerted. "What about your father, Edward?"

He pulled off his cap and began to wring it like a wet dish towel. "My father abandoned my mother as soon as she told him she was pregnant. She had no idea where he went, and he never made any effort to get in touch with her. Maybe he thought she'd get an abortion." He gave me a wry smile. "She didn't, obviously."

"Obviously," I said. I could think of only one reason why he was telling me this, and I really didn't want to hear it. I desperately tried to think of a delicate way to terminate the conversation. Clutching my throat and crumpling behind the counter seemed extreme. I crossed my fingers and prayed to any deity on duty that Fiona, Julius, and a battalion of knights would storm the bookstore, giving me a chance to escape into the office and out the back door. A short dash down the railroad tracks, an undignified scramble up to the street, two blocks, and then the sanctuary of my apartment and a stiff drink. Ten minutes, max.

"She didn't have any family members to help her out," Edward blithely continued, "so she had to drop out of school and get a full-time job. She's always been pretty bitter about that. She got married when I was six or seven to a nice guy, who adopted me and really tried to make it work, but he was killed during a drug deal. Things were pretty tough after that. Luckily, my grades were good enough to earn me a scholarship to Berkeley; otherwise, I would have had to settle for a community college in Oakland."

Clearly something was expected from me. As much as I wanted to jam his cap back on his head, congratulate him on his academic success, and usher him out the door, I realized that I was doomed to be regaled with the rest of his story. "What's the connection between your father and Farberville?"

"My mother didn't tell me the truth about him when I was a kid. Her story was that he was just somebody she'd met at a bar and slept with, that she never even knew his name. When I turned eighteen, she told me the real story. They'd lived together for a summer, so, of course, she knew his name and a few things about him. I think that she'd never tried to find out what happened to him, because if she ever found out, she'd do everything she could to destroy him."

"That's a long time to stay so angry."

"She had a lot of menial jobs. Ten years

ago she injured her back and had to go on permanent disability. We lost the apartment and slept in the van for almost a year before we could even get into public housing. We relied on food stamps and charity stores. Friends would occasionally slip her marijuana, since she couldn't afford pain medication. Other drugs, too. She drank cheap wine when she could get it. I was in and out of foster care. It was hardly the life she'd envisioned when she was young and quite beautiful." He came over to the counter and gazed intently at me. "After she told me his name, I started trying to track him down on the Internet. It took awhile, since he'd never done anything newsworthy. Eventually, I discovered that he'd moved here."

"And here you are," I said flatly. Flatly, because I had only minimal control of my face. I couldn't tell if I was grinning or grimacing; I hoped I wasn't drooling. My feet had turned to concrete. I was sure my organs had shut down, including my lungs, heart, and brain.

"And here I am," he agreed.

"Why are you telling me this?"

"I don't really know. I just wanted to share it, and you seem like the most obvious person."

"Me?" I clamped down on my lower lip

until I could trust myself not to start babbling or bawling. I stared at his face, searching for some resemblance to Carlton. None of Edward's standard features brought back any memories, but I was too distraught to be sure. His eyes were blue, granted, and his mouth was slightly wider than average. His teeth were not perfectly aligned, but this might be because of the expense of braces. There was a slightly smug arrogance that had been one of Carlton's less admirable characteristics, but such traits were more apt to be the product of nurture than of genetics. Carlton had boasted of previous relationships, but I had not asked for details. I would never have married him if I thought him capable of deserting a pregnant woman. Then again, I had never thought him capable of carrying on sleazy affairs with his own students — and I'd certainly gotten that one wrong. I felt a sudden urge to walk over to the cemetery, dig him up, and demand an explanation.

I finally took a deep breath and said, "What's your father's name?"

Edward shook the wrinkles out of his cap and put it back on his head. "Sorry, I shouldn't have said anything about it. I don't know what I'm going to do. It's kind of scary. Looking for his name on the Internet was a game with obscure clues to be followed. Lots of false leads and dead ends."

"You haven't made any effort to contact him since you arrived?" I didn't add that it might require a shovel or a séance.

"I guess I'm afraid to try. He doesn't even know I'm alive. Maybe he won't care, and just shrug or deny it. He's probably married with kids and a nice, respectable life. He'll see me as a threat and assume I want money from him to make up for all those years." Edward turned his back and pretended to study the covers of the paperbacks on the rack. "Even worse, he could be a nasty, alcoholic failure who'll expect me to help him out. Then again, he could be dead. That would mean I'd have to decide whether or not to approach his family."

"I might be able to help if you tell me his name," I said, aware that both of us might be on separate paths that converged in an emotional crisis.

"Thanks, Mrs. Malloy, but not yet. I'm going to stay low, check out the situation, and then decide what to do. I haven't had any experience in this situation."

"Very few of us have." Guilt kicked in with the severity of a thunderstorm, as if I in some obscure way was responsible for Carlton's . . . irresponsibility. Edward was only a few years older than Caron. My eyes began to sting. "I want you to know that you can always talk to me, Edward. I may not have any advice, but I'll listen."

He looked over his shoulder at me, his expression indecipherable, then disappeared behind the rack. I heard snuffling, and then a suggestion that he was blowing his nose. I waited silently, not at all sure what to expect. I was about to say something, although I had no idea what, when he said, "I'm surprised you've never heard of ARSE. The fiefdom's been around for ten years."

"I'm not into organizations."

He reappeared. "Forget about all that stuff I told you, okay? I'm just waiting for Julius. I told him I'd help with the sound system, even though about all I know how to do is mumble 'testing, testing,' into a microphone."

"Exactly what's planned for today?" I asked. "Should I be worried that some sort of anachronistic Renaissance rock band will be belting out the greatest hits from the fourteen hundreds? Christopher Columbus on lead guitar, with Niña, Pinta, and Santa Maria playing backup."

"I'm going to juggle and do hokey tricks, then there'll be a sword fight with steel weapons. Fiona will show up in garb to pass out fliers and sell admission and banquet tickets. We need to get enough cash to put deposits on the tents, chairs, tables, and whatever."

"There won't be any bloodshed, will there? I've never been good with stains."

"Just bruises and scratches. ARSE members aren't allowed to fight until they've completed a supervised training program. Off the battlefield, they're all friends, but they're competitive once they've put on helmets and mail armor."

"Made from soda can pop tops, I presume."

Edward looked appalled. "Milady underestimates the neurotic obsession of fierce ARSE knights. Some of them spend close to a thousand dollars for a helmet, mail shirt, coif, shield, sword, boots, and gauntlets — and that's just the basic equipment. It's heavy, too, as much as sixty or seventy pounds. Any fatalities in the summer are from heat stroke and dehydration." He waggled his head to make the bell on his hat jingle as he gave me an impish smile. "That's why I prefer to play the fool. I do it well, don't you think?"

"Quite well, from what I've seen thus far," I said. I tried to envision Carlton with an impish smile, but his had tended to be condescending. He'd certainly never allowed even a hint of a dimple. "I hope Farber College isn't too conservative for your taste. It certainly lacks the ambicnce of Berkeley. I've heard rumors that the male art majors wear ties to class."

"I'm not taking any classes until the fall semester. I moved here last week to — well, let's just say to check things out. I was lucky enough to find a cheap apartment close to the campus so I can use my bicycle."

"Bicycle or unicycle?"

"I'll have to see how bad the traffic is. The unicycle is a bit tipsy. Have you ever tried one?"

"Me?" I squeaked, beginning to retreat.

Edward grabbed my wrist. "Don't be a coward; it's not as hard as it looks. Let's go outside and I'll teach you. I promise that I won't let you fall." He began to pull me toward the front door. "C'mon, Claire. Can't you see yourself unicycling up the street to buy a cup of coffee?"

"I can see myself hobbling around on crutches for six months. No, thank you, Edward. I can barely ride a bicycle. I spent my formative years with scabs on my knees and elbows. When I was twelve, I collided with a parked car and nearly knocked out my front teeth. I never attempted to roller-skate. I can't look out a third-floor window without getting queasy."

He ignored my bleats of protest, and hung on to my wrist until we were in front of the store. A few pedestrians stopped to gawk at him, as well they should have. All I could do was hope that they were too blinded by his purple tights to notice me. The arrival of an ambulance — which seemed inevitable — would attract more attention.

He released me and fiddled with the unicycle, then leered at me for the benefit of his audience. "Come hither, Mistress Malloy."

"No, Edward. I'm not about to get on that contraption. My upstairs apartment is not wheelchair-accessible."

"Upon my soul, I promise I won't alloweth thee to fall," he said, widening his eyes as he dropped to one knee and held out his arms. "Doth thou not trust poor Pester the Jester?"

"No, but that's not the issue." I paused as I heard giggles from the audience, then lowered my voice to a whisper. "Why don't you teach me how to juggle?"

"Just try this first."

"Absolutely not!"

He stood up and thrust his hips forward to offer the audience a view of his codpiece.

"Mistress Malloy, art thou afeared of my toy? It doth not sting like a bee nor bite like an adder. Wilt thou not touch it?"

"Not with a ten-foot pole!" I snapped.

"My mistress knows it well," he countered, eliciting brays of laughter and whistles from the audience.

I was saved by the arrival of a van next to the portico. Julius climbed out and waved. "Hey, Edward, glad you're here. I had a helluva time loading the amps by myself. The darn things weigh a ton." He frowned at the crowd, then added, "Hello, Mrs. Malloy. How are you?"

"Just dandy," I said as I stepped around the unicycle and hurried into the store. Through the dusty windows, I watched them carry mysterious black equipment from the van to selected vantage points. Edward seemed quite strong for a man in pointy shoes and tights, but Julius was panting and his face was streaked with sweat when he came inside with a tangle of cords and began to plug them into the sockets. Edward remained outside, standing on a wobbly aluminum ladder to hang brightly colored triangular flags and a banner between the pillars that supported the tiled roof. It made for a very odd scene, I thought, hardly evocative of the fifteenth century. Sir Gawain and the Green Knight would not have known what to make of it.

Eventually Edward was given the opportunity to intone "testing, testing" into a microphone. His voice echoed down the weedy tracks like a phantom train from earlier decades. When the clinging and clanging started, I had a feeling the cacophony would be heard at the truck stops at the edges of town. The Farberville town council had enacted a sound ordinance several years ago after complaints about the live music in the beer garden on weekend nights. Fines could run high, based on the decibel number. The roars from the football stadium are tactfully overlooked, since the local economy thrives on the generosity of hordes of fans. The bars, restaurants, and motels, anyway. I usually close the Book Depot and stay home to avoid the inebriated drivers, and spend the following morning picking up litter and broken glass in the parking lot adjacent the store.

Reminding myself that I could simply unplug all the equipment should the tiles on the roof begin to rattle, I went to the rack of literary works read only under duress. I collected an armload of trade paperbacks, although I wasn't sure I could concoct a window display that would have the same appeal as the current collection of thrillers, celebrity memoirs, and romance novels. Recreational reading rarely includes such classics as Sir Thomas More's *Utopia* or Spenser's *Faerie Queene*. It was worth a shot, however, and if Peter didn't call, I could spend the evening twisting aluminum foil to make figurines of knights. Dressing dolls as duchesses and damsels would challenge my artistic capabilities, since I had not yet mastered the skill of threading a needle. Anything to avoid thinking about Edward's paternity issue.

The door banged open. I turned around, expecting to find Julius frantically fiddling with more miles of wires. Instead, I found myself gaping at a very large man clad in what appeared to be authentic armor, a helmet tucked under one arm. Very large, as in well over six feet tall. His wavy, dark hair was combed back, accenting his broad forehead and retreating hairline. He had a trimmed beard and mustache, and glittering eyes.

He looked less menacing as he grinned at me. "Milady."

"I gather you're one of the combatants?"

"The Duke of Glenbarrens, at your service." His sword clinked in its scabbard as he clumped into the bookstore.

"The squire of the shire?"

His grin widened. "Also known as Anderson Peru. In the mundane world, I'm a computer geek at a wholesale distributor in Waverly. With a mere keyboard stroke, I can create a shortage of toilet paper in Portland or send a truckload of snowblowers to Pensacola. You, Mrs. Malloy, are not what I expected. I've always assumed booksellers would resemble the ninety-year-old librarian at my high school. She was formidable, to put it nicely. You, on the other hand, are tall and willowy, with lovely skin, gossamer curls, and a mischievous glint in your emerald-green eyes. I would fall to my knees and confess undying adoration, but then you'd have to help me up and the mood would be shattered. One of the drawbacks to wearing armor."

"I suppose so," I said, nearly dropping the books. I sternly reminded myself I was well beyond the age of adolescent swoons, although I wouldn't have put it past Caron and Inez. He'd probably left his black stallion at home and driven up in a rusty Volkswagen Bug cluttered with fast food wrappers and crumpled beer cans, the glove compartment jammed with unpaid parking tickets. Picturing this was not enough to keep me from blushing, however, and my knees were decidedly unsteady. Before I further embarrassed myself, I cleared my throat and added, "I was told the Renaissance Fair is going to take place at your farm."

"I trust we'll have the pleasure of your winsome company. After the banquet, you and I can take a stroll and I'll show you the apiary. The scent of honey, the glittering stars, the moonlight catching sparkles of gold in your hair . . ."

Before I could come up with a response, a second knight stumbled into the bookstore, roaring incoherently and thrashing his arms. He crashed into Anderson, sending him flailing into a rack of fiction. It was hard to tell much about him, since he was wearing a helmet that covered his head and face. The two began to roll around, kicking and pummeling each other. The noise was worse than hail on a tin roof. Some of the invectives they hurled at each other were of a crude Anglo-Saxon nature, others more contemporary and concerned with lineage and procreative prowess. Both of them were guffawing like donkeys — or in this case, asses. All the while, books were being flung everywhere and other racks were increasingly imperiled. Edward came to the doorway and stared, but made no effort to intervene. I could not fault him when he went back outside.

"Stop it!" I shouted, doubting they could hear me over the escalating din. "Get out of here!" Kicking one of them would be gratifying, but a broken toe would be a nuisance. I finally settled for banging on them with the ledger and contributing some of my favorite Anglo-Saxon expletives.

Anderson pushed his assailant off him and looked up at me. "Oh, dear, we've upset you. Benny, cut it out or she'll come after you with a can opener."

The second knight, now identified as Benny, sat up and pulled off his helmet. His beard was wild and bushy, and his mustache hung down over his lips. His thick reddish orange hair stuck up in tufts. His face, like Anderson's, was red. "My apologies, milady," he said between gasps. "I haven't seen this smarmy bastard in three months."

I crossed my arms and waited as the two struggled to their feet. "If you have a dispute to settle, then take it outside. This is not Bosworth Field." I grimaced as I looked at the overturned rack and scattered books.

Anderson draped his arm over Benny's shoulder. "You'll have to forgive Sir Kenneth of Gweek. He can be overly exuberant."

"So I noticed," I said, unappeased.

"I'm sorry if I alarmed you," Benny said as he righted the rack and began to gather up books. Each time he bent over, his armor creaked. "My company sent me overseas, and I just got back yesterday. Duke Pumpernickel here is my best friend. It was just my little way of letting him know I was back."

Anderson kicked Benny's backside, but without enough force to knock him down. "Benny's a crude, lice-ridden Viking. He should be locked up, but not in a petting zoo. He spits and slobbers, and is capable of biting off some little tyke's finger."

"Perhaps, but I do not sweat like a pig, and stink like a sty."

"Ah, but the vile miasma of your breath has put many a comely wench on the floor."

"Or on my bed, her lips moist and her eyes glittering with lust. Speaking of such, how is the Duchess of Glenbarrens? Did she pine in my absence?"

"I'm sure she would have if she'd noticed it." Anderson laughed, but with an edge of hostility. "Why don't you come over later and tell us about your trip?"

"Lanya's already invited me to dinner," said Benny. "She called this morning to make sure I was back and willing to partici-pate in the demo. She wanted me to surprise you, so she had to cut short the call when you blundered in." He put the last of the paperbacks on the rack and nodded at me. "My apologies, milady. I would be delighted if you would allow me to make it up to you in a more intimate setting. My abode is humble, but I can offer a bottle of wine, candles, a simple meal —"

"Sorry, but I'm not available," I said.

Anderson thumped his fellow warrior. "C'mon, Benny. Let's go beat each other's brains out. Loser supplies the wine tonight."

Benny gave me a forlorn look as he waited while Anderson put on his helmet, and then followed him outside. I took a moment to catch my breath. A bull in a china shop could not rival what had seemed like a herd of buffalos in a bookstore. That, along with Edward Cobbinwood's extraordinary compulsion to confide in me, was more than enough to give me the stirrings of a headache. I wished I could close the bookstore for the rest of the day, but I couldn't lock the door until the wires were unplugged and the sound system removed — or brought inside to be stashed in a corner until the next debacle. And then the next, and so forth until the weekend of the Renaissance Fair arrived.

I went into the office and started searching through desk drawers for a bottle of aspirin. Ignoring the withered corpses of moths and beetles, I finally found the bottle, poured myself a cup of coffee, gulped down a couple of tablets, and settled down in the chair, resigned to wait. From the portico, I could hear Edward's voice and the appreciative laughter and bouts of applause from what sounded like a decent-sized crowd of spectators. The specter of blood and violence would undoubtedly draw even more of them. I could only hope I would not be held accountable if traffic backed up in both directions.

And I could only hope that Edward Cobbinwood was not the product of a relationship in which Carlton had engaged before he met me. Carlton had lived in California for a year, fancying himself to be a soulful literary novelist in search of the ultimate truth found only in the core of American decadence (or something like that). He'd mentioned going to rock concerts in San Francisco and the Bay area. He'd never said much about his jobs, which had led me to believe they must have been ignoble rather than worthy of his delicate sensibilities. He'd finally come to his senses when he realized he could make more money by droning about Cannery Row than by living there.

If Carlton was indeed Edward's father, then Edward would not be related to me in any form or fashion. Caron, however, would be Edward's half sister. Her reaction was difficult to predict, but I doubted it would be accented with whoops of delight. Nor would Carlton's family be thrilled. I'd met them once and been appalled by their pedigreed pomposity and hypocrisy.

I was still lost in dark thoughts when Caron and Inez came into the office through the back door.

"What Is Going On?" Caron demanded, quivering with indignation.

I shrugged. "Beats me."

"She means out front," Inez said helpfully.

I realized I'd been too preoccupied to notice the noise from the portico. Edward's cheerful babble had been replaced with the jarring sounds of metal on metal. The crowd was no longer laughing, but instead was roaring with approval or groaning. Individual voices bellowed encouragement. The din was worse than I'd imagined it might be.

"Oh, that," I said. "Cling and Clang are attempting to cause grievous injury upon each other. Bloodshed is not allowed." I flinched at a particularly loud clash. "In theory, anyway. Is there a first-aid kit in the bathroom?"

Caron peered through the doorway at the windows in front, then brushed a few papers off the corner of my desk and perched there. "This is so embarrassing, Mother. We could hear them from three blocks away, and the traffic's so snarled that we gave up and left the car behind Luanne's store. Those two men look ridiculous."

"Like comic book characters," Inez said, still standing since she didn't have the nerve to clear off a corner of the desk for herself. "Or toys, anyway. My nephew got a set of action figures for his birthday. It came with a cardboard castle and all these little weapons and shields, as well as plastic horses and a green dragon. His dog chewed off the dragon's head the same night."

I looked at Caron. "This is all your fault, dear. If you'd signed up for home ec, all we'd have to worry about is a cooking demonstration."

"That's so not fair! You told me I *had* to take all the AP classes so I could get through college in three years. The only reason Rhonda's taking AP history is because Louis Wilderberry is. She's terrified that he'll dump her for somebody else, so she clings to him like a tick. She'd probably follow him into the locker room if the coach would let her."

"She waits outside after every practice and game," added Inez. "She'd better hope he doesn't get into a college that requires decent SAT and ACT scores. The only way she'll get into any college is if her father pays for a library wing or endows a chair."

"I thought she made good grades," I said.

Caron rolled her eyes. "A toadstool could make good grades if it took typing, home ec, basic English, beginning Spanish, and math for morons. She gets straight A's in phys ed because she's a cheerleader."

"Enough," I said as I stood up. "I'm going home. You'll have to stay until that nonsense out front is finished and you can lock up."

Caron glared at me. "What if we have other things to do?"

"Then you'll have to do them later. I'll slip out the back door and walk, so you can have the car to go do your other things. Should the issue of bail arise, don't call me."

Inez cut me off before I could make my escape. "Are you okay, Ms. Malloy? You look kind of pale. You shouldn't worry about those guys in armor. Miss Thackery explained how they're actually careful not to hurt each other, that they just like to make a lot of noise."

"No, Inez," I said, "I can promise I'm not

worried about them. I have a headache, that's all."

Caron was not about to be upstaged, even if it required feigning compassion. "Do you want one of us to go with you in case you get dizzy?"

"I'll just have to risk it on my own," I said. "There's a stack of books on the counter. Arrange them in the window and put the ones currently there back on the racks. I'll see you later."

"We were going to have dinner at Inez's and then get her mother to help us with our costumes, but if you're getting sick or something, I can stay home."

I held up my hand. "No, you go work on your costumes. I'll see you much later." I went out the back door, paused to listen to the uproar — much ado about nothing — and then walked along the railroad tracks to the bridge. There was a well-worn path that led up to the sidewalk across from the Azalea Inn, a charming mansion that predates the Civil War and is rumored to have been a stop on the Underground Railroad. Despite its picturesque façade, it had housed more than one murderer in recent times. Lieutenant Peter Rosen had failed to appreciate my investigative prowess in the matter, as always, and I'd solemnly promised to mind my own business in the future. Which I had, for at least a month. I wondered if FBI camp might teach him to be a tad more skeptical. He was much too young for ulcers and premature wrinkles.

As I trudged up the side street toward the campus, I heard music from inside one of the rental houses. For the most part, these were inhabited by those students without the funds to live in dorms, sorority and fraternity houses, or even the bland apartment complexes. This music, rather than the raucous dissonance that was more common, was light and melodic. Curiosity slowed me down briefly, but I thought of the cold drink awaiting me and turned at the alley behind the duplex. I went up the back steps and into the kitchen. The sound of ice clinking in my glass was equally melodic, as was the splashing of scotch.

Carrying the glass, I continued to the bathroom, and within a few minutes was immersed in steamy water and bubbles. Willing myself not to entertain troublesome thoughts, I imagined myself curled up next to Peter in a variety of exotic locales, all of them uninhabited except for faceless waiters delivering cocktails made with freshly squeezed fruit juices.

We were heading for reckless passion

when the phone rang. I opened my eyes and realized the bubbles had long since dissipated and the bathwater was chilly. The jarring rings were not coming from a cozy cabana, but from the living room. I hastily wrapped a towel around myself, grabbed my watery drink, and dashed for the phone.

"Hello?" I gasped, trying to keep the towel from slipping.

"Is something wrong?" asked Peter. "You sound upset."

"Nothing's wrong, but you owe me big-time." I put down the drink, tucked in the towel, and sat down on the sofa. "Tracked down any terrorists lately?"

"Are you sure nothing's wrong? I called the store, but there was no answer. I was ready to catch the next flight home."

He could be so adorable when he dithered over me, I thought with a small smile. "Nothing's wrong." I told him where I'd been and what I'd been envisioning, which led to a most satisfying conversation that included some scandalous details and promises. I then told him about the upcoming Renaissance Fair and my reluctant involvement, omitting any reference to Edward Cobbinwood's paternal dilemma. He found the wrestling match in the bookstore much funnier than I did, but I tried to keep any tinge of annoyance out of my voice and admitted that, in retrospect, it had been an inimitable experience.

"So when do you graduate?" I asked.

"Ten days, and then a week in Rhode Island with my mother. There's something I suppose I should tell you, but you have to promise not to get upset."

"I never get upset," I said stiffly, although the hairs on my arms were prickling.

"Well, Mother thinks I should tell Leslie about the marriage."

"Send her a telegram. 'Getting married. Stop. None of your business. Stop.' That ought to cover it."

"In person," he mumbled.

"Why? She's your ex-wife, for pity's sake!"

"Mother just thinks I should tell her in person, so she invited her to the house. Listen, I've got to go. There's a lab class on identifying and classifying fragments from explosive devices, and it's mandatory. I'll call you later. I love you."

He hung up before I could have the satisfaction of hanging up first. Lovely Leslie, lioness of the Wall Street jungle, manicured, pedicured, and polished, who owned Russian wolfhounds and never missed the St. Petersburg opera season. Who sailed in Newport and skied in Aspen. Who'd probably been taught to ride a unicycle by her nanny.

I sat on the sofa as the sun sank behind Old Main and the room grew dark.

CHAPTER THREE

I'd freshened my drink, sliced an apple and some cheese, and was sitting on my small balcony above the duplex porch when Caron came up the sidewalk. She glanced at me, then continued inside and upstairs. The downstairs apartment was vacant, a nice change from the endless procession of tenants that my landlord seemed to recruit from caves, psychiatric wards, or maximum security prisons. Some of them appeared to have experienced all three, although in no particular order.

"Did anybody call me?" she asked as she joined me.

"I wouldn't know. I unplugged the phone."

"You did *what?*"

I smiled serenely. "I unclipped the little doodad that connects the receiver to the vast electronic universe of buzzing and humming. Thus liberated from the shackles of societal demands that exhaust our souls, we are free to watch the moon rising above Old Main and listen to the plaintive bleats of lovesick sorority girls. 'To-morrow and to-morrow and to-morrow, creeps in this petty pace from day to day, to the last syllable of recorded time; and all our yesterdays have lighted fools the way to dusty death.' "

Caron looked at me for a long while. "Maybe I should call Luanne."

"So she can listen to a tale told by an idiot, full of sound and fury, signifying nothing?"

"Something like that."

"I'm fine, dear. I just wanted a little peace and quiet." I settled my feet on the railing and picked up my drink. "Did you and Inez make progress on your costumes?"

"Mrs. Thornton got kind of upset after all the thread started spewing out of the sewing machine and the bobbin flew off and hit her on the forehead. I think we're going to have to figure out another way. Staples and duct tape, maybe. You want anything from the kitchen?" When I shook my head, she went inside for a moment, then returned with a can of soda and a handful of cookies made by generic elves. "Did Peter call you?"

"I believe he did," I said. "Did anything happen at the bookstore after I left?"

"Not really. The knights declared the bout

to be a draw, took off their armor, and drove away. Miss Thackery started passing out fliers and selling tickets. She was dressed in a really fancy lavender gown with long sleeves and all kinds of lace and beads. It was cut so low in front that I kept hoping somebody would bump her in the back and she'd . . . pop out." Caron popped open the soda can to emphasize her comment. "Some nerdy man and the jester person moved all the amps inside and stashed them in a corner. As soon as they were done, we locked up and went to get the car."

"Did you redo the window display?"

"Partway," she said as she finished her soda and set the can on the rail. After a glance at me, she hastily picked it up. "Can I use the phone? Emily told Carrie that Rhonda and her little clique had to go to a dance session this afternoon. According to the reports, they are not happy fairies. I'm absolutely frantic to hear about it."

I remembered the odd music I'd heard while walking home. "Do you know where they went?"

Caron started for the apartment door, then hesitated. "No, but I can ask if it matters, as long as you swear you're not going to start prancing around in a green leotard. You've already got a reputation for being weird. Inez's father says your name's in the newspaper more often than the mayor's. If you want me to graduate, I have to show up at the high school for two more years. Once I've gone away to college, feel free to put on a feather boa and pirouette on the sidewalk."

"Do you think I'm weird?"

"Let's just say you seem to know more murderers than other people's mothers."

"I suppose I do," I murmured.

"Oh, and Miss Thackery wants you to go to an ARSE meeting tomorrow at six thirty. It's out at the farm where the fair's going to be. It's a potluck picnic, but you don't need to bring anything."

"I don't go to meetings."

Caron's lower lip began to quiver. "You have to go, Mother. AP history is rumored to be harder than Brain Surgery 101. I don't need to start the semester with Miss Thackery pissed at me. There will just be a few people, since most of the members are gone for the summer. All you have to do is eat their potato salad and nod every now and then. It's not like there's going to be jousting after dessert."

As appalled as I was at the idea of a meeting, much less a potluck, it would mean that I wouldn't be home in the evening. With luck, Peter would be too busy during the day to call, and I would have a legitimate excuse for not being available should he try to call later. On the other hand, it was likely that Edward Cobbinwood would be there. "I'll think about it," I finally said. "Didn't you and Inez go out there earlier today?"

"Yeah, we had to meet with the woman who's helping us organize the concessions. She's okay, if you like that sort."

"What sort?" I asked, remembering the flicker of hostility that I'd heard in the Duke of Glenbarren's voice when his faithful knight, Sir Kenneth of Gweek, had mentioned her.

"One of those seventies earth mothers, all Woodstock and Birkenstock. Thick build, with a big butt, dingy brown hair in a braid, worn sandals, and a long skirt straight from a yard sale. Four children — a petulant preadolescent girl, a snotty-nosed eight-year-old boy, and bratty six-year-old twin boys. She has dogs, cats, bees, chickens, and an herb garden, and makes her own soap. The farmhouse is old and messy, and smells funny. She offered us tea, but we were afraid to drink it."

Caron's description hardly fit my image of a seductive Guinevere. However, I'd already decided that at least some of the ARSE members were less than grounded in reality.

As were Caron and Inez, on occasion. "She's a duchess," I said, "so she's entitled to her eccentricities. Was she helpful?"

"She's already arranged for the food and drink. All we have to do is pick up a few things the day before, and then make sure all our workers show up for their shifts. Can I please call Emily?"

"Go on, but if anyone calls for me, say I've gone to bed."

"Including Peter? Is there something going on that I should know about?"

I held up my glass of scotch. "Alas, poor Cutty Sark, I knew him well."

She started to say something, then sighed loudly and went inside. Within a minute, I heard her on the phone, cackling with malicious glee.

The next morning I was arranging a display of bestsellers from the fourteenth, fifteenth, and sixteenth centuries when a short figure in a hooded black cape came into the store. It was already getting to be too much, I thought wearily, and the Renaissance Fair was still ten days away. Before too long, Fiona Thackery would ask if she might tether a dragon outside the store on Tuesdays and Thursdays, and Celtic warriors would besiege the beer garden across the street during happy hour.

The hood was brushed back, exposing Sally Fromberger's rosy cheeks and daffodil-yellow hair. I could tell from the brightness of her eyes that she'd already been indulging in her daily regime of bran fiber, raw oats, and tofu kibble.

"Guess who I am?" she demanded.

"A cheerleader at the Spanish Inquisition."

"Claire, you are so droll! I'm a prioress." She twirled so I could appreciate the fullness of her cape and the scarlet lining. "You may address me as Madam Marsilia d'Anjou. I don't know how to go about finding a habit. It's not as if I could call a Catholic church to rent one. They would think it was for a frivolous prank or a costume party. You don't happen to know any nuns, do you?"

"I'll check my address book. May I presume this has something to do with the Renaissance Fair?" I dearly hoped I was right, because otherwise one of us was drinking from the wrong tap.

Sally giggled. "Well, of course. As members of the Thurber Street Merchants Association, we all have an obligation to support the fair so that it will become an annual affair that draws people from all across the country. I've already talked with Fiona about staging some events in this area. You had quite a crowd in front of the Book Depot yesterday, and that was without any advance publicity." She gave me a disgruntled look. "Had the rest of us been informed, we would have taken advantage of the situation. Tomorrow many of us will have display tables on the sidewalks in front of our establishments. I thought I'd sell cups of cold herbal tea, cider, and carob cookies. The pottery shop, the art gallery, the boutique — all of those merchants are already making plans. I'm sure Luanne will want to display some of her beaded belts and purses."

I was clearly guilty of betraying my fellow merchants, but I was hardly overwhelmed with remorse. "I didn't have much warning," I said in my defense.

Madam Marsilia d'Anjou graciously accepted my apology with a nod. "Tomorrow there will be a more genteel demonstration of medieval and Renaissance music. Several members of the college orchestra, along with a few high school students, will play lutes, piccolos, recorders, mandolins, tambourines, and so forth. A group will sing madrigals. A pleasant change from that crude sword fight, don't you think?"

"Indeed," I said, thinking of the hours I'd spent earlier in the day reshelving paperbacks. I doubted madrigal singers and piccolo players were inclined to wrestle on the floor, although I'd never actually met any.

I resumed arranging books in the window, hoping Sally might take the hint and leave. However, she was much too enthusiastic to be sidetracked by subtlety.

"I hear Caron and Inez are involved in concessions at the fair," she said. "Such a big responsibility for girls their age."

"If it is, they're holding up well. The duchess — I can't remember her mundane name — is making all the arrangements. Caron and Inez are merely in charge of peasant labor."

"Oh," Sally said, her smile wavering. "I was hoping to be invited to sell hot cross buns and little loaves of oat bread. Fiona will know this woman's name, don't you think?"

Before I could respond, my science fiction hippie slinked through the door. He drops by almost every day, ostensibly to browse. Luckily for me, he's an inept shoplifter, and rarely makes it out with anything. He's done a few favors for me in the past, so I tend to regard him with guarded benevolence. I also frisk him.

"Wow," he said, gaping at Sally, "are you a sorceress? Cool."

"You know precisely who I am," Sally said. "Don't I give you a discount on day-old bread several times a week?"

He winked at her. "Yeah, great cover. Don't worry, I won't tell anybody." He drifted behind a rack of paperbacks. "A sorceress. Like, very cool."

Madam Marsilia d'Anjou looked very much as though she'd like to punch him in the nose, assuming she could find it under his matted beard and mustache, but settled for a sniff and swept out the door. I doubted my hippie would be munching any day-old hot cross buns in his immediate future.

I waited until the middle of the afternoon to call Luanne. Skipping preliminaries, I said, "Do you want to go to a gourmet dinner and ARSE meeting with me this evening?"

"I'm sorry — did you ask me if I wanted to have my leg amputated? I'm too busy these days, but maybe next year."

"If I have to go, I don't see why you shouldn't, too. We're both members of the Thurber Street Merchants Association."

Luanne chuckled. "I heard about the sword fight yesterday. For that matter, I could hear it from the doorway of my shop,

71

but it sounded entirely too violent for me." She hesitated. "I tried to call you last night to hear the gory details, but no one answered. Were you the trophy swept off by the victorious knight for purposes of debauchery and wantonness? Peter's not going to like it if he has to do battle to win back your hand."

My throat tightened, but I managed a halfhearted laugh. "The peril of leaving a lady in waiting. If you'll go to this meeting, I'll owe you. Surely it won't last more than an hour or two. All we'll have to do is eat their potato salad and nod."

"Nod — or nod off?"

I took my last shot. "I met the knights before the demonstration. They're both sexy guys, Luanne. I can't attest to their manhood, since they were in full stainless steel drag, but I'm fairly certain one of them is single."

"Nice try," she said dryly, "but I've already suffered through one textbook case of arrested adolescence. His suits were handmade rather than forged, but the end result was the same."

"A pox upon your house," I said as I hung up. I had two hours in which to develop an acute appendicitis or malaria. Since my appendix had been removed twenty years ago and we were quite a distance from the nearest swamp, my chances were not good. I went to the nonfiction shelf and began to look for books on early symptoms of infectious diseases.

The realm of the Duke and Duchess of Glenbarrens was a few miles west of Farberville, no more than a twenty-minute drive from my apartment. I dawdled, dragging it out to half an hour, but eventually turned by a mailbox with the names of Anderson and Lanya Peru painted in Gothic script on one side. The house was as unappealing as Caron had said, and a few outbuildings looked as though they could topple on a whim. There were flower beds in front of the house; a large vegetable garden was partially visible in the backyard. Toys were scattered in the grass, and several bicycles lay about like rusting fossils. On one side of the house, clotheslines sagged under the weight of jeans, socks, and towels. The pasture was rutted and weedy, hardly conducive to trampling about after a cup of mead or ale. The structures and property were protected not by a moat, but by woods and steep hills.

"Beyond this place be dragons," I muttered as I parked among dusty cars and trucks. As I walked up the steps to the porch, children came whooping out the front door and headed in the direction of the pasture. Caron had mentioned four children, but I felt as though there were at least twice that many. I closed my eyes for a moment, then took a deep breath and knocked on the door.

Fiona Thackery appeared almost immediately. "Mrs. Malloy," she said as she held open the door, "we are delighted that you decided to come so we can express our appreciation for your generosity. Caron was afraid you might have had other plans. Come in, please. The others are in the back room. Would you like something to drink? The mead is homemade. Lanya collects the honey from her apiary and ferments it in jars in the basement. It's . . . ah, potent. We also have wine, sodas, and beer."

I glanced at the living room as she herded me along. It smelled of mold, dirty socks, and patchouli oil (a fad that fortunately had faded from favor decades ago). Amateurish tapestries did not quite cover peeling wallpaper and water stains. The upholstered furniture was worn, the cushions lumpy and uninviting. Lanya's interests seemed to lie in areas of procreation and mead, rather than interior decoration.

"Yesterday went very well," continued Fiona. "I was sorry to hear that you had to leave early because of a headache."

I felt as though I needed a written excuse from a doctor. "I had some errands to do, and Caron and Inez were eager to stay and watch the demonstration. They were very impressed with the authenticity of the armor."

She gave me a wry smile. "Yes, so they told me several times."

We went into the kitchen. It had the ambience of a Depression-era farmhouse, with ancient appliances and open shelves cluttered with oddments of plates, bowls, glasses, jars, and bottles of spices. A cast-iron skillet on the stove held an inch-thick layer of congealed grease, and a saucepan next to it was splattered with what appeared to be dried tomato soup or spaghetti sauce. A rickety table was cluttered with bottles of wine, gallon jars of what I assumed was mead, paper cups, and empty aluminum cans. A cooler on the floor was filled with ice, beer, and sodas. I could hear voices and laughter from the room beyond, mostly male. I wondered, albeit briefly, which of the battling knights had been obliged to supply the wine the previous evening.

Fiona's nose was slightly wrinkled, but she

forced a smile and said, "Lanya must have her hands full with all those children and animals. It's no wonder that Anderson prefers to work late at his office rather than come home to this. There's something to be said for population control, even if it means putting up with a smallpox epidemic or a plague every fifty years. What would you like to drink, Mrs. Malloy?"

"A soda will be fine." I would have chosen wine, but it seemed wise to stick with something that was tamperproof.

After I'd been issued a can and a cup, I was escorted out to join the party. The room was encased by screened window panels to convert it into a sleeping porch, once considered a necessity during hot summer nights. Now it held a hodgepodge of wicker and ladderback chairs with splintery seats. Two card tables had been pushed together and covered with a vinyl tablecloth for the potluck offerings. There was a preponderance of undefinable casseroles, along with the obligatory potato salad, a plate of curling cheese slices, and a bowl of fruit. Flies buzzed about, as unsure as I was about the wisdom of sampling any of the fare.

Fiona clung to my arm. "This is Claire Malloy, who owns the bookstore on Thurber Street. Claire, you've already met Julius and

Edward."

Julius, who was perched on a low stool, smiled nervously. From a corner, Edward fluttered his fingers at me. He wore a faded cotton shirt and cutoffs, and did not appear to be in the mood to entertain us with juggling and magic tricks. I hoped he had no intention of pulling me aside for further confidences about his father. All I intended to do was survive the meeting and depart without ptomaine poisoning.

Fiona gestured at an elderly couple sitting to one side. "Glynnis and William Threet, known also as Lord and Lady Bicklesham. Glynnis makes wonderful tapestries."

Tears began to dribble down Glynnis's cheeks as she looked at me. "Needlework keeps me busy these days. I used to work at the admissions office at the college, but after we lost Percival . . ."

Her husband handed her his handkerchief. "Try not to think about it, my dear."

"I'm very sorry for your loss," I said weakly.

"Ah, thank you," he said with a small cough. "You're welcome to come by and visit him. We had him stuffed so he can be with us in the living room."

Glynnis wiped her eyes. "He makes a lovely footstool."

I glanced at Fiona, who merely said, "And you met our gallant knights. Anderson Peru and Benny Stallings."

Anderson rose from a wicker rocking chair. "I had the honor of meeting her ladyship yesterday," he said, "although she may not have fond memories of our encounter. I would not fault her for that. I was behaving with great gallantry when I was beset upon by a lumpish, knotty-pated moldwarp with the manners of a pig herder. I had no choice but to beat him senseless in the ensuing brawl."

"The hell you did," said Benny as he winked at me. Even dressed in jeans and a T-shirt, he was a bearish man, with thick arms and an obvious fondness for beer. I mentally revised my assessment of them; Anderson was sexy, but Benny radiated unadulterated animal lust. He would not have been a suitable candidate to teach at a girls' school. "You were thrashed until you mewled for mercy, you beslubbering puttock. Only out of pity for Your Grace's weakened condition did I allow you to concede. I do hope milady understands that now that I've defended her honor, I have every intention of claiming my prize."

"Just what did you juvenile delinquents do?" demanded the woman sitting next to

Anderson. "Every time you put on armor, your brains shut down and your testicles take over." She looked me over carefully, as if I were guilty of provoking them. "I'm Lanya Peru."

Caron had described her well, although she was now wearing a peasant blouse that exposed her heavily freckled shoulders and ample cleavage. Her hair was braided and pinned into a sloppy bun, exposing gray hairs at the edges of her round face. When dressed in her medieval finery, she would make a most imposing duchess, I thought. "Nice to meet you," I said.

"I wouldn't worry about it, Lanya." The speaker, a clean-shaven man with pale blue eyes and the sculpted cheekbones of a malnourished poet, was sprawled in a wicker chair. His sandy-blond hair was untidy, but in what I suspected was a studiously intentional way. He took a sip of wine, then made a face and set the cup down on the floor. "They're no more dangerous than Tweedledee and Tweedledum."

"Salvador Davis," said Fiona, her fingers pressing into my arm. "He's the one who's dangerous, or so I've heard."

He shrugged. "Also known as Lord Galsworth, Baron of Firthforth, and master of the archers' guild. Should you ever desire to have an apple shot off your head, I shall be overjoyed to oblige you. Come, you must sit by me, my fair Claire, and tell me more about yourself. There is a serenity in your features, not unlike that seen in the finest Italian Renaissance depictions of the Madonna."

I did not tell him that my so-called serenity was nothing more than paralytic panic. They were entirely too intense, and staring at me as if I were a shoplifter who'd been caught by a security guard. Anderson and Benny were both leering, and Salvador's smile was predatory, if not outright carnivorous. Lanya seemed to be considering the likelihood that I was a wanton bar wench intent on seducing her husband and any other man within my grasp. The same thought must have been passing through Fiona's mind, since she was squeezing my arm so tightly that I felt my fingers turning numb. Glynnis and William eyed me nervously, as if I'd been responsible for Percival's demise. Edward seemed to be waiting for me to say or do something of great significance. Julius was the only one who showed no interest in me, and instead was frowning at Fiona. I wished I were wearing Sally's cloak so that I could put on the hood and vanish in a puff of smoke. I spotted a chair at the edge of the circle, pried off Fiona's hand, and sat down.

Fiona remained standing. "I thought Angie was coming tonight. Has anybody heard from her?"

"Who's Angie?" asked Glynnis. "Is she a member of the fiefdom? Why haven't we met her? Or have we met her?"

"I'm quite sure we haven't," said William firmly.

"None of us has," Lanya said. "She moved to Farberville earlier in the summer, she told me, and found my name and number in the ARSE national directory. When we decided to hold the Ren Fair, I called her to see if she might want to participate. She's had some training as a dancer and agreed to take on the fairies. I gave her Fiona's number."

Fiona nodded. "She was very nice about it. I offered to escort the girls to her house, but she said that she preferred them to come on their own. I've been so busy that I was grateful not to have something else on my list."

"So no one has actually met Angie?" murmured Anderson. "Did you ask her for references?"

Lanya glared at him. "She volunteered, which is reference enough for me. She called this morning to say she sprained her ankle yesterday during the dance class with the fairies, and wants to stay off it as much as possible. I would have volunteered to go to the grocery store for her, but I had to stay here all day to meet with various people. I've arranged for enough small tents for the vendors and concessions, but I'm still working on a large tent for the Royal Pavilion. There are a lot of weddings and family reunions this month. It would have been much easier if we'd had more notice, Fiona."

"You can't blame her for that," Julius said, doing his best to bluster.

Lanya glared at him. "I wasn't blaming anyone, Julius. I was merely pointing out that most events of this magnitude are planned months in advance."

Salvador leaned forward and ruffled Julius's hair. "Back off, Lanya, the little fellow is just defending whatever vestiges remain of his lady's honor. We can't all don armor and smack each other with swords. What we must do, Julius, is assign you a name and title befitting your talents. How about . . . Squire Squarepockets? That has a nice ring, don't you think? Solid, dependable, like a village greengrocer or a bank clerk."

"You're not nearly as clever as you think

you are," Fiona said coldly. She sat down next to Julius, who was looking at the floor.

"May I suggest," Anderson said, "that we get back to business? Lanya has the tents and concessions under control. Julius will see to the technical systems and will liaison with the media for whatever coverage we can get. Fiona is in charge of scheduling the stage entertainment during the day and also the banquet performances. Edward will herd the performers to their proper venues. Salvador is in charge of the archery. Benny and I will oversee the sword fights and contact the adjoining fiefdoms to find out if we can scrounge up knights. Glynnis and William have agreed to supervise the decorations. Any questions?"

"The schedule will be finalized by Monday," said Fiona. "Since this was my idea, I feel as though I should help during the actual event."

He sat back and crossed his legs. "You, dear, will have your hands full with your students. They will all need to arrive at seven in the morning to help set everything up and decorate. During the day, the pirates, fairies, and musicians will be expected to perform on stage, so check with Edward and make sure they understand when and where to assemble. Be careful to keep them away from the alcoholic spirits, especially during the banquet. The Duchess will not be amused if one of the serving wenches barfs in her lap."

"I anticipate no problems in seeing that they behave according to Your Grace's wishes," she said.

Benny chuckled. "And you certainly should be aware of those."

Fiona abruptly rose and went into the kitchen. I wondered if I was the only one who noticed her tightly clenched fists. After an awkward moment, Lanya suggested that we help ourselves to the food. She offered her arm to Julius, who glanced at the kitchen doorway but obediently stood up to escort her to the makeshift serving table. Benny and Anderson jostled each other and exchanged insults as they began to pile spoonfuls of the bizarre casseroles on paper plates. I took a cracker and a few grapes and sat back down. Edward had remained in the corner, watching the group with the impartiality of a surveillance camera. It took me a moment to realize that Salvador had disappeared, most likely into the kitchen.

Everyone was still chattering around the table when I heard a car drive away. I had no idea if the driver was Fiona, Salvador, both of them, or one of the barbarian Peru children, but it seemed like an excellent idea. I caught Lanya before she could sit down, and said, "Thank you so much for inviting me tonight. I hope the Renaissance Fair raises a lot of money for Safe Haven. I really must go now."

"So early? I was looking forward to having a nice talk with you. Even though we've lived in Farberville for more than ten years, I'm so busy out here that I rarely come into town. Your daughter hinted that you're quite a remarkable woman."

"She exaggerates," I said lightly. "Now if you'll excuse me, I'll be on my way."

Anderson joined us. "What a shame that we shall not have the pleasure of your company. Are you keeping late hours at the bookstore? You must be nervous by yourself after dark. Sometimes I have to go back to the office to straighten out a mixup, and I'm keenly aware of every little noise in the building."

"I'm quite a remarkable woman," I said, "or so it's been said. Good night, everybody."

I hurried through the kitchen and living room, both unoccupied, and out to my car. I was fumbling through my purse for the keys when Lanya loomed at the window beside me. My undeniable quick wit failed me, and all I could do was look up at her.

She thrust a basket at me. "These are a few things for Angie to tide her over until I can shop for her. She lives just around the corner from you in a small blue house with white shutters. Would you please drop them off for me?"

At that point I would have gladly given her all my money and jewelry, including the discreet diamond engagement ring on my left hand, just to get away. "Sure, glad to," I said as I snatched the basket out of her hands. I jammed the key into the ignition switch, started the engine, and drove away as if I were being pursued by a ferocious clan of Scottish warriors, blue theatrical makeup and all.

When I reached the highway, I stopped and looked at my watch. I had been at the meeting for all of half an hour, and would be home before eight o'clock unless I had a flat tire or got caught behind a gypsy caravan. Caron had mentioned that Inez was going with her parents to a lecture on the exhilarating developments in electronic card cataloging, which meant Caron would be on her own — and on the telephone. My daughter is a gifted liar when telling the truth is not to her advantage, but if Peter managed to call during a lull, she might very happily supply him with the details of my behavior the previous evening. I did not want to be there if he asked to speak to me.

I looked through the contents of the basket that Lanya had asked me to deliver to Angie, last name unknown. It contained a pint jar with a handwritten label proclaiming it to be red clover honey, a larger jar of mead, a loaf of bread, a bar of soap wrapped in torn tissue paper, and several plastic bags of dried herbs and spices. Since nothing would spoil, I decided to drop off the basket in the morning.

After a quick stop at a liquor store to buy a bottle of wine, I went to Luanne's apartment above her shop and pounded on the door. She opened it, a slice of pizza in her free hand.

"You lasted longer than I thought you would," she said as I came inside. "The pizza just got here. I'll open the wine."

I sat down at the kitchen table. I was hungry, but the idea of eating did not appeal. "How long did you think I'd last?"

"Considering the snit you're in, no more than ten minutes." She brought two glasses of wine and sat down across from me. "Caron called me."

I took a drink and shuddered. "I should have known better than to take the advice of a salesclerk with a ponytail."

"Why do I have an eerie sensation that you're avoiding the subject?" Luanne asked, gazing steadily at me. "If you don't want to talk about it, fine. You're entitled to your feelings. However, we're going to talk about it anyway, even if it means I have to tie you to the chair and pour this entire gallon of cheap wine down your throat. So what did he say?"

"You'll have to be more specific. The Duke of Glenbarrens? Sir Kenneth of Gweek? Pester the Jester? My accountant? The sales rep from Truculent Press? The college kid who wanted to buy a guide to growing marijuana for fun and profit?"

"Peter — and I don't mean O'Toole, the pumpkin eater, or the rabbit."

I related the conversation, then added, "Yes, I know I'm being ridiculous. It's his mother's idea, not his. He's just going along with it to appease her. I have absolutely no reason to be upset." I finished the wine and got up to pour myself another glass. "See? Now that we've talked it over, I'm not upset. I'm as tranquil as a field of daisies on a sunny afternoon."

"And I am Anastasia, daughter of Tsar Nicholas and Alexandria. I'm hiding in Farberville until the Russian Revolution ends, surviving as best I can on caviar, vodka, and Botox injections three times a week."

I picked up a slice of pizza, inspected it, and put it back in the box. "There's nothing I can do about it. If Peter feels that he should tell his ex-wife in person, so be it. I can hardly fly to Rhode Island and ring the doorbell, can I?"

"Can you? How much would it cost?"

"A bloody fortune," I said, grimacing. "I called a couple of airlines this morning. And even if I could afford it, what would I do? Smile politely and say, 'Peter, I love you so much that I want to marry you, but I don't trust you'? That wouldn't go over so well."

"Do you trust him?" asked Luanne.

"Of course I do. I just don't trust his mother and his ever so lovely ex-wife. They might be scheming to spike his food with tranquilizers, and when he's too spaced out to realize what's going on, stuff him into a tuxedo and drag him down the aisle. Before he comes to, he'll be on a honeymoon cruise in the South Pacific, and his house here will be for sale."

"Now I really am beginning to think I'm Anastasia. If I had coffee liqueur and vodka, we could drink a toast to the Romanov dynasty."

I slumped back in the chair. "Or to self-pity and petty jealousy," I said with a sigh. "Peter's too intelligent to fall for his mother's transparent trap. I suppose I ought to feel some sympathy for the ex-wife. Leslie was the wealthy, well-bred girl next door. His parents and hers were in favor of the match long before their offspring were potty-trained and taught to ride their wee polo ponies. They shared a limo on their way to their first day at some exclusive preschool. Peter said he never had a chance, that his destiny had been determined by the merging of stock portfolios. They went to different prep schools, naturally, and in theory dated other people, but he never dared bring a date home for a weekend, much less a holiday. It was a given that he would escort Leslie to all the fancy parties. They announced their engagement one Christmas while they were both in grad school, and married the month after graduation. The only thing they failed to do, according to their Emily Post world, was produce adorable little heirs."

"And the reason they divorced?" Luanne asked, plying me with more wine.

"Peter said it was a mutual decision. Basically, they'd always bored each other. She wanted the glitzy, high-powered world of a penthouse in Manhattan and a summer place within a few minutes' drive of the yacht club. He wanted to live in a small town, mow his own lawn, and grill steaks on the patio."

"But now you're afraid he'll be seduced by all that?"

"No," I said irritably as I put the wine glass in the sink. The last thing I wanted was to lapse into maudlin snuffling, or get stopped for driving while under the influence of the Gallo boys. "I've already admitted I'm being ridiculous, okay? Maybe it is prewedding jitters, or PMS, or the stress of dealing with these Renaissance weirdos. In case Sally hasn't caught you, I'm having musicians and madrigal singers tomorrow afternoon. After that, who knows? It could be a full-scale production of *A Midsummer Night's Dream,* with hot cross buns and lemonade available at intermission."

Luanne refused to be distracted. "If Peter calls, are you going to talk to him?"

"Why wouldn't I? We're getting married in September." I found my purse and took out my keys. "I need to go. Caron's undoubtedly convinced by now that I did or said something so outrageous at the meeting that she'll have no hope of passing AP history. This will, of course, ruin her chances of getting into college, so she'll have to earn a living as a Welsh miner or an Australian bush pilot."

"And we wouldn't want that, would we?"

I will admit I hesitated for a moment, envisioning the scenarios, then shook my head. "No, we wouldn't want that."

CHAPTER FOUR

I took a circuitous route home to avoid the traffic on Thurber Street, which can be tedious even in the summer because of the bars, restaurants, pool halls, and performances at the art center. I was vaguely aware of some sort of annual biker gathering in progress, but their presence was minimal during the day. This meant the presence of police was maximal at night. I certainly didn't want any citations with my name on them to find their way into the hands of Sergeant Jorgeson — or onto Lieutenant Rosen's desk when he returned.

As I crossed one of the two bridges over the railroad tracks, I realized that I would be driving past Angie's house. If I could spot it, it would be easier to drop off the basket before I arrived home. Blue with white shutters, Lanya had said. I slowed down to a crawl and began to watch for it. The streetlights were doing their best, but the neighborhood had been there for decades and large trees kept many of the houses in shadows. There were lights on in some of them; others were dark, possibly vacant for the summer. Two college girls came walking down the hill, too fascinated with their conversation to notice me. In one of the houses, a baby began to wail. In another, a TV set flickered.

I was almost to the alley when I spotted the blue house on the right side of the street. The front porch light was on, not only attracting moths and other winged insects, but also a visitor. His back was to me, and his arm propped against the frame, blocking the view of whoever was on the other side of the screened door. As my car went by, he turned and looked over his shoulder. I was pretty sure it was Edward Cobbinwood, dressed as he had been at the ARSE meeting two hours ago. I doubted he could see my face, and there was no reason to think he would recognize my car.

Even if Edward had identified me, it didn't matter, I thought as I turned left into the alley and pulled into my garage. Although he'd looked a bit startled, it seemed perfectly reasonable for him to go by Angie's to express concern for her ankle — and deliver the basket. It would have been helpful if he'd announced his intention before I fled the potluck.

Caron was not home. I found a note on the kitchen table that explained her whereabouts: Inez's father had offered to take them out for ice cream after the lecture. She'd added a hasty scrawl that read, "Peter called, didn't believe me." I frowned at it, not at all sure what she'd told him that he'd failed to believe. That she was to be a damsel? That a young man in purple tights was haunting Thurber Street? That I'd taken to unplugging the telephone and quoting Shakespeare to a glass of scotch?

I made a cup of tea, found my novel, and crawled into bed. I was half awake when Caron came home, but I decided I could wait until the next day to determine the source of Peter's skepticism.

Caron was asleep the next morning when I got up. After performing the mundane daily rituals, I went downstairs to the car, took out the basket, and walked down the side street to drop it off at Angie's house. I knocked on the door and waited, but no one appeared. I was uneasy about leaving the basket on the porch, where it would be visible, but disinclined to take it to the bookstore and bring it by later. For all I knew, red clover honey and homemade bread were all that stood between starvation and salvation.

As I hesitated, an elderly woman came out of the house next door and sat down on a porch swing to read the newspaper. "Hello," I called. "Have you seen Angie this morning?"

The woman stared at me. "Who?"

"Angie. I believe she's a dance teacher."

She pondered this for a moment, then shook her head. "No, but I don't recollect that I've ever seen her. She's been here two months, give or take, but she keeps her curtains drawn like she's allergic to sunshine. Yesterday or maybe the day before, I saw some teenaged hussies go inside. Didn't stay long, though. I could hear 'em snickering and laughing when they left."

I was annoyed that I'd allowed Lanya to burden me with her errand. I made a mental note to find a book on assertiveness in the self-help section when I got to the bookstore. "Do you think it'll be okay if I leave this basket on the porch?"

"I don't care if you climb onto the roof and drop it down the chimney." The woman folded her newspaper, tucked it under her arm, and went inside.

After some further hesitation, I set the

basket by the door and went down the steps to the sidewalk. Most people could make do for a day or two with what was in their refrigerator and cabinets. Or maybe Edward had come by with sustenance from a fast food place. Lanya might be on her way to the grocery store that very minute. Angie had a telephone, after all. If she didn't want to order a pizza, she could call 911 and feast on hospital food.

Instead of scrambling down the path to the railroad tracks, I turned in front of the Azalea Inn and continued to Thurber Street. This required me to go past Sally Fromberger's health food eatery, but I did so without being ambushed or coerced into sampling a hot cross bun. The Book Depot was not quite the haven it had been before the onslaught of Renaissance scholars, but it was cool and dim. I turned on lights, flipped the sign in the door to indicate I was willing to sell literature brimming with insights into the nature of good and evil, as well as pulp fiction, recipe books, travel guides, and anything else that would make the cash register chirp with pleasure. Peter and I had agreed that we would both continue in our present careers, although he'd mentioned that I would be able to hire a full-time clerk whenever we decided to take off for a long weekend or an extended trip. I couldn't remember when I'd last kept the store closed for more than a few days, and even then I'd been aware of the loss of income. Now I could look forward to Caribbean resorts, spacious suites, and four-star restaurants. Hedonism, despite its negative connotations, has a certain charm.

I made a pot of coffee, filled a chipped mug, and was on my stool behind the counter, immersed in the newspaper, when Salvador Davis entered the store.

"Good morning," he said as if greeting a colleague in an adjoining cubicle. "I'd love a cup of coffee if you have any to spare."

"Sure," I said warily. "Sugar? Powdered cream?"

"Black, thank you." He held up a bag. "Fresh croissants. I made them myself from a secret recipe given to me by an octogenarian who owned a *boulangerie* in Normandy. Have you ever been in that region?"

"No, although it's likely some of my ancestors lived there ten centuries ago, and immigrated across the English Channel only after William had exterminated the Cornish gentry. You'll have to come in the office if you want to sit down."

He did as instructed, and after we were settled on opposite sides of the desk, said,

"Did you enjoy your first fiefdom meeting?"

I hesitated, then said, "This croissant is delicious. I'd ask for the recipe, but I don't even have measuring cups and mixing bowls. Well, I probably do, but I don't know where they are."

"Does that imply that you won't be applying for membership in ARSE? I heard that you left before Lanya could persuade you to sample the goat cheese and barley quiche. It's less authentic but more palatable than Anderson's venison pot pie."

I brushed flakes off my fingers. "I left right after you did."

Salvador studied me over the rim of his coffee mug. "How observant you are. Are you equally discreet?"

"Absolutely not. I am the worst gossip on Thurber Street, and I cannot be trusted with anyone's darkest secrets. No one should ever confide in me." I took my coffee mug into the tiny bathroom and rinsed it out, turned off the coffeepot, and picked up a stack of invoices. "Thank you so much for the croissant, but I have some work to do. If you're interested in a book, I'll be happy to point you in the right direction."

He remained seated, watching me with an amused look. "I don't believe you."

"I seem to have a poor credibility rating

these days." I flapped the invoices at him. "My credit rating's not so hot, either. If I don't reconcile these with my current stock and settle the accounts, then the distributors won't send me any more books. If I don't have books to sell, then I'll go out of business. Some entrepreneur will buy the building and turn it into a quaint little bistro. My daughter will become a Welsh miner. So if you don't mind —"

"A Welsh miner?"

"It's an honest living."

Salvador put down his mug and gestured for me to precede him into the front room, which I did. "Are you always so difficult to converse with?" he asked.

"Not always," I said as I sat down on the stool and picked up a pen.

"Do I make you nervous?"

"Don't flatter yourself."

He sighed, but not convincingly. "I see that I've offended you, Claire, and I apologize. My behavior last night was . . . well, boorish. As soon as I got there, I realized I should have stayed home. I've been working sixteen hours a day on a project, and finally got it packed off. I thought I would enjoy socializing, but I would have been better off to sit on my deck and drink champagne with the whippoorwills."

"What is it that you do?" I asked.

"I'm a writer, and I also illustrate my work. I'm embarrassed that I've never been in your bookstore before, but I'm sure you don't carry my particular genre."

I puzzled over this for a moment. "I don't know why you're so sure, unless you write pornography. I refuse to sell it, and I don't want the people who read it loitering around here."

"Hardly," he said. "I usually throw in some romance and passion, but nothing too lurid. Most of my readers are too young for that sort of thing. I have some older readers, but they have a pubescent mentality." He put his elbows on the counter and leaned toward me. "You, on the other hand, are mature, candid, and self-confident, as well as alluring. Could I entice you to forget your misconceptions about me and come to my house so that I can impress you with my more commendable qualities?"

"No, you cannot," I said firmly. "I'm engaged and in September will be marrying a man whom I love and respect. You'll have better luck stalking girls at the mall, so why don't you run along?"

Salvador held up his hands. "My profound apologies. Allow me to rephrase my invitation. I'm having a few people over tonight for drinks. Would you and your fiancé care to join us? It will be very civilized. I have two unexpected houseguests from Japan and a demented amateur geologist from Australia who disappears for weeks at a time and then pops back up. Most of the people you met last night. We'll sit on the deck unless the mosquitoes make it intolerable. I can promise you we will not talk about politics, religion, or anything that happened before the twentieth century."

A wicked idea came to mind. "My fiancé is out of town," I said, "but I'd like to come if I may bring a guest."

"Certainly." He gave me directions to his house, which was on the far side of the hill near the football stadium. "Around six thirty or seven?"

I agreed, then waited until he left before calling Luanne. "I hope you're free tonight," I said when she answered. "We're going to a very civilized little cocktail party."

"How long are you going to dodge Peter's calls?"

"I have no idea what you're talking about," I said with great innocence. "I'm doing this for you, Luanne. I am wounded that you should think I'm doing this for personal reasons. Your social life is appalling. What were you planning to do tonight? Wash your hair and watch reruns of *Law & Order?* Clean out a closet or two?"

"My closets are impeccable."

"I'll pick you up at seven. If it turns out to be dreadful, we won't stay. Oops, I have a customer, so I'd better go."

I hung up before she could ask any questions, then went into the front room to study real estate ads in the newspaper. I wanted authentic Victorian charm, Peter wanted modern plumbing, and Caron wanted a pool. The ones I'd found thus far had two of the three, but I wasn't prepared to compromise just yet — or be dragged all over town by a rabid real estate salesperson determined to sell us one of a dozen matching faux mansions in a cow pasture. Five bedrooms, four bathrooms, walk-in closets, marble countertops, and no soul.

Nothing of note happened until the middle of the afternoon, when Julius and Fiona arrived. While he moved his sound equipment outside, she peered at the window display, which was not especially artful. Edward Cobbinwood pedaled up on a bicycle, decked out in his jovial jester attire, but remained outside to help Julius. I watched from my stool, not inclined to offer assistance or make conversation. To my regret, Fiona eventually came into the bookstore and spotted me.

"Did you have a nice time last night?" she asked.

Since there was no one else in the store, it seemed obvious that she was speaking to me. "Lovely," I said.

"I'm sorry that things got so . . . intense," she said. "Sometimes I think my high school students behave more maturely than the ARSE members. In any small group, there are always some undercurrents. There are times that I come away from a meeting feeling as though I'd run the gauntlet."

"Edward did say that sometimes it's hard to define the line between camaraderie and competitiveness. I hope Julius wasn't too upset."

Fiona glanced out the window at him. "He was perturbed, but he has to learn to stand up for himself. He practically begs people to walk all over him. Then, when they do, he sulks and whines. He's thirty-two and still lives with his parents, if you can imagine. They're perfectly nice, but their idea of a wild adventure is to try a new laundry detergent. Julius claims that he's saving himself for marriage, but I suspect he's afraid to drop his trousers in front of anyone but his pediatrician. When we travel, he always arranges for separate rooms. I'm surprised he doesn't bring along his mother as a chaperone."

"I understand you two are engaged," I said mildly.

"Yes, he is a dear at times. Once I get him away from his parents, he'll do better. Last night was awful, wasn't it? Salvador can be brutal when he gets in one of his moods. Last year Anderson wanted to banish him from the fiefdom, but that requires King Leopold's approval and all sorts of paperwork and a hearing. I don't know what started it, but there's some ill will between them."

"How unfortunate," I said, wishing everybody would stop confiding in me. I happen to be extraordinarily tactful and sensitive, but I was not in the mood to proffer wisdom on a daily basis. "I understand there will be musicians today."

"It's on one of the printouts I gave you," Fiona said. "Have you read through the folder?"

I wanted to tell her my dog ate it. "Some of it. Caron said you were wearing a stunning gown the other day."

"I do like to participate," she said with a modest smile. "I'm going to run home shortly and change. I hope you'll be able to stay this afternoon and listen to the performance."

"I plan to be here."

"I think you'll enjoy it. On Monday we're scheduled for more music and some dancing, if Angie can bully the fairies into shape. I may have made a mistake when I chose that particular group of girls. They are not taking it as seriously as I'd assumed they would." She paused for a moment, her eyes narrowed. "They may regret it when the semester begins."

"How is Angie?" I asked. "When I took Lanya's basket by her house, she didn't answer the door. I was concerned."

Fiona shrugged. "I thought about dropping by her house, but I was on the phone all morning, arranging publicity. We're going to make a tape this afternoon and send it to the local radio station, and I'm going to be on the noon talk show on KFAR later in the week. There are so many details that sometimes I regret ever suggesting we stage the fair. I know I should have made a point of meeting Angie, and I feel awful that I haven't had a chance. But Angie knows what she's doing, and anyone who volunteers is always welcome." She paused to catch her breath. "Even your friend, Sally Fromberger, although I must say . . ."

"Yes?" I prompted, eager to find out how

she was going to continue. Perhaps some volunteers were a wee bit more welcome than others. And in this situation, Sally was on the other side of the clipboard, so to speak. She was more adept at issuing orders than taking them. I prefer to do neither.

"She's — well, highly enthusiastic," Fiona said without any enthusiasm whatsoever. "She proclaimed herself to be a prioress, Madam Marsilia d' someplace, and has recruited her book club ladies to be nuns. They want to set up a booth and sell indulgences, along with hot cross buns, rosary beads, and crosses made from scraps of tin. Lanya put her foot down when Sally mentioned religious relics, like bone slivers and flecks of dried skin purported to be from saints. From poultry, supposedly, but it's still grisly."

Julius and Edward came inside to haul the microphone and the amps out to the portico. Fiona gathered up an armload of plastic banners and followed them. Madrigal singers in red cloaks began to arrive, and after them a dozen musicians in blue and yellow tunics and floppy caps. A few of both species wandered into the store to use the restroom. It was all very colorful and pleasant, especially compared to the chaotic scene two days earlier. I'd expected Caron and Inez to show up, but concluded they'd gone off to work on their costumes.

As a crowd began to gather, I saw Sally Fromberger in her cape, accompanied by half a dozen pasty-faced nuns in what looked like tattered graduation robes and black scarves. Rhonda Maguire and some of her clique stayed at the edge of the crowd, waiting for Fiona to notice their presence before they slinked away to the mall — or their dance lesson at Angie's house. My science fiction hippie stared at the scene, scratched his head, and ambled away to ponder this latest manifestation of life's little mysteries. William and Glynnis Threet arrived, unaccompanied by the late Percival.

The performance went nicely. Edward juggled and balanced things on his nose, the singers sang, and the musicians did their best to start and stop at the same time. Fiona returned, wearing a lemony gown adorned with seed pearls and ribbon, and announced that she would be selling tickets. Julius trailed after her with a cash box and a foppish grin.

As Fiona had predicted, the demonstration did draw in a few customers. It was well after six before I shooed out the stragglers and locked up. On my way home, I walked by the blue house and noted that the basket was no longer on the porch. I considered stopping to ring the bell to make sure that she, rather than a neighborhood dog, had retrieved it, but decided I didn't really care.

There was no sign of Caron except for a cereal bowl in the sink. I tidied myself up, changed into clothes slightly less casual than my customary shorts and T-shirt, rinsed out the bowl, and left a note that I'd gone out with Luanne. With Salvador's directions tucked in my pocket, I drove to Luanne's store and parked by the curb until she came out. The bikers were beginning to descend on the Thurber Street bars and pool halls. Most of them could have been the original extras from *The Wild Bunch,* now old and paunchy enough to be grandparents or eccentric old aunts and uncles who belched at the dinner table and bored the kiddies with long stories.

Luanne was dressed to kill, in a manner of speaking. She was wearing a skimpy black skirt, a semitransparent blouse, and sandals with three-inch heels. She climbed into the car and studied me. "This is how you dress for a cocktail party?"

"I'm not on the prowl these days."

She laughed. "I should hope not. If I

could find a guy like Peter, I'd turn in my hunting license and learn to bake brownies. Have you spoken to him?"

"No," I said as I turned off Thurber Street to avoid the congestion. I handed her the directions. "You'll have to help me when we get past the stadium. I don't know those little streets. They're named after trees and birds. I can tell the difference between a mockingbird and a blue jay, but I'm not so good with white oaks, black oaks, sycamores, hickory trees —"

"I get the point," she said dryly. "So who's coming to this party?"

I told her as much as I knew. "And you may be interested in our host, Salvador Davis," I continued. "Tall, gorgeous, well traveled, ruthless, egotistical. You two have a lot in common."

"I should think so," she said, nodding as she thought this over. "You don't have any idea what he writes?"

"Not a clue. I looked him up in *Books in Print,* but couldn't find his name. If you're interested in him, I'll try some of the online booksellers and sources. I may not get anywhere if he uses a pen name."

"Not only tall and gorgeous, but also mysterious . . ."

I slowed down to peer at a street sign hidden behind some sort of flowering tree. "And ruthless and egotistical," I reminded her. "Maybe he writes how-to books for assassins and terrorists. I don't carry those, either."

We turned this way and that until we saw several cars parked on the street. I found a spot and waited while Luanne inspected herself in the rearview mirror. Once she was satisfied, we walked up a winding sidewalk to a house made of redwood, natural stone, and expanses of windows. It was definitely not a bungalow.

The front door was open. We went inside and paused to assess the scene. The living room was large, and furnished in a contemporary style that focused on color rather than comfort. Large oil paintings dominated the walls; they were filled with images of nudes swirling in fog, demons swarming like army ants, and body parts suspended in opaque liquids.

"My goodness," Luanne murmured. "You forgot to mention his peculiar taste in art."

I heard voices at the back of the house. As we started in that direction, Salvador appeared in a doorway. He was dressed in khakis and a shirt that discreetly advertised its designer, but his hair was tousled and his feet bare to assure us that beneath his *GQ* attire lurked the soul of a tortured artist.

"I'm delighted that you came, Claire — both you and your charming friend." He took Luanne's hand and bent over to kiss it. "I'll look forward to getting to know you better, my darling creature. What can I offer you to drink? I have everything from absinthe to zinfandel, as well as the customary bar offerings."

We allowed him to escort us through a dining room and out to a deck. While he poured me a glass of scotch and opened a bottle of wine for Luanne, I checked out the guests. Two Japanese boys were beside a table laden with a variety of seafood, cheeses, and puffy tidbits. Neither of them looked to be more than sixteen or seventeen, and I suspected from their red complexions and unfocused expressions that they had already worn a path to the bar. Lanya was seated on a deck chair next to a man with a gray beard, straggly hair, and harshly weathered skin. He had a smoldering pipe clenched between his teeth. In his dirty fatigue jacket and heavy shoes, he looked as though he'd just walked in from a covert mission in uncharted territory. If he was the Aussie, he was not the sort Luanne preferred. Anderson was leaning against a railing, deep in conversation with Fiona. Neither looked pleased. Julius was attempting to talk to the Threets, although she was dribbling steadily and her husband appeared to be dozing. Edward Cobbinwood was perched on the railing in the corner.

Since I was unwilling to intrude on Luanne's less than subtle interest in Salvador, and appalled by the idea of joining any of the other conversations, I went over to Edward.

He raised an eyebrow. "I didn't expect to see you here. It's so — I don't know — middle-class. Cocktails and canapés. I can hardly wait for the women to retreat to the kitchen to moan about carpooling and the men to talk about baseball."

"Don't hold your breath," I said. "So why are you here? Shouldn't you be drinking beer on Farber Street with your fellow grad students?"

"I didn't plan to come, but Fiona insisted on dragging me along. It seems that meek Julius Valens can turn into slobbering Mr. Hyde when he's had too much to drink. Hard to imagine, isn't it? I would have thought that at his worst, he might loosen his bow tie. I was surprised when Salvador invited me. Maybe he thought his Japanese friends might enjoy meeting someone their own age."

"Did they?"

Edward shook his head. "Salvador left them here all afternoon to let in the caterers and the deliveryman from the liquor store. Their party started several hours ago. The guy from Brisbane went rock climbing today, he told me. In that he hasn't had a shower since, I believed him. So here I am in the corner, drinking fizzy water and fated to be a designated driver."

"Is that why you were in the corner last night, too?" I asked. I took a sip of scotch as I waited for his response. In a sense, it was a very middle-class scene, although I doubted that car pools and baseball were likely topics. Fiona and Anderson were now hissing angrily at each other. Julius was keeping an eye on them between gulps of what looked like straight bourbon. As was Salvador, I noticed, although he had his hand on Luanne's shoulder and was cooing in her ear. Lanya was nodding at the Aussie as he rambled on, but I could tell she was also very aware of her husband and Fiona. There was a distinct chill in the air.

I'd about given up on Edward when he said, "I can't decide what to do about my father. How would you feel if someone dropped a bomb like that on you?"

"Women tend to know if they've given

birth," I said slowly. "But if I'd had a baby when I was young and put it up for adoption, and twenty years later a young person appeared on the porch . . . I don't know how I'd react, Edward. I'd be shocked, maybe skeptical at first. Would I feel an immediate bond between the two of us? I think — but keep in mind this is speculation — that once I was convinced, I would. Men might feel differently, since they're basically sperm donors."

"So you're saying I should just forget about it?"

"No, I'm not saying that at all. I simply don't know." I took a deep breath while I tried to compose myself. "If I knew his name, I might be able to offer an opinion. Bear in mind that's all it would be. No one can predict how someone else will react." That wasn't quite true, since I knew precisely how Carlton would react, which would be not at all. Dead men do not have emotional outbursts. Teenaged girls, on the other hand, most certainly do. One in particular has been known to go into paroxysms of hysteria when a spider creeps out of the bathtub drain.

"You're a widow, aren't you?" he said abruptly.

I almost spilled my drink. "How do you

know that?"

Edward slipped down from the railing. "I must have heard something. I think I'll have a drink. May I bring you something, Claire?"

I shook my head and watched him as he headed for the bar. Salvador had deserted Luanne and was now sitting with Lanya on a wicker bench. Julius had found the nerve to join Anderson and Fiona. The Aussie crooked a finger at me, but I ignored him and went over to Luanne, who was attempting to fend off the Japanese visitors. Luckily for her, they were too far gone to do more than make clumsy attempts to fondle her.

"Shall we go?" I said to her.

"Not quite yet," she murmured with a smug smile. "Salvador wants to show me his studio after he's played host for a few minutes. You can come along to protect my reputation."

"Since when have you been worried about your reputation? Your first debutante ball?"

"What a night that was. One of the girls who had an unfortunate tendency to whinny was escorted by her older brother, who was a midshipman at Annapolis. There's something about a man in uniform that's utterly impossible to resist. Regrettably, his sister caught us in the backseat of a Grand Prix and all hell broke loose. I refused to set foot in the country club the rest of the summer, even though it meant I couldn't defend my title in the tennis tournament. Damned if his sister didn't win, even with her wobbly serves."

"You are such a slut," I said as I replenished my glass.

"What were you and the codpiece whispering about in the corner?"

I dropped an ice cube in my drink. "We were not whispering. We were having a conversation about various things. I'm surprised you noticed anything but Salvador's meaningful gazes and quasi-erotic blathering. Are you sure you want me to stay? If I leave, you'll have to ask him to give you a ride after the party's over. That's not to imply you'll make it home before dawn."

Luanne glanced at him. "No, I'm going to keep him at arm's length for awhile. He's used to women falling all over him, and I suspect some of them are here right now. I'm just not sure who's sleeping with whom."

I brushed away the hand of one of the Japanese boys before he could make contact with my derriere. After he'd retreated a few feet, I continued. "Did Salvador say anything about the group dynamics?"

"He was uneasy. As soon as he noticed Lanya looking at him, he suggested I try the shrimp rolls and hurried over to rescue her from that Aussie. It could have been a simple act of mercy. I asked him about all three of his houseguests, but he was vague about why they were staying with him. He implied that he met them while he was traveling and offered a generic invitation, not expecting them to actually show up."

"Maybe," I said, not convinced. I noticed the Japanese boys were edging toward us again. "Are you sure you want to hang around, Luanne? Why don't you tell Salvador that you'll look at his etchings another time? We can pick up Chinese and go to your place."

Before she could answer, Edward joined us. He'd switched from fizzy water to fizzy wine, thus endangering his status as a designated driver. I hoped he was better able to handle it than the Japanese boys. He glanced guiltily at Fiona, who was trapped between Anderson and Julius and might be planning to dive off the deck at any moment.

Edward seemed to have the same thought. "She'd survive. It's only a three-foot fall onto the forsythia bushes. Anderson would go leaping after her, while Julius sat down to take off his shoes and jacket before he took the plunge. Then again, milady is too much concerned with her appearance to risk unsightly bruises and scratches. It would liven things up, though, don't you think?"

Luanne raised her eyebrows in genteel reproach. "This would amuse you?"

"You're the woman with the vintage clothing store," Edward said. "Are you one of Salvador's pursuers? You'd better get in line." He stepped back and retrieved the bottle of wine, then refilled his glass and drank half of it.

"I beg your pardon," Luanne said huffily. "I do not pursue men, and the only place I stand in line is at the grocery store. Why don't you go away and juggle corks or something?"

I hate to admit that I was finding this highly entertaining. The two were staring at each other as if they were feral cats. I could have intervened, but I decided to find out if Edward could insult Luanne to the point that she stalked out of the party. Which meant I could trail after her. Cocktail parties were now on the list just below meetings and potluck suppers. I had no desire to stand there for another hour or two, hazarding guesses about secret sexual liaisons. I didn't know these people, nor did I have any inclination to feel kindly toward them.

Abruptly, Edward looked at me. "I'm going to make an announcement. I could use some support."

"Announcement?" Luanne said. "About what?"

"The identity of my biological father."

I gaped most unbecomingly. "Now? Don't you think you should wait a while longer and reconsider the ramifications?"

He drained his glass and refilled it. "No, I've made up my mind."

"Edward, you should do this privately," I said, alarmed. "It's nobody else's business but yours and his. There's no reason to embarrass a bunch of innocent bystanders." I was so distressed that I ignored a pinch from behind. "Let's go inside and talk about this."

Luanne was puzzled, and rightfully so. "What is all this about, Claire? Why would you care about the identity of his father unless . . ." She stopped and stared at me. "You didn't tell me about this."

"Why should she?" drawled Edward.

I was desperately trying to come up with a response when the Aussie stood up. "Your attention, mates! Salvador here is too modest to crow, so I reckon I'll do it for him. Lift your booze and bottom-up to the bugger, winner of this year's Gryphon Award to be presented in Paris next month! Not only does he get a silver platter, he also gets a big fat check and a worldwide publicity tour. I'm proud to be one of his publishers, and I know you're all proud to be his friends."

Salvador smiled as we all obediently drank. "Thank you, Gudgeon. If I were a modest man, I'd claim that I didn't deserve the award. Since I am not, shall I open a couple of bottles of champagne?"

Before anyone could respond, a voice erupted from the dining room. "Bring on the saucy, dizzy-eyed, rump-fed wenches!" howled Benny Stallings as he staggered onto the deck, tripped over a chair, and went sprawling across Glynnis Threet's lap. "The beslubbering strumpets and the impertinent giglets! A pint of ale and a piece of tail! Sir Kenneth of Gweek is ready to rumble!"

CHAPTER FIVE

Glynnis began to caterwaul as she tried to shove Benny off her. Her husband grabbed a pillow to defend himself should the assault shift in his direction. Julius blustered incoherently, while Fiona fluttered her hands. Gudgeon began waving his arms. "See here, release that woman at once!" he shouted. "I flogged many a bloke better'n you when I was a warrant officer in the Australian Royal Navy!"

Benny draped his arms around Glynnis's neck. "Let's go waltzing, Matilda! Waltzing on the billabong!"

William hit him with the pillow. "How dare you speak to my wife like that!"

"Tie me kangaroo down, boy!" Benny roared. "Tie me kangaroo down!"

"Do something!" screeched Glynnis. "Get him off me!" The harder she tried to free herself, the more tightly he wrapped himself around her with the tenacity of an octopus.

She pounded on his back with her fists. "Anderson! I demand you get him off me this instant! I can't breathe!"

This last statement lacked credibility, since she had more than ample lung power and was using it. Unseen dogs barked and howled. Houselights came on beyond the trees. A car alarm went off, although that was likely to be an ill-timed coincidence. I wondered if the neighbors were debating whom to call: the police, an ambulance dispatcher, or a squad of animal control officers armed with tranquilizer guns.

Lanya went over and grabbed a handful of orange hair. "You are a drunken disgrace, Benny Stallings! Stop this immediately! Anderson, get over here!"

Luanne glanced at me. "Aren't you glad we stayed?"

"It does beat chicken chow mein," I admitted as Anderson tried to unwrap Benny's legs from around Glynnis's waist. The Aussie snared one of Benny's feet and began to yank on it. This motivated Benny to cling with greater determination as he continued to bellow about Matilda and billabongs, as well as billboards and billy goats gruff. Glynnis's screeches grew louder despite her claims of suffocation. Salvador reluctantly joined the rescue operation. Behind us, the

Japanese boys were shrieking with laughter. Edward, I noticed, had edged into a corner before he was enlisted into duty.

After several more minutes, Benny was at last disentangled and manhandled into a neutral corner. William offered Glynnis his handkerchief. She snatched it out of his hand and began to mop her face. Anderson, Salvador, and Gudgeon were panting as they stepped back.

"What's gotten into him?" demanded Lanya, glaring at Anderson as if he were the culprit.

"I guess I'd better take him home," he said. "Sorry if he ruined your party, Salvador."

Salvador smiled coldly. "Not at all, but I do think it would be best if you remove him before he launches another attack."

Benny did not look capable of launching anything as Anderson grabbed his arm and pulled him to his feet. "Well met, my Lord Duke of Dingleberry." He waved at Lanya. "And her Ladyship. Thou art a beauteous sight to behold 'neath the moonlight."

"Get him out of here," Lanya growled.

"And Lord Zormurd!" Benny shouted, gesturing in Salvador's direction. "I prayeth thou will not have me thrown to the zombies! I am sorely afeared of their ravenous appetites for mortal morsels such as I, your faithful servant."

Julius took Benny's other arm. "I'll help you get him to your car."

The three staggered past us. Benny gave me a calculating look before he was escorted into the dining room, then lapsed back into inebriated babble. We could hear him singing until at last the front door closed.

"A peculiar chap, that one," Gudgeon said as he headed for the bar. Lanya followed him, shaking her head.

Luanne made a remark under her breath, but I was too puzzled by Benny's peculiar flicker of sobriety — if that's what it had been — to answer. If he'd been pretending to be drunk, he'd failed to amuse anyone except the teenagers, who would have been amused by pretty much anything short of a heatstroke. It was more probable that I'd misinterpreted his look.

William and Glynnis stood up, expressed their gratitude for being invited (although with a marked lack of sincerity), and left. The Japanese boys made it down the steps to the yard without deleterious effects on their anatomies, and began to fence with sticks, all the while jabbering shrilly about Lord Zormurd. Fiona stood at the railing and stared at them, her expression grim.

"Not quite what I anticipated," Salvador said as he joined us. "I shouldn't have left Dazai and Hoshi alone with the liquor all afternoon. As for Benny, I didn't invite him simply because I was worried he might pull a stunt like this. He's likable, but so are bears — at a distance. My civilized cocktail party wasn't all that civilized, was it?" He put his hand on Luanne's arm. "Promise me you'll stay so that I can show you my studio. I had to badger the architect in order to get maximum natural light during the day."

"You paint by candlelight at night, I suppose," said Luanne.

"You'll have to find out for yourself." He gave me a faint smile. "And you, too, Claire. Once Anderson and Julius return, everyone will leave except us. Gudgeon will stay out here and keep an eye on Dazai and Hoshi. What happened to Edward?"

I looked around the deck. "He must have left during the melee," I said, trying to hide my relief.

"Understandable. Would you ladies care for another drink? Have you tried the caviar mousse?"

"I suspect the Japanese lads found it first," Luanne said as we all regarded the unappetizing red-speckled mush.

"The idea of eating fish eggs makes me queasy," said Fiona, who'd come up behind us with the stealth of a cat stalking a chipmunk. "I can't help thinking of them as tiny fetuses. What could be more precious than the first manifestations of life?"

"Then you're a vegetarian?" Luanne asked sweetly.

"Not precisely. I'm aware of the necessity of the food chain, but I do not condone unnecessary suffering. I refuse to eat veal or lamb, or the flesh of any animal that is not raised in a humane environment."

"Nothing better than a kangaroo steak fresh off the barbie," Gudgeon said with a chuckle. He stuffed a piece of cheese in his mouth and grabbed a bottle of bourbon. "Reckon I'll go see if our young Japanese friends want to go snake hunting under the deck. I damn near stepped on a real beaut of a copperhead this afternoon, nigh onto six feet long and right proud of his fangs, he was." He bounded down the steps to the yard.

"Where did you find these people?" Fiona asked Salvador.

I waited with interest for his answer, since it was a very good question. Etiquette precluded asking such things. It did not preclude allowing someone else to breach the rules.

Salvador shifted uneasily. "Gudgeon's my Australian publisher. I stayed with him for a few weeks last year, and felt obliged to reciprocate. I met Hoshi and Dazai at a fan convention in Osaka." He hesitated, aware that we were not satisfied. "They're good boys, both in school. They came with a group this summer to improve their English, and then took off on their own. You know how impulsive kids can be."

"A fan convention?" I prodded.

"Ah, yes, well . . . I mentioned I was a writer, didn't I? Hoshi's father plays golf with a relative of my editor over there. I suppose that's how the boys found out my address. When they showed up on my doorstep yesterday, I really had no choice . . ."

"What is it you write?" asked Luanne.

"Nothing you've read."

Luanne gestured at his house. "But you must do very well to have a house this large and a Lamborghini in the carport. I knew some writers back on the East Coast. They wrote genre fiction and could barely afford wigwams and quart bottles of beer."

Salvador tried to stare her down, but it was futile. Finally he shrugged and said, "I really don't care to discuss my financial situation with anyone. I've just finished a project, and now I'd rather forget about it and relax. Surely you can sympathize with that."

"Well, I do," Lanya said from the shadowy niche behind the bar. "Last week I started a batch of cranberry mead for Thanksgiving, as well as a few gallons of sweet raspberry melomel to give as presents at the Feast of St. Stephen. My fingers were so waterlogged I could barely flip through my recipe files. It was such a relief when I finally had all of it fermenting in the cellar."

"*Melomel?*" said Fiona. "That sounds like some kind of disgusting candy."

Lanya gave her a pitying smile. "I would have thought someone who claims to be well versed in British history would be familiar with it. Do you remember that rhubarb melomel I made last year, Salvador? I thought it came out well, even though I substituted lemon juice for the pectic enzyme."

"It was tasty," Salvador said reluctantly. "An excellent after-dinner drink."

Fiona shrugged. "I don't care for sweet wines. One might as well drink soda pop." She smiled at Lanya. "In your case, you might be better off with diet drinks."

"And you might be better off with a chastity belt," countered Lanya. "Don't forget to have several copies made of the key."

Gudgeon was being attacked by stick-wielding Samurai warriors, but Salvador was in greater danger, I decided. His only hope lay in the return of Julius and Anderson. I nudged Luanne and rolled my eyes in the direction of the door.

"Would you look at the time!" she said, no more eager than I to serve as a referee when the spitting and hair-pulling began. "I have a shipment arriving first thing in the morning. Three steamer trunks from an estate sale in Frederick, Maryland. I can hardly wait to see what's in them."

We expressed our thanks for being invited, wished everyone well, and fled through the dining to the living room. Luanne caught my arm before I could open the front door. "I'm going to find a bathroom," she said. "All that excitement is agitating my bladder."

"Not to mention all that wine."

"That, too. Don't you dare desert me. Benny may have escaped and be hiding behind a door somewhere — and there are a lot of doors in this place." She went down a hall, her footsteps hesitant.

I was idly gazing at Salvador's art collection when I realized that a woman was seated on the black leather sofa. Her frizzy black hair and black clothes made her nearly invisible. Her face was coated with black and white grease paint, her eyes nearly lost under eyeliner and mascara, her lips a dark magenta. For a somewhat hysterical moment, I wondered if she might be a mannequin left over from a macabre Halloween party.

To my dismay, she turned her head to look at me. Almost imperceptibly, her lips moved as she whispered, "Wet."

"Me?" I squeaked. "No, not at all. I'm waiting for my friend. She went to find a bathroom. It may take her a while. This is such a large house for the neighborhood. Quite elegant, though. There must be a wonderful view from these windows." I finally stopped myself before I forfeited the last vestiges of any remaining dignity.

"Wet," she repeated in the same slithery hiss.

"What's wet?"

"The paint."

"Then I won't poke it with my finger," I said. "Are you a friend of Salvador's?"

"I don't like it when people ask me that."

The conversation was not going well. If I'd had a clue how to find Luanne, I would have barged in and dragged her out the front door, no matter the condition of her bladder. "I'm Claire Malloy. My friend and I have been out on the deck with the others. Perhaps you should join what's left of them."

"My name is Serengeti."

"How interesting," I said. "Were you born there?"

"I don't like it when people ask me that."

It was getting monotonous. "Is there anything you do like people to ask you?"

She pondered this for a moment. "No, and I don't like it when people ask me that, either."

I was hardly in the mood to apologize. Wishing Luanne would hurry, I returned my attention to the paintings. They reminded me of posters from the 1970s, when marijuana and LSD were two of the four basic food groups. I looked more carefully at a particularly lurid collection of body parts and tortured faces, then at Serengeti. "Do you model for Salvador?"

"I don't like it when —"

"Never mind," I said wearily.

Eventually Luanne emerged from the hallway. "You would not believe this place," she began, then noticed the motionless figure on the sofa. "Who's that?"

"She doesn't like it when people ask her

that," I said as I propelled Luanne out the door. Giggling like teenaged girls, we went down to my car.

"Well?" she said as I started the car.

I recounted my lame conversation with Serengeti, and added, "I'm almost sure I could see her depiction in a few of the paintings, but with all that black makeup and hair, I could be wrong. It's happened before. Not often, of course."

"That particular affectation is called goth," Luanne said. "It was faddish when heavy-metal rock became popular back in the eighties. All those pathetic kids, rebelling against societal conformity by knocking themselves silly to look identical. At least this girl didn't have paper clips stuck through her eyebrows and staples in her cheeks. That's not to imply she hasn't had other parts of her body pierced."

I didn't want to think about it. "Well, at least we escaped. Couldn't you have come up with something more original — or at least been wearing a wristwatch?"

"Would you have preferred me to swoon?"

"No," I said, "since Salvador would have insisted that he carry you upstairs to his bed. Lanya and Fiona would have turned on me, since they saw us arrive together. He seems to have gotten himself into a bit of mess, don't you think?"

"Don Juan ended up being dragged to hell, at least according to George Bernard Shaw. Our boy may feel like he's on his way as we speak."

I laughed. "And hell hath no fury like two women scorned."

"I'm not so sure about that," Luanne said thoughtfully.

"That hell hath no fury?"

"Of that I'm sure," she said, then refused to discuss it further.

Sergeant Jorgeson came into the Book Depot the following afternoon. He never looked cheerful, but he seemed gloomier than usual. Instead of his customary brown suit and muted tie, he was wearing slacks and a pale blue cotton sweater.

"Ms. Malloy," he said, "I trust you're well?"

"I'm fine, thank you," I said cautiously. Jorgeson was not a customer, nor the type to make social calls. "You look very nice in your civilian clothes."

"Mrs. Jorgeson wants to know if you prefer yellow or red chrysanthemums."

"Please tell her that I'll be delighted with whichever she selects. It's very kind of both of you to offer your garden for the wedding."

"Happy to do it," he mumbled, looking around to make sure we were alone. "Then the wedding's still on, I guess."

I stiffened. "Why wouldn't it be?"

"Well, the lieutenant called me last night, said he was worried about you." Jorgeson held up his hands. "It's not like he said much, Ms. Malloy. He can't call during the day on account of how busy they keep him, but when he's tried to call you in the evenings, there's been no answer."

"So he sent you to check on me? How thoughtful, Sergeant Jorgeson. Perhaps you'll be so thoughtful as to check on him next week while he's at his mother's house with his ex-wife. He seems to feel as though he should tell her in person about the wedding."

Jorgeson rubbed his jaw as he looked at me. "Do I detect a certain note of coolness in your voice, Ms. Malloy?"

"You're the detective, not I."

"But I'm not the one you should be talking to." His lips pinched as he fell silent, either hoping I'd say something or praying I wouldn't. When I opted for the latter, he sighed and said, "Well, then, Ms. Malloy, I'll be on my way. Mrs. Jorgeson wants me

135

to go to the nursery and find a special brand of potting soil. She worries about things like that, even if the plants don't. One more thing. The head of the traffic control wanted to know if you'll be staging these outside performances today or tomorrow. What with the bikers arriving, Thurber Street's going to be a three-block nightmare."

"Not until Monday, but I'm not responsible for any of it. The events are being arranged by Fiona Thackery and members of ARSE. Did you hear about the knights in armor last Wednesday?"

"I did. I do not think you should expect a fruitcake from the chief of police at Christmas, Ms. Malloy."

He left before I could point out that I'd never had a fruitcake from the chief, or even a greeting card. In truth, the chief held me in such regard that if Farberville had a MOST WANTED: DEAD OR ALIVE poster, I'd be featured. I could easily imagine his expression when he'd learned that Peter and I were getting married. Which we most assuredly were, even if the lovely Leslie sat on a folding chair in Jorgeson's backyard and wept throughout the ceremony. So what if she was beautiful, intelligent, independently rich, charmingly eccentric, well bred, sophisticated, and chic? So what if Peter's mother doted on her?

No good answer came to mind, so I collected a stack of books on self-esteem and assertiveness, sat down at the counter, and looked through them. Outside, thunderous motorcycles began to make their way toward the strip of bars and restaurants up the street from the Book Depot. Engines revved in the parking lot of the beer garden across the street. Men and women clad in black leather jackets walked along the sidewalk, no doubt sweltering in the July heat. The ones who were dressed in more humdrum attire had graced tattoo parlors in their past. A few resembled ambulatory comic books. The plastic cups they carried most likely did not contain lemonade or one of Sally's chilled herbal teas.

They seemed harmless and more interested in impressing each other than in creating problems for the police. However, I decided I might as well lock up and go home, since my customers were not daring enough to venture out among potential road warriors and Hell's Angels, even if most of them qualified for Medicare.

Caron had gone to a bunking party the previous evening, so I had the car. I rarely had a chance to shop for groceries during the day, and the cupboard was nigh onto bare. An hour later I parked in my garage, grabbed a couple of heavy sacks out of the backseat, and lugged them upstairs. Two trips later my mission was completed, but my arms and shoulders ached. I poured a drink and flopped down on the sofa to recover before I faced the final chore of putting everything away. If Caron was home, she was holed up in her bedroom, aware that I might demand her help. She was a devious child, but she was the product of a gene pool that might have been murkier than I'd formerly thought.

On this occasion, however, she was blameless. The groceries had been dispersed to the cabinets, refrigerator, and freezer, and I was sitting on the balcony when she came home. A few minutes later she came out to join me.

"The telephone is not unplugged," I said, wincing as a motorcycle cruised past with the subtlety of a 747. "I am simply enjoying the view of the campus. It's much more attractive without students cluttering it up."

Caron was not interested in my serenity or my sanity. "The most incredible thing happened this afternoon, Mother! Inez and I went to the bookstore, hoping you'd let us have the car. You were gone. While we were deciding what to do, Miss Thackery came by to see you about something or other. She had her fiancé with her, the squirrelly guy who teaches drama at the college. He told us that if we volunteer to help out at some dorky community theater production for the next two nights, he'll let us borrow costumes from the drama department wardrobe for the Renaissance Fair. Miss Thackery got all indignant because we're supposed to make the costumes ourselves, so they had a squabble right there on the sidewalk. Inez and I were About To Die. Mr. Valens kept saying that all four members of the stage crew had quit because the director yelled at them, and the dress rehearsal was tonight. Miss Thackery said it wasn't fair for us to get special treatment, but he said —"

"Who won?" I asked, unwilling to hear a blow-by-blow recitation.

"He did," Caron said smugly. "Miss Thackery was fuming, but she wasn't about to agree to help him herself and risk breaking a fingernail. We have to go to the dress rehearsal tonight and the performance tomorrow night, and then Mr. Valens will meet us on campus and let us try on costumes." She sank down and leaned her back against the railing. "We are going to look utterly cool. We still have to dress as bar wenches, but Mr. Valens says there are all kinds of off-the-shoulder blouses and tight leather bodices. He even says they have special padded undergarments to make you look . . ."

"Brazen?" I suggested.

"Yeah, brazen. We're going to keep them here until the fair. Inez is convinced that if her mother sees them in advance, she'll freak out and make Inez wear a sweater. You don't mind, do you? I've always felt like Raggedy Ann instead of Barbie. This time I may catch Louis Wilderberry's eye, especially when Rhonda's tiptoeing around in a green leotard, tissue paper wings, and pointy ears."

Her eyes were watery, I realized with a flicker of guilt. I could still remember the horrid Halloween school carnival when she was in first grade. Despite my better judgment, I'd allowed her to dress as a prosecuting attorney, while her friends all dressed as princesses and ballerinas. Surely she deserved to exact her revenge after ten years.

"As long as Miss Thackery doesn't bear a grudge, you may wear whatever you like," I said. "And without a sweater. Whatever happens between Inez and her mother is none of my business."

Caron got up and gave me a hug. "Thanks, Mother. The rehearsal's at six, in the town hall of some retirement village near Hasty. Mr. Valens said it's likely to last until midnight because nobody has a clue what to do. The regular performance will be over at ten. He offered to drive us, but I'd rather take the car if you don't mind. He's kind of creepy."

"Why do you think that?"

She made a face. "I don't know how to explain it. He looks all meek and toady, but when he and Miss Thackery were arguing, I was afraid he was going to — to get violent and slap her or something. She must have seen it, too, because all of a sudden she capitulated and walked away from him. It was like he was simmering right below the skin. Inez said she didn't get that feeling, but half the time she was staring at those biker people. There was a little kid, maybe four or five, who already has tattoos on his arms and hands. That's child abuse. I mean, what if he's really smart and gets all these scholarships and becomes a famous judge and is in line to be nominated for the Supreme Court — but he has a swastika tattooed on his hand? Or he's short-listed to be president of Harvard? Somebody ought to call Social Services and have that child removed before his parents can really screw him up for life."

"Go for it," I said. "You'll find the number in the telephone directory, listed under Stump County offices. They may want you to go with them to spot the child on the sidewalk. Last year the unofficial estimate was five thousand bikers, but it's predicted that there will be more this year. It may take hours to find him."

Caron's lower lip shot out, which was as good as any response to a moral dilemma of this magnitude. "Well, somebody ought to call them," she said as she went inside and slammed the door.

I stayed where I was. Caron called good-bye as she went out the kitchen door and down the steps to the garage. After a half hour or so, I went inside to watch the news. The local TV station had live coverage from Thurber Street, but to the reporter's dismay, everybody appeared to be congenial and reasonably sober. She did her best by stressing the potential for destruction, disaster, and death should the situation deteriorate. I waited for her to suggest that viewers stock up on bottled water and batteries, but eventually coverage moved on to a goat show at the county fair ground.

I was debating which delectable gourmet dinner to nuke when the phone rang. I grabbed my drink, went into the living room, and picked up the receiver with only the mildest flutter of apprehension. "Yes?"

"Ah, Claire, I wasn't sure I'd catch you at home," Salvador said in a curiously flat voice, as though he'd have preferred that he hadn't.

"I can leave if you wish. There's rumored to be a lot of action on Thurber Street this evening. Nothing like a couple of thousand Harley-Davidson hawgs to stir things up."

"No, I would like to talk to you — that is, if you're not busy. I don't want to interrupt if you have plans. I shouldn't have called. It was a terrible idea, and I'm really sorry. We barely know each other. Why don't I let you get back to whatever you're doing?"

"Why do you want to talk to me, Salvador?" I said. "I am an exceptional conversationalist, I grant, but I am not a licensed therapist or an attorney. If you're suggesting some sort of libidinous liaison, you seem to have several willing candidates."

He took a moment to respond. "No, nothing like that. You've already made that clear. I just need to talk to someone who's . . . well, a disinterested party. Someone who can be objective. I don't even want advice. No, that's not true, but I have to make the decision. Talking to you will force me to sort out the situation in my own mind. Everybody wants to slap a label on me: I'm rich, I'm a womanizer, I'm a celebrity, I'm a cynic. So maybe I am all of those things, but that's not all I am. Right now I'm just a very confused, forty-year-old guy without a clue what I should do."

He sounded so miserable that I felt my dislike of him beginning to waver. "And there's no one else you can talk to except me?"

"I sent Hoshi and Dazai back to their group in Iowa. They were too hungover to protest. Gudgeon's gone caving in Kentucky. As for the ARSE group, there are obvious complications." He exhaled loudly. "Forget it, Claire. It might do me good to figure this out on my own. If I'm still around, I'll see you at the Renaissance Fair next weekend." A dial tone suggested the discussion was over.

I replaced the receiver and took a swallow of scotch. His final remark could have meant he might go out of town, or it might have been an oblique reference to his demise. His remark about "obvious complications" was less than enlightening. I was in an awkward position, which is my least favorite kind. I clearly could not call Lanya or Anderson for a chat about Salvador's mental stability. He'd tried his best to impress me with his urbanity and wit, but that did not rule out the possibility that his ego was not invulnerable. Inside even the most pretentious twit is an inner child, although in Salvador's case, said child was likely to have been bound and gagged at an early age.

"Drat," I muttered as I put the epicurean delight back in the freezer. I couldn't call Luanne, since she and some of her gay friends had decided to check out biker chic. By now they were undoubtedly sharing a pitcher of beer with men named Fat Daddy and Mongo. I looked for Salvador's number in the phone book, but he was not listed. Caron had the car. Farberville's only attempt at public transit was a fleet of two taxis, and they were in perpetual use by drunks needing a ride home or escort service employees making house calls.

I switched on the TV, but news had been replaced with a game show in which celebrities attempted to be adorable by exposing their ignorance. Competition was fierce. I flipped through more channels, all of them apparently showing commercials all the time. Why bother with a cast and a script, when there are SUVs to be sold, germs to be eradicated, and pills to be popped? I gave up and tried to read, but somewhere in the corner of my mind I was waiting to hear the scream of a siren as Salvador was rushed to the hospital. Of course, it was more likely that if he had done himself grievous injury, his body would lie undisturbed until Gudgeon came back with a bag of bat guano.

It wasn't that I simply didn't want to get involved. I really, most sincerely didn't want to get involved. I disliked Salvador, but in a passive way. When the Renaissance Fair was done, the only person in ARSE I would ever encounter was Fiona Thackery — unless I could arrange to be in the ICU on the night of parent-teacher conferences. That would require planning. I was thinking of other potential escapes when the phone rang. My book tumbled to the floor as I leaped up and grabbed the receiver.

"Are you okay?" I demanded, perhaps more shrilly than necessary.

"Are you?" asked Peter.

I caught my breath. "Yes, of course. Why wouldn't I be?"

"You sounded frantic."

"I am never frantic," I said coolly. "I may have been perturbed on occasion, but had I been frantic, my hair and clothing would have been in disarray and I would have been shrieking. That is hardly seemly behavior, is it?"

"No, I suppose not," he said, sounding a bit bewildered for some reason. "So how are you?"

"I'm fine, thank you. Are you still at spy camp?"

"Tonight's the final exercise. We have to crawl around in the dark and infiltrate the terrorists' campsite. Why any terrorists would set up camp near Farberville is a little hard to imagine. They'd be much more comfortable in a motel."

I sat down on the sofa and reached for my drink. "Then tomorrow you're going to Rhode Island? Your mother must be excited."

"I'm taking the shuttle to La Guardia. She's sending the car to pick me up. It's a three-hour drive, if we don't get caught in construction. I'll call you when I get there, probably around five or so."

"Are you going to bounce around the backseat of the limo all by yourself?" I asked, then bit my lip.

"No, I'll sit in the front seat with Witbred, just like I did when he drove me to nursery school. My mother has always believed he's been with us all these years out of devotion to the family. The truth is that he takes advantage of free room and board so that he can spend all his money at the racetrack.

His loyalty lies with his bookies." Peter paused, but I wasn't about to come to his rescue. "I don't know when Leslie's coming out to the house. She's in Paris right now, and my mother is uncertain when she'll get back. It's not a big deal, Claire."

"Did I imply it was?"

"The jury's out, but rumor has it they're leaning toward a conviction on all counts. Is there anything I can do or say to reassure you that I love you and want to marry you? That Leslie's no more than a part of my history? I don't have to go to Rhode Island. I can be on a flight to Farberville tomorrow afternoon, and back in time for dinner."

"No, Peter, you should go see your mother," I said, trying not to sound like a martyr. Even though his offer had come promptly, it had lacked enthusiasm. "She's been counting on it for a month — and if you cancel, she'll assume that I'm manipulative and spiteful. Just make sure she intends to put you and Leslie in separate bedrooms, preferably on different floors. Better yet, why don't you stay with Witbred in the servants' quarters?"

"I'll ask him if he wants a roommate," Peter said. "So what's happening there? When I spoke to Caron a couple of days ago, she didn't make much sense. From what I could make of it, she's going to work in a tavern. You've been out every night."

"That sums it up fairly well. Of course Caron doesn't know about Carlton's illegitimate son, or the writer who may or may not be committing suicide as we speak, or the goth who doesn't like to be asked things. Do you have any opinion about the color of the chrysanthemums in Mrs. Jorgeson's garden? We have a choice between red and yellow. Oh, and there's a house on the market in the historic district. I drove by it this afternoon on the way to the grocery store. It needs work, but it has bay windows and a wide front porch."

The distraction was a success. We chatted cheerfully until he ran out of time. After a few murmurs of an intimate fashion, he rang off in order to slather on black greasepaint, suitably dark clothes, and penetrate the mock enemy encampment. In that it looked as though I would be a blushing bride within two months, I decided to treat myself to a facial. I put on the teakettle, changed into my bathrobe, twisted a towel into a makeshift turban, and did a bit of slathering of my own with green goop. I was housebound for the evening, and blessedly free of Caron's sardonic allusions to wicked witches with pea-green complexions and warts on their chins. I still worried about Salvador, but not so much that I was willing to walk two miles in the dark to make sure he was all right.

I was in the kitchen adding a dollop of milk to my cup of tea when I smelled smoke.

CHAPTER SIX

I stepped out on the small screened porch at the top of the back steps. The smell of smoke was more intense. Everything seemed peaceful in the neighborhood, with the exception of the faint sounds of music and motors from the Thurber Street festivities. The smoke lacked the pleasant redolence of meat charring on a barbecue grill, but it could have been from burning trash or dead tree limbs. I went to the bottom of the steps and, wincing as my bare feet met gravel, continued slowly out to the side street. My eyes stung as the air grew more acrid. I could hear no sirens in the distance, or see flashing lights at the bottom of the street. I started down the sidewalk. Calling 911 prematurely would not be popular, as I had discovered earlier in the summer.

I was about to give up when I saw the yellow glint of flames through the front windows of the blue and white house. Angie's house. I ran across the street and onto the porch, and began to pound on the front door. According to Lanya, Angie had sprained her ankle, but the report might be out of date. If Angie had broken her ankle and required crutches, she might be trapped inside. The door was locked. I knew better than to break a window and send a fresh supply of oxygen to the fire.

My apartment wasn't far, but the house next door was closer. I bounded over a bed of begonias, flapping my arms like a wounded goose. Lights were on inside, although the curtains were drawn securely. I began to beat on the door with my fist while pushing the doorbell. I was preparing to throw a potted plant through the window when the door opened a few inches and a face peered out at me.

"Get off my porch before I call the police!"

It was the woman I'd seen in the porch swing earlier in the week, and she was in an even nastier temper. "There's a fire next door! Call 911 and make sure they get the address. I don't know if anyone's in there. The front door's locked. I'm going around to the back to see if I can get in that way."

As I rebounded over the begonias, I saw the woman come out to her porch. She would smell the smoke immediately, I assured myself, and make the call, even if she thought I was a lunatic. Before I could find a path through the untamed shrubs, I heard a deafening noise behind me. I reeled around. Stopping in front of Angie's house were two mammoth motorcycles. The drivers and passengers wore black helmets and would have made convincing alien insectoids in a B-grade science fiction movie. Moderately convincing, anyway.

Luanne yanked off a helmet and said, "Good grief, Claire! Have you lost your mind?" She climbed down and came across the yard. "It is you, isn't it? Halloween's a good three months from now. Do you realize what you look like?"

In that she was wearing skintight leather pants, boots, and a bright red T-shirt cropped to expose her navel, I could have asked her the same question, but instead said, "There's a fire inside and someone may be in there! I can't get in through the front door. Help me find a way around to the back."

Luanne gestured at the two men and the woman, who'd removed their helmets and were huddled uneasily at the curb. They'd apparently already seen the flames in the front room, and wasted no time busting through the shrubs. We shoved and shouted at each other until we arrived at the back of the house. The door was locked.

"Break it down," Luanne commanded her troops. The larger man flung himself against the door until it splintered and gave way. Smoke billowed out like a suffocating sand storm. It was impossible to see across the room. We all recoiled and retreated to the sparse grass.

"Did you call the fire department?" the woman gasped.

"The next-door neighbor did," I said, then paused. "I hope she did, anyway."

Luanne gave me a curious look. "She may not have believed you. Lance, use your cell phone."

The fire was nearly as loud as the motorcycles had been. By this point, I knew it was consuming the walls, and the roof would go next. I am not a fool, and most certainly not foolhardy. "We'd better go around front and wait for the firefighters!" I yelled over the din from inside the house.

We went back through the shrubbery, Lance trailing as he dutifully kept the cell phone to his ear. I could hear him attempting to answer questions, but since he didn't know the address, the owner's name, the number of occupants, or the cause of the fire, his responses were short.

When we reached the sidewalk, Luanne pulled me aside. "What are you doing outside like this?"

"My bathrobe is tattered but hardly provocative," I said. I knew my hair was mussed, since the towel I'd been using as a turban had fallen off, and my feet were bare. "You can throw me a lingerie shower if it'll make you happy."

"We'd better move our bikes out of the way," the big man said. He was rubbing his shoulder as he tried to pretend he wasn't staring at me. Which he was.

"Maybe in that alley across the street," the woman said. "All hell's going to break loose in about three minutes when the fire trucks, police cars, and ambulance arrive."

We looked at the house. The interior was lost in a conflagration of smoke and flames. Sparks shot from the roof. The neighbor was in her yard with a hose, attempting to defend her house and begonias. The back of the house on the other side of Angie's was buffered by an alley and a graveled parking area. Luckily, there was not even a mild breeze.

After the bikers had moved their precious vehicles, they joined Luanne, Lance, and me on the sidewalk across from Angie's house. I was mesmerized by the fire, and struggling to keep myself from imagining what must have happened to anyone trapped inside. Angie could have escaped through the back door and slammed it behind her. For that matter, she could be among the thousands of people on Thurber Street, or be having dinner at Lanya and Anderson's house. I'd never laid eyes on her. She could be twenty-one or seventy-five.

All hell did indeed break loose. Three fire trucks came roaring up the street, sirens screaming. As the firefighters began to dash around purposefully, an ambulance squealed around the corner. Police cars descended in a drove. Porch lights came on in most of the houses on the block, and their residents spilled out to the sidewalks to gawk.

Lance, who'd been on his cell phone with the 911 dispatcher, clicked his phone closed and sat down on a low wall. "They seem to have found it."

Luanne abruptly switched into her genteel-hostess mode. "This is Claire Malloy," she said to the others. "Claire, this is Lance, my hairdresser. I believe you met last year at a wine-tasting at the arts center. We ran into these two at the beer garden. This is Shellie Morrison, a caterer from

Manhattan, and Phillip Leiberman, a lawyer from . . ."

"Longboat Key in Florida," he supplied. "I specialize in trusts and estate planning. It's a very lucrative area for a nice Jewish boy from Brooklyn."

"You came all this way for the biker rally?" I asked.

"Every year," Shellie said. "I'd much rather deal with bikers than hysterical brides."

It was ludicrous, I thought, and as surreal as any of the paintings of Salvador, Davis and/or Dali. It was fortuitous that I was no longer in high school and required to write the essay on what I did last summer. It might be several hundred pages long.

They were staring at me, as if expecting me to say something clever or even invite them to my apartment for a drink. Before I could come up with a response (or a platter of cheese and crackers), a pair of uniformed officers loomed in front of us. Over the next hour, the fire was extinguished and some of the vehicles departed quietly. A van from the local TV station inched by, then sped off. We were asked the same questions by what felt like dozens of police and fire department investigators. When it became evident that none of us had anything further to contribute, I asked one of the officers if they'd found a body.

"Not yet," he said, "but we can't do a thorough check until we ascertain the condition of the roof and floors." He stopped and frowned at me. "Aren't you Lieutenant Rosen's . . . ?"

"Yes, I am."

The officer was not happy. He consulted one of his fellow officers, then told the bikers and Luanne that they could leave, then added that I'd better stay where I was until he returned. Ignoring my protests, he hurriedly walked away.

"This is ridiculous," I said to Luanne. "Do I look like a pyromaniac?"

"Oh, no," she said. "You most definitely don't look like a pyromaniac. We came by to see if you wanted to go for a ride, but it looks as though you're in for a long night." She picked up a helmet. "There's no reason for the rest of us to hang around. I need a very cold beer."

"You're deserting me?" I squawked.

Shellie and Phillip shrugged as they stood up, neither of them willing to comment. Lance pressed his business card in my hand and told me to call for an appointment at my first opportunity. Considering what we had just gone through, I'd expected some sense of camaraderie. Luanne, who should have insisted that she stay by my side (or at least called a lawyer), grinned at me before she turned into the alley. Seconds later, the bikes rumbled away toward Thurber Street.

My feet hurt from the harsh contact with the gravel, pavement, and stubbly grass. I examined them for signs of blood and blisters, willing to demand immediate medical attention. The stone wall was not padded, nor was my derriere. I was clammy from the perspiration that had flowed copiously from the unwarranted exertion. As I waited, irritation turned to anger. Being mild-mannered, I generally refrain from expressing extreme emotions, and I fully subscribe to the adage that revenge is best served cold. In this case, however, I was already cold, as well as thirsty and exhausted.

I finally snapped and stood up, prepared to go home, fix a drink, and thumb through the phone directory for a lawyer who specialized in arson and, if it came to it, false imprisonment.

The young officer, who must have been lurking behind or in a tree, caught my arm. "Ma'am, if you won't wait voluntarily, I'll have to take you into custody."

"For what?" I jerked myself free. "I have

already explained umpteen times that I smelled smoke, went outside, saw the fire, and asked the neighbor to call 911. I've never met the woman who lives — or lived — in that house. Her first name was Angie. She was teaching the fairies to dance. You need to get in touch with Lanya and Anderson Peru. They're the duke and duchess of whatever."

"Have you been drinking, ma'am?"

"Much earlier in the evening. I am now going home to resume drinking. I live on the top floor of that duplex fifty feet from here. Just follow the sounds of the tinkling ice cubes."

A car pulled up and Sergeant Jorgeson emerged. "Ms. Malloy," he began, then stopped, gaping at me.

"Et tu, Brute?" I snapped.

"Are you ill?"

"I am ill-tempered," I said. "I am also bruised and battered. Will you please tell this barbarian to step back and let me go home?"

Jorgeson shooed away the officer. "If this is some kind of prank, Ms. Malloy, I fear I must admit its intent escapes me. I'm sure you have a very good explanation, since you always do. I would like very much to hear it."

I gestured at the firefighters near the sole remaining truck, the fire chief huddled with investigators, the milling police officers, and the few residents still loitering in their front yards. "Ask any of them. I've been detained for over two hours, Jorgeson, and told my story so many times it's become rote. Why would you even suggest this is some kind of prank? That house burned down, for pity's sake, and there may be a body inside. It's not the same as stringing toilet paper in the tree branches or throwing eggs at the front door, is it?"

Did I mention I was angry?

Jorgeson gave this some thought, then sighed. "You're right, Ms. Malloy. This was not a prank. I'll still need to talk to you, but it can wait until tomorrow. You go on home and wash your face, then have a cold drink."

"Wash my . . . ?" My hand moved slowly to my face. I'd totally forgotten about the facial mask I'd so whimsically put on earlier. Most of it had melted from the heat and perspiration, but there were still crusty patches clinging to my cheeks and chin. I undoubtedly resembled some hideous monster rising from the depths of a murky swamp. Gulping, I said, "Yes, Jorgeson, we can continue this tomorrow. Now if you'll excuse me, I really must go."

■ ■ ■ ■

I was picking up discarded cups and other debris in the Book Depot parking area the next morning when Lanya drove up.

"This is terrible business," she said as she got out of a vintage station wagon. "I understand you reported the fire. I'm just so — I don't know — not devastated, but —" She dabbed her eyes with the cuff of her faded blue work shirt. "You must be, too."

I suggested she come inside for coffee. After we were seated by my desk, I said, "Did they find . . . Angie?"

"I'm sorry to say they did. In the bedroom, on the floor." Her hand was trembling as she slurped some coffee, and her tanned face had a sallow undertone. "They wanted my help to identify the body. That was impossible, of course. I talked to Angie on the phone a few times, but I never met her. I can't even remember her last name, if she ever told me. She called me early in the summer to ask about Avalon." She noticed my blank look. "The local fiefdom, in the county of Mistymont."

"But all she did was call? She didn't want to meet the local members?"

Lanya shook her head. "From what she said, I got the feeling she was a recluse. I offered to come by and visit, but she rattled off a lot of flimsy excuses. If I hadn't happened to come across her name in my notebook, I wouldn't have thought to ask her if she might want to participate in the Renaissance Fair."

"If she didn't want to meet anyone, why did she volunteer to coach the fairies?"

"I was surprised that she did. This fairy business is silly, but Fiona insisted. It seems the fair she went to last month had fairies, and they were wildly popular with the children. I thought we should stick to the maypole and folk dancers, but Anderson sided with Fiona." Her mouth curled unpleasantly. "As did Salvador and Benny, especially after Fiona mentioned recruiting some of her high school girls. William Threet didn't say a word, but his eyes were bright. Glynnis was too busy glaring at him to comment."

"And Edward?"

She thought about it for a moment. "The potluck last Thursday was his first meeting, so maybe he didn't think he should offer his opinion. I doubt I mentioned it to him when he called a couple of weeks ago to ask about joining the fiefdom. Anyway, I told Fiona she could schedule the fairies in however she wished, and that I would have no part in violating the basic tenet of ARSE. It's hardly authentic, is it?"

"Well," I began, "Shakespeare —"

"Rarely," Lanya said curtly. "The obsession with delicate, winged fairies was more of a Victorian thing. Supernatural creatures in earlier fiction were wicked and ugly. Monsters, witches, ogres, trolls, even elves — none of them were romantic figures."

"Perhaps not." I grabbed some papers and stood up. "I'm sorry about Angie, Lanya. I guess she was a recluse. The morning after the meeting I stopped by with your basket, and she wouldn't answer the door. Her neighbor had never seen her. The authorities will locate her next of kin. There's nothing you or any of the rest of us can do."

She acknowledged my less than subtle hint and put down her mug. "No, there isn't. I feel bad about it, though. I should have made more of an effort to reach out to her, but I've been canning tomatoes and beans. I have two bushel baskets of peaches to tackle next. The children need supervision night and day. Last week they took the roof off the shed and made it into a raft. They were in the middle of the pond when it sank. Anderson finds ways to work late so he doesn't have to deal with them. So typical of men. They're happy to make babies, but they aren't so happy to follow through for the next eighteen years."

I felt a sudden pang, but it was not from sympathy for Lanya. "Typical," I said, nudging her out of the office. "By the way," I added ever so casually, "have you spoken to Salvador recently?"

She gave me a sharp look. "Since the cocktail party that Benny disrupted, you mean?"

"Like this morning," I murmured, trying to hold my own and not squirm. If she wanted to pour out all the lurid details of whatever sexual shenanigans were taking place in the idyllic fiefdom of Avalon, that was fine with me. It was not, however, what I wanted to know at the moment.

"As it happens, I dropped by his house this morning after I finished my interview at the police department. I thought he should know about Angie. He was appalled, as we all were, but he didn't know her. He insisted that I stay for coffee so that we could discuss another issue." A grin spread across her face, and her face turned rosy. "It was a most rewarding conversation."

I wasn't sure if she was implying the conversation had taken place between the sheets. If so, I didn't want to know. "Oh, really?" I said lamely.

"Yes." Still beaming, Lanya went out to her station wagon and drove away.

Relieved to know Salvador hadn't done anything dreadful to himself, I resumed picking up litter in the parking lot. A couple of my regular customers ambled by, clutching hefty *New York Times* newspapers that arrived by special arrangement to a newsstand up the street. I decided that as soon as the parking lot was acceptably tidy, I would close the bookstore for an hour to go collect my newspaper, along with a cappuccino and a pastry. Business was usually marginal on Sunday afternoons, allowing me to tackle the crossword puzzle in pleasant solitude. Jorgeson would come by to pester me, but I had nothing more to add to the previous night's statement. I knew even less than Lanya about Angie and her unfortunate demise. Jorgeson would have better luck with the flock of fairies, who'd at least been in the house and presumably met Angie. As had Edward Cobbinwood after the ghastly potluck on Thursday.

I had just lugged a garbage bag to the Dumpster behind the bookstore when I spotted my science fiction hippie wandering along the railroad tracks. He was bobbling his head and beaming at the wildflowers on the embankment. There were times that I envied his detachment from reality, even though I suspected it came from an overindulgence of illegal substances in the seventies. He was whistling as he followed me into the store.

"Peace be with us all," he said in the benign voice of a priest dismissing his flock.

"Amen," I added under my breath.

"Did you catch the scene with the burning house last night? It was fantastic."

I nodded. "You were there?"

"Not in that sense, no." He went behind the rack to browse through the science fiction and fantasy paperbacks. "I was looking for a cat when I saw all the flashing lights and people running around in the dark. I thought it might be a wedding or something like that. When Princess Zirconia got married, her husband had to fight an albino tigress with twelve-inch claws before he could claim his marital prerogative."

"Did you find your cat?"

"I didn't say it was *my* cat."

I didn't even want to think about the possibilities. I let him alone for a few minutes while I rinsed out the coffee mugs and the pot. When I returned, he was shuffling toward the front door. "Wait a minute," I said, as I always did. "Empty your pockets."

Unabashed, he put three paperbacks on the counter. "Did you see the swamp man last night? I was surprised, since everyone knows they're terrified of fire. Lord Zormurd used torches to hold them back while his men searched their cave for the Crusaders' gold relics, but then it started to rain. I thought His Lordship was a goner."

I tried to think where I'd heard the name Zormurd. After a moment, I realized Benny Stallings had yelled something about it when he'd crashed Salvador's cocktail party. "Who's Lord Zormurd?"

The hippie headed back to the rack to make a second attempt to shoplift. "He's the fiercest warlord of fourteenth-century Waldsenke, and a direct descendent of Attila. His beloved Lady Maves was kidnapped on the eve of their wedding by the Duke of Plendark. Zormurd spends all of his time trying to rescue her, but so far all he's been able to do is slay a couple of dragons and defeat the Plendarkian cavalry. Of course he doesn't know that Princess Zirconia's husband — the one who fought the albino tigress — is a spy."

"Oh," I said. "If you run into him, give him my best wishes."

I allowed him to leave despite the suspicious bulge in the pocket of his fatigue jacket. He was amiable and often amusing, but his prime virtue was that he wanted nothing more from me than a purloined paperback book. In his befuddled mind, I did not exist outside the bookstore. I wasn't sure he did, either. Ours was a very uncomplicated relationship.

I walked up the hill to fetch my newspaper. When I returned, Sergeant Jorgeson was waiting on the portico. "Ms. Malloy," he said as he took the key from me and unlocked the door. "I was beginning to wonder if you'd decided not to open the bookstore today. You were rather high-strung last night, according to the reports."

"If you read them, then you know why," I said. I set the newspaper and a small sack on the counter. "Lanya Peru came by earlier. She mentioned that someone from the department had called her about the body found after the fire."

"We were hoping she could enlighten us."

"In England, the term is 'assist us in our inquiries.' It has a much classier ring to it. You might suggest it to the chief."

"I'll keep it in mind, Ms. Malloy. Ms. Peru said that she'd never met the deceased. When we spoke to the neighbor, however, she was able to describe a woman who'd visited the house earlier in the week. She mentioned that this visitor had messy red hair and was skinny, and appeared to be on foot. Being unimaginative, I could think of only one person who met the description."

"I am not skinny," I said indignantly. "I am svelte. And my hair wasn't messy, it was damp. I will have to admit I was on foot in the tradition of Little Red Riding Hood. It was a pleasant morning, and I do my best to be environmentally conscious of the damage caused by excessive reliance on petroleum products. Did she mention that?"

"No, she did not," Jorgeson said. He crossed his arms and waited.

I was eager to have my cappuccino and get to the crossword puzzle, so I relented. "I went to an ARSE meeting the night before, and Lanya asked me to drop off a basket of edibles. I knocked on the door, but no one answered. I eventually left the basket on the porch. So, Sergeant Jorgeson, I'm even less help than Lanya. What about the fairies?"

He took a small notebook out of his pocket and opened it. "We're trying to locate a teacher named Fiona Thackery to get their names. In the cop dramas on TV, the witnesses are always at home. Alas, in the real world, people are less cooperative. We'll keep trying."

"Caron knows," I told him. "When I left this morning, she was still in bed. If she's not home now, you might try Inez's house. And if you can't locate them, I'll give you the names of some more of the high school kids. One of them can help you."

"An excellent idea, Ms. Malloy. I will assure the lieutenant that you assisted us in our inquiries with your customary charm. Have you two . . . ah, resolved your differences?"

"Meddling does not become you, Jorgeson. Your ears turn redder than chrysanthemums. Nevertheless, the answer is yes. He's cn route to his mother's house as we speak. Leslie is in Paraguay or Prague, or someplace like that. I might not be terribly upset if she were arrested at an airport for smuggling cocaine, but I don't suppose that's likely to happen. Peter's planning to be home next Sunday." I hesitated, then plunged ahead. "You will have this wrapped up by then, won't you? I'd hate for Peter to get back and have to deal with this case."

"And see your name?"

"That would be a factor," I admitted, wondering if Jorgeson could be bribed with a hazelnut muffin. "My involvement is minuscule. All I did was perform a minor act of charity by dropping off the basket. I can swear truthfully I never met the victim. The houses in the neighborhood are old and likely to have the original wiring. Shouldn't you be going after the landlord for violating the fire code?"

"He's already been interviewed, but it doesn't matter if the wiring was faulty. The fire was set intentionally, according to the arson investigator at the fire department. Some sort of accelerant like gasoline or kerosene was used."

"Ooh, that's nasty," I said. "I wouldn't think Angie had been in Farberville long enough to make an enemy like that. What have you found out about her, Jorgeson? The landlord must have known something."

"Only her first name. She rented the house by telephone, and mailed a deposit and three months' rent in cash. The landlord left the key under a mat by the back door. We're tracing the call from his end, and all we know so far is that it was local. He thinks she was calling from a pay phone because of the traffic in the background."

"What about fingerprints?"

"On what, Ms. Malloy? He put the cash in his bank account, and threw the envelope and note away. No car of unknown owner- ship has been found in the area. Our lab guys will try to pull up some prints from the exterior doorknobs, but even if they find a decent one, it'll have to match one in a data bank. Maybe someone will report a missing person, and we'll be able to identify her by whatever the autopsy indicates. It won't be much, though. Height, gender, a ballpark estimate of age, old fractures. Dental records, if they exist." He shrugged, then surprised me with a wry smile. "I asked Mrs. Jorgeson about the green substance on your face. She herself doesn't care for that sort of thing, but she was kind enough to explain it for me. There are certain female rituals that are difficult for men to understand."

He was chuckling as he left. I was annoyed at his minor display of chauvinistic superiority, but decided to forget about it since he had allowed me to avoid questioning at the police department. Peter would have been more than appalled if I'd been paraded into the building for the entertainment of the night shift. At least the written reports would be dry recitations riddled with poor grammar and misspelled words. It occurred to me that it might be prudent to assist the detectives in their investigation in hopes the whole matter would be resolved quickly.

Regrettably, I didn't know any more than Jorgeson. He was on his way to round up whichever of the fairies he could find on a sunny Sunday afternoon. Instead of following in his wake, I could let Caron and Inez handle it. Rhonda Maguire was their nemesis, but some of the other cheerleaders could be wheedled into describing the dance lesson. Not that a physical description would be useful, I thought, since it didn't really matter. Angie might have said something about her past, however, that would explain where she'd lived previously and why she'd moved to Farberville. Or why she'd bothered to call Lanya if she didn't want to meet the local members.

Edward had not lived in Farberville long enough to be in the telephone directory. I called information, but his name was not listed. The college information operator assured me his name was not in the student directory. There was no point in trying the art department office on a Sunday afternoon. He'd said he lived close enough to bicycle to the campus, which meant nothing. Neighborhoods like mine ringed the campus for blocks.

Obviously, I could have called Sergeant Jorgeson and told him I'd just remembered that I might have seen Edward on Angie's porch. I'd have to do it eventually, no matter what. I wanted to talk to Edward first, though, and get the paternity issue resolved quietly. Whatever had happened between Carlton and Edward's mother did not need to be dragged into the investigation. Gossip was staple fare in Farberville. Caron would be mortified if her half brother (aka, the guy in purple tights) became the topic of conversation at the high school, the mall, and the pizza places. I would be no happier about it, but she was the one who would be bombarded with catty questions and snarky comments.

"Lord, what fools these mortals be," I muttered as I put the crossword puzzle in a drawer for future consideration. I spotted the file Fiona had given me and found the schedule of events to be performed on the portico. Tomorrow I could expect musicians and dancing fairies. I hoped they'd attained some level of proficiency in their class with Angie. On Wednesday, the dank and steamy knights returned to do battle. This time perhaps Madam Marsilia d'Anjou would seize the opportunity to peddle her hot cross buns.

Since business was nonexistent, I locked the store and went out to my car. Caron and Inez would need the car to go to the theater for the performance, but not for a couple of hours. I decided to drive to

Salvador's and ask him if he knew how to get in touch with Edward. That, and find out why he'd sounded so urgent the previous night.

I still had his written instructions in my purse. Without treacherous Luanne's navigating skills, it took me nearly twenty minutes to find his house. It was larger than I'd realized, with the second story extending over the carport. The only car in sight was the Lamborghni in the carport, glittering as though it had been freshly waxed.

I pulled up the driveway and stopped. I ran my fingers through my hair, and would have checked my lipstick had I been wearing any. After all, I was nothing more than a disinterested party. I rang the doorbell and waited, growing uneasier as each second passed. I was about to leave when the door opened.

Serengeti stared at me.

CHAPTER SEVEN

In full sunlight, Serengeti looked even more garish. Her complexion was grayish white, either from the theatrical makeup or entirely too much time lying in a coffin during the day. Untamed black hair kept her features in shadows. Her dark eyes were heavily outlined in black, as were her lips. I tried to imagine her sitting at the family dining table with doting parents and genial relatives, while small cousins climbed in her lap. The image eluded me.

"Hi," I managed to say. "I came by to see Salvador. Is he here?"

"I don't like it when people ask me that." Leaving the door open, she silently faded into the interior of the house.

I licked my lips, then ventured into the living room. There was no sign of her, or of anyone else. It could have been a room in an art gallery, if said gallery also served as a funeral home for the Addams family. I continued through the dining room, saw Salvador through the sliding doors, and went out to the deck. Newspaper sections were piled sloppily on the floor next to his chair, and a cigar smoldered in an ashtray on a nearby table. As I opened the door, he turned around and smiled.

"Claire, my dear," he said as he stood up, "you're just in time for a martini. Sunday afternoons can be so boring, don't you agree? Make yourself comfortable." Without waiting for a response, he went over to the bar and began to take out the necessary accouterments. "I suppose if one liked to watch sports on TV, it wouldn't be so dull. Despite my all-American upbringing, I never developed a taste for watching men swing iron sticks at innocent white balls. What about you? Did you grow up playing lacrosse and field hockey?"

"Not really." I sat down at a distance from the cigar, crossed my legs, and waited. After he'd brought a pitcher and glasses to the table and resumed his seat, I said, "I'm sorry for barging in like this. Serengeti left the front door open, so I just came inside."

"Serengeti? What's she doing here?"

"I have no idea. It's your house, Salvador."

"And she's here?" He glanced back at the sliding door. "Did she say anything?"

I couldn't help glancing back, either, as if she might be there, listening to us. "Only that she didn't like it when I asked her if you were home. She models for you, doesn't she?"

"Sometimes," he said, "but not for the last week or so. We settled up after the final session, so I don't owe her any money. You know, I thought I saw her on the second floor a few days ago. It was dark, and by the time I turned on thc light, nobody was there. I decided I'd had too much wine. You think she's in the house now?"

"She was ten minutcs ago. She was here Friday evening, too. Luanne and I met her in the living room. Does she have a house key?"

Salvador rumbled unhappily. "I don't know. With the exception of my studio, I rarely bother to lock doors when I'm in town. I don't like the idea of her wandering around the house, especially when I'm home. I'd have a heart attack if she came into my bedroom in the middle of the night."

"Then talk to her," I said sensibly.

"Maybe later," he said, glancing once again at the door. "She and I don't communicate very well. I have no idea about her personal life, but I wouldn't be surprised if she lived under a rock in the woods. When I need her to model, I leave a note on the bulletin board at that coffee shop across from the arts center. She simply shows up. Afterward, I pay her in cash and she leaves." He stared at the olives in his glass. "I think she does. Is it possible that she doesn't? This is a big house, and I hardly ever go into some of the rooms. You know, in the last month I've noticed that I was running low on orange juice or bread when I thought I was well stocked."

I wasn't going to offer to help him search the house for her, so I changed the subject before he could suggest it. "Lanya came by the bookstore today. She said she told you about Angie and the fire."

"A terrible thing," he said, grimacing. "I didn't know her. As far as I know, none of us did. I've been to a few big tournaments, but I can't remember ever meeting anybody named Angie. There are legions of people at these things, with elaborate tents and RVs in camps that cover several acres. Almost all of the attendees use their ARSE titles instead of their real names. There are usually a thousand lords a-leaping and nine hundred ladies dancing, and the partridge is served at the royal banquet."

"And the five gold rings?"

"Sovereignty of the kingdom until the next tournament. Whoever scores the most points in sword fights and jousts is coronated King or Queen. Same thing at the county level to become Duke or Duchess. Lanya and Anderson have won numerous times over the years."

"Women engage in sword fights?" I asked. I didn't object to the idea, but it seemed as odd as women playing professional football. There was no reason why they shouldn't, if they had the physical aptitude and the desire. I just couldn't think of a reason why they would want to engage in such a potentially painful activity.

"There's no gender bias or age discrimination on the battlefield. Once the armor's on, everybody's an equal. Luckily, experience almost always wins over youthful bravado. Lanya is renowned for her ferocity and cunning." Salvador leaned over and picked up the pitcher. "Ready for a refill?"

"No, thank you. I came by to ask you if you happen to have Edward's address or phone number."

Salvador sat forward so abruptly that the martini glass slipped out of his hand. Luckily, it rolled under a chair instead of shattering. Cursing to himself, he went to the bar and refilled a new glass, then sat down. He tried to look at me, but his eyes shifted away as if I'd said something ludicrous. "The jester? Don't you think he's a bit young for you?"

"Because I'm old enough to be his mother? Is that your point?"

"I was teasing, since you've made it clear that your virtues are beyond corruption. No, I don't know much of anything about him. Lanya waits until October to put together a directory. After the semester begins, we do a few demonstrations on the campus to recruit new members. For now, you'll have to ask her about Edward. Do you have an urgent reason to find him today?"

I did, but I wasn't about to admit it. "No, nothing that can't wait. So all your house-guests have gone?"

"The Japanese boys are back with their group. Gudgeon will probably show up again before he goes back to Australia. For the moment, I'm on my own. I presume you are, too."

"Why would you presume that?"

"You were home alone last night."

"My fiancé is still out of town," I said. "Luanne invited me to go to the biker festival, but I declined. Too noisy for my taste."

"Mine, too. Lovely day, isn't it?"

We both gazed at the backyard. Birds were twittering in the oak trees. A cat leaped on the top of the fence, stared at us, and disappeared. No motorcycles roared, not even in the distance. It was a pleasant neighborhood, I thought. If Peter and I couldn't find anything suitable in the historic district, I might consider the area. A house as large as Salvador's would unsettle me, but surely there were more reasonable ones. A pool would be nice, as long as someone other than I handled the maintenance. After certain distasteful events earlier in the summer, I had established an amiable relationship with a gentleman who owned a pool service. As long as I would provide him with coffee and listen to stories about his dog, he'd give us a reasonable deal. Peter had made a secret bargain with Caron; it occurred to me that it might include a pool, rather than a Porsche.

"Sorry about the disruption at the cocktail party the other night," Salvador said, interrupting my meandering thoughts. "Benny's a good sort, but he can be overly exuberant. He would have been a splendid Viking back when raping and pillaging were acceptable social activities. He's a well-known structural engineer, so his employers tolerate him. That doesn't mean I have to. We used to be close friends, but we've drifted apart. When I'm not locked in my studio working, I travel. I'm getting older, and he's getting younger. Strange, isn't it?"

"Why did Benny call you 'Lord Zormurd'? That's a fictional character, isn't it?" I tried to remember the details my science fiction hippie had been burbling. "He's out to rescue his bride from dragons and people who reside in swamps."

Salvador snorted. "Something like that. Benny's preferences in literature do not include the classics. He tends to get carried away with this knight business, and fancies himself to be an incredibly romantic figure. He has his eye on some of the ladies in our little group. They're not always as eager as he is to indulge in lustful trysts in the moonlight, although he and Lanya . . . well, you know what I mean. I don't know the details, but she broke it off because she was afraid Anderson would find out — or so she said. The three of them met back in college when they joined an ARSE fiefdom. I don't know who was sleeping with whom during that time, but Anderson and Lanya ended up married."

"How do you know all this?"

"Lanya told me. She drops by every now

and then when Anderson is working late. She suspects that he's having an affair with his secretary, which is likely to be true. I can't blame him for not wanting to go home at the end of the day. He told me he'd file for divorce if he weren't terrified that he'd end up with custody of the kids." He shook his head, presumably in sympathy for one of the Perus. "I don't know if it's a blessing or a curse to be cast in the role of confidant. Sometimes I feel like a bartender."

"A disinterested party, so to speak?"

"You're referring to my call last night, I assume. Please forget about it. I overreacted to an unsettling piece of information. One of those things that's hard to assimilate, like a punch in the gut when you're not expecting it." Salvador held up his hand, then realized it was trembling and quickly put it on the arm of the chair. His eyes were too bright and his voice too hearty as he continued. "Not to imply violence was involved. Nothing like that. In any case, a bottle of chablis washed away my woes. Or maybe it was a case of chablis. The details are fuzzy."

"You sounded suicidal."

"Now you're overreacting, dear Claire. I may have a touch of romanticism in my soul, but I'm far too pragmatic to cause myself physical pain. At midnight I decided to absolve myself of sin through generosity. Luckily, my financial situation is such that I will feel nothing more than pinpricks. I will even give up my misanthropic ways, although that will be painful. However, all's well that ends well, as the bard opined."

"He wrote some tragedies, too."

"I never cared for those." He held up the pitcher and looked inquiringly at me. When I shook my head, he added a splash to his own glass. "I hear your daughter and her friend scored in the costume department. They'll be a couple of sexy wenches."

I didn't care for his tone. "But they'll still be less than half your age, and I'll be there to keep an eye on them. You may think Lanya's ferocious, but you've never seen me with a mace."

"Do come by the archery stall and say hello. Will you be dressed in garb? Julius could probably find something for you, as well. Lady Clarissa of Farberville. You can waft about the fair, looking down your lovely nose at all the uncouth peasants and ruffians."

"I don't think so," I said. I thanked him for my untouched martini and left. I did not spot Serengeti as I went through the house and out to my car. I peered in the backseat, just in case, and then drove home.

The only thing I'd learned was that Salvador was a first-class gossip and had seemingly vanquished his personal devils. In exactly one week, the Renaissance Fair would be over and Peter would be home. If he wasn't too tired, I would allow him to take me out to dinner. I would not mention Leslie, and if he had any sense, he wouldn't, either. At least not on his first night home.

Caron and Inez were sprawled in the living room when I arrived at the apartment. The remains of a pizza were in a box on the coffee table, along with cans of soda, cartons of dip, chips, and a package of cookies. Sally Fromberger would faint on the spot at their idea of a well-balanced meal.

"How was the dress rehearsal last night?" I asked as I joined them.

"It lasted until two in the morning," Inez said. "The so-called actors tripped, fell, giggled, sneezed, and forgot their lines. Two of them cried. One of them threw a vase at another one, who stalked off and locked himself in the ladies' room for an hour."

Caron rolled her eyes. "And those were the high points. The curtain collapsed. One of the stage lights started smoking. Mr. Valens blew the fuses three times, resulting in total darkness and wild accusations of groping from the wings."

"Oh, dear," I said. "I hope things go better tonight. What are they performing?"

"A tragedy."

"*Agamemnon? Oedipus Rex?*" I suggested. "Something by Euripedes?"

"*The Sound of Music,*" Caron said with a groan.

"That's not a tragedy."

"It will be. Trust me."

Inez began to snicker. "The youngest von Trapp child is thirty-five, the oldest about sixty. They wear lederhosen. All of them have hairy legs, including the women. The nun yodels."

"One performance, and then you'll have earned your bodices," I said. "Please stick to modest for Inez's parents' sake, if not mine." When they ignored my remark, I added, "Did you hear about the fire last night?"

"Oh, yes," Caron said. "We also heard about you. Are you sure you should be lecturing *us* about modesty? At least we don't run around the neighborhood in bathrobes and bare feet, not to mention green, scaly faces. What if the news camera crew had shown up? Haven't you already done enough to Ruin My Reputation?"

I raised my eyebrows. "Was I carted off to the animal shelter in a gorilla suit? Did I serve six weeks in detention for stealing the frozen frogs from the biology department?"

Inez blinked with impressive (if less than convincing) sincerity. "But none of that was our fault, Ms. Malloy. You said so yourself."

"I most certainly did not," I said, "and whatever I did say was an attempt to keep you out of juvenile court. When you turn eighteen, you're on your own. I understand that even minimum security prisons lack spas and tennis courts."

"Whatever," Caron growled. She does not care to be reminded of certain undignified activities in the past few years.

I waited a moment, then said, "Are the fairies upset about their teacher's death?"

"Some of them are creeped out," said Inez. "I mean, they were in the house. They thought Madam, as they were instructed to address her, was kind of a freak and obsessed with perfection, but they were sad when they heard about her. That must be a terrible way to die."

"Duh," said Caron, who was still annoyed at me, and therefore at everyone else within spitting range. "Would you rather be disemboweled while you're alive, or be trampled by a herd of buffalo? Thrown in a pot of boiling oil?"

"My three greatest fears," Inez retorted.

"They're right up there with being accused of mooning over Louis Wilderberry in the cafeteria. Rhonda snickered about it the rest of the day. She did everything but announce it over the PA system."

I realized I'd better intervene. "Did Sergeant Jorgeson get in touch with you earlier?"

Caron was still glowering. "Yes, and I gave him some names and telephone numbers. It's not like he could have found anybody this afternoon. They all went to the lake. Rhonda's uncle has a cabin and a party barge. Why don't you have any cool relatives, Mother?"

This was not a question I cared to answer. Years ago, when I thought she was old enough to understand, I'd explained the situation. Now all three of us were annoyed. I went into the kitchen and poured myself a drink, then returned with a forced smile. "Did the fairies say anything about Madam? Did she tell them where she was from or why she'd moved here?"

"Not really," Inez said. "She sort of slouched around while she poked them with an umbrella and made nasty remarks about how clumsy they were."

"She didn't mention any friends or enemies?"

"You'll have to call Rhonda and ask her. They should be back from the lake in an hour or two," Caron said. "Can we have the car now, Mother? Mr. Valens wants us to come early so he can redo the lighting. I told him the play would be better if it was performed in the dark — and in pantomime. He looked pissed, but I could tell he agreed."

"I doubt the retirees of Hasty are ready for alternative theater," I said, then told them they could go search the hills for the sound of music, as well as a few of their favorite things. I was relieved to be rid of them for the evening. I tidied up, turned on the news, and settled down on the sofa. Peter had promised to call once he arrived at his mother's house. I wanted to tell him about the area where Salvador lived, but it might be tricky to explain why I'd spent part of the afternoon sitting on Salvador's deck, with a martini glass nearby. Then again, it might be the moment to remind him that I was not without appeal to others of his gender.

As for Edward Cobbinwood, there was nothing I could do until he showed up at the bookstore. If I called Lanya to ask for his phone number, she would demand to know why. I wasn't ready to implicate him in the arson investigation, and I wasn't about to mention his parentage until I talked to him in private. Without a reasonable explanation, she would conclude, as Salvador had done, that I had designs on him.

If I ended up in court, I would do so with my dignity intact.

Luanne called while I was eating dinner. I allowed her to grovel, then accepted her apology and gave her an update. We agreed that it was all very peculiar and puzzling. After we'd run out of speculation, we planned an evening of popcorn and movies later in the week. Peter finally called to say that his flight had been delayed by weather, but he was at his mother's house and was looking forward to a hot shower and a decent bed. Caron came home much later, took a soda out of the refrigerator, and retreated to her bedroom.

And so to sleep, perchance to dream.

The next few days passed uneventfully. The fairies performed as scheduled on the portico, drawing attention primarily from children, college boys, and geezers clad in Bermuda shorts. Caron and Inez had chosen costumes from the theater department, but refused to model them. I finished the

Sunday crossword puzzle (in ink, of course) and resumed reading the real estate ads. Anderson and Benny appeared in armor once again to whack at each other, while Fiona watched from the sidelines. Madrigals were sung. Lutes were strummed. Tickets were sold. Edward Cobbinwood did not appear, however, so I'd finally told Sergeant Jorgeson that it was possible that there might be a link between Edward and Angie. Underwhelmed by my revelation, Jorgeson agreed to look into it. Peter's calls were infrequent and inevitably cut short by a whimsical demand from his mother. Sally and her entourage had paraded past the Book Depot several times, perhaps readying themselves for a crusade. Best of all, I'd had minimal contact with the ARSE members, limited to watching Julius struggle with his sound equipment.

By Friday, I was optimistic that the Renaissance Fair would come and go without any demands on me. Luanne and I planned to attend on Saturday afternoon, both out of curiosity and to support Safe Haven, the battered-women's shelter. I'd just sold a guide to indigenous wildflowers to a retired couple when Edward came into the store.

He waited until the transaction was finished and the couple gone, then said, "Good morrow, Claire, for that is your name, I hear."

"Good morrow," I said politely.

"I guess you've been wondering where I was all week."

I pretended to consider this while I put away the sales slip. "No, Edward, I haven't." This was, of course, a lie of immeasurable magnitude. I'd imagined him in a endless variety of situations, including one in which he approached Caron to give her a brotherly hug. Half of one, anyway. I turned around and looked at him. His face was pale and his hair uncombed, and he looked as though he'd lost weight. Dark smudges under his eyes suggested he hadn't been sleeping. "A police detective questioned me this morning. He wouldn't say why he thought I'd known Angie. I finally figured out that you were in the car that drove by her house when I was there."

"I had no choice," I said. "They're investigating arson, if not murder. The fire was set intentionally. As far as I know, they haven't had much luck learning anything about her past or present. You knew her?"

"Yeah, sort of. I met her at a Ren Fair in Sacramento. She was selling fairy wings and wands, and junk like that. We sat at a picnic table and had a couple of pints of ale, talked about ourselves. When Lanya mentioned that a woman named Angie was going to work with the fairies, I wondered if it might be the same woman. Funny, the two of us running into each other fifteen hundred miles from California. I went by to say hello and to ask if I could shop for her or anything. She stayed in the doorway, said she didn't need any help, and thanked me for coming by. I'm not sure she even remembered me. I felt like an idiot."

"She never told you where she was living when you met her?"

"Some little town in Arizona. If she told me the name, it didn't register. All I could tell the detective was that she was about forty years old, brown hair, and was using an umbrella as a cane. Not much help, I'm afraid."

I was watching him closely, unsure that he was telling me not only the truth, but the whole truth. "You said the two of you talked about yourselves over ale. She must have said something."

He blushed. "I guess I did most of the talking. I'd just found out about my father, and I didn't know how I felt about it. Up until then, I'd never had a father. I mean, well, I knew some guy had impregnated my mother, but he didn't have a name or a face.

He wasn't real. When I was a kid, I used to fantasize that he was a cowboy or an astronaut, then later that he was a celebrity. I didn't hide girlie magazines under my mattress; I had issues of *People* and *Entertainment Weekly.* Whenever I was in San Francisco, I'd stare at the restored Victorian houses along the trolley route, picturing him living in one with his perfect wife and two adorable, polite children. His name would be Michael, his wife's Stephanie. Mike Junior and Julia would attend a private school and take music lessons. I even gave them a dog."

"I can understand that," I said. "I'm sure a lot of children in your situation do the same thing."

Edward tried to blink away the tears welling in his eyes. "One day I saw them — all four of them — walking on Fisherman's Wharf. Michael and Stephanie were holding hands. The children had balloons. I followed them all afternoon. I'd just gotten up the courage to approach them when they got in a car with a Nevada license plate and drove away. I felt like I'd been slapped." He turned away, his shoulders hunched and trembling.

It was almost — but not quite — enough to move me to tears as well. I went around the counter to pat him on the back. "Edward, you're going to have to tell me your father's name. You told me that you came to Farberville specifically to find him. By now you surely know enough to step forward and acknowledge him. Instead, you're playing some silly game that only hurts you all the more."

"I just can't get up my nerve," he said in a low voice. "It could go so wrong. Another slap in the face, but this one would sting forever. No more silly fantasies about Michael and Stephanie, or anybody else."

"You'd still have your mother."

"She packed up and left two years ago. She didn't even warn me before she disappeared, but later I heard that she was living on a farm up north. Not long after that, one of her old friends told me that she died and was buried courtesy of the state. No funeral, nothing." He paused and wiped his eyes. "My college friends made more of a fuss when their goldfish died and was flushed into eternal bliss. We had to crowd into the bathroom and sing hymns."

I felt worse than what might euphemistically be considered evidence of the proximity of livestock. He was still a kid, despite his college diploma. I was begrudging him what family he might have. Carlton's relatives were not likable. In truth, most of them were loathsome, and that was putting it kindly. However, Edward would have aunts, uncles, and cousins, as well as Caron and me.

"Okay, Edward," I said, "let's cut to it. Tell me your father's name."

"When the time is right."

My sympathy was rapidly being replaced with exasperation. "I have no idea why you're being so coy about this, unless you enjoy tormenting me."

"Why would I do that?"

"I really don't know, Edward. Just tell me his name and get it over with — okay?"

He fidgeted for a moment, then said, "I promised Fiona that I'd go out to the mall and draw a crowd so she can sell tickets. She's picking me up in half an hour, so I need to get home and change into my garb. You'll be at the Renaissance Fair tomorrow. We can talk then." He dug into a pocket and handed me a folded envelope. "These are free tickets for admission and the banquet. The Duke and Duchess have requested your presence at the royal table. You don't have to wear garb if you don't want to, but it would be better. Lanya said she'll find a gown for you. I'll see you there."

He scurried out the door, leaving me to

gape at the envelope.

I went into the office, picked up the phone, and dialed a familiar number. "Lu- anne," I whimpered, "we have a problem . . ."

CHAPTER EIGHT

On Saturday morning Caron was long gone before I bestirred myself to crawl out of bed. I'd yet to see what she and Inez were wearing, so I could only hope that they had anticipated Fiona Thackery's wintry judgment. If they incurred her disapproval, she'd have two semesters to exact her retribution. Julius Valens had supervised their selection from the theater department's wardrobe. He, too, would have enough sense to keep the girls' cleavage covered. Caron's, at least. Inez had expectations.

Luanne had agreed to go with me to the fair, but had balked at the idea of attending the banquet. Her comments about eating greasy food with one's fingers while seated on a long wooden bench had not imbued me with enthusiasm. I could see no way out of it. I was to be an honored guest of the Duke and Duchess of Glenbarrens, who might call for my beheading if I snubbed them. Sally had lost herself in the role of Madam Marsalia d'Anjou to such an extent that I was concerned about her unraveling sanity. If I failed to take my place with the Duke and Duchess, as well as Lord and Lady Bicklesham (the Threets), the Baron of Firthforth (Salvador), Sir Kenneth of Gweek (Benny), Squire Squarepockets (Julius), Lady Olivia of Ravenmoor (Fiona), and whomever else, I would hear about it for months, if not years. Sally has not only the bulk of an elephant, but also its memory. A rogue elephant that tramples villages and everything else in its path, including bookstores.

And after all, with the exception of slippery fingers, how bad could it be? There would be lots of pomp and pomposity, processions, heralds, trumpets, and so forth to amuse the bourgeois. Wine, as well as lemonade. Entertainment from Pester the Jester, the musicians, the madrigal singers, the dancers, and, of course, the fairies. Their faces might be green with greasepaint, but they would be bright red underneath it. Two hours, max. I'd spent longer than that in a sadistic plastic chair in an airport.

I avoided the side street when I walked to the bookstore. Business was brisk, as it usually was on Saturday mornings when my regulars discover the need for books on gardening, decorating, grilling, or escaping into fantasy in a hammock. The sky was dotted with only a scattering of clouds, boding well for those who would park in a pasture and slog through weeds. Toothy Dan, the weatherman on the local TV station, had predicted sunshine and temperatures in the mid-eighties. A lovely day for parsley, sage, rosemary, and mead.

Sergeant Jorgeson came into the store late in the morning, dressed in slacks and a cotton shirt. "Ms. Malloy," he said with a nod, "I thought you might be at the Renaissance Fair."

"Luanne's picking me up at one. Aren't you and Mrs. Jorgeson going?"

"I fear we are not. A number of her relatives — sisters and cousins and aunts and such — are arriving later this afternoon. Maybe nieces and nephews. Ex-husbands and stepmothers. She comes from a large family prone to divorces and remarriages, and I have difficulties figuring out who they are. Instead of spending the weekend relaxing on my deck, I am working my way through a list of chores."

I tried not to smile. "And I made the list? How fascinating."

"Technically, I am on the way to the paint

store. Mrs. Jorgeson has decided the guest bathroom is dingy, so we're going to paint it lilac. I just stopped by to tell you that we've made no progress identifying the victim of the fire. The remains have been sent to the state lab. We won't hear from them for several weeks."

"And the arsonist?"

He shrugged. "No one has admitted seeing anything. Most of the residents on the block were either at the biker rally or in their living rooms watching TV. The woman next door had her blinds drawn. All of the residential fires in the county in the last year were caused by wiring, space heaters, or stupidity on the part of the homeowners, so there's no reason to think we have an arsonist in the area. Until we identify the victim, we have no leads as to motive. The young man whose name you finally brought to my attention had nothing useful to contribute. We are at a standstill, which is a very unsatisfactory position to be in. Lieutenant Rosen will not be pleased to find the open file awaiting him when he returns."

"Tomorrow," I said firmly. "He called two nights ago and said he'd be home late in the afternoon. I've made dinner reservations."

Jorgeson hesitated. "Have you? Well, I

must continue on in search of the perfect shade of lilac, which I believe is a fancy name for purple. Please permit me to ask a small favor of you, Ms. Malloy. I have a feeling that some members of the Renaissance society are not being entirely candid about this woman named Angie. I've interviewed all of them. There's a sense of conspiracy, although I have no idea what it involves." He stopped, struggling to clarify his thoughts. "Odd comments, shaky laughs, evasiveness. I've learned over the years that even the most innocent witnesses can be unnerved when questioned by the police. These people, however, are keeping secrets that may or may not be relevant." Looking straight at me, he added, "As you have been known to do, Ms. Malloy."

"Me?" I said huffily.

"It has happened," he said. "I would appreciate it if you could talk to them, and see if you get the same feeling. I don't mean you should interrogate them or anything like that, but chat."

"They're not my close friends, Jorgeson. I doubt anyone is going to mention buying kerosene on the afternoon of the fire. That sort of thing rarely comes up in casual conversation."

"Perhaps you underestimate their fondness for you, Lady Clarissa."

My mouth was still open as he left. Had I missed something on the nightly news or on a banner outside the bookstore? I found the local newspaper and leafed through it until I came to an ad promoting the Renaissance Fair. Dates, times, location, events. A map indicating the location of Lanya and Anderson's realm. And a list of dignitaries at the banquet, including one Lady Clarissa of Farberville, better known as local bookseller Claire Malloy. I could almost see Salvador's smirk as he'd made sure my name was prominently displayed in the ad. I could only hope that Serengeti smothered him in his bed one night.

When Luanne arrived, I locked the store and got into her car. "Shall we have lunch before we join the festivities?" she asked sweetly. "Or would you rather not be seen in public with a lowly peasant?"

"Don't you dare say that name," I growled.

"Whatever pleases Your Ladyship. I suppose we can make do with charred turkey legs and tepid ale."

I let my head fall back against the seat. " 'Now is the winter of our discontent,' " I intoned, " 'made glorious summer by this sun of York . . .' "

"So it's the summer of our discontent."

"Don't split hairs." I told her about my brief conversation with Edward. "I still have no idea what he's going to do," I went on, "but I may have to move to York. Not New York, though. With my luck, I'd bump into the lovely Leslie as she came dashing out of some *très chic* boutique. I'd be wearing sweats and sneakers. Baggy sweats and sneakers with holes."

"Has she shown up in Mommie Dearest's mansion yet?"

"I don't know. It's a touchy subject. Peter didn't say anything when we spoke, and I didn't ask. Of course I had to bite my lip so hard that it swelled up as if I'd run into a door." I gazed out the window at the passing array of fast food joints and used-car lots. "Jorgeson came by earlier, too. He hasn't made any progress finding out about Angie. He thinks some of the ARSE people know more than they told him."

"Do you?" Luanne asked as she serenely drove through a yellow light.

I considered this for a minute. "Not really," I said slowly. "Edward's the only person in the group who admits to having met her. Rhonda Maguire and her coterie did go to her house for one dance session, so we know she was more than a voice on the telephone. According to Caron, they did not enjoy it. A couple of them cried, and one has bruises from being wacked with an umbrella. If somebody had thrown eggs at Angie's front door, I'd suspect them. Arson, no."

Luanne began to curse under her breath. "Look at this traffic! You'd think this was a Grateful Dead concert if it weren't for all the children hanging out car windows. This is going to be a nightmare, unless Your Ladyship has special parking privileges. Where are the cops when you need them?"

The cops proved to be a hundred yards farther up the road, uniformed and already sweaty. We were directed into a pasture where acned teenagers in plastic orange vests pointed and blew whistles as drivers obediently pulled into designated spots. One particularly grim teenager marched over to an errant driver who was attempting to turn around and began to screech at him. I could see the kid had a promising career as a drill sergeant in the military — if he wasn't run down in the immediate future.

"Guess this is where we park," Luanne said. "I hope I can find it when I leave. What are you going to do? The banquet's not until six."

"This is not what I expected. I was planning to go back with you, and then have Caron come pick me up later. She and the other workers had to be here early. They're probably parked at the far end of a pasture in a different area code. She and I may be stuck here until the banquet's over. I shouldn't have agreed to any of it, including the demonstrations on the portico. I may not be a doormat, but I seem to have a lot of footprints on my back." I caught Luanne's arm as we began to trudge across the pasture. "And if you refer to me as 'Your Ladyship' one more time, I'm going to tell Gudgeon you have a mad crush on him but are hopelessly shy. He can climb rock walls, you know. He could scuttle up the side of your building and be in your apartment in ten seconds — and in your bed in another five."

"As you wish," Luanne said meekly. "It's just that I've always been entranced by royalty. I'm not completely sure Charles won't ditch Camilla and come riding up Thurber Street in a twenty-four-carat carriage to whisk me away. Now that you're titled, you can be one of my ladies-in-waiting. Imagine what a jolly time we'll have frolicking with the corgis on the grounds of Balmoral and riding to the hounds."

"Balmoral or Bellevue?"

At the corner of the pasture, we were herded down a path that led to the fair. Above the gate was an arch decorated with plastic roses and brightly painted cardboard shields. Two teenaged girls sat behind a table, selling tickets. Ten dollars for adults, five dollars for children under twelve, free for those six and younger. I gave the girls the two complimentary tickets, twenty dollars for the women's shelter, and accepted site maps indicating the locations of stages, food tents, vendors, portable toilet facilities, the first-aid station, and a list of the times for performances. Visitors were warned to watch out for beggars and pickpockets.

Luanne and I moved out of the stream of chattering ticket buyers and tried to make sense of the map. The pasture was cluttered with tents sporting banners, stalls, picnic tables, and temporary stages. I could hear musicians playing enthusiastically. A loudspeaker crackled as the time of the next competition was announced. The crowd surged along the walkways between the tents. Most wore shorts and T-shirts, but a few were in their version of medieval attire. The loudspeaker crackled again, this time urging people to attend an exhibition of falconry next to the pony rides. A juggler in a top hat and a ragged tuxedo was setting off squeals from a herd of children.

"Goodness," I murmured, having expected a much dinkier production. Instead, the scene looked as though a medieval circus had rolled into town the night before. "Shall we see if we can find the food court? Caron and Inez are likely to be there."

"Where did all these people come from?" asked Luanne, as awed as I. "Some of them . . . well, some of them need to be sent back right away. Look at them! If that woman so much as sneezes, her buttons will go flying off like bullets. And those oafs in burlap-bag tunics and boots. Talk about beer bellies. If I were married to one of them, I'd be wearing the burlap bag over my head. Sheesh!"

"Be charitable," I said. "Think of yourself as a social anthropologist doing field work."

"I'd rather think of myself as a pampered princess drinking gin and tonics in the garden behind Buckingham Palace."

"I hope you're not frittering away your life savings while you wait for Charles."

"What about Grace Kelly?" she countered. "Or Mrs. Wallace Simpson and Queen Noor? Rita Hayworth married Ali Khan. It happens all the time."

"Keep telling yourself that when your children put you in a home for delusional indigents."

We joined the crowd, doing our best to stay on the sidelines. It was slow going, since the vendors' tents were held up by ropes staked to the ground. Luanne stopped to admire a display of beadwork. I wandered ahead, keeping an eye out for familiar faces (and potential escape routes). It wasn't possible that the entire population of Farberville had turned out for the fair, but it certainly felt like it. I spotted the mayor and his wife eating ice cream bars at a picnic table. The young couple who owned the newsstand were dressed in garb. She was quite fetching in a blue gown, and he seemed at ease in a wizard's cloak. A member of the English department with a secret craving for romance novels waved at me. His wife, whose stash consisted of fantasy paperbacks, was wearing a tight suede jacket and long skirt; she looked ready to have a sunstroke at the first opportunity. A stooped crone hobbled by, her robe and broad-brimmed hat so thickly covered with scraps of rags, ribbons, and tin trinkets that she resembled a heap of rejects from a donation bin. Robin Hood and Friar Tuck stood outside a booth, talking on their cell phones. A beggar in black rags tried to wheedle money from a monk with a pierced lip.

Somewhere to the left of us, a roar of laughter indicated a performance that was apt to be bawdy.

I was beginning to enjoy the sense of frivolity when Edward, now clad as Pester the Jester, wobbled up on his unicycle. "Good day, Lady Clarissa," he said as he teetered in front of me, somehow managing to stay atop his contraption. Several people stopped in hopes of seeing an undignified sprawl. "The Duchess of Glenbarrens bids you wait upon her at your earliest convenience. She and the Duke are in the Royal Pavilion. What say you, milady?"

I looked back, but Luanne had disappeared. She was a pushover for jewelry, and was no doubt having a fine time. I nodded at Edward. "I shall heed the Duchess's request. Alas, I must admit I know naught of the location of the Royal Pavilion. Whither might it be found?"

"I will show thee the way." He spun around and went wobbling off, dodging children with painted faces and clothes streaked with dribbles of ice cream.

The Royal Pavilion was in the center of the activities, near a maypole with dangling ribbons. It wasn't as grand as the name implied, consisting of a large tarp that provided shade, tapestries tacked on the back wall, a piece of worn carpet on the ground, and an assortment of props and a wooden trunk partially hidden behind a blanket draped over a clothes rack. The scattering of chairs looked suspiciously like the ones in Lanya's kitchen. Anderson sat on one of them, his legs extended and his arms crossed, looking imperially bored. He was wearing a long, embroidered vest over a silky tunic, and a gaudy crown. Lanya's dress was tight, with a scooped neckline adorned with lace and sequins. She, too, wore a crown. The Threets, dressed for court, hovered nearby. Benny, or so I assumed, stood behind them in full armor, a three-foot battle-ax in hand to ward off marauders.

Lanya gestured at me to join them. "Tut, tut, my dear. We can't have Lady Clarissa roaming about in shorts. I found a few of my old gowns that might fit you. They're on the bed in the first bedroom on the left. Why don't you run up to the house and change?"

Anderson raised his eyebrows. "The Duchess has a point, Lady Clarissa. Now that you have been bestowed with a title, you must dress the part. Sir Kenneth will be happy to escort you to the house, and wait for you."

The Threets shuffled forward. Benny

moved next to Lanya. I glanced over my shoulder, fully prepared to see Madam Marsilia d'Anjou and her black-clad coven closing in from the rear. Lanya's stare made it clear that the Duchess was not accustomed to insubordination from her subjects.

I wavered, then finally succumbed to what amounted to coercion. "Oh, all right," I said ungraciously. "I don't need an escort, though." I turned around to ask Edward to let Luanne know where I was, but he had disappeared. It was a good trick, since his seat on the unicycle made him conspicuously higher than everyone else.

Benny raised his visor as he came over to me. "A gallant knight such as I would never allow milady to make an arduous trek by herself. There are highwaymen and thieves aplenty roaming this fair fiefdom." He lowered his voice. "What's more, I need to get out of this thing to answer a call of nature. We tapped the cask several hours ago."

I felt as if I'd been arrested as he took my elbow in a steel grip and led me through the crowd. Fearless children darted up to pound on him, then fled before he could grab them. A group of college girls in shorts and skimpy halters giggled as we went by. Eventually we emerged from the chaos and walked along the driveway to the house. I was relieved to be out of the fifteenth century, if only for a few minutes.

Benny pulled off his helmet and rubbed his face. "It's damn hot in this thing. The concept of ventilation was unknown back then."

"Have you been fighting?"

He grinned. "I'm ahead by three points. A bunch of knights from the fiefdoms of Merrivale and Verdant drove over last night and set up camp down the road. We had some good rounds earlier today. The championship's at four o'clock. You should come watch. I'm looking forward to taking on Anderson, the sorry bastard. He's a dirty fighter. King Leopold lets him get away with a lot of crap that's banned in the rule book. He won't get away with it today, though. He's not the only one who knows how to inflict some damage."

"I thought you two were friends," I said as we reached the porch. "From college, someone mentioned."

Benny opened the door for me. "Yeah, I suppose so. He, Lanya, and I used to go to the tournaments and wars together. The good ol' days, when knighthood was in flower and barefoot lasses roamed the camps after dark. Lanya and I were the couple back then, up until she caught me fooling around with a raven-haired lute player. She didn't handle it well. Soon afterward, she and Anderson got married under an oak tree. Jumped the broom and all that."

"Must have been hard on you," I said with as much sympathy as I could muster.

He stopped in the living room and began to remove his armor. "I got over it. Got married myself, but it didn't work out. At least I admitted it. I suppose Lanya and Anderson feel like they have to wait until the children are older before they can get divorced. He's not sitting on the sidelines until then. You're likely to be the first woman who hasn't succumbed to his flattery."

It didn't seem appropriate to bring up Salvador's remark about Lanya's consort in infidelity. "I'm going to try on the gowns, Benny. You don't need to wait for me."

"I was hoping you'd let me lace up your bodice."

"Don't hold your breath." I went into the bedroom and closed the door, and then locked it. On our walk to the house, Benny had been a bit unstable on his feet, either from the weight of the armor or from excessive tippling. He could break down the door within a matter of seconds. However, I was reasonably confident he wouldn't try, not with the likelihood that other members of ARSE might prefer to use the bathroom in the house rather than the more primitive facilities in the pasture. Within minutes, I heard several doors open and close, indicating we were not alone.

The gowns on the bed smelled musty, and one of them had been packed away with a stain on the sleeve. Lanya had been slim in her earlier days, I thought as I held up a pale blue gown (with a subtle undertone of lilac, which Mrs. Jorgeson would appreciate). Attractive enough to have at least two men panting after her. Even flirtatious, although it was harder to envision. I put down the blue gown and eyed an emerald green one with a low neckline and gold piping on the sleeves and waistline. Lady Clarissa might as well seize the moment, I decided. I had just slipped off my shirt and shorts when I heard voices.

I do not condone eavesdropping. A large percentage of what is heard is trivial, and hardly worth the effort. The rest of it would have been better left unspoken. Had I not been mostly unclothed, I would have opened the bedroom door and made known my presence. At the moment, all I could do was struggle with the gown, which was failing to cooperate.

"What am I going to do?" Fiona demanded from the living room. "Don't just shake your head at me! It's your problem, too." The response was low, nearly inaudible, but clearly male. It could have been Benny, but I'd heard other members of the royal entourage coming and going, too. In any case, whatever was said displeased Fiona. "I don't even want to hear it! You lied to me, you son of a bitch! I could get fired if this gets out."

I gave up trying to pull the gown up over my hips. I made sure all the tiny hooks on the back were undone, then began to wiggle it on over my head. It wasn't too small for me, and there had to be a way to get the waistline past my shoulders. Dresses, even faux Renaissance gowns, were designed to be worn. This one had obviously been designed by a man. Conceived, sketched, and sent to production without a thought given to practicality.

Fiona's voice shot up an octave. "You're lying, and we both know it! How dare you stand there and offer these pitiful excuses!" Again, I could not make out the response. "No, you have an obligation, and you're going to live up to it. Otherwise, I swear I'll dance on your grave!"

I was so startled that I lost my balance. Unable to see anything with the dress over my head, I stumbled into the bed and then fell back on the floor. I yelped in surprise, as well as pain. For a brief moment, I fought to figure out where I was and why everything was dark.

The front door slammed. I took several deep breaths until I began to regain my senses. I wondered if I resembled a stalk of broccoli on the bedroom floor. As I pushed the dress back over my face, I heard the door close once again, this time softly. A moment later, yet another door slammed somewhere farther away. A busy house, considering everyone was supposedly in the pasture. Fiona had made a dramatic exit and was surely back there by now. I had no idea about the man upon whose grave she would dance if he failed to fall into line. Julius might have backed out on the engagement, but that would not have an impact on her teaching position . . . unless she was pregnant. Farberville was a fairly liberal place, but the conservative faction made itself heard whenever old-fashioned family values were at risk. Creationism had not yet crept into the school curriculum, but neither had any mention of alternative lifestyles, sexually transmitted diseases, gun control, political dissent, or other heresies that might warp young minds that had grown up watching R-rated movies and playing violent video games.

I realized I was ready to throw Fiona a baby shower, based solely on speculation. She just as well could have been embezzling money from the math club coffers, sending poison-pen letters to her colleagues, or even moonlighting as a dancer at one of the so-called gentlemen's clubs.

The green gown was crumpled on the floor. I picked it up, flapped it to shake out the wrinkles, and dedicated my wiles to getting into it. I succeeded at last, although I was unable to hook it up properly. Without a lady-in-waiting waiting, I did what I could, put on my sandals, then stood in front of the dresser mirror to run my fingers through my hair. I must admit I looked quite elegant. The gown fit loosely, but at least part of that would be rectified when it was secured in back. The neckline stopped short of scandalous by a fraction of an inch. Pearls would have been nice, an emerald necklace superb.

I opened the bedroom door and peered out. Benny's armor was gone. The house felt empty. I hurried out the front door and headed along the driveway toward the fair. As I reached the back of a row of tents and stalls, I spotted one of the college girls smoking a cigarette and gazing at the sky, no doubt pondering a problem in quantum mechanics or the impact of a free-trade agreement with a South American country on the global economy. I approached her just as she ground out her cigarette, and asked her to help me with the dress.

"How quaint," she said in a patronizing voice as she deftly dealt with the hooks. "If you're looking for your knight, he came by a while ago. Sexy guy, for his age, and a real sweetie. He invited me to take a stroll after the sword fighting." She smiled knowingly at me. "I suppose he can get in and out of his armor pretty damn fast, with the right encouragement. I told him I have a date tonight, but that he could call me sometime."

"How lovely for both of you," I said. "Thanks for your help — and good luck with Benny."

"You sure you don't mind?"

"Not in the least." I went between two tents and found myself on the main walkway. There was no sign of Luanne, but I figured we'd meet up at the food court sooner or later. I was eager to see Caron and Inez. As I hesitated, trying to remember the locations on the map, an unfamiliar woman asked if she might take my photograph with her grandsons. Surprised, I nodded. As I posed with two grimy little boys dressed in shorts, black galoshes, and plastic pirate hats, I noticed I was garnering admiring looks from the crowd. I take small satisfaction in my modesty, but this was fun. Lady Clarissa of Farberville, benevolent patron of booksellers, kind to small children, gracious to smirky college girls. My smile was, to be candid, radiant.

I patted the little beasts on the head and fell into step with the crowd. As I went by the Royal Pavilion, I noticed that neither the Duke nor the Duchess was holding court. Glynnis and William Threet were doing their best to organize a platoon of Brownie scouts to participate in a maypole dance. Unsurprisingly, Glynnis appeared to be on the verge of tears. I didn't blame her.

I paused to look at a display of metallic wind chimes, and then at ceramic gargoyles and dragons. I cut across the traffic to a stall with crystal figurines, tempted by an array of unicorns. After careful study, I bought a small one for Caron as a souvenir and waited while the pleasant young woman wrapped it in several layers of tissue paper.

Pleased with myself, I returned to the ceramics stall and bought a whimsical elf for Mrs. Jorgeson's garden. As I hesitated, wondering what I might buy for Peter, a band of teenaged pirates swaggered by. Presumably, Louis Wilderberry was among them, although I had no idea which one he might be. They had not taken pains with their costumes; they wore old jeans hacked off below the knees, striped T-shirts, scarves around their necks, and cardboard hats with sloppily painted skull-and-crossbones insignias. A few had glued on mustaches, and others sported eye patches. They were lustily shouting pirate sorts of phrases like "yo ho ho" and "shiver me timbers." Brawn, but sadly lacking in imagination. They looked incapable of boarding even the Peru children's makeshift raft.

I knew it wouldn't be prudent to offer my opinion to Caron. One of these days, I thought as I moved on toward what I hoped was the food court, she would snap out of her infatuation. And the sooner, the better.

Instead of picnic tables and stalls with turkey legs and lemonade, I found myself at the archery range. Salvador smiled at me as he helped a child position an arrow and draw back on the string. He, too, was dressed in garb, in this case consisting of an embroidered shirt with billowy sleeves, a leather vest, and noticeably tight breeches. The arrow flew well over the paper target taped on a bale of hay and into the thicket of scrub pines. Scowling, the child threw down the bow and stalked away, muttering phrases he should not even know.

"Three tries for a dollar," Salvador called to me.

"And what do I win?"

"My heart and my undying devotion, Lady Clarissa. Or perhaps milady fancies becoming a baroness. Firthforth would gladly welcome an heir with auburn locks and inquisitive green eyes." He picked up the bow and joined me. "You are most becoming in that gown, although I am sure you would look more splendid without it. What say you to a walk in the woods to collect the errant arrows?"

Despite his gleaming smile, he looked pale. I frowned at him as I said, "Are you okay, Salvador? Do you need to sit down in the shade?"

"I can think of a very shady spot near the creek."

"I'm serious," I said. "You look ill. If I could find the food court, I'd get you a glass of lemonade. You'll have to give me directions, though. I looked at a map, but now

I'm totally confused."

"So am I," he said softly.

"Oh, look," boomed a woman dressed in a kilt for reasons difficult to fathom. "Give me a dollar, Earl. I want to shoot an arrow into the air, and let it fall I know not where. Stop gaping and get out your wallet."

Earl was gaping at me, naturally. After his wife elbowed him in the ribs, he took out his wallet and found a dollar. "You ain't gonna win yourself a stuffed animal like at the county fair, Eileen," he said as he handed the bill to Salvador. "There ain't no rides, neither, and I'm gettin' tired of all these pretty boys prancin' around. Shoot your damn arrows and let's go home. I can still catch the last couple of innings of the ball game."

Eileen looked as if she were considering a target other than the one on the bale of hay. However, she allowed Salvador to put his arms around her and help her with the bow, and on her third attempt managed to nick the target. "All right, Earl," she said coldly as she handed to the bow to Salvador, "we can go home soon as I have a chance to buy some little presents for the grandbabies. Fairy wings and a wand for Rose Marie, and maybe a pirate hat for Kevvie Junior."

Grumbling, Earl followed her back toward

the vendors' tents. I sat down on a bench and watched Salvador as he put the bow on a rack and counted the arrows remaining in a pile. I was about to continue our conversation when the Brownie scouts descended, chirping excitedly like a flock of chickadees. Their two leaders, most likely mothers, were too busy counting heads to acknowledge my smile as I left.

Once in the labyrinth, I tried a different direction. The sun was relentless. I ducked into shade whenever I could, and finally arrived at a low wooden platform that functioned as a stage. One of the local librarians was dressed in a pink Cinderella outfit topped with a rhinestone tiara. She was telling a story to a rapt group of children. Each time she swished her wand through the air, glitter sparkled in the sunlight. Behind her a row of fairies, clad as Caron had described, fluttered on cue. They were somewhat cute, I supposed, although their green faces and pointed ears gave them a faintly menacing demeanor. Although I had met some of them, it was difficult to differentiate one from another. Which isn't to imply I gave it much effort.

I tried again to find the food court, and after an unfortunate glimpse of a mud-wrestling competition, arrived at an area with a dozen picnic tables and the heady aroma of food, glorious food. It was now well into the afternoon, and I'd had nothing since a skimpy breakfast and my daily overdose of caffeine. Luanne was seated at one of the tables, a turkey leg bone on a paper plate nearby.

As I approached, she raised her eyebrows. "Why, how nice to see you. Been off vying for the role of prom queen? No roses, I see. Were you first runner-up?"

I was more interested in eating than engaging in witty repartee. "How was the turkey leg?"

"Greasy, but not too bad. Your face is flushed. Sit down and I'll go get you something to gnaw on. Ale or lemonade?"

"Lemonade," I said. "Have you seen Caron and Inez?"

"Indeed I have. A couple of their crew didn't show up, so they're peddling ice cream bars in that stall right over there."

"I don't see them."

Luanne grinned. "They must have seen you coming. It may take me a while to convince them to stop cowering behind the counter. Instead of lemonade, you'd better have a cup of ale. Maybe two."

"That bad?" I said, glancing at the stall that appeared to be uninhabited.

"I don't think so, but I'm not one of their mothers."

CHAPTER NINE

I sat numbly, expecting the worst — even though I wasn't sure what it might be. I do not consider myself to be an overly protective mother, but I do tend to forget that my baby is old enough to drive a car. As well as old enough to drive me crazy. Despite the increasingly oppressive heat, I felt a chill. Somewhere in a befuddled corner of my mind I heard Luanne pointing out that they couldn't dodge me indefinitely. I wished they could.

Caron and Inez materialized in front of me. They were wearing long brown skirts that brushed their ankles. The epitome of modesty. I moistened my lips as I lifted my head. Leather bodices laced tightly enough to interfere with breathing. And blouses that exposed not only their freckled shoulders, but also entirely too much of their amazingly full bosoms. Whatever undergarments they'd found in the theater wardrobe added an illusion of several inches and cup sizes. They were perilously close to bursting forth in a mammary explosion. I'd seen more decorous dress on the prostitutes in the film version of *Tom Jones.*

"Goodness," I said weakly.

Caron opted to brazen it out. Her hands on her hips and her head tilted, she did her best to imitate a Cockney flower girl. "So what do you think, Mum? Not 'arf bad, if I sez so meself."

"I'm not sure yet. Inez, have your parents seen you?"

"Not exactly. I brought a sweater that I happened to be wearing at the time. My mother looked kind of funny, but she didn't say anything. My father was distracted by the madrigal singers on the stage over there. He's a big fan." She cleared her throat. "I was thinking maybe I could spend the night at your place."

Luanne intervened. "Both of you can stay with me if you'd prefer. Caron's mother is looking a teensy bit ashen. Probably coming down with a cold."

"That's a classy dress," Caron said to me. "You didn't tell me you were going to wear garb."

I explained how I'd been coerced, unhappily aware that I was exposing my fair share of cleavage, too. I certainly didn't want to run into Inez's parents. "So you two got stuck behind a counter, I hear."

Caron scowled. "Somebody's going to pay for it when school starts. You'd think even sophomores could handle some responsibility. I mean, how hard would it have been for Jason to call me during the week and mention the motorcycle wreck? It's not like he's in intensive care anymore. He's such a dork."

"Don't forget about Wendy, either. It's not her fault that her uncle had a heart attack and her parents made her go with them to the funeral in Vermont, but she should have let us know," added Inez, emphasizing her point with an indignant squeak.

" 'Whether 'tis nobler in the mind to suffer the slings and arrows of outrageous fortune . . .' " I murmured. "You two may resume your duties. I'll see you at the banquet."

Caron rolled her eyes. "Where *we* have to wait tables. Lanya said to tell you that she and some of the others will knock off about five and go to the house to relax. You can join them if you want to."

I remembered the peculiar conversation I'd heard while changing clothes. "Has Miss Thackery seen you?"

"Yeah," Inez said, "and we might as well start reading Chaucer. Mr. Valens was so smitten with how we looked that he dragged her over to see. She wasn't pleased."

"Mostly because he was drooling on us," Caron said smugly. "She didn't like that one bit. They were bickering when they left. She's been by a few more times, but not him. She must have threatened him with a session in the dungeon if he dared come within a hundred yards of the food court."

A distasteful thought popped into my mind. "He wasn't in the dressing room while you were trying on costumes, was he?"

"Of course not, Mother! He brought in a bunch of clothes and said he'd be in his office down the hall."

Inez grimaced. "I told Caron he probably had a secret camera or a peephole. We stayed in the corner with our backs to the room while we tried on stuff."

"You two need to get to work," I said, gesturing at their stall. "You've got customers waiting."

The girls trudged away. Luanne sat down across from me, her expression perplexed. "Who is this guy? Is he on the sexual offenders list?"

"That's hard to imagine," I said as I nibbled on the turkey leg. "He seems perfectly normal to me, a little henpecked and toady at worst. He lives with his parents and, according to Fiona, is a virgin. Or was, until he met her. I didn't ask for details. The girls talk about him as if he's Mr. Hyde in disguise, but they weren't at all nervous about working alongside him at the play in the community center. The only thing Caron's said about him since then is that his deodorant was inadequate. I'm sure she and Inez exemplified grace under pressure, since they didn't have their reputations on the line with the Hasty retirees."

We giggled and snickered while I finished eating. She showed me the earrings she'd bought, and admitted she was tempted by the crystal figurines. I wiped my fingers on a napkin, tossed the trash in a mundane bin, and suggested we take a stroll. I caught a glimpse of Fiona sailing by while we watched Pester the Jester juggle apples and oranges. Her gown of the day was of a deep cranberry that accentuated the whiteness of her shoulders and neck. She exuded an aura of innocence and fragility, but I wasn't fooled. I had yet to spot Julius, but he might be busy with the sound system. Announcements were spitting out with growing urgency: a few tickets still available for the banquet, pony rides closing in one hour, free tastes of sweet raspberry mead in the food court, under-twelve mud-wrestling championship to begin shortly. It was quite as bad as the relentless warnings and reprimands at airports.

At four o'clock, we followed the crowd to the sword-fighting arena, which was nothing more than a patch of ground demarcated by ropes strung on poles. I was relieved to see there were no bloodstains on the grass or severed limbs in a pile. Lanya was officiating as emcee, referee, and scorer. The bouts were mercifully brief, and the swords were nonlethal, made of wood wrapped in duct tape. Infractions were penalized and winners announced. One knight in black armor knelt in front of Luanne and begged her Ladyship to allow him to fight in her honor. His eyes were so blue and twinkly that I expected Luanne to drag him behind the nearest tent. To her dismay, he was defeated and walked away, shaking his head and mumbling to a fellow knight.

"Chivalry is dead," she said with a sigh. "He didn't even ask for my phone number."

"A blackguard of the worst kind. He's undoubtedly pledged his loyalty to Lord Zormurd, evil ruler of some silly mythical country."

Luanne looked at me out of the corner of

her eye. "Has Lady Clarissa been out in the sun too long?"

I refused to tarnish my dignity with a response. Edward joined us as Lanya introduced the next combatants, the Duke of Glenbarrens and Sir Kenneth of Gweek. "Ten bucks on Benny," he whispered in my ear.

"You have no faith in your sovereign?" I whispered back.

"They're evenly matched, but Lanya makes the rulings. Right now she's furious with Anderson, so she may throw the match to Benny out of spite."

"How do you know she's furious with him?"

Edward shrugged. "Even jesters need a break. I grabbed a cup of ale and went over to that clump of trees near the house. They were in the backyard. I heard them say some very nasty things to each other — I assumed they were nasty, anyway. He called her a pathetic wagtail, and she called him a sodding clotpole. There's nothing quite like a good old medieval marital spat. So, you going to take my bet?"

"Do I look like a bookie?" I said.

He grinned. "No, you look like a very fine Renaissance lady. Your portrait should be hanging in the Louvre. Not in the Vatican, though. You're much too sexy for that. The cardinals would cast aside their red hats and go dashing out into the streets to search for you. The pope would be too distracted by lewd thoughts to bless the throngs in St. Peter's Square. Tourists would be trampled in the ensuing bedlam. You, of course, would be so overwhelmed with remorse that you would take to your bed chambers indefinitely. How about five bucks, then?"

Luanne jabbed me. "They're about to start."

I considered what he'd said about Lanya and Anderson, then shook my head. "No bet. Try that couple over there. His name's Earl, and he's sulking because he didn't get to watch his ball game."

The fight appeared to be choreographed. The combatants circled each other as they looked for an opening, although I wasn't sure they could actually see much through the heavy visors. A lunge, a parry. More circling. The crowd, hungry for bloodshed, shouted derogatory comments. Another lunge, another parry. A heart-stopping moment of blades wildly banging against thick armor. Cheers and boos. I had nothing to contribute, and if I did, I'd forgotten who was who. I finally spotted a wisp of Benny's beard poking through his visor.

This particular bout seemed to go on interminably. There was no shade nearby, or even a bench. Some of the large women who'd stuffed themselves into tight costumes were turning pink and beginning to sway. The men in burlap tunics were scratching themselves as sweat dribbled down their necks. I noticed Fiona and Julius at one corner of the arena. She was watching the bout without expression, her mouth set, her arms crossed. Julius kept glancing warily at her, as though anticipating a sudden outburst.

"How long can this last?" Luanne muttered. "It's going to take forever to get my car out of the pasture, and I have a date at seven."

"With the biker from Florida? Is he going to plan your estate?"

"In my dreams. No, with a corporate vice-president who's suffering from PMS, as in postmarriage syndrome. His wife ran off with his secretary. The poor man's totally lost. You're planning to drive home with the girls after the banquet, right?"

I was about to reply when there was a veritable cacophony from the combatants. Swords flailed. The crowd livened up and began to shout. Babies and toddlers wailed. Anderson caught Benny off guard and sent him staggering back. Undaunted, Benny rushed him, his sword above his head. Both went sprawling on the ground. Benny had gone down on his back, and was struggling like a turtle on its shell as Anderson lumbered to his feet and stamped his foot on Benny's chest.

"I proclaim the Duke of Glenbarrens to be the grand champion!" Lanya said.

Everyone clapped and cheered, but most of them were staring at Benny, who was motionless. I heard whispers and mutterings as we waited. Anderson removed his foot, calmly placed his sword in its scabbard, and offered his hand to Benny. I was ready to go for medical help when Benny at last knocked aside Anderson's hand and made it to his feet. They pulled off their helmets, bowed to Lanya, then acknowledged the crowd with nods. Their faces were as red as stewed tomatoes. Benny's beard was a sodden mass. His eyes narrowed as Anderson joined Lanya and held up his fist.

"You should have taken my bet," Edward said as he slipped by us.

Luanne exhaled. "That's enough combat for me. I'm going to see if I can beat the traffic out of the pasture. Call me tomorrow and tell me about the banquet."

"Are you sure you'll be home?"

"No, but the veep gets maudlin after a couple of glasses of wine. He was having an affair with his secretary, so he feels betrayed by both her *and* his wife. The last time we went out, he locked himself in a stall in the men's room for forty-five minutes and sobbed so loudly the maître d' called for an ambulance."

"This is your idea of a hot date?" I asked. "Maybe you should pick up a pizza and head for the psych ward at the hospital."

"Talk to you tomorrow," she said, fluttering her fingers above her shoulder as she disappeared into the crowd moving toward the tents.

She had made good her escape by the time I reached the food court. On a nearby stage, a play was in progress, presumably a farce since one of the actors was wearing a donkey's head while a woman in a white apron and cap chased him with a rolling pin. A banner taped on the backdrop identified them as the FOOLS APLENTY TRAVELING THESPIANS. I wryly noted that their choice of obscenities, such as "bollocks" and "sodding," were carefully chosen from early English literature to protect the sensibilities of young ears.

Caron and Inez were dealing with a long line of whiny children and grumpy parents.

Lady Marsilia d'Anjou and her flock of ravens were doing a brisk business from a wooden cart, although I suspected the hot cross buns were cold. If she was selling relics on the side, I didn't want to know about it. The Brownies trooped by, all sporting pointed ears. It seemed appropriate.

I browsed the stalls and tents for another twenty minutes, looking for something for Peter. Nothing caught my fancy. I conceded defeat and headed for the farmhouse, where I could slip into my civilian clothes for a while and drink something with ice cubes in it. Tepid ale might be authentic, but it was hardly satisfying.

The living room was uninhabited. I went into the bedroom to change, then realized I was at the mercy of the innumerable hooks on the back of the gown. I limited myself to obscure yet colorful Anglo-Saxon swear words as I went into the kitchen. I heard low voices in from the screened porch. Having no excuse for eavesdropping this time, I continued out and found the Threets sitting on the sofa.

"You look very nice, m'dear," William said. "You must seriously consider joining ARSE. Too many of our members are either college kids or old fogies like us."

Glynnis sniffled. "Percival so loved attending the fairs."

"I'm sure he did," I said. "Would you please help me with the hooks?"

"You're not leaving?" William said, alarmed. "You're supposed to sit at the head table at the banquet. It's a rare honor to be invited. Lanya and Anderson sat at King Leopold's table at the last tournament, but only because they're old friends. We usually find ourselves at the back, where we can barely see the entertainment."

"Percival was despondent," Glynnis added, taking a lace handkerchief from under her cuff. "Inconsolable."

"The hooks?" I said brightly.

She rose and released all the hooks. I assured them I would attend the banquet, then fled to the bedroom and put on my shorts and T-shirt. Feeling as if I'd been released from a straitjacket, I returned to the kitchen and found a cup and a cooler of sodas and ice. Anderson came into the kitchen and caught my wrist before I could pull up the pop top. His hair was damp from a shower, and he'd changed back into his duke suit.

"Would you prefer something else?" he asked as he rubbed his thumb on my hand. "There's a liquor cabinet in the dining room. I keep it locked because of the kids, but I think you've earned a sip of scotch or gin. What dost milady prefer?"

I freed my wrist. "Scotch on the rocks would be nice."

He ran the tip of his tongue over his lips. "I saw you at the arena. Did you enjoy the fight?"

"I'm not a fan of brutality, even when it's make-believe."

"I can assure you it wasn't make-believe. Benny was coming at me as though he intended to cut off my head in one slash. He was completely out of control, which was why I won. It may seem mindless to you, but it requires strategy."

"Benny was fine earlier," I said.

Anderson gave me a patronizing grin as he took my cup and went into another room, presumably to unlock the liquor cabinet. I noticed that all of the chairs had vanished, but this was not extraordinary in a household with children. Anything that was not bolted down or too heavy and cumbersome to be carried off was fair game. I was thinking about some of Caron's more creative endeavors when Lanya came into the kitchen.

She'd exchanged her aristocratic finery for a bathrobe, and was fanning herself with a magazine. "We're lucky it isn't any hotter out there. I did okay in the Royal Pavilion, but I thought I was going to pass out at the fighting arena. Da Vinci is credited with the invention of collapsible campstools. I keep meaning to order one from a catalog. Would you like to try some mead?"

"No, thank you," I said. "Anderson's fixing me a drink."

"Is he?" she said dryly. "I'm not surprised. You're a knockout in that gown, Lady Clarissa. I remember when I used to be that slim. I had long, dark hair with gold highlights. Four kids later, and look at me. A frumpy housewife with a husband who prefers to seek his carnal pleasures elsewhere. He thinks I'm content to stay home all day and work in the garden, wipe runny noses, tend the bees, bake bread, and brew my little concoctions to sell at fairs and tournaments." She filled a cup with what I assumed was one of her little concoctions. "You want to know what I dream about when I'm yanking up weeds?"

I truly did not, but I couldn't see a polite way to escape. "Getting away for a few days?"

"A hysterectomy — with complications. I want to lie in a hospital bed for weeks, while orderlies bring me trays and friends drop by with flowers and fruit. I want to read, undisturbed, until I can't keep my eyes open. I want to watch old movies. All of this and a morphine drip so that whenever I hear the merest hint of children's voices, I can send myself into oblivion. What's more, I won't have to think about my husband's latest fling."

"My last duchess," said Anderson as he entered the room and handed me a nicely filled cup. "Only she would stoop to blame this sort of trifling." He winked at me. "I did a minor in English lit."

Lanya snorted. "As well as one in American slut."

"I do believe I'll join the others," I said, then scurried out to the screened porch and sat down next to Glynnis. "A lovely day for the Renaissance Fair, don't you think?"

"Yes, lovely. Did you notice the gypsy with all the sparkly trinkets on her hat and cape? I was tempted to ask her if she conducts séances. Wouldn't that be fascinating?"

"It's all fascinating," I said, wishing I'd sat down in a corner, preferably in another room.

"You're enjoying it, then?" said Fiona as she came up the steps from the yard. She seemed to be oblivious to the heat, and if she had been dancing on anyone's grave, it had not required excessive exertion or soiled her slippers. "I do believe it's going well thus far. There have been glitches, but one expects them. The green gown suits you. I do hope you're planning to wear it at the banquet. It's customary for those at the head table to be clad in proper garb."

"Just taking a break," I told her. Glynnis began to pluck at the handkerchief tucked in her cuff. I hastily got up and went to stand next to Fiona. "Where are the others?"

"Edward's upstairs, resting. He's going to be the Master of the Revelries at the banquet, so he has a lot of material he wants to review. Julius is supervising the arrangement of the picnic tables in front of the Royal Pavilion. Benny's off somewhere, probably crying in his ale. I haven't seen Salvador since the middle of the afternoon."

"This 'Lady Clarissa' business was his idea, wasn't it?"

Fiona gave me a sharp look. "He told me it was *your* idea. I was a member of ARSE for six months before I was given the title Lady Olivia of Ravenmoor. I was on two committees and volunteered to organize the rummage sale." She waited for me to explain my impertinent usurpation of a title. When I didn't, she said, "I must say I'm upset with your daughter and Inez. Part of the assignment was to make one's costume. I haven't had time to decide how I'll handle this."

"They *did* have to work to earn them," I pointed out. I did not say this from the perspective of a mother defending her offspring from unjust accusations, as I'd done countless times in the last sixteen years. I just didn't want to have to live in proximity to Caron if she was obliged to write the dreaded paper. She does not suffer in silence, and she does not hesitate to share her misery. "The gown you're wearing now is lovely. You must be a very talented seamstress."

Her smile was bland. "Thank you. It's my favorite. I save it for very special occasions. If you'll excuse me, I'm going to freshen up before the banquet." She went into the kitchen.

Anderson did not seem to have noticed her as he came out to the porch and joined me. "Shall we sit here with the others, or would you prefer a more intimate chat elsewhere?"

What I preferred was to have been elsewhere, such as at home or on the way to a funeral in Vermont. "This is fine," I said. "Where are your children?"

"Terrorizing the fair, I suppose. When things wind down at six, they'll be hauled away to spend the rest of the weekend with friends."

"Four of them, right?"

He shrugged. "More or less. It's hard to get an accurate head count on a pack of wolves. Why don't you sit down and rest?"

After twenty minutes of aimless chatter about the weather and the high turnout at the gate, Lanya came to the doorway to announce that we would leave shortly. I went into the bedroom and put on the green gown, paused in front of the mirror to frown at my sunburned nose, and returned to the living room. Glynnis assisted me with the hooks. Fiona was brushing invisible lint off her gown as she joined us. Edward came downstairs, carrying a rolled-up scroll and looking drowsy. William hurried to the door and held it open as the Duke and Duchess of Glenbarrens led our noble procession to the Royal Pavilion.

The picnic tables formed a two-row semicircle to create a stage area in front of the pavilion. The banquet attendees, some in garb, sat on the benches, already supplied with beverages and place settings of ordinary flatware. The musicians were playing one of the pieces in their limited repertory (I would be haunted by "Greensleeves" for weeks, if not longer). They stopped as trumpets blared to announce our arrival. Our table was long and graced with a linen tablecloth, as befitting our exalted status. Fiona directed me to a seat near one end, with the Threets on one side of me and an empty chair on the other. Neither Salvador nor Benny had shown up. I would have been happy to have either one of them take the empty chair, saving me from trying to make conversation with Glynnis.

Edward stepped in front of the table and bowed so deeply to the audience that he lost his balance. After a theatrical recovery amid laughter and catcalls, he introduced the royal personages, promised entertainment throughout the evening, and gestured for the musicians to resume playing. The students began to bring out platters of fruit, cheese, and bread. Caron and Inez had been assigned to serve picnic tables in the second row. I noticed they were receiving bold stares from some of the men, which I found unsettling. They, on the other hand, seemed to be having a fine time. Caron leaned down much farther than I felt was necessary as she refilled cups from a pitcher, and her smile was impudent. Inez was more reserved, but she bestowed a few winks on the customers.

I was watching them when Benny sat

down next to me. He was wearing a vest and a slightly grimy white shirt. His beard was damp and neatly combed. He hadn't showered at the house, as far as I knew, which meant he might have bathed in a more authentic tin tub.

"Did I miss anything?" he said as he filled his cup with wine.

"Not really." I passed the platter to him. "You must be hungry."

He chuckled. "After having been beaten so soundly? Is that what milady is supposing?" He took a roll and a wedge of cheddar. "It was my fault. I lost my temper, which was my undoing. I could tell Anderson was tired. All I had to do was wear him down before I went after him. Damn it all, I really wanted to beat the son of a bitch."

"There seems to be a lot of animosity among the ARSE members today."

He grunted in response. I took a slice of apple from the platter and resumed watching Caron and Inez. William and Glynnis were having a whispered conversation, saving me from attempting to be sociable. Lanya kept an indulgent smile on her face as Anderson regaled the audience with bawdy remarks about her Ladyship's remarkable talents in the bedchamber. Edward played the fool, asking naïve questions and feigning shock and bewilderment at Anderson's replies.

As the first course was being removed, Edward again came forward and began to entertain the children at the picnic tables with riddles and magic tricks. The musicians were sent to a corner and the madrigal singers took over. Bowls of thick vegetable soup were brought out by the servers.

"Who's doing the cooking?" I asked Benny. "Surely not the home ec classes at the high school."

"Caterers," he said. "Their van is parked behind the tents."

"Oh," I said. As a dinner companion, he was not sparkling. I'd left my watch in my bag in the farmhouse. The banquet was scheduled to last until eight, but I was ready to leave. I'd warned Peter that I wouldn't be home. Not that I thought he'd try to call, I thought with a sigh. It was likely that his mother was hosting an elegant dinner party, with candles and glittering china and silver. Unobtrusive servants moving deftly behind the seated guests. Leslie, dressed in diamonds and a little black dress she'd picked up in Paris during her visit, seated next to him, finding occasion to squeeze his hand and remind him of private jokes they'd shared. While I was seated between a surly, noncommunicative knight and a woman inclined to snivel.

The soup bowls were replaced with plates of chicken breasts in sauce, new potatoes, and green beans. Benny ate steadily and with fierce dedication, as if this were his last meal. I took a few bites, then refilled my glass and sat back. There were seventy or eighty banquet guests, some of them known to me in varying degrees. Sally and her nuns sat at one table, mutely bent over their plates. The crone with all the rags and ribbons sat alone at the end of one table; the brim of her misshapen hat hid her face. It was good to know Madam Marsilia was handy to exorcize demons if she was in the process of casting an evil spell over us. Robin Hood and Friar Tuck were still talking on their cell phones. Several of my bookstore patrons smiled at me. The mayor appeared to be grumpy, as though convinced he'd already fulfilled his civic obligation and would prefer to be dining in a more elegant milieu. The pirates sat together at a front-row table. Based on their boisterous behavior, it seemed likely they'd been paddling about in a cask of ale. The fairies were behind the pavilion, preparing to perform. Others of Caron's friends were lugging trays and refilling glasses from the pitchers. Carrie had a bruise on her shoulder, possibly from a playful pony nip. Emily was limping. None of them was dressed as stylishly (or indecently) as Caron and Inez.

A bowl of bread pudding was set down in front of me. I wrinkled my nose, having always been suspicious of what might be masquerading as raisins and currents. No one else seemed to share my reservations. I was making a few exploratory jabs with a spoon when Pester the Jester stepped into the stage area.

"While my ladies and gentlemen partake of this most splendid dish, what say you to a ballad of mine own doing? I bid you listen well, though I have but naught to compel you." He snapped his fingers and a very nervous high school boy with a guitar came from behind the tent and kneeled. Edward tweaked the boy's nose, smiled, and then began to sing.

I'd expected a facsimile of one of the traditional ballads, with references to knights of noble worth and courage, bonny brides, heroic deeds, and plenty of gore. Edward's ballad did not qualify. I can't quote the lyrics, but the gist of the tale was that a baby boy was found abandoned in the king's stable and raised as a page. As he approached maturity, he yearned to know the name of his father. (I was turning paler than the bread pudding by this point.) The boy went to a series of knights and pleaded for each to acknowledge him as a son. Each rejection wounded him, and he became increasingly despondent. Finally, he approached the man he assumed to be the Royal Gamekeeper of the Imperial Forest and fell to the ground, begging to be killed as a poacher. (I was now befuddled, since I hadn't run across any gamekeepers.) The man cradled the boy in his arms and admitted that he himself was the boy's father. (Okay, this was good. Carlton wouldn't have known a pheasant from a stork.) But then, just as I was about to jump to my feet and applaud madly, Edward finished the ballad on a happy note. The gamekeeper was in reality the wealthy Baron of Firthforth and a master archer, who happily acknowledged the page as his long-lost son, and trained him to follow in his footsteps. The son achieved glory in tournaments and the two lived happily ever after in a stone house on a hillside.

I sat back, stunned, then glanced down the table. William and Glynnis were hissing at each other, their faces as animated as I'd ever seen them. Anderson and Lanya sat like marble figures in a cathedral. Fiona's lips had disappeared and her cheeks were flushed. Edward bowed to the audience, patted his accompanist on the head, and went behind the tent. Julius stared at him from near the exit. In contrast, the audience clapped with enthusiasm. Some of the women were dabbing at their eyes. The pirates, well beyond comprehension, cheered lustily and demanded an encore.

Benny jabbed me in the ribs. "What the hell was that about?"

"Autobiographical, I'm afraid," I murmured. "Edward told me a couple of weeks ago that he'd come to Farberville to find his father."

"And he thinks it's Salvador? This is friggin' bizarre. What did Salvador say about it?"

"Nothing to me. We may be stretching here. Edward's ballad could just be about wish fulfillment. The end may be nothing more than fiction. It wouldn't have been much of a ballad if the gamekeeper had obliged and killed the page. It certainly wouldn't make the *New York Times* Bestseller Ballad list without a satisfactory conclusion."

Benny craned his head to look past me. "Where's Salvador?"

"I have no idea," I said. "I saw him at the

254

archery range earlier. He didn't show up at the house at five. Maybe he left."

"He wouldn't do that," Glynnis interjected. "He knew that he was expected at the royal table. He is a baron, after all. It's more likely that he's collecting arrows that overshot the target and has lost track of the time."

I didn't buy that. "And didn't hear the trumpets when we came here an hour ago, or any of the music since then? He's not lost in Sherwood Forest, for pity's sake."

"I'll go look for him if he doesn't show up before too long," Benny said, then sat back and crossed his arms. "He may have persuaded some lusty wench to wander into the woods with him. He won't appreciate it if I blunder onto the scene."

"Or he could have sprained his ankle," Glynnis said helpfully. "Just like that poor woman who died in the fire. What was her name, William?"

"Angie," he supplied.

"Yes, Angie," she continued. "It's obvious what happened. Unable to walk, she tried to crawl to the front door, but the smoke was so thick that she collapsed on her bedroom floor. She must have been terrified, lying there all alone. And from what I've heard, the police have been unable to identify her so they can contact her relatives. How tragic to end up in a pauper's grave."

"More likely in a box on a shelf in the medical examiner's storeroom," Benny said. "There wasn't much left of her."

Glynnis's eyes watered. "Dreadful, simply dreadful."

I was about to mumble something comforting when I realized Glynnis was referring to the fairies, who were flittering around the staging area while the musicians played. Clearly no one had choreographed their chaotic attempts to dance. Bodies thudded and toes were trampled. One fairy whacked another with her wand, resulting in a howl of fury. The victim snatched off her attacker's pointed ear and flung it at the lute players. Hair was yanked. Derrieres landed on the ground. The pirates were standing on their table, shouting encouragement. Eyes in the audience were wide. Parents began dragging children behind the picnic tables. One fairy grabbed my bowl of pudding, scooped out the contents, and squashed them into her opponent's gaping mouth.

Fiona came out of her stupor and banged on the edge of the table with a spoon. "Girls, stop this! Stop this right now or I'll

—" Tears were racing down her cheeks as she shook Anderson's shoulder. "Make them stop! You're the damn duke! Do something!"

Anderson shook his head. "What can I do? You make them stop."

"They won't listen to me," she wailed.

For reasons known only to themselves, the trumpeters decided to add to the fun. This provoked the musicians to play louder. The expletives from the fairies were not of Anglo-Saxon origin. The pirates leaped off the table and stumbled into the melee with their cardboard cutlasses raised. Edward reappeared and began to juggle plates and bowls. A few members of the audience participated by throwing rolls, fruit, and handfuls of pudding.

It was much more entertaining than madrigals, I thought as I watched. Caron and Inez, standing at a prudent distance, seemed to agree with me. Benny was grinning as he gulped down ale. The Threets cowered behind the table. Fiona continued to bang the table and wail. Only Lanya appeared unperturbed. She had not, as best I could tell, so much as twitched since the end of Edward's ballad. She was gazing not at the combatants, but into the distance. She did not flinch when Anderson shoved back his chair and started thundering for order. I was beginning to wonder if she was breathing when Julius appeared from behind the back wall, tapped her on the shoulder, then bent down and whispered in her ear.

Her reaction was extreme, to put it mildly. She jerked herself to her feet and toppled the table. Dishes, pitchers, and flatware crashed onto the carpet. Her wail outdid Fiona's best efforts, and was so anguished that everyone fell silent. Fists were retracted. Feet raised to execute well-aimed kicks were lowered. The musicians froze. Edward's plates and bowls fell to the ground. Fiona's mouth snapped closed.

"Salvador," Lanya said brokenly, "is dead."

CHAPTER TEN

Lanya buried her face in her hands. Anderson stared at her, then went around the table and pulled Julius aside. The fairies and pirates melted away into the audience, leaving Edward alone in the staging area. His face gnarled with anguish, he crumpled to the ground and hugged his knees. Fiona looked as if she might do the same, but she grabbed the back of a chair and managed to stay on her feet.

"Dead?" Benny said to me, his voice so low I could barely hear him. "What happened to him?"

"How would I know?"

"You think he's really dead? Is this supposed to be a joke?"

Glynnis glared at him. "If it is, it's in very bad taste."

"Oh, yes," William added, nodding emphatically. "Very bad taste."

The three of them seemed to expect me

to explain the situation. I shrugged, then got up and joined Anderson and Julius. "What's going on?" I demanded.

"I'm not sure," Julius said. He looked away and gulped several times as if trying to hold back a gush of acid. Each time his eyes bulged like those of a bullfrog. I inched backward and prayed I would be out of range. He finally rallied enough control to continue. "I was behind the tent, talking to the caterer. One of the students — I don't know his name — came up and told me that he'd gone down past the archery range to . . . ah, relieve himself, because the toilets here have been used all day. I couldn't argue with that since I" — he stopped himself — "anyway, he saw a body on the ground."

"Is the student sure it was Salvador — and that he was dead?" asked Anderson.

"The kid swears it was." Julius gulped again, then took a handkerchief from his pocket and mopped his face. "There was a lot of blood, he said, and no doubt that Salvador was dead."

I frowned. "Some kind of accident?"

It took Julius several seconds to answer. "It wasn't an accident, unless Salvador found a way to smash the back of his own head with an ax."

"Oh, God," Anderson said, shuddering.

"You have a cell phone?"

"Not on me, but I told the caterer to call 911. If you'll excuse me, I think I'm going to throw up."

Julius went back around the edge of the tent. Anderson and I looked at each other, then he said, "I'd better go find the caterer and call the police myself. They may need directions." He stopped as Lanya began to wail once again. "I don't know what to do. I guess I ought to say something so we won't have a stampede. How could this happen? I feeling like a blithering idiot. What should I say?"

I squeezed his arm. "Announce that there's been an accident, and everybody needs to stay here until the police arrive. Have the servers refill the pitchers. And please see if you can calm down Lanya. I'll make the call."

Benny and the Threets were already hovering over her. Anderson pushed them aside and knelt next to her. Fiona had disappeared, although I doubted she was holding Julius's head over a bucket. I beckoned to Caron and Inez, then pointed at Edward. They headed toward him. Satisfied I'd done what I could, I left the pavilion and found the catering van. I ordered the student servers who were huddled nearby to sit down at the picnic tables. The caterer held a cell phone to his ear, and was struggling to talk to the 911 dispatcher while also issuing orders to his assistants. I took the phone and waved him away.

"Do you need directions?" I asked briskly.

"No, ma'am, but I need more information. Now what exactly happened? Is there a doctor with the victim?"

"Good idea," I said. "I'll call you back in two minutes." I carried the phone with me as I went back into the pavilion. I pulled Benny aside. "Ask if there's a doctor present. If so, take him or her with you and go find Salvador's body. I'm going to stay here until the ambulance and the police arrive, and then send them to the archery range."

"That's where . . . ?"

"Either at the range or just beyond it in the woods. One of the students went down there to take a leak and saw the body."

"He's sure it's Salvador?"

"He claims to have recognized him," I said. "I'd send this student with you, but I don't know who he is and Julius isn't going to be much help for a while. Just find out if there's a doctor, and then go — okay?" I noted that Caron and Inez had gotten Edward to his feet and were guiding him away from the pavilion. I returned to the area by the van and called 911. "All right, I'm back. I can't answer your questions because I have no idea what happened. How long will it take for the ambulance and police to get here? There are at least a hundred very nervous people."

"Your name, ma'am?"

"Claire Malloy, if you must know. The victim's name is Salvador Davis. He was hit on the back of his head with an ax."

"An ax? Just what's going on out there?"

"I'm at the Renaissance Fair on the property of Anderson and Lanya Peru, and I'm going to save the explanations for the police when they get here. Oh, and call Sergeant Jorgeson. He's off duty, but he'll want to know."

"Hey, aren't you the lieutenant's —"

I cut him off before he could say "meddlesome girlfriend" or other unflattering phrase. "Yes, I am. Now please call Sergeant Jorgeson. I'd give you my number, but I'm on someone's cell phone and I have no idea what the number is. Presumably you can determine it from your end. Tell the sergeant I'll keep the phone with me if he wants to call me back. Do you understand?"

"I thought I recognized your name," the dispatcher said, chortling as if he expected to be praised for his acumen. "You and your daughter must have called us a dozen times last month about a body that kept vanishing. Me and the other guys was going start a pool to guess how many times you'd call, but the captain —"

"Was not amused," I said, then turned off the phone. I would have slipped it in a pocket, but Renaissance gowns did not offer such conveniences. I considered slipping it in my bodice, then dismissed the idea since it would be less than decorous to have to retrieve it should Jorgeson call.

The audience had been somewhat pacified by fresh pitchers of wine and ale. The fairies and pirates were jammed together at one picnic table. There was a great deal of hissing and sputtering going on, but they kept their voices low. I found Emily and Carrie, and sent them to the gate to make sure the table was moved aside to allow entry to the ambulance and police vehicles. I thought I could hear sirens in the distance, although I might have been deluding myself. Anderson escorted Lanya out of the pavilion. Her face was blotchy, and her entire body was trembling so hard that she was scarcely able to walk, but Anderson had a good grip on her. The musicians and madrigal singers milled about like brightly clad cows. The scene was eerily quiet.

I told William Threet to order the musicians to play anything but "Greensleeves," then sank onto a chair and rubbed the back of my neck. All afternoon, and up until ten minutes previously, the pasture had been filled with colors, flags, banners, screaming children, activity, noise, and good-natured rowdiness. The transition had been too abrupt. And Salvador was dead, or so we thought. One could certainly do significant damage to one's body with an ax, but only a contortionist could clobber himself in the back of the head.

Benny put his hand on my shoulder. "The best I could do was a podiatrist. I guess I'll go by myself to find the body and wait for you and the others. Surely whoever did this to Salvador wouldn't hang around afterward. That'd be asking to get caught, wouldn't it? It was probably some homeless guy living down by the creek who got upset by the noise from the fair. A lot of guys getting back from a war zone are like that, you know. Almost psychotic. They have flashbacks, and —"

"I'll send a couple of the pirates with you, if I can find any that aren't too drunk to walk." I went over to the picnic table inhabited by pea-green fairies and flushed buccaneers. Rather than ask for volunteers, I grabbed two of the boys by their collars and yanked them to their feet. They were not eager to oblige, but Benny had made it clear he would have preferred to discuss post-traumatic stress syndrome for an hour rather than go alone.

Once they'd gone, I surveyed the scene. Most of the adults in the audience were looking worried. The children had lost enthusiasm for the music, and were squirming or squabbling. Edward was in no shape to entertain them with juggling and magic tricks. I had no idea where Caron and Inez had taken him, or how he was handling the unexpected and potentially devastating news of Salvador's death. I wondered if he'd already told Salvador, or planned to surprise him at the banquet. If the latter were true, Edward had certainly climbed out on a limb.

I was pondering this when I finally heard sirens. I went to the tents nearest the entrance and watched an ambulance and several police vehicles bounce across the pasture. Lights continued to flash, but the sirens whined into silence as uniformed officers got out of the cars.

"You the one who called?" demanded one of them.

I acknowledged that indeed I was, explained what little I knew, and gave them directions to drive around the tents, stalls, and battlefield to arrive at the archery range. I did so briskly and with more confidence than I felt, since the layout had seemed like a maze that afternoon.

He stared at my gown, and then at the tents and banners flapping in the breeze. "Is this a play or something? All I can say is it better not be a prank. If it is, you're gonna be in big trouble."

I squared my shoulders. "This is not a prank, as far as I know. It may turn out to be one, but I can assure you that I am not the instigator or a conspirator. A student reported finding the body. He made the assumption, based on his observations of blood and other distasteful material, that the man he was looking at was dead. I sent two other students and an adult to wait near the body for your arrival."

"So you haven't seen this body yourself?"

"No, I just told you what I know — for the second time. Perhaps you might want to see for yourselves," I said sharply. "It's remotely possible that the victim is not dead, in which case he needs immediate medical assistance."

"Hey," said a second officer, "I recognize you. You're the lieutenant's —"

"I am the person who has reported what may have been a vicious assault or a homicide."

The first officer chewed on his lower lip as he studied me. "Weren't you at that fire last week, dressed up like a witch? I asked Sergeant Jorgeson the next day why it is you always seem to be loitering around when there's a crime. He said it was hard to explain."

The other whiz kid sniggered. "Like Einstein's theory about relatives. My wife tried to tell me how her third cousin twice removed was also her grandmother's first cousin once removed or something like that, but I just turned up the TV."

I wanted to snatch off their badges and stuff them in their mouths. However, since I was mild-mannered as well as courteous, I merely said, "There is a body at the archery range. There are approximately a hundred potential witnesses on the verge of bolting for their cars. As much as I myself am enjoying our little chat, I do think you might want to take charge of the situation. I believe the techniques for preserving the scene are taught at the police academy, but I could be mistaken."

A paramedic from the ambulance joined us. "What's the deal? It's Saturday night, fellows, and the calls are gonna start coming in pretty soon." He took in my admittedly fetching attire and let out a low whistle. "Begging your pardon, miss. You in need of my very finest medical attention?"

I held up both hands. "I've told you where the body is to be found. The mob is stirring down that walkway behind me. There are also some very upset people wandering around, although I don't know where they may be by now. You're professionals, so for God's sake act like it!" I wheeled around and headed toward the Royal Pavilion, ignoring barked orders to stop. I knew Lanya would be distressed if her gown was returned with bloodstains in the middle of its back, but that was the least of my concerns.

By the time I reached the Royal Pavilion, the only people remaining at the Duke's table were the Threets. They did not appear to be displeased by their sudden promotion in prestige, if not rank. Glynnis was waving a fork as the musicians struggled through a number. William beamed at his motley collection of pirates, peasants, and mall shoppers as if they'd come to offer homage. Said subjects were beginning to look surly.

The two police officers on my heels stopped at the edge of the pavilion. "What the hell's going on?" one demanded. "Why are these people dressed up like this? Wait, I think I saw something about it on the news earlier this week. Sounded kind a lame."

I gestured at the head table. "Those two are Lord and Lady Bicklesham. They will be delighted to explain."

"What about those green girls?" asked the second officer.

"Fairies."

"Well, excuse me," he said. "How could I miss the obvious explanation?" He stared at the crone. "What about her? Is she the bad fairy godmother?"

He was going to add more, but several members of the audience approached and began to badger him for information. Small children who'd watched the bloodthirsty knights with wide-eyed glee now began to cry at the sight of uniformed police officers. I glided behind the tent and gave myself a few moments to savor the solitude. There were lights on in the farmhouse. Lanya and Anderson were there, I assumed, as well as Fiona. Julius had last been seen staggering away to throw up. Once he'd recovered, he might have taken refuge there, too. I had no idea what Caron and Inez had done with Edward.

I was still standing there, not quite dithering and wringing my hands, when one of the pirates came blundering across the rutted pasture. "Mrs. Malloy," he said between gasps, "they want you at the archery range."

"They?" I inquired politely.

"Yeah, you know, like the police. It's real crazy down there. All kinds of lights and people shouting and stuff."

"It sounds as though they have the situation under control with officious and energetic efficacy. Why on earth do they want me to clutter up the proceedings?"

He gave me a startled look, as though I'd spoken to him in a foreign dialect. I have noticed that certain members of his age group are often perplexed by multisyllabic words. Their vocabulary seems to consist of acronyms for mysterious state-of-the-art technological jargon.

"They just told me to get you," he said at last. "Can you find your way, or do you want me to show you?"

"Milady does not require an escort. Run along and find some breath mints. You smell like a distillery, and the police will question you and your fellow buccaneers sooner or later. Miss Thackery will be displeased if the lot of you end up being arrested for underage drinking. Dante's Inferno will sound like a holiday destination."

"Yeah, right," he mumbled, then made his way in the direction of the Royal Pavilion.

I, on the other hand, did my best to avoid it. I went behind the caterer's van and various tents until I felt confident enough to emerge. The walkways were unpopulated. The vendors had packed up earlier and slipped away to peddle their wares at other festivals (or go home and watch TV). The food court looked particularly desolate. A few paper plates and cups had fallen out of the trash bins and were quaking in the light breeze. The moon, as well as the lights from the area around the Royal Pavilion, were adequate for me to avoid blundering into any of the picnic tables or stumbling over tent pegs. Dressed as I was, I felt like a character in a gothic novel. Lady Clarissa, back from the netherworld, in search of her brooding lover, haunting the palace grounds on moonlit nights. Her pale shoulders and graceful neck gleam in contrast to her emerald gown. How lightly she moves on her feet, as if drifting above the trampled grass. She pauses, her lips pursed. Her fingertips flutter to her mouth as she peers into the fathomless shadows.

"Claire!"

Lady Clarissa almost wet her satin panties.

"Who's there?" I croaked.

"Sssh! It's Edward. I'm behind the stage."

"Doing what?" I wrinkled my nose as I tried to locate him. The shadows were by no means fathomless, but they were dark. "Why don't you come out here?"

"I want to talk to you. Please, just for a few minutes. We can sit on the edge of the stage. I found a frying pan in the prop box. You can hold on to it in case you want to clobber me with it."

"Is there a reason why I'd want to clobber you?" I asked. I remained where I was, not at all willing to accept his invitation. I wasn't afraid of Edward. However, I was aware of the adage about fools rushing in where angels fear to tread. Edward might enjoy playing the fool, but I wasn't as eager. "Why are you hiding, Edward? Is somebody after you?"

"I don't know," he said piteously. "You're the only person I trust, Claire, and I have to talk to somebody. I think I'm going crazy."

"All the more reason for me to stay right here."

"No, not that kind of crazy." He hiccuped noisily, leading me to wonder how much he'd imbibed between his short performances. It was likely that he'd been unable to eat prior to his ballad. It could make for an unpleasant situation.

"Where are Caron and Inez?" I asked, still unable to see him.

"I told them I was about to be sick, so they aimed me at one of those portable toilets. They're probably still waiting for me."

That was credible. Neither girl was a likely candidate for nursing school, which was just as well for patients everywhere. Caron once fainted when I removed a splinter from her finger. Inez, who was watching, did, too. They'd recovered only when I offered to take them out for lunch.

I came to a decision. "Okay, Edward, but I'll meet you at the battle arena. Nobody will see us, but there's enough light for me to keep an eye on you." I waited for a few seconds, then frowned and said, "Edward? Are you still there?"

The beam from an industrial-strength flashlight caught me in the face. "Are you Mrs. Malloy, ma'am? Sergeant Jorgeson's waiting for you. He thought you might get lost on the way."

I shaded my eyes with my hand. "Get that out of my eyes, please. Yes, I'm Claire Malloy. What does Sergeant Jorgeson want?"

"You, ma'am. Do you want me to hold your arm? The ground's kind of rough on account of the weeds."

"That will not be necessary, Officer. I have slogged across deserts during raging sand-storms, and used a machete to fight my way through a jungle. Once, when I was captured by a tribe of headhunters in the Amazon rain forest, I ended up teaching them how to make soup from lizards and dung beetles. I am more than capable of walking down to the archery range without assistance."

"Of course you are," he replied with a smirk. "No encounters with aliens?"

"I am a demigoddess in the mythology of Alpha Centauri." I took a quick look at the stage, then turned and followed the officer. I realized I'd yet to have a conversation with Edward that had not been cut short, usually by his abrupt departure. I was more than curious to question him about Salvador.

Sergeant Jorgeson managed a faint smile as I joined him. Beyond the bales of hay that had served as targets, lights glared and police officers moved purposefully. Whether or not they were actually doing anything useful was impossible to determine, but they were keeping themselves occupied.

"You're in charge?" I asked Jorgeson. "What about your wife's relatives?"

"I can't say I argued when I got the call,"

he said. "What a mess, Ms. Malloy. People in costumes, drunken pirates, bitchy fairies, and all these lords and ladies. It is not your typical crime background." He paused, then tilted his head. "You look particularly charming, if I may be so bold to mention it."

"I don't feel charming. What's going on?"

"The victim was dead when we found him. The back of his head is a mess. The medical examiner is on his way. He'll come up with a reasonably good estimate for the time of death, but I'd guess at least a couple of hours."

"And you're sure it's Salvador Davis?"

"His friend over there talking to Corporal Cooper says so. Do you want to take a look?"

I shook my head. "I'll trust Benny's identification. Salvador drove out here. If his wallet's not in his pocket, you can look for it in his car. Anderson Peru will know where it's parked. What do you think happened?"

"Hard to begin to say, Ms. Malloy. From what Mr. Stallings has said, it sounds like Davis arrived around eight o'clock this morning. He brought some archery equipment and paper targets. Some of the high school boys lugged the bales of hay down here and attached the targets and taped up banners. We'll locate them and ask questions, but I doubt they'll have anything to contribute. Mr. Stallings says he took Davis a cup of ale and a turkey leg shortly before noon and they had lunch at the edge of the woods. He didn't see him after that."

"Several hundred people did, though," I said. "Lots of would-be William Tells willing to put out a dollar to shoot three arrows."

"Were you among them?"

"I wandered down to say hello early in the afternoon, maybe around three o'clock. I stayed for no more than five minutes, then left when a troop of Brownies arrived. I presume other people came after that. I don't know how on earth you can locate the last person to see Salvador."

"It will present difficulties," Jorgeson said with a sigh. "According to Mr. Stallings, there were five or six hundred people here today. We can question the ones who remained for the banquet, but there's no way to locate the others. Nobody was required to show identification to gain entry."

I sat down on a bale of hay. "No telltale footprints near the body or fingerprints on the ax handle?"

"We're looking for footprints, but the ground is dry. The lab will check for fingerprints. According to Mr. Stallings, every now and then Davis would have to go trample around in the area behind you and collect stray arrows. He also would take breaks whenever he wished." Jorgeson glanced at his officers, then sank down on another bale. "I do not understand these people, Ms. Malloy. I am hoping you can help me out."

"I'll do my best. They're not as peculiar as you seem to think they are. They all have jobs and responsibilities. They put on garb and indulge in make-believe merely for entertainment. They spend more money on their hobby than, say, quilters or gardeners, but I haven't met anyone who's unaware that this is not the fifteenth century. What I don't understand is the dynamics of this particular group."

Benny came over and looked down at Sergeant Jorgeson. "Do you still need me here? Everybody's upset, and I'd like to let them know what's happening. I'll be at the farmhouse."

"Yeah, go on," Jorgeson said, wearily flapping his hand. "I'll need to speak to all of you who organized this thing. One of my officers will go with you and wait outside so that you won't be disturbed by reporters."

"Reporters?" I echoed. Would all of Farberville be treated to footage of Lady Clarissa trying to sneak up the steps to the Perus' porch in her emerald gown? What if, by some quirk, the story caught the fancy of the big news organizations and the said footage was aired across the entire country? Would Peter's mother and the lovely Leslie have a splendid time the next morning watching the news while they nibbled triangles of toast and sipped mimosas on the patio? With any luck, Peter would be at the airport when he glanced up at one of the ubiquitous TV screens and saw me. Although he could hardly blame me for meddling, he might be a bit testy.

"Jorgeson," I began in my most genteel voice, "would it be at all possible for one of your officers to take me home now? I swear that I will be available all day tomorrow to give a statement and do whatever I can to assist you."

"No, Ms. Malloy, that is not possible."

I allowed the tiniest hint of desperation to enter my voice. "Please, Jorgeson. I feel faint and my stomach is in turmoil. Salvador was a friend, in a way. I am overwhelmed by his death and this horrible act of violence. I'll set my alarm for seven and be in your office at eight o'clock. I'll make the coffee and bring some muffins."

Benny did not help matters. "You and Salvador were friends? I would have thought you had enough sense not to be seduced by that artistic posturing. The paintings in his living room are nothing but nineteen-seventies rip-offs. Everything he did was a rip-off. Everything! All he did was find his niche market and exploit it. That was his only real talent. That, and insinuating himself with adoring women."

Jorgeson gazed at me but said nothing.

"Now wait just a minute!" I said, trying not to sound shrill. "I was not seduced by anyone, including Salvador. What's more, I didn't admire him or his so-called talent. I felt sorry for him. Who wouldn't, considering the unpleasant reality that his only purported friends were you ARSE wackos? You're all a bunch of manipulators, hiding behind your grandiose titles and silly clothes."

"That's not true!" Benny snapped.

"Oh, really, Sir Kenneth of Gweek?" I took a breath, aware of Jorgeson's bemused expression. As much as I wanted to grab a handful of Benny's orange beard and give it a yank, I realized such a gesture would not get me any closer to home in the next few hours. "If you see any dragons on your way to the farmhouse, be sure and slay them. It will certainly impress the college girls."

"Maybe so," Benny said. He headed up the slope, followed at a discreet distance by a uniformed officer who kept glancing over his shoulder at the woods.

"He's more likely to encounter lions, tigers, and bears," I said. "Well, bears, anyway."

"Would you care to elaborate?" asked Jorgeson.

"Lions are indigenous to Africa, and tigers to India. I've been told there are small black bears in this —"

"I was thinking more of your use of the words 'manipulators' and 'purported.' It sounded to me as though you have quite a few insights that might be of value to the investigation."

"Tomorrow I will be brimming with insights, all of which I will share in the most intricate detail. Right now I'm too shocked to pull my thoughts together. You may not get much from the others, either. I don't know how any of them truly felt about Salvador, but he was a significant part of the group." For some reason I couldn't explain (or justify), I was reluctant to mention Edward's revelation at the banquet. I most certainly had no idea how Edward felt about Salvador, since I didn't know if

281

Edward had confronted him previously or was just hoping for the best. One of the others would tell Jorgeson when he interviewed them. I would claim it was merely a minor sin of omission brought on by the trauma of the murder.

"All right, Ms. Malloy," Jorgeson said as he stood up. "I'll let you go home, and we'll talk tomorrow. I can't spare an officer to take you, but I assume you can get a ride with Caron and Inez."

"You're letting them leave, too?"

"We can't keep all these people here all night. We're getting a list of names and contact numbers, and telling them we'll need statements in a few days. Right now I'm going to focus on the members of this screwy club. What did you call it?"

"ARSE. The Association for Renaissance Scholarship and . . . Enlightenment, I think. It's a national organization. This is the fiefdom of Avalon." I brushed bits of hay off my gown as I rose. "Do you want me to come to the police department in the morning, or shall I wait for your call?"

Jorgeson surveyed the crime scene, then sat back down on the bale of hay. "I'll be lucky to get home by dawn, and there will be a ton of paperwork waiting for me on my desk. Let's plan on meeting tomorrow afternoon, Ms. Malloy."

"As early as possible," I said. "Peter's getting home about six, and I'd like time to get ready for our date."

I couldn't see his expression as he looked up at me. "Probably about one o'clock or so. I'll let you know."

"Is something wrong, Jorgeson? Have you heard from Peter? He is coming tomorrow, isn't he?"

"Run along, Ms. Malloy," he said. "I need to find out if we've found any evidence."

"Fine, then." I walked back up the slope toward the tents, keenly aware that he hadn't answered my questions. Peter had had ample opportunities to call me during the last few days if his plans had changed. He knew the telephone number at the bookstore, as well as my home number. I stopped and looked back, but Jorgeson was no longer on the bale of hay.

When I reached the food court, I went over to the stage and whispered Edward's name. There was no reply. Clouds had covered the moon, and now the area was even darker. I edged forward and promptly banged my knee against the edge of the stage. Resisting the impulse to curse, I again whispered Edward's name. He could have gone to the battle arena to wait for me, I supposed, but I was no longer in the mood to be taken into his confidence. Not that I ever had, it occurred to me. The best he'd offered thus far was a proposal for a scene. Characters, setting, and dialogue had not been disclosed. His hints had led to me to an erroneous conclusion — but not an illogical one. Had that been his intention since he'd first come into the bookstore two weeks ago? Or, to his credit, it might have never entered his mind that I would even consider Carlton to be a likely suspect. Edward was young, I reminded myself, and confused.

And I was not so young, but decidedly confused. I desperately wanted to go home, slip into something less medieval, and sleep.

"Good night, sweet prince," I whispered, then went to find Caron and Inez.

CHAPTER ELEVEN

Caron and Inez were sitting at a picnic table, pointedly ignoring everyone around them. I told one of the uniformed officers who was scribbling down names and phone numbers that we had Sergeant Jorgeson's permission to leave, then hauled the girls out of the Royal Pavilion before I could be ordered to produce a hall pass.

"I hope you weren't lying," Caron said as she led me toward a pasture well behind the farmhouse. "I don't want the police pounding on my bedroom door in the middle of the night. That would be Too Much."

"It's already been too much," Inez grumbled.

"It certainly was for the murder victim," I said. "How far is the car?"

"Miles," Caron said, as if we were setting off on a transcontinental trek. "I can't believe we don't even have a flashlight. If I fall and break my ankle, it's your fault,

Mother. I'll be in traction for three months, and hobble on crutches all semester. You'll have to rent a maid of honor for the wedding."

"Why would it be my fault?"

Caron tripped on a clump of weeds but recovered without an orthopedic catastrophe. "Because you didn't tell us to bring a flashlight. Emily's mother gave her a little one to keep in her purse. Rhonda Maguire and her circle can hang on to their boyfriends' arms."

"The pirates aren't too steady on their feet," I commented. "Didn't you notice?"

Inez smiled. "Miss Thackery did. If she hadn't needed them for entertainment, she would have sent them home. She may waft around in her fancy dresses and twinkle at everybody, but she can be really mean. You know how you told us to get Edward away from the pavilion? Well, we were sort of just standing behind the tents when she came over and slapped him."

"His head nearly flew off," added Caron. "I don't think she noticed us at first. When she realized we were there, she mumbled something about it being for his own good and took off for the farmhouse. The three of us just stood there and gaped at each other for like forever."

I tried to envision the scene. "Was Edward hysterical before she . . . ah, tried to calm him down?"

"No, not really. He was mostly stunned, and blubbering about how he couldn't believe this had happened. It was way too pathetic. I mean, it's too bad that man got killed, but there was no excuse for him to get so carried away over it."

"Did you listen to his ballad?" I asked her.

"Yeah, like everybody else." She stopped and thought for a long moment. "The dead guy was his father?"

"Apparently he thought so," I said.

"How was I supposed to know that? Nobody said anything about it."

"Nobody knew," I said, shaking my head. "I'm not sure Salvador did, either."

Inez clutched my arm. "What's that?" she whispered. "Over there by the cars. Something moved."

Caron snickered. "A cow, Inez. This is a pasture, remember? That's usually where cows hang out. If we were in a desert, it'd be a camel, but it's not hot and sandy. I saw you tasting the mead. Maybe you're tipsy."

"I only took one sip," Inez said hotly. "That was not a cow."

"So you're saying it was a camel?"

I shoved both of them into motion. "I

don't care if it was a cow riding on a camel. I'm ready to go home." I did not add that I intended to make a long-distance call to Rhode Island.

When we arrived at the car, I realized I'd left my purse in the farmhouse, which meant I didn't have my driver's license with me. Caron drove us to my apartment. Conversation was nonexistent. As I came into the kitchen, I caught a whiff of soy sauce and ginger. I followed the scent into the living room. Peter was sprawled on the sofa, holding the remote control. Carry-out cartons of Chinese food, a plate, and chopsticks cluttered the coffee table. I was faintly aware of Caron and Inez scuttling down the hall to the former's bedroom.

"I wasn't expecting you until tomorrow," I said inanely.

"Is that your idea of a warm welcome?"

I continued to stare at him as if he were an apparition. "I'm surprised, that's all. I thought you were still in Newport. You told me you weren't coming home until tomorrow. I made dinner reservations."

Peter pretended to ponder this. "Then the only thing for me to do is go spend the night at the airport. I will admit I was hoping for a bed and some cozy companionship, but if you say tomorrow, then tomorrow it must be." He put down the remote. "There's still some sesame chicken and garlic shrimp, and a spoonful of fried rice. Help yourself."

I grabbed him before he could get to his feet and pushed him back on the sofa. My welcome was more than warm. After ten minutes or so, I sat up and ran my fingers through my disheveled curls. "Was that more in line with your expectations, Super Cop?"

He put his arms around me and expressed his appreciation for another few minutes. He has many talents, and my appreciation rivaled his. Eventually he surfaced. "How was your day at the fair, milady? Were you pursued by effeminate earls and fat, middle-aged barons?"

"You may wish you'd stayed in Newport," I said, then told him what had happened. "Jorgeson's out there now, hoping the murderer dropped his business card at the scene. He seemed overwhelmed by the number of potential witnesses. There were a hundred or so people at the banquet, and a lot of them will recall friends they saw during the day. If the medical examiner puts the death prior to six o'clock, then any one of five or six hundred people could have done it."

"Damnation," Peter said. "I put some beer

in the refrigerator. Why don't you get me one, and make yourself a drink? I'd better call Jorgeson and find out what's going on."

"Fine," I said mendaciously. I left him on the sofa with his cell phone, and went to my bedroom to change into shorts and a T-shirt. The hooks on the back of the gown were undone during the episode on the sofa (further elaboration will not be forthcoming), so it took me only a few minutes. I then knocked on Caron's door. She was still wearing her garb, although in the light I could see stains on the skirt and sleeves. Inez was seated on the bed with the phone, assuring her parents that she was safe. Their noses were less sunburned than mine, since they'd been in the stall most of the day. Nevertheless, Caron had acquired a few new freckles.

"Did you know Peter was coming today?" I asked her in a low voice.

"Maybe."

"Why didn't you warn me?"

"Why would I? It's not like he was going to catch you in bed with someone else. Are you afraid he'll find all the empty scotch bottles in the trash?"

I wasn't sure about the legal definition of infanticide; there might have been a cutoff birthday, when the crime became homicide.

Justifiable homicide, I might add. "There is precisely one empty bottle in the trash, and that's partly because Luanne came by one evening and we sat on the balcony discussing Nietzsche and Schopenhauer."

"I'm sure it was fascinating. Now if you don't mind, I'd like to change clothes. I haven't been able to breathe all day. Can we keep the phone?"

"Just don't call Nietzsche," I said. "Overseas calls are expensive."

Peter was still on his cell phone when I returned with a beer and a drink. I didn't bother to listen, but I could see that he wasn't pleased. As I put the beer in front of him, he shot me a look that did not bode well. Jorgeson was clearly telling tales not of damsels in distress and knights in shining armor, but of Lady Clarissa and her involvement. I was very glad I'd changed clothes.

After yet another look, he went out to the balcony to continue his conversation. I was gathering up the cartons when Inez, now dressed in shorts and a wrinkled blouse, came down the hall. "It's going to be on the news," she said, blinking at me. "Carrie's parents told her that the local station is promising a live story at ten o'clock. Will it be okay if Caron and I come out and watch it?"

"By all means," I muttered. "Are you the volunteer who sticks her toe in the river rumored to be infested with giant leeches?"

"Something like that." She fled back down the hall.

I dumped the cartons in the trash, noting with satisfaction that the only other bottle besides the scotch held the dregs of moldy pickle relish. I washed my hands and was on my way to the living room when Peter cut me off.

"I'm going out there," he said. "I'm not officially back in town, but Jorgeson sounded harried. He said you could give me directions. He also said you knew the victim, as well as all the other members of this goofy club."

"That's not true. I only know the ones who are in town this summer and helping organize the fair." I hesitated, then virtuously added, "And the victim. I had a martini on his deck Sunday afternoon. He prepared one for me, anyway. I didn't drink it because I don't especially care for gin. We didn't really talk about much of anything except Serengeti. He doesn't know whether or not she lives in his house. I find that a very unsettling idea — having someone prowl around the house. We'll have to keep that in mind if we buy a large house."

Peter seemed a bit perplexed by this. Once he found his voice, he said, "I'll be out at this blasted place all night with Jorgeson. We can talk tomorrow."

"About large versus modest houses?"

"Not exactly," he said. I told him how to find the Perus' farm. He gave me a quick kiss, then left through the kitchen door. A minute later I heard a car drive away.

Caron and Inez were on the sofa. As I sat down, Caron turned on the TV and settled back to appreciate the drama. Although we'd left through a back gate and never even glimpsed the news van, she seemed to think that she would have a starring roll.

The news came on. The two current anchors stared solemnly at us. One was an aging male with suspiciously black hair; the other was a distressingly young woman with a perky nose and artfully applied makeup. Ken and Barbie, eager to share Farberville's celebrations and calamities. After a quick teaser about the "purported" homicide, they took turns relating tidbits about car wrecks, a factory closing with "a major impact on our regional economy," and the deadline for a children's essay contest in which tykes could express their innermost feelings about Labor Day. I doubted Caron and Inez would hole up one afternoon to produce the winning entry and be rewarded with a kiddie burger and fries from a fast food restaurant. After all, mailing in their entry would eat up a third of the value of their winnings.

"What a wonderful opportunity for the children in our viewing area," Barbie said, squinting at us. "As I told you at the beginning of the broadcast, police have been called to what is likely to be homicide at Farberville's first Renaissance Fair. Channel Five's own field reporter, Penelope Poplin, is at the scene. Penelope, what's going on?"

Penelope's grim visage appeared on the screen. She was standing below the arch at the entry gate, apparently having been stopped there. To her annoyance, people were jostling her as they left. No one seemed inclined to stop for an interview. As hard as she tried to sound as if she were at the edge of the crime scene and privy to updates from the investigators, the best she could produce was a lame story about the police and paramedics arriving earlier. Someone leaving had told her that the police had detained an astounding number of people well into the night and — she paused to allow us to realize the significance — had asked for identification and telephone numbers. She did her best until at last she acknowledged that we could expect more information on the morning news show and smiled bravely at the camera until Ken and Barbie took over with a promise to give us the weather outlook for the upcoming week.

"Sheesh," Caron said as she turned off the TV, "I was hoping we'd get to see the fairies and the drunken pirates. The only person I recognized is that guy who works part-time at the pizza place. He's a dork."

Inez nodded. "Worse than my brother."

Having never met either of them, I had no opinion. "I'm surprised Madam Marsilia d'Anjou didn't demand her fifteen seconds of fame." When they looked blankly at me, I added, "Sally Fromberger, Farberville's very own prioress."

Caron has minimal tolerance for adults who behave foolishly. "Can you believe she had the nerve to park her stupid cart in the middle of the food court and badger everybody who walked by. If ever there was a reason not to become a nun . . ."

"She wasn't as creepy as that lady with the rags and trinkets pinned all over her," Inez said. "Half the little kids in town will be having nightmares about her."

"Very creepy," I said. "I'm sure you have phone calls to make, but let me ask you a question first. Did either of you go to the archery range during the afternoon?"

Inez glanced at Caron, then said, "We took turns wandering around to look at things. I went to the archery range, but only for a minute. The guy — I guess the one who was killed — was talking to Mrs. Peru. You know, the Duchess. She had the same look that Miss Thackery had when she slapped Edward. Well, she was talking. He just looked pissed. I didn't get close enough to hear what she was saying."

"Any idea what time?" I asked her.

"An hour or so after the rush at lunch. I wasn't paying attention."

"It doesn't matter," I said, mentally trying to formulate a timetable. "You two are dismissed. Don't stay up all night."

Caron pursed her lips for a moment. "I guess we didn't do a very good job of taking care of Edward, Mother. Is he okay?"

"I don't know. I spoke with him after the police arrived, so Miss Thackery didn't do him any permanent injury."

"As long as he's not locked in one of those awful portable potties," she said, having absolved herself of guilt. "By late in the afternoon, we could smell them."

"But very authentic," I pointed out. "Indoor plumbing was not a concept in the

Renaissance era. Chamber pots were emptied on the street."

"Eeew," Caron said as she went into the kitchen and opened the refrigerator. "Why is there never anything to eat in this house?"

Somehow she managed to scrounge up enough to sustain them, and they retreated to her bedroom with chips, crackers, cookies, and sodas. I went out to the balcony and idly gazed at the campus lawn across the street while I tried to piece together the day's events. In retrospect, the Renaissance Fair seemed more garish than a county fair midway. I could not retrieve the faintly euphoric glow when I'd swished down the walkways in my emerald-green gown. My clothes were at the farmhouse, but there was no urgency to fetch them. It would be no great loss if they were pitched. I would need my purse as soon as I could retrieve it, along with the nonmedieval plastic bag with the unicorn and Mrs. Jorgeson's garden gnome.

I wondered how Lanya, Anderson, and the members of their court were holding up to intensive questioning by the police. Lieutenant Peter Rosen could be daunting, as I knew from personal experience. From what Caron and Inez had said, it sounded as though Fiona Thackery were already teeter-

ing on the threshold of an emotional break-
down. I could think of no other reason to
explain her attack on Edward, unless she
had convinced herself that he was responsible for Salvador's death. But why would
he be? He'd spent four years chasing down
his biological father, who had turned out to
be intelligent, successful, and reasonable (as
far as I could tell). Likable when he was in
the mood. If Edward had already presented
him with the facts, then Salvador's obtuse
comments about being confused and wanting to talk it over with me made sense.

Lanya had been devastated by the announcement of Salvador's death, but it was
hard to decide if that was because they'd
been friends or they'd been lovers. I wasn't
convinced she'd halted her affair with
Benny, despite what Salvador had told me.
It was also possible that all of his gossip had
been fabricated to intrigue me.

I went back inside, locked the door, and
headed for bed. I could hear squeals and
giggles from Caron's bedroom, which was
normal on almost any night. If by some
bizarre series of events, she landed in a
priory under the benign guidance of Sally
Fromberger, my daughter would undoubtedly be cloistered with her fellow novices,
babbling about Sister Beatitude's midnight

cookie binges and Sister Sylvestor's obsession with rosary beads.

I was ambiguous about Peter's unexpected
arrival. I was delighted to see him, naturally,
but his timing was inopportune — and his
motive suspect. Jorgeson had been in com-
munication with Peter, but he knew perfectly well that I wasn't really involved in
the recent peculiar happenings. Peter would
not have been worried that I'd discovered a
latent fondness for arson. But he wanted to
talk. Something was afoot.

I ground my teeth for a long while before
I fell asleep.

When I arose the next morning, I peeked
into Caron's room. Their outfits from the
drama department were piled on the floor
amid the remnants of their junk food fest. I
found the telephone on the floor next to the
bed and took it with me to the living room.
I wasn't in the mood to open the bookstore,
but I'd promised Jorgeson that I would be
available and I didn't want to sit around
and wait for his call. Half an hour later I
went out through the kitchen and down the
steps to the alley. I had no particular reason
not to walk to the store and enjoy the fresh
air and sunshine, since it was likely that I
might be spending numerous hours in the

police department later in the day. I'd done so in the past, and the ambience was not to be savored. The walls were painted a shade best described as municipal green, and the floors were grimy. The redolence was that of sweat and burned coffee.

I was surprised to see a police car parked in front of the remains of Angie's house. Being of a moderately curious nature, I stopped and waited until an officer came outside. Her face, hands, and uniform were caked with sooty ashes, and she was limping. She gave me a chilly smile. "We're not conducting tours, ma'am, so you might as well move along. If you cross the yellow tape, you'll be charged with trespassing and interfering with an investigation."

"And good morning to you," I said politely. "What are you looking for?"

"Evidence."

I eyed her, not sure how to elicit information without landing in the backseat of one of the vehicles. Although I've never worn handcuffs, I doubted they were comfortable. The officer was shorter than I, but stocky and clearly not having much fun inside the house. "I saw the investigators several times last week. I guess I thought the investigation had been completed. It must be dreadful in there. You look exhausted."

She allowed herself to sigh. "It's no damn picnic, that's for sure. It's filthy and it stinks. All I want to do is go home and take a long, hot shower, but we'll probably be stuck here most of the day." She clasped her hands together and stretched her arms above her head. "My back is killing me, and I've only been here an hour. I'm usually assigned to a desk job. I'd give anything to be filing reports and making coffee. My softball team's playing tonight, but I'll be too tired to swing a bat."

I grimaced as if I'd been in that very same predicament. "They certainly stuck you with a rotten job. Maybe you'll get lucky and find whatever you're looking for before too long. Is it something specific?"

"I wish," she said with a groan. "We have a lead on the woman who was killed in the fire last week. This morning someone at DHS called to report that one of their clients went missing two weeks ago. Her description matches what the lab has been able to determine about age and height. The missing woman broke her arm in a fall last February. The victim had a healed fracture just below the elbow, same arm. They also matched some kind of congenital jaw deformity. I don't know why the captain has us here to sift through debris for more evidence to confirm the identity. It's not like we're going to find her driver's license."

"Did the social worker have any idea how Angie came up with enough money to rent this house?"

"The name wasn't Angie," the officer said. "Rose or Rosalyn, something like that. A sad case. Mid-forties, no relatives, in and out of psychiatric wards since she was a teenager. A couple of months ago, when she was on her meds, the social worker found her a minimum-wage job and a rooming house. Then two weeks ago the social worker dropped by to check on her. She'd disappeared — moved out of the rooming house and quit her job without giving notice. One of her coworkers overheard her say she'd found an easier job. It took the social worker a while to get around to filing a report with us. I guess they're more concerned about children."

"I guess so," I murmured.

"Wilcoxen," a male officer shouted from the precarious doorway, "what do you think you're doing? The captain'll bust you back to traffic control if he finds out you were giving information to a civilian."

"Oooh, what a threat," she said wryly, then went back inside the skeletal structure.

I continued toward the Book Depot, mulling over what I'd learned. Rose did not fit my impression of Angie, a card-carrying member of ARSE and a volunteer dance instructor. Edward could have met her at a fair when she was between bouts of hospitalization, but it was hard to imagine. Even if she'd found a better job, she'd been working for minimum wage. How could she have saved enough money to send a deposit to the owner of the blue house? All things were possible, I concluded as I arrived at the back door of the bookstore and dug through my purse for my key.

The door was already unlocked. I stepped back and tried to think if there was any way I could have failed to lock it when I left the previous day. I had not left in a panic. I'd kept an eye on the time, and when Luanne drove up, I'd been ready to go. I was looking forward to the Renaissance Fair, but I wasn't in a mad tizzy to get there and start buying unicorns. I could remember locking the front door, turning off the lights, unplugging the coffeepot, and locking the back door on my way out.

I couldn't stand in the parking lot indefinitely. Neither of the two options that came to mind appealed. Going inside might lead to an awkward encounter with an intruder.

Trotting up to Sally's health food restaurant to use her phone to call the police would result in a bothersome conversation with her. She might force me to eat a multigrain muffin or a carob cookie while we waited. I was still trying to decide when the door opened and Edward looked out at me.

"Aren't you going to come inside, Claire?" he asked. "I've already started the coffee."

"How did you unlock the door?"

"Magic shops stock more than top hats and rabbits. Look, if you're afraid to come in, then say so and I'll leave. You don't happen to keep any clothes here, do you? I'm going to be conspicuous if I have to walk home in my jester's garb. I really don't want to attract any attention at the moment and end up at the police station."

"Are the police looking for you?" I asked, still unsure what to do.

He shrugged. "I should think so. I can tell that I'm making you nervous, so I'll go. Maybe I'll find out where the railroad tracks lead. I'd rather sleep under a bridge than in a cell with a bunch of drunken rednecks."

Despite his nonchalant tone, I could see that he was exhausted and close to tears. "No, I'm not nervous," I said, since I was too apprehensive to be merely nervous. "We'll have some coffee and talk, but afterward you have to call the police. Do you promise?"

"Scout's honor." He opened the door wider and waited until I came inside. "Do you mind not opening the store just yet? I don't want to have to hide behind the boiler while you deal with customers." He wiped his eyes with the back of his hand. "Sorry. It's all too much for me. It's crazy. None of it makes any sense. If I don't talk to someone, I — I don't know what I'll do. Kiss off grad school and become a wandering minstrel. 'Will juggle for food.' It's a career I never considered." He abruptly went into the tiny bathroom and closed the door.

I poured myself a cup of coffee and sat down behind my desk. The only weapon I had in a drawer was a bottle opener given to me by a sales rep as a promotional gimmick. It lacked panache. I hoped Edward was pulling himself together, since I tend to be softhearted when faced with tremulous youth. I crossed my fingers as Edward emerged, relieved to note that he seemed more composed.

"All right," I said briskly, "let's hear the whole story. When did you tell Salvador that he was your father?"

Edward hesitated, perhaps disconcerted by my bluntness, then sat down across from me. "Friday afternoon — the day before yesterday. Less than forty-eight hours ago. I went to his house. Some peculiar woman let me in and told me he was in his studio. I couldn't figure out who she was. Really spooky and not exactly glad to see me. Is she like a housekeeper or something?"

"Close enough. So what happened?"

"Salvador — I can't bring myself to call him anything else — was cleaning brushes. I told him I had something important to tell him, so he suggested we go sit on the deck. All I could think to do was just blurt it out. He didn't say anything at first, just went to the bar and made himself a drink, then sat back down and looked at me. I didn't know what to say, so we sat there in silence for maybe ten minutes. Finally, he asked me if I had any proof. He didn't sound upset or angry, just interested."

"Do you have any proof?" I asked.

Edward slumped in the chair. "His name's not on my birth certificate, but I have the legal right to require him to give a DNA sample."

"Even though you're not a minor?"

"Yeah, I looked into it. Judges order the parties to do it all the time, mostly in child support or custody cases, but also in ones like this. The test costs a couple of hundred dollars, and the results are entered into the record. Salvador said he'd cooperate voluntarily, but he figured that the results would show that he was my father. He said my mother's story was basically true, that they'd lived together one summer. He was really angry when she told him she was pregnant, because she was supposed to be on birth control pills. He was planning to go to New York and get into the art scene, and he had no intention of being stuck with a wife and kid. He gave her as much money as he could and left. Never heard from her again, never tried to get in touch with her."

"How do you think he felt about discovering he was a father twenty-two years after the fact?" I asked, trying to imagine the scene on the deck. "Did he act as though it was just a pesky little problem that could be resolved with an apology and a handshake?"

"No," Edward said. "He didn't hug me and profess his affection, but he looked kind of pleased at the idea. Not thrilled, but not upset. He asked about my mother, and I told him about everything that she'd gone through to support me. He just sat there and nodded the whole time. Finally, when I couldn't think of anything else to say, he said that we should probably have the DNA test, but he was willing to accept me as his son. Once he got used to the idea, he wanted to make things right. I told him I didn't want anything from him, but he said he would acknowledge me publicly, support me while I was in grad school, and help me get my career started. We talked about my painting, and he insisted that he would take me to New York in the fall and introduce me to his important friends. If I wanted, I could use the room over the carport as a studio. It was better than any of my fantasies."

"So you went home and wrote the ballad," I said.

He grinned. "I wrote it ten years ago, when I was into King Arthur and those legends. Except for the archery stuff, of course. In my original version, the foundling's father turns out to be a claimant to the throne who had some sort of dalliance with Guinevere while Arthur was off in battle. I revised it Friday night. It was supposed to be a surprise for . . . my father." His grin vanished. "I was so happy yesterday. Then it all blew up in my face, like a damn grenade."

I got up and went around the desk to refill my coffee cup while I considered what he'd told me. "But you must have noticed Salvador wasn't at the banquet, Edward. Why did you sing the ballad?"

"I noticed," he said in a low voice. "I suppose it occurred to me that he might have taken off again, the same way he did when my mother told him she was pregnant. Then I realized that I was being paranoid. I mean, earlier in the afternoon I went down to the archery range and he was there. A bunch of little girls were squealing at him and fighting over the bows, so he and I just smiled at each other for a second. If he were going to split, he wouldn't have shown up at the Ren Fair. He would have been halfway to New York or on a flight to Paris. When I didn't see him at the banquet, I assumed he was around somewhere. Maybe I shouldn't have sung the ballad, but I wanted everyone to know that Salvador was my father. The people at the head table, anyway."

"They do now. Not of all them were enchanted by the idea, though."

"Like Fiona, for instance?" Edward went to the doorway and looked at the dimly lit rows of racks, as if he thought she might be lurking with the intent of renewing her assault. "Did Caron and her friend tell you what happened? We were just standing there in the pasture. I was so bewildered that I didn't even know how to process what I'd heard. I couldn't decide if I should be crying or laughing at the ultimate irony. This man I'd been searching for since I turned eighteen — my father — I finally found him and confronted him. He didn't call me a lying bastard and throw me out of his house. Even after the DNA test came back, he could have refused to have anything to do with me. But no, he was happy. You have to believe me, Claire. Salvador wanted me as his son. He told me so. And the next day he's dead — murdered. Can't you see the irony?" His voice rose. "It took me four years to find him, but only one day to lose him again — forever."

"Sit down, Edward," I said in my sternest maternal tone. "You need to collect yourself. I understand that you're bewildered and in pain. Anyone in your situation would feel the same way." Not that I could imagine anyone ever finding himself in that situation. It was the second act in a poorly plotted, overwrought melodrama from the Victorian era. Shakespeare would have treated it as a comedy fraught with mistaken identities and a happy ending, in which nobody had died and all the characters were properly sorted out by gender and wedded. Dickens would have at least allowed the son to inherit a great fortune and a title.

Edward sniveled for a few minutes, then

wiped his face. "Okay, so now what? Have the police caught the person who did it?"

"If they have, they haven't shared it with me. Why do you assume they're looking for you? You talked to them last night, didn't you?"

"I couldn't handle it, so I stayed away from the Royal Pavilion. I'd left my street clothes at Lanya and Anderson's house, but there was a cop on the porch and maybe more inside. I finally found an unlocked hatchback in the pasture and hid behind the backseat. A comely lady of the realm and her two dimpled damsels gave me a lift back to town."

"You escaped in my car?" I said, appalled. "You had no business involving us in your premature departure! How could you do such a thing, Edward? You might have had the courtesy to announce your presence instead of eavesdropping like that."

"Nobody said much of anything," he said, trying to smile. "And if I'd asked for a ride, you would have said no. After the three of you went upstairs, I went down that side street and along the railroad tracks. I didn't have anyplace else to go, and I was hoping you and I could have a private conversation this morning. Would you like me to make another pot of coffee?"

Before I could tell him that I most certainly did not, the door opened and Sergeant Jorgeson came inside. "Ms. Malloy," he began, then spotted Edward. "My goodness, look who's here. We've been trying to locate Mr. Cobbinwood since last night. I trust, Ms. Malloy, that you can explain this."

CHAPTER TWELVE

Jorgeson declined the offer of a cup of coffee, and summoned an officer to escort Edward to a vehicle. I waited silently, not at all sure how much trouble I might be in. Albeit without my complicity, I had helped Edward flee before he could be questioned — and I'd provided a sanctuary for the night. Ignorance seemed like a perfectly reasonable excuse for those transgressions. Although I do have my moments, I am not omniscient.

I gave Jorgeson an accusatory look. "I thought you said one o'clock."

"I seem to recall saying something like that, Ms. Malloy, but I did not interpret it as an appointment. I assumed you might be eager to share your insights as soon as possible."

"I am, but at the moment I'd prefer to open the store and read the newspaper. Is there anything else?"

Fifteen minutes later I was ushered into Lieutenant Peter Rosen's office and left to wait. The air was stale, so I opened a window. I resisted an urge to straighten up his desk, which was covered with piles of folders, bulletins, and interdepartmental communiqués involving such portentous matters as the softball team schedule and dirty dishes in the break room. The view from his window was of a chain-link fence, an alley, and the back of a building. The FBI facility in Quantico may well have seemed like a summer camp.

"Have a seat, Claire," Peter said in a stony voice as he came into the office.

"Is that your idea of a warm welcome?"

He put a cup on the corner of his desk. "I brought you some coffee. I'd like to review your story before you make an official statement. Shall we get started?"

"In that case," I said as I dusted off a chair seat and sat down, "I should call a lawyer. I'd hate to be in a prison cell on my wedding day. Perhaps my fellow inmates can make me a bouquet out of tissue paper, and the warden can be your best man. Will we be allowed a conjugal visit afterward?"

He made a few uncouth remarks under his breath, then took his sweet time reading through notes on a legal pad. He was in a grumpy mood, I decided, so I busied myself pouring the coffee out the window and watching men share a cigarette on the loading dock of the building. Peter continue to shuffle papers. I tried to remember if I had any change to buy a soda from the vending machine in the hall. There were no magazines in the office, only catalogs for cop paraphernalia. There wasn't a feather duster, either, or I might have tidied up his collection of plaques and awards.

"Please stop sniffing around and sit down," Peter said. After I'd obliged, he continued. "I was gone for three weeks, not three months. Even though you promised not to get involved in any more potential crimes, you managed to meet these screwy people, allowed them to perform in front of your store, thereby snarling up traffic in a six-block radius, went to their meetings, heard their woes, reported the fire that killed one of them —"

"I'm sorry to interrupt, but the fire did not kill one of the them. The victim appears to be a woman who'd been under the supervision of the DHS. The officers who were at the scene earlier this morning told me —"

"— helped sponsor this Renaissance Fair, participated by calling yourself some silly name and wearing a costume —"

"It wasn't a costume," I said. "It was garb. You saw it yourself last night when I got home. You were on my sofa, and unless I'm confused, in a much nicer mood. Stop barking at me, Peter. We're supposedly getting married in two months. Right now I'm more inclined to go to the animal shelter and find a nice, quiet mutt."

"I apologize," he said. Before I could reply, however, he snatched up the sheaf of papers and pecked at it with his finger. "Your name is mentioned in almost every paragraph. You're getting better coverage than a doped-up Hollywood celebrity who can't stay married for fifteen minutes. Why couldn't you just stay home and read bridal magazines?"

"As that celebrity would say, I'm out of here." I picked up my purse and started for the door. "If you have anything further to say, I'll be at the airport, waiting for the next flight to Camelot. Fare thee well, milord."

"Claire," he said, then stopped.

I turned around. Despite his week in Newport, no doubt occupied by sailing and playing tennis with his ex-wife, he looked dreadfully wan and exhausted. He'd found time to shave and put on a jacket and tie, but his eyes were bloodshot. I resumed my seat, took a breath, and said, "I didn't tell Jorgeson quite everything."

"Surprise, surprise."

"Don't push your luck, Peter. Do you want the generic version, or the true one?"

He raised his eyebrows. "Door number two."

Although I knew I would sound like an idiot, I related the conversations I'd had with Edward concerning his biological father. "I didn't just jump to a conclusion," I added. "I flung myself at it. I was convinced Carlton was his father, and therefore Caron was his half sister. I was worried sick about how to handle it. I didn't know if I should welcome Edward into the family or tell him he was out of luck as far as finding his father." To my dismay, my voice began to quiver as if I were a hapless heroine. "He's just a kid, but so is Caron."

"It never occurred to you that he might be looking for me?"

"No," I said firmly. "I misjudged Carlton. We were grad students, caught up in our cleverness as we ruthlessly shredded authors for their shallow insights and lack of literary merit. It was a departmental pastime to deconstruct books and disparage them for such trivial concepts as plot. We fueled ourselves with cheap red wine and moldy cheese. When our friends started getting married, so did we. Once we landed here in Farberville, isolated and forced to rely on each other, we began to see the folly of it. I got pregnant, and Carlton looked for adulation from his students. Gratuities for grades, so to speak." I stood up and went to the window to breathe in some fresh air. "What I just said was not an excuse. I knew what I was doing, although even at the time I was already having misgivings." I gave myself a minute to recover from admitting frailty, which is not among my favorite activities, and to think how best to continue. "To contemplate for even one second that you might be Edward's father would mean that I am totally incapable of judging character."

"So basically it was about you, not me or Edward or Caron or any of the other players?" Peter said.

"I did not wish to precipitate the decline of civilization as we know it," I said. "If we can't trust a bookseller to carry forward the beacon of enlightenment, we might as well rely on cable reality shows." I waited to see if he wished to argue the point, but he seemed to be at a loss how best to refute my remark. "Now that we've cleared that up, you can understand why I was reluctant to discuss it with Jorgeson. We really should look into the timing of all this. I'm not sure how Edward's paternity issue fits in, but it's hard to dismiss it as coincidental. He was singing his ballad when Salvador's body was discovered. Very peculiar, don't you agree?"

"*We* won't look into anything. All *you* need to do is give a detailed and precise statement that includes all these tidbits you failed to mention. One of the officers will meet you in the interview room and keep you supplied with sharpened pencils. After you're done, someone will take you back to the bookstore so that you can snatch up the beacon and carry it forward. I have an appointment with the captain in ten minutes, and I need to organize these reports."

"Shall I cancel our dinner reservations?" I asked.

"I don't know. I'll call you later."

I went around the desk and reaffirmed my faith in his character, then trooped down the hall to the interview room. The next two hours were tedious and unworthy of further description.

The officer who drove me back to the store had agreed to a small detour by the newsstand, and I was working on the *Sunday New York Times* crossword puzzle when

Anderson Peru came inside. He was carrying a purse, which I found rather unnerving until I recognized it as mine. As he dropped it on the counter, I glanced up and said, "Do you know a seven-letter word for a medieval scourge?"

"See if 'Clarissa' fits," he said sourly.

"That's eight letters. Should I be honored by your unexpected visit, or alarmed?"

Anderson grimaced. "Neither. All I want to know is what the hell is going on. The police made it clear that Salvador was killed yesterday afternoon. How could that happen when all those people were wandering around the site? The archery range was away from the tents and stalls because of safety concerns, but it wasn't in a remote corner of the pasture. Salvador knew what he was doing — he'd done it dozens of times. We all have."

"He wasn't shot with an arrow," I said.

"No, he wasn't." Anderson looked around the store. "Is there somewhere we can sit down? I didn't get any sleep last night. The police questioned everybody at the house, and then had me give them a tour of the fairgrounds. It looked like a video game version of a ghost town. I kept thinking Benny was going to spring out from behind a stall and attack me with his sword. By the time I was allowed to go back to the house, I was too freaked out to try to sleep. You seem to have some sort of connection with the detectives, Claire. What happened? Who killed Salvador?"

Anderson looked worse than Peter. His hair was unkempt and he hadn't shaved. His regal finery had been replaced with torn jeans and an unironed shirt. It was obvious, even from a distance, that he'd unwound with whiskey into the early hours of the morning. The Duke of Glenbarrens was less than impressive.

I suggested coffee in my office. As he settled himself with a groan, I said, "What about the battle-ax? Was it Salvador's?"

"Benny's," he muttered. "He had it earlier, but he stashed it in the prop box at the Royal Pavilion when he went took off his armor after the preliminary rounds. He doesn't remember seeing the ax when he retrieved his armor for the final battle. That's understandable, since the box had all of the jester's toys, as well as my armor and oddments of garb, and, as always, the Threats' lunch basket."

"William and Glynnis don't partake of the turkey legs and ale?"

"They prefer chicken salad sandwiches and martinis," Anderson said, rolling his eyes in the same way Caron did when particularly vexed. "Anyway, I didn't notice the ax when I took out my armor just before four o'clock, but I wasn't paying attention. I was . . . I guess you'd say I was distracted. The box is supposed to be padlocked to prevent theft. It wasn't, though, because all of us needed access throughout the day. Benny admits it was a dumb mistake not to take the ax to the house, but he said he was tired of lugging it around with him. Mine cost more than a hundred dollars, and I keep it locked in a closet most of the time. If my kids ever got their hands on it, they'd hack up all the furniture and make a bonfire."

"He must be feeling pretty bad about leaving the ax where anyone could take it."

Anderson accepted a mug of coffee and leaned back in the chair. "I can assure you that he's feeling bad. As soon as we got to the house, he headed for the liquor cabinet. The detectives were not pleased when they arrived to question us and found Benny sprawled on the sofa, watching a movie on the VCR and doing a steady critique of the dialogue and characters. It was one of the kids' movies, animated. Benny found it as fascinating as a documentary by Jacques Cousteau."

"Oh, dear," I said as I sat down. "He has a serious drinking problem, doesn't he? Has he acknowledged it?"

"It's not as bad as it appears. When he's away on a project, he's a fantastic engineer, and in a crisis, he's the first person they call. He's so intelligent that it's frightening. When he gets home, he indulges himself to the extreme. He really is a Viking at heart, even when he's wearing a hard hat and supervising the construction of a bridge or an oil rig in the Middle East."

"A lusty Viking, from what I've seen," I said tactfully.

"If you're referring to his purported affair with Lanya, you can forget about it. You've seen her. She has the sex appeal of a turnip — make that an organic turnip from her garden. Benny chases college girls, and has remarkable success. Did Salvador say something to you about it?"

I almost choked on a swallow of coffee. "Obliquely. I am not unobservant, Anderson. There's more to your fiefdom than devotion to the study of the Renaissance."

"You have an active imagination, Lady Clarissa. You really should send in an application to the central office and get a membership card. You might enjoy making tapestries of lovesick virgins and valiant knights astride stallions."

"I'll put that on my to-do list, right below self-flagellation. Benny himself told me about his relationship with Lanya when the three of you were in college. Was he lying?"

Anderson's forehead creased with annoyance. "That was twenty years ago. After we graduated, Benny went on for another degree and Lanya and I lived in a couple of places before settling here. Benny's company is headquartered in Chicago. He didn't like the weather, so he moved here. When he's not overseeing a project, he uses his computer to communicate with his department. They're content to keep him several hundred miles away from the men in suits. As for Lanya, she was delighted when Benny decided to live here. He flatters her with his avowals of undying adoration and pretends she's still sexy and desirable. They're not having an affair, though. Benny's not that desperate."

I wasn't as convinced as he was, but I couldn't see what it had to do with Salvador's murder so I let it go. "Were you surprised by Edward's ballad?"

"In a way," said Anderson, relaxing. "Salvador seemed adept at avoiding sticky relationships. For some reason, women found him attractive. I thought he looked like he'd just recovered from a life-threatening disease. If I were a woman, I'd be afraid I'd catch something from him. But he'd always show up at parties and ARSE events with a new one gazing at him like he was friggin' Zeus."

"So you believed it?"

"Why not? Men make mistakes when they're young. Look at me — father of four, married to a woman obsessed with bees and herbal teas. She makes soap. Do you know how much a bar of soap costs at the grocery store? Lanya prefers to spend a whole day in the kitchen, stirring a pot of lye, ashes, and who knows what else. She'd build a generator out of scrap metal if she knew how to do it. It's ridiculous. As for Salvador, I think it's credible that he got some woman pregnant and abandoned her. He played the role of a sensitive artist, but he was pure ice inside. A manipulator with no conscience to slow him down."

"You don't sound as though you were fond of him," I said, wondering if Anderson realized he shared those traits as well. Birth control has been readily available for decades, yet he blamed Lanya for their offspring. He hadn't abandoned her outright, but he had no sympathy for her daily grind at the farmhouse. He worked off his anger

325

at the battle arena, and his sexual frustration at his office in the evenings. I shuddered as I remembered his reference to my late hours at the Book Depot.

"Are you okay?" he asked. "Would you like some more coffee?"

"I'm fine," I said. "Lanya seemed upset last night. Is she better today?"

Anderson shrugged. "I don't know. After she finished with the detectives last night, she locked herself in the front bedroom. She was still there this morning. I made a call to make sure the children can stay with their friends for another day or two, then left. Fiona and Julius are at the fair site, supervising the removal of the tents, trash bins, picnic tables, and all that. I didn't want to talk to them, so I came into town to drop off your purse and see what I could find out about the murder investigation. What's your connection with the police, Claire? You took charge last night as if you were used to this sort of thing, and then you were allowed to leave without answering interminable questions at the house until two o'clock in the morning. One of the detectives winced every time your name was mentioned. Are you out on parole?"

"It's more like probation," I murmured. "Don't you think you should go home and check on Lanya?"

"Yeah, I suppose so." He stood up and looked at me. "I'm puzzled about you. If ARSE were doing anything remotely illegal, I'd suspect you of being an undercover government agent. Regrettably, we're too disorganized to engage in subterfuge. We're barely able to pull off a potluck. Your superiors will be disappointed with your reports."

"I promise you that I'm a member of only one organization known by an acronym, and that's the ACLU. I had no intention of getting caught up in any of this ARSE business. Fiona bullied me into letting you use the portico. After that, it simply escalated. Rest assured that I will not be applying for membership in the future."

He grinned, then left. I returned to the crossword puzzle and filled in a few obvious words, but I was unable to focus on it. The customers who drifted in were more interested in gossiping about the Renaissance Fair than purchasing books. Several of them inquired about my role as Lady Clarissa, which did not amuse me. My responses became terser until I realized I was imperiling my source of income and hung the CLOSED sign on the door. When my science fiction hippie tapped on the glass, I shook my head at him and retreated to the office. Peter had not instructed me to remain available for the rest of the day. I suspected he thought I would be, but I was not responsible for his imperious assumption.

I carefully locked the back door before I headed along the railroad tracks. The sky was dark, and I could hear distant thunder. The temperature was cooler than it had been earlier, which would have been a relief had it not been for the suffocating humidity. It was definitely a day to curl up with the crossword puzzle or immerse myself in a genteel murder in a country house at the edge of the moors. There was no point in fretting about Edward, Lanya, or even Salvador.

The police cars in front of Angie's house were gone. Yellow tape fluttered in the sporadic gusts of wind. I ignored my impulse to poke around, and was feeling noble as I went up the back steps and into the kitchen. Caron had left a note on the counter stating that she was sick and tired of calls from reporters (my fault, no doubt) and that she and Inez had decamped for the afternoon. Whither they'd gone was not mentioned.

I put on the teakettle, made a sandwich,

and settled on the sofa to fret about medieval scourges and South American tapirs. Ten minutes later, I was on the balcony, sipping tea and thinking about the peculiar dynamics of the local fiefdom. Lanya might be having an affair with Benny — or with Salvador. Fiona might have been having an affair with Salvador as well, although Julius might be more than a little perturbed. Anderson might have been having an affair with Fiona. Edward might be having an affair with Glynnis Threet, for all I knew. That would leave William Threet and Julius out of the loop. Then again, the staid meetings could have been a cover for madcap orgies with all combinations possible. I indulged myself for a moment with a vision of ripped bodices and bits of armor strewn about the porch, lawn, and pasture.

Peter and Jorgeson had most likely solved the crime, and were petitioning a judge for a search warrant while the guilty party sweated in an interview room. Although there had been at least five hundred people wandering around the previous afternoon, it was impossible to imagine someone without a motive attacking with a battle-ax.

Unless someone had a grudge.

The only thing I could come up with was Salvador's casual mention of his books.

They had to be the source of his income, unless his paintings were wildly popular. It was hard to believe that what had once graced album covers for ostentatiously primitive rock bands was now a hot item in Manhattan galleries. If he had written under a pseudonym, and I assumed he had since I'd been unable to find his name on the computer, he could have written most anything. Had he uncovered proof of a terrorists' cell in Farberville? A plot to unleash a virus or take hostages at the next city board meeting? He'd mentioned that his readers were young, and therefore unlikely to be concerned about anything that happened out of the range of their cell phones. Caron and Inez could not name the prime minister of Canada; Rhonda Maguire could not find it on a map.

The answer was likely to be at his house, stuffed in a desk drawer or neatly filed in a cabinet. Peter would not find this minor puzzle worthy of his attention. I had nothing else to do. I went back inside, put my cup in the sink, and went downstairs to the garage. After a quick look to make sure Edward was not lurking beneath the window of the hatchback, I drove to Salvador's house.

Rain arrived at the same time I did. I

parked in the carport, then skittered along the porch and tried the door. Unlike Edward, I had no need of a gadget from a magic shop. Only when I stepped inside did I think about Serengeti. If she was living in the house, she might not even know that Salvador was dead. Or she might not be taking the news well.

I switched on a light and peered around the room. She was not blending into the black upholstery. I continued into the dining room and the kitchen. The only indication of inhabitancy was a glass in the sink. I turned around and went down the hallway, reminding myself that I was not a prowler. It may have been true that I had no legitimate excuse to be in the house, but neither did anyone else. The police investigators had most likely already been there and gone, although it was curious that they hadn't locked the door. I found a bathroom, a dimly lit spare bedroom, and a den with a large television and a pathetically plebeian recliner. A remote control was within reach on an end table. I wondered if Salvador had been a closet soap opera fan. Luanne was, although it had taken me a while to figure out why she closed her store at precisely the same hour every weekday afternoon. We all have secret vices. Mine, of course, shall remain so. Luanne had paid for my silence with a nice bottle of scotch.

There were more bedrooms on the second floor, none of them looking as if anyone had ever slept in them. On the other side of the hall was the master bedroom, outfitted with a black satin bedspread on a king-sized bed, a dresser cluttered with typical oddments, and a master bath with a shower, Jacuzzi, mannish toys, and enough ferns to crowd a greenhouse. The paintings hung on the walls were graphic, to put it politely. The exuberant exaltation of anatomy made me queasy.

His studio took up the rest of the second floor. It contained the standard easels, a table with tubes of paint and icky palettes, and canvases propped against the wall. Salvador was prolific, if not noticeably talented. Rain beating on the skylights accentuated my uneasiness as I explored. At one end of the room was a large desk, and next to it a drawing table of the sort used by architects. Pencils, pens, and markers stuck out of a coffee mug. The filing cabinet was locked, as were the desk drawers. The waste basket was empty. He'd said that he had recently finished a project, but any evidence of it was locked in a drawer or tossed out with the trash.

I was sadly lacking in crowbars, or even a

nail file. Salvador had been a sloppy and careless painter, but a meticulously organized writer. I could almost see the contracts tucked away in files in the cabinet, each labeled and containing the specifics of dates and deals, agents and editors, foreign sales, clipped reviews, maybe movie rights. I sized up the computer. No doubt a fourteen-year-old boy could switch it on, break the password, and pull up the pertinent files, but I was barely able to order books online — and I never did so with any confidence (having once received a carton of books written in Finnish).

The key to the filing cabinet was the level of my expertise. Although it was probably in Salvador's pocket, I decided to prowl before I crept away in defeat. I opened the drawers of the drafting table. They contained erasers, colored pencils, calligraphy pens, a pad of tracing paper, a stained note reminding him to buy coffee and olives, a dozen photographs of Serengeti in a leather bikini with shiny metallic studs, a catalog from a mail-order medieval outfitter, utility knives, and a pencil sharpener. Only someone more devious than I could arrange them into a clue.

I crammed everything back in the drawer. After a futile tug at the top drawer of the filing cabinet, I went back downstairs. As I came into the living room, lightning flashed. The thunder that followed seconds later rattled the house. I was startled, but not unduly alarmed. Summer storms are blessedly short. The rain was apt to abate within ten minutes, at which time I would give up and go home. The whole house was gloomy, but I would hardly find myself blundering about in the dark.

What light there was reflected on the polished surface of the dining room table. Rain poured on the deck, the drops bouncing like silver pellets. I stared, trying to think how best to utilize the next few minutes. If Salvador was a writer (and I had to assume he was), then surely he would have copies of his masterpieces somewhere in the house. He was secretive, however, so they would not be displayed on the mantel or arranged on the shelves of a bookcase in the living room. I'd looked in all the rooms in the main area of the house. Still to be explored was the room above the garage that I'd noticed earlier. I continued through the kitchen and opened a door. It proved to lead to a utility room, I brilliantly deduced as I saw a washer, dryer, and metal shelves holding laundry and cleaning supplies. I felt a flicker of hope when I spotted a garbage can, but instead of letters and envelopes, it contained cans, wine bottles, an empty cereal box, and some scraps of food that were decidedly inedible. Next to it was a door that led to the carport.

Behind me was a staircase. Restraining myself from chortling, I went upstairs to a large, dim room. Old deck chairs with worn pads were in a corner. A rather nice walnut desk was piled high with travel and gourmet magazines; its drawers were empty. Several battered suitcases were coated with dust. I knew I'd start sneezing if I disturbed them, but it appeared no one else had in a long while. A spider crawled along a rolled-up carpet that had no suspicious bulges worthy of investigation. In another corner were neat stacks of cardboard boxes. Although it was probable that they contained sweaters and coats, I opened the top one.

Apparently, Salvador had been unable to part with his boyhood treasures. The box was filled with comic books featuring muscle-bound heroes in tights and capes, scantily clad buxom heroines, and fiendish villains with peculiar disfigurements. In my childhood, I'd preferred Huey, Dewey, and Little Lulu. Maybe these were collector's items now, I surmised, and I was riffling through a million dollars. I opened another box and found more of the same.

"Keep looking," commanded a raspy voice behind me.

I stood up and looked over my shoulder at Benny. "You startled me."

"Sorry," he said. "For a minute, I thought you were a burglar. What are you doing here?"

A fair question, but hard to answer. "I should ask you the same thing, and since I was here first . . ."

"Just driving by, and saw your car. Well, I didn't know it was your car, so I thought I'd better stop and check. I was expecting to find a next-of-kin sort of person." He winked at me. "You're not, are you?"

"No," I said, since he wouldn't believe some idiotic story about being a second cousin. A better one came to mind. "That's why I'm here. Someone needs to be notified about Salvador's death. The desk and filing cabinets are locked, so I came up here to see if I might find some old letters or a family photo album." I dusted off my hands. "No luck, though. The only thing he seems to have saved were these boxes of comic books. I guess I'll leave it to the police."

Benny stayed in the doorway. "I don't think he ever mentioned any family members. Now, of course, there's Edward — if we believe his story. An incredible coincidence, don't you think? The young starving artist finds his long-lost father, who just happens to be wealthy and without other heirs. Our jester will be juggling his inheritance all the way to the bank."

I sat down on a suitcase. "I hadn't thought about that," I admitted. "Edward told me that Salvador had been stunned when he found out, but had agreed to acknowledge Edward as his son and help him with his career."

"You believed that?" Benny laughed, his bushy beard rippling. "It's not what I heard Friday night, once Salvador polished off a second bottle of wine. I can't remember when I've seen him that drunk. I had to roll him upstairs to bed."

"You knew about Edward's claim?"

"Yeah, but I swore that I'd keep my mouth shut. The bottom line is that it wasn't any of my damn business. For all I know, there could be paunchy, red-haired babies all over the world. Maybe I'm just lucky none of them has shown up on my front porch."

"Oh," I said slowly. "So is that why you pretended to be surprised at the banquet?"

Benny ignored my question. "Salvador was a tightfisted egotist. The only reason he'd brake for a kitten was to avoid getting blood on his precious car. And he lied, either to cover his back or just for malicious pleasure. He could charm the panties off every woman he met. Are you sure you didn't come here to make sure yours aren't displayed in his trophy case?"

My jaw quivered with outrage. After a moment to compose myself, I uncurled my fingers and said, "Please leave now."

"As milady wishes," he said, then turned around and went downstairs. Seconds later the door to the carport opened and closed.

I stayed seated while I cooled down to a low simmer. At least I'd had the sense not to attack him with a rolled copy of *The Amazing Amazon Warriors.* Despite myself, I mentally replayed the ridiculous encounter. Benny's first words were peculiar, I decided. Rather than ask the more obvious question of what I was doing, he'd advised me to keep looking. Looking for what? A will made in favor of the publishers of *Dart Boy* and *Master Gangsters?*

I stood up and opened another box. More comic books of the same ilk, none of them carefully wrapped in plastic covers to protect them. They'd been read, ripped, dog-eared, and used as coasters. Boyhood souvenirs. A sneeze exploded from my aristocratic nose, loud enough to alarm any residential rodents. A second caught me before I could wipe my eyes. I was clearly stirring up thirty years of dust and mold.

I hurried downstairs before another sneeze could send my head flying across the room. A few years ago my delicate sensibilities had led me to the identity of a murderer. This time they were more likely to send me to the emergency room. I stopped in the kitchen to blot my watery eyes and damp nose with a paper towel. If Salvador's treasure trove was in that room, the police would have to deal with it.

I dropped the towel in the garbage can. Concluding I'd wasted my time, I went into the living room to turn off the light before I left. Serengeti was seated on the black sofa. I wasn't overwhelmed with shock.

"Do you know about Salvador?" I asked her.

"Yes."

"Then why are you here?"

She turned her face toward the window. "I don't like it when people ask me that."

I was getting very tired of her affectation. "I can assure you that you'll like it even less when the police ask you that. You'll be in a cramped interrogation room with bright lights. The table will be grimy and the chair will be hard. The officers won't simply accept your answer and send you back to wherever it is you go. You may end up in a cell. If you're lucky, you'll have it to yourself, but sometimes they have to double up. The food's awful and there's no wine list."

"Why do you care?" she whispered.

I thought about it, then said, "I don't care. The detectives do, though. I gave them a very detailed statement this morning, and your name came up several times. I even told them that Salvador thought you might be living here. Are you?"

"I am living when I am here. Do the police know who killed him?"

"The detectives don't keep me informed, Serengeti. They may have arrested someone by now, or they may be looking at suspects. You're on the list."

"Why would I kill him?"

"I really don't know." I went over to the switch and turned off the light. The storm had passed, but the gray sky lingered. I was still prickly from Benny's lewd remark, and the only remedy was a drink on my balcony, followed by a phone call to Luanne to grouse about pretty much every last soul I'd run into since dawn. "Good luck," I said to the motionless figure on the sofa. "The police have a description of you, so unless you take off that ridiculous makeup they'll

340

find you sooner or later."

"Please don't leave."

I stopped, exasperated. "I don't want to participate in your silly game. You're on drugs, deeply neurotic, or pretending to be both. If you want sympathy, hunt up your goth buddies and complain about the indignities forced upon you by our evil society. I'm going home."

"I'll do better," she said with the first hint of emotion I'd heard. "We could open a bottle of wine."

"And you'll talk?"

"I don't like it when —" She caught my glare. "Yes."

Chapter Thirteen

"Is there any chance that you'll take off that ghastly makeup?" I said to Serengeti as we sat down at the dining room table.

She busied herself with a corkscrew. "I prefer not to. I hope chablis is okay. How about something to eat?"

"This is not a social call. I feel as if I'm talking to something that goes bump in the night. The police will insist, so you might as well get it over with now." I watched her fill my glass. "I assumed you were going to be candid with me."

"Oh, all right," she said sulkily. She stalked out of the room and down the hall, muttering to herself.

I wasn't sure that she might not climb out a window and continue on her way, but I heard the sound of water running in a sink. It might take her a long time to remove the heavy greasepaint, eyeliner, magenta lipstick, and mascara, I thought with a sigh, and it was past the middle of the afternoon. Peter was likely to be looking for me. As Benny had pointed out earlier, my car was visible in the carport. I needed to concoct a reasonable explanation for being in the victim's house, although nothing came to mind. I wondered if I could claim that I was worried about Edward, who might have come to brood about his father's death. Admittedly, it was feeble.

Serengeti came back into the dining room. "Well?"

I stared at her. She was older than I'd suspected, at least in her late thirties. With her hair pulled back, gray hairs were visible. More disconcertingly, she had a puckered white scar that ran from the outer corner of one eye to her jaw. The cheek sagged, as if muscles had been permanently damaged. "Satisfied?" she asked as she poured herself a glass of wine. Smirking at my expression, she leaned against the edge of the table and looked down at me. "I got that from a guy who attacked me when I was walking home from a bar. He was angry because I owed him a lot of money. I was scared to report it to the police, since he was my supplier. The perils of dealing with the scum of the earth."

"So it seems," I said.

"If people are going to laugh at me, I'd

just as soon give them something really worth the effort. I considered becoming a mime, but they're pathetic. Goths make people uncomfortable. That's more my style."

"Did you go to goth school?"

She looked at me as though I'd lost my mind. "Sure, it was an elective in high school."

"Oh." I took a sip of wine. "Let's talk about Salvador and this house. Do you live here?"

"I do now, but I suppose I'd better clear out until the police finish with it. After that, I'll move back in. Don't bother to ask me if I have a key. I borrowed Salvador's and had a copy made. He was very sloppy about leaving things like that lying around in plain view. I could count on enough loose change for coffee at the café. I never took any real money, although I could have."

"Where do you sleep?"

"Wherever I choose. I keep my things in a box in the room above the garage. I was worried that you might start opening them. That vulgar man arrived before I could create a diversion. He's such a cocky creep. It will be a pleasure to make him squirm."

I frowned at her. "You're going to make him squirm?"

"Don't underestimate me." She parted her lips and hissed. "I know how to take care of myself."

"I agree that he's vulgar," I said uneasily. "He wasn't very fond of Salvador, either. Why do you suppose he came here?"

"I really don't know," she said. She examined her fingernails, which gleamed like ebony talons. "I didn't care for any of those silly people. So pretentious and full of themselves, just like Salvador. Whenever Lanya came over, she'd insist on cooking some disgusting casserole to go with her freshly baked loaf of seventy-six-grain bread. I gagged when I tasted some of her concoctions. As soon as she left, Salvador dumped all of it in the garbage."

"You're avoiding the issue, Serengeti. Why are you here?"

"Don't you think that's an impertinent question? Why are *you* here?" she replied coolly.

I toyed with the glass of wine. I was clearly losing control of the conversation, which was not my nature after sixteen years of dealing with my daughter. "I came to see if I could find information about Salvador's next of kin. And you?"

"Ironies of ironies; all is ironies." She giggled rather shrilly. "I'm Salvador's favorite model. The first time I showed up at his door, he knew he had to have me. He smiles to himself when he sketches my body. He begs me to stay whenever I tell him that I'm too bored to pose any longer. His eyes dwell on my breasts and buttocks. He needs and desires me, but he's afraid that I'll run away if he so much as touches me. I've warned him not to even try. I like to make him suffer. Sometimes when he's sleeping, I go stand beside his bed and poison his dreams. I move things in his cabinets so he'll worry that he's becoming forgetful."

"He's dead," I said softly.

"There is that." She raised her glass. "Shall we drink a toast to him?"

This was becoming too macabre for my taste. "I don't think so, Serengeti. If this is all you're going to say, then I'd better go home."

"He needed me, and now he's made me famous," she continued, her tongue licking the corner of her mouth as if she were a satiated predator. "Therein lies the irony. He won't be around to see it happen. I was going to tell him, you know, but I wanted to wait for the perfect moment to humiliate him in the same way he humiliated me. He was such a swine. He deserved to be punished."

"He's made you famous?" I asked. "I doubt his paintings are all that well known."

She giggled again. "Painting was his hobby. He liked to fancy himself a prestigious artist, but he never sold anything or had a show. Who'd want to buy his crap? Fans, maybe. Now that's a thought . . . We might be able to get quite a lot of money for them, just because he signed them. I must make a note of that. Fans will buy the most gawd-awful things."

"His fans?" I no longer had any desire to leave. Serengeti was quite a talker; her pose as a nonverbal goth must have required a great deal of self-discipline. "Who are his fans? He made them sound like teenagers."

"Those are the ones who show up in public, dressed in costumes and waving plastic weapons at each other. His older readers stay in the closet, quietly collecting his work and driving up the prices. First printings in mint condition sell for upwards of ten thousand dollars. Of course he took great care to write under a pseudonym in order to protect his privacy."

"What exactly did he write?" I asked ever so casually. "Porn?"

"Don't be ridiculous!" she snapped. "Do you think I'd allow myself to be portrayed in sleazy work like that? I have standards, just like everybody else. I am Queen Zanthra, leader of the glorious goth nation! I allow men to seduce me, but when my carnal pleasures are fulfilled, I cut off their heads and rip out their entrails. Only one brave warrior eludes my cunning game. One day he will weaken, and I'll pounce on him like a sleek leopard. His head will be displayed on a stake in the middle of my compound deep in the forest."

"By any chance, would that be Lord Zormurd?"

"He is clever, but he will not escape his fate." Scowling, she banged her fist on the table with enough fury to slosh wine out of her glass. "He is no match for Queen Zanthra!"

My mouth felt dry. "No, he's not," I said soothingly. "Queen Zanthra is more clever and more devious than any mere man. I'd like to read all about you."

Serengeti shrugged. "No, Salvador only sent it off a few weeks ago. It ought to be out in six months or so." She stopped as someone rang the doorbell. "Wait here, Claire. I'll be right back."

I held my breath as she opened the front door. After a moment, she said, "No, I'm the housekeeper. Salvador's dead, in case you haven't heard. Someone bashed in his head with a battle-ax. I understand it was very bloody. It didn't happen here, so there's no reason for you to come inside."

An argument ensued as Serengeti tried to hold down the compound. To my regret, I recognized Sergeant Jorgeson's voice politely insisting that they were coming inside all the same. There was no point in ducking out the door to the deck, since the evidence of my presence was parked in the carport.

"Why, if it isn't Ms. Malloy," Jorgeson said as he came into the dining room. "We seem to bump into each other in the oddest places."

"I came looking for Edward. I was worried about his mental state. He was devastated this morning, and capable of almost anything."

"Not bad," Jorgeson murmured, "but surely not one of your better fabrications. Would you care to try again?"

I shook my head. "It's about time you got around to searching the victim's house. Aren't you supposed to attempt to locate the next of kin as quickly as possible?"

"A uniformed officer came by earlier, and reported that we needed a locksmith. Our specialist is off for the weekend on a fishing trip. It took a while to find someone else to open the desk and file cabinet drawers. I presume you've already tried."

I raised my eyebrows. "I was trying to be helpful by making sure no unauthorized person or persons had access to the studio. That's what good citizens do. Now that you have the situation under control, I'll run along. I have a dinner date."

"Lieutenant Rosen's supervising the interrogations of approximately four hundred of the people who attended the Renaissance Fair yesterday. He'll probably be at the department past midnight. You might want to cancel your dinner reservation, Ms. Malloy."

"An excellent idea, Jorgeson. I'll go straight home and call the restaurant." I breezed past him, and by a couple of uniformed men gaping at Serengeti. There were no vehicles blocking the driveway. I backed down carefully, then drove away as quickly as I dared. And found myself in a cul-de-sac. Benny's story about driving by and noticing my car was absurd, unless he lived in one of the houses on the same street. I suspected he did not.

The telephone was ringing when I arrived home. Afraid that it might be Peter, I went into the bathroom, stripped off my clothes, and took a bath to wash away the dust from the storeroom. I dearly hoped Jorgeson was correct in his opinion that Peter would be at the police department until midnight. Caron and Inez had not returned. If I was lucky, they would spend the night at Inez's house and I would be left alone to consider what Serengeti had told me.

I called the restaurant, then settled down on the sofa with a notebook. Lord Zormurd was a fictional character, as was Queen Zanthra. Salvador had boxes of old comic books from his childhood. Some of the boxes might contain newer ones — ones written and illustrated by himself. There was a trade term for that sort of action comic book, but I couldn't remember what it was. He hid behind a pseudonym to keep fans like Dazia and Honshi from tracking him down, but he may have also done so to protect his reputation. It was certainly more dignified to pose as a serious painter than as a comic book writer. A noncomical comic book, along the lines of the venerable Prince Valiant comic strip I'd never bothered to read.

I wasn't meddling, I reminded myself. I felt as if I owed it to Edward to identify his father's killer. If there were no other heirs, he would receive a hefty estate that included money, a pricy car, and a house with a studio. Even if he were unaware of the true situation and naïvely assumed Salvador's paintings were valuable, would that give him an adequate motive for murder? Wouldn't it have been wiser to allow Salvador to openly acknowledge paternity and bide his time?

My thoughts continued to flounder until dark. The telephone rang periodically, but I ignored it. When the doorbell rang, I was tempted to ignore it as well, but I grudgingly went downstairs. Fiona was standing in the glow from the porch light, wearing jeans and a faded sweatshirt. Her face was pale, and she looked as though she needed sleep.

"Fiona?" I said as I opened the door. "Are you okay?"

"May I come in, if it's not an imposition?"

"Sure," I said. I was surprised by her timid demeanor. She did not look capable of squelching a classroom of noisy teenagers or arguing with her elderly compatriots in the teachers' lounge. She looked more like a freshman on the first day of class, unable to find her locker in the chaotic hallway. "I live in the upstairs apartment."

She followed me to the living room. "This is very nice. Have you lived here long?"

"Quite a few years. Shall I make tea?"

"That would be lovely. With milk and

sugar, please. I don't think I've had anything all day. It took forever to get things packed up at the fairgrounds this morning. When I finally dragged home, I couldn't bear to just sit there. I've been walking for hours. When I came around the corner, I remembered your address. Are you sure I'm not disturbing you?"

"No, not at all." I went into the kitchen, started the kettle, and made some sandwiches. Caron and Inez had missed a package of cookies, so I put several on a plate. When I returned with a tray, she was looking out the window at the campus. "Come sit down and have something to eat," I said.

She gave me a blank look but obediently sat on the sofa and accepted a cup of tea. "This is kind of you, Claire. I know I've behaved badly in the past, and I want to apologize for it. I thought the Renaissance Fair would be a lighthearted affair. Music, entertainment for all ages, pageantry, colors, gaiety." Her eyes filled with tears. "Then everything went wrong. I'm the one who'll be blamed, since it was all my idea. I don't know what I was thinking."

"It wasn't that bad," I said, attempting to sound sincere. "Except for that . . . ah, unfortunate incident, everyone had a good time."

"Principal Kirkpatrick was there. He said to see him in his office tomorrow to talk about the pirates. Julius barely spoke to me today while we were supervising the removal of the tents and all. According to Anderson, Lanya's still locked in her bedroom. And, of course, Salvador's dead. I overheard the students talking about how horrible the scene was. Bloodstains on the ground. The back of his head. That awful ax lying near him. How could anyone do something as terrible as that? Salvador didn't have any enemies. Well, he wasn't always nice, but that's hardly a reason for someone to kill him." She set down the cup and dabbed her eyes with a napkin. "It's all my fault. All of it."

"It's not all your fault," I said. "How could you have known someone would — do that to Salvador?"

"I wish Edward had never come here!"

I must admit I was startled by the incongruity of her bitter remark. "You believe that Edward killed Salvador?"

She picked the crust off a sandwich while she thought. "No, not really. I shouldn't have said that. Did he tell you before the fair that he thought Salvador was his father?"

"No," I said, "but he did tell me that he

believed his father was in Farberville. I thought it was someone else. I was as surprised as everyone else when he sang the ballad. When I talked to him earlier today, he told me that he'd gone to Salvador's on Friday and confronted him."

"Edward's lying," Fiona said flatly. "Salvador would have told me if he had a son. We talked about that sort of thing. He admitted he'd slept with a lot of women over the years, but he was never deeply involved with anyone. He was an artist. He didn't want to be tied down by some demanding, shrewish wife. He told me I was different. I was going to be his model."

"You and Salvador were . . . ?"

Tears began to dribble down her cheeks. "He was going to announce our engagement last night after the banquet, when we were all at the farmhouse. When I took him a cup of lemonade at the archery range, he promised me that we'd get married in a week. How could this have happened to me?" She leaned forward and covered her face with her hands. Her shoulders twitched as she sobbed. "What am I supposed to do?" she said between gulps and hiccups. "Tell me what I'm supposed to do!"

I decided she needed something stronger than tea. I patted her shoulder, then went into the kitchen and took out glasses and scotch. I could point out that she shouldn't book the church or order a cake, but I doubted that was what she meant. I recalled the conversation I'd overheard while putting on the Renaissance gown, in which I'd suspected she was pregnant. If that were the case, her situation was grim. "What about Julius?" I asked as I reentered the room. "Does he know you and Salvador were having a relationship?"

The tea may not have been to her liking, but she had no problem tossing back a hefty gulp of scotch. "I don't know. Maybe he suspected. I tried to catch him earlier in the afternoon, but he was having trouble with the sound system and running around the fairgrounds to adjust this or that. I never could find him. I decided all I could do was pull him aside after the banquet and prepare him. But then — well, you know what happened. I couldn't see any reason to bring it up after that."

"So Julius still believes the two of you are unofficially engaged? Will he believe he's the father of your baby?"

"What?" she said, choking so violently that scotch spewed out of her mouth. "Who says I'm pregnant? You have no right to say something like that!"

I sat back and waited while she attempted to compose herself. I had to agree that I had no right to say it, and it was none of my business, in any case. It would, however, explain her anger toward Edward. My silence finally got to her.

"Okay," she said, wiping her hands with a napkin before she refilled her glass, "so maybe I'm pregnant and Salvador's the father. Julius will know he sure as hell isn't. I had to do something, Claire. Can you imagine what it's like to stand in front of a classroom and lecture about the French Revolution when you know the boys are staring at your breasts and the girls are daydreaming about their upcoming dates? Some days I'd sit in the teachers' lounge watching all these gray-haired teachers get older by the minute. They're obsessed with their lesson plans, tests, grades, and bringing cupcakes for little birthday parties at lunch. I'm twenty-nine. I am not going to still be sitting there when I'm fifty-nine, volunteering to chaperone the prom and supervise the chess club, or take up a collection to buy flowers for the secretary. At least you've been married and had a child. That's something."

I felt as if she considered me a scrap of flotsam on the beach, to be pitied and then carefully stepped over so as not to soil one's feet. "Julius was your safety net, I gather."

Her face flushed as she considered her outburst. "He's very sweet. Well, he does have a temper at times, but I'll be able to manage him. I don't know what to do about this baby, though. It's going to complicate things no end. Damn that Edward! He probably figured out what was going on and murdered Salvador so he could have everything that was going to be mine." Her eyes slitted in a most unbecoming fashion. "He's not the only heir, however. In seven months, he'll have a half sibling. I wonder just how much the estate is worth . . ."

"I have no idea," I said.

"I ought to look into it," Fiona continued, now lost in her mental calculations. "I'll lose my job, that's for sure. But I won't need it — or Julius — if I'm wealthy. I can move to another area, buy a house by the ocean, hire a nanny, and find a husband worthy of being my child's father."

I had an eerie feeling that she had rehearsed her lines and was presenting them for my benefit. They had flowed from her too easily. We had covered the so-called predictable stages of grief in ten minutes, and she was now on the road to recovery. I wondered if I was missing my cue to squeeze her hand, sympathize with her loss, admire her courage, and assure her that she would be fine, just fine.

"Edward may be able to prove paternity," she went on, "but I can, too. Amniocentesis is a routine procedure these days." She began to eat a sandwich. "I didn't realize how hungry I was. It's very thoughtful of you to fix me something, Claire. Why don't we have lunch someday? My treat, of course."

"Aren't you overlooking the possibility that Salvador made a will?"

Fiona stopped chewing and stared at me. "Did he?"

"I have no idea," I said. "People with a lot of money tend to have financial managers, as well as brokers and lawyers."

She managed to swallow. "And life insurance?"

"I guess you'll have to wait seven months to find out. I'm not a lawyer, but I doubt those in utero can inherit. Probate will take at least a year. If there is a will leaving his estate to some obscure artists' colony, then there are bound to be lawsuits that drag out for years. You may not collect anything until your offspring is ready for college."

"Salvador wouldn't have made out a will to anybody. He was just forty-one. His paintings may seem morbid, but he wasn't at all like that. I would have known. We used to lie in bed and talk about sailing around the world, stopping whenever and wherever we wanted. We were going to buy a house in Vail and another one in Bimini. He was full of life."

"Whatever you say," I murmured as I put the cups and glasses on a tray. "Good luck explaining the situation to Julius."

She stood up. "He'll get over it, dear boy that he is. Maybe his parents will take him on a vacation to Disney World. He can have his picture taken with Mickey Mouse. Thank you for the tea and sandwich. I'd better go home now."

I walked her downstairs and out to the porch, then watched her as she strolled in the direction of Thurber Street. She seemed rather jaunty, considering the father of her baby had been hacked to death the previous evening. If her story was true. That I did not know, but I couldn't come up with a reason why she would lie about it. DNA tests would prove — or disprove — paternity, within a zillionth level of probability. Courts bought them.

I turned the opposite way and walked to the corner of the street that ran along the side of my duplex. That which had been Angie's house was a black hole. No lights reflected from the charred remains. Lights were on inside most of the other houses; Sunday was not a night for sociability. I continued to walk until I was standing in front of it. Drooping yellow tape glinted in the dim light. The corpse had most likely been identified by now as the woman named Rose or Rosalyn. The police would close the case, and the landlord would collect a check from his insurance company. No one would ask why the woman had called Lanya and offered to teach the fairies how to flutter convincingly. Or ask Edward more about his previous meeting in California with a woman calling herself Angie. Or even, I thought, ask the fairies to look at the photo of Rose (as I decided to call her) that was surely in the social worker's file.

Lieutenant Rosen and Sergeant Jorgeson were much too busy with their more newsworthy case. A minimum-wage worker who died in a house fire would not interest the national news vultures, but a participant in a Renaissance Fair, dressed in garb, who was attacked with a replica of a medieval battle-ax was picturesque, as well as grotesque.

Someone ought to look into it. Someone who would not be privy to whatever was discovered in Salvador's file cabinets. Someone who would not be given any information about the interviews with the members of ARSE. All I needed to do was go to the DHS and speak to the caseworker. Any tiny detail that could remotely be relevant would be promptly reported to the police, of course. Peter would be grateful that his bride-to-be was not the sort to fly to Paris when the going got tough. Jorgeson might even apologize for his unnecessarily snide remark about my presence in Salvador's dining room earlier in the afternoon.

I returned to my apartment and forced myself to read until I began to nod off in the vicar's parlor. Caron and Inez came in and collected food from the refrigerator before coming into the living room.

"I thought you were going to dinner with Peter," Caron said accusingly.

"He's tied up with the investigation."

"Oh," she said, "then that's all right, I guess. We're going to watch movies and paint our toenails."

I yawned. "What a splendid idea."

"Did anybody call, besides those reporters? I thought I was Going To Scream."

Inez nodded solemnly. "Every ten minutes, and nobody wanted to ask us anything. Caron tried a couple of times."

"Jerks," Caron said, flaring her nostrils to emphasize her disdain. "They all wanted to talk to you. It was like we weren't even at the stupid fair. The only student who'll get his picture in the paper is that guy who found the body. He's not even taking AP history."

"He has acne and bad teeth," added Inez.

"Better luck next time," I said. "By the way, I want you two to open the store tomorrow at ten. I should be back by noon."

"This happens to be our summer vacation," Caron said. "We're planning to watch movies till dawn, and sleep in. Why can't you open your own store, Mother?"

"I have something important to do." I crossed my fingers between the pages of the book. "I'm going to look for a wedding dress at the mall. If you recall, I'm getting married in two months. I can hardly wear shorts and a T-shirt."

"You're going shopping?" said Caron. "By yourself, at the mall?"

Inez made a funny little noise, as if swallowing a giggle. "Really, Ms. Malloy? When's the last time you went to the mall?"

I would have taken the high road had there been one. "I am going to the mall, okay? I'll wake you up at nine and expect you to be at the bookstore by no later than ten." I swept out of the room and to my bedroom. In reality, I was going to have to go to the mall sooner or later. Luanne had promised to accompany me, hold my hand in the parking lot, and blot the perspiration off my brow before we went into trendy little boutiques. She would also stop me from buying the first thing that I found passable, which I would do if left on my own. The mall is a dangerous place, filled with reptilian salesclerks, sniveling children, grim-faced matrons, and gaggles of teen-aged girls. Each store blasts its own music. Speakers crackle with orders for various personnel to report hither and yon. Bodies are probably hidden under mounds of clothes in obscure fitting rooms. Whenever one attempts to purchase something, it requires at least two salesclerks and a supervisor.

When I fell asleep, I was tormented with dreams of being locked in a fitting room, hounded by leering salesclerks holding up miniskirts and leather bikinis.

The next morning I sat in the living room and drank coffee while I tried to figure out how best to talk my way into being allowed to see Rose's file. I rejected schemes involving claims I was a relative. Presumably,

Rose's family history would be in the file. Impersonating a detective would lead to complications. Reporters would not be allowed to see the file, nor would concerned friends from work (as if I knew where she'd been working). I finally came up with an idea, although it required panty hose and a major dose of bravado.

I put on said panty hose, a navy skirt, a white blouse, and sensible pumps, and took Carlton's old briefcase from a closet. After I'd parked outside the DHS office, I applied lipstick and wished myself luck.

The receptionist glanced up from her computer as I came into the office. "May I help you?"

I gazed down at her. "I'm from the law office of Steel, Robbins, and Ruthless. We represent the landlord of the property on Willoughby Street that burned last week. Our client is having difficulties with the insurance company. I need to speak to the caseworker of the unfortunate woman who was killed."

"Poor Rosie Neely," the receptionist said, shaking her head. "A nice woman."

"Yes, Rosie Neely. Is her caseworker available? I have another appointment this morning, but I'd like to get the preliminary information as soon as possible. The insurance company is claiming that Rosie set the fire herself."

"She'd never do that. She was doing so well. Her boss was pleased with her, and she was making friends at last."

I took a notebook out of the briefcase and scribbled a note. "That's very encouraging. Her caseworker?"

Before the receptionist could reply, the phone rang. She answered it, took a message, and replaced the receiver. "Mrs. Hartly is out of the office for the next three days. She went to a conference in Tucson or Phoenix or someplace like that. I'd turn you over to our director, but she's at the conference, too. Why don't you come back on Friday?"

I smiled ruefully. "I wish that would work, but we're having a pretrial hearing tomorrow morning. If we have no way to document Rosie's mental stability, I'm afraid the hearing will go badly. Perhaps if I could have a quick look at her file? Just a peek so I can get the name of her psychiatrist."

"No one's allowed to read the files without authorization or a court order. I wish I could be more helpful."

Having cornered my prey, I went in for the kill. "I wish you could, too. I hope whatever family she had won't be devastated when her death is ruled a suicide. They often feel so terribly guilty that they didn't do more, even simply making the effort to stay in touch more often. That sort of guilt can tear families apart." I paused for a moment. "And our client will suffer as well. He and his wife are retired, and use the small profit from their one rental property to pay medical bills. The property was mortgaged. They're likely to lose their own little home and their life savings."

"This is dreadful," the receptionist said, shredding a tissue. "Maybe I can try to reach Mrs. Hartly at the conference. She left the telephone number of the hotel."

I glanced at my watch. "Yes, please try to call her."

I tapped my foot as I waited. Any conference worthy of drawing in DHS personnel from across the country would surely be having lectures and meetings by this hour — or at least a breakfast buffet. Mrs. Hartly might be a tad slipshod about her work, having taken two weeks to report Rosie's absence, but she was there with her supervisor. I watched the traffic, halfway expecting police cars to pull up, when the receptionist replaced the receiver.

"Mrs. Hartly's not in her room. I left a message, but she may not get it until late in the afternoon," the receptionist said, shrugging apologetically. "You say this hearing is tomorrow morning?"

"At nine o'clock. We only found out about it late Friday." I picked up my briefcase and gave the woman a faint smile. "I know you have to abide by departmental regulations. It's such a shame when other innocent parties are punished by all those faceless bureaucrats in their offices in the state capitol. Nothing we can do, though."

"You wouldn't take the file with you, would you?"

"Heavens, no. In fact, I could make photocopies of the most recent pages and be gone in less than five minutes. No one would know that I was even here."

The receptionist opened a drawer and placed a thick manila folder on her desk. "If you'll excuse me, I'm going to visit the little girls' room. I'll just be gone a few minutes." As she left the room, she pushed a button on the photocopy machine, eliciting a blinking green light and a low hum.

I dropped the briefcase on my foot in my haste to open the folder. I took out the top three pages and a small photo paper-clipped to the edge of the cover. Without bothering to glance at the material, I made photocopies, replaced everything, and left the

DHS office. My instinct was to drive to the Book Depot, but I realized that I would have to face Caron and Inez. Sans shopping bag. I continued to Luanne's shop, Second-hand Rose, and parked in back.

I found her at the counter, reading the newspaper and wolfing down cookies. "How do you get away with a diet like that?" I asked. "It's not as if you go to a gym every day or run marathons."

She licked her finger. "Cookies are on my personal food pyramid, along with caffeine, alcohol, and nachos. You look like the secretary of a greasy-haired ambulance chaser. I didn't realize you were changing careers."

"Put on some fresh coffee and get comfortable," I said as I reached for a cookie. "Even if I fast-forward through the dull bits, it's a long story."

We'd finished the box of cookies by the time I'd related the tawdry sham at the DHS office. "I haven't looked at the papers yet," I added as I took them out of the briefcase.

"Maybe you shouldn't. If Peter ever finds out how you got them, he won't applaud your deviousness."

"Maybe I shouldn't," I said, "but I'm going to, anyway."

CHAPTER FOURTEEN

I studied Rosie's photo, then handed it to Luanne. "An unremarkable woman," I said, "but pleasant. She must have been on her meds when it was taken."

Luanne nodded. "I could have been in line with her at the grocery store a dozen times."

I moved on to the first page. "Rosamunde Emerson Neely, born in some obscure town in the county, would have been forty-four next month, parents deceased, only sibling is a brother in Vermont. Married when she was twenty. One child, a daughter who was born prematurely and died. Divorced two years later, whereabouts of former husband unknown, possibly Alaska. History of mental illness starting when she was in elementary school." I looked up. "Sad story."

"And probably more typical than we think," Luanne said. "Where was she working?"

I scanned the page. "Bud's Automotive

Emporium, out on the bypass. Her case-worker found the job and persuaded the owner, presumably Bud, to give Rosie a chance. I suppose I'll try to talk to him."

"Bear in mind you don't know a carburetor from a carbuncle."

"I doubt it will come up," I said. "If Caron should happen to call, don't admit I was here. I told her and Inez that I was going to the mall."

"You? Going to the mall? Why didn't you tell them you have a skydiving lesson? That's more plausible."

"Humph," I said, then went out to my car. I sat there for a few minutes, considering Rosie's life history. She had not, according to the file, been in California, and if she'd had any connection to ARSE, she hadn't admitted it to her caseworker. Perhaps she had mentioned it to her coworkers, I thought as I drove toward the edge of Farberville. That, and her sudden influx of cash to pay the deposit and rent for the little blue house. It was hard to imagine her stumbling onto a vast blackmarket industry involving auto parts. Then again, carburetors and carbuncles. What did I know?

Bud's Automotive Emporium was housed in a massive metal building with a flat roof and numerous flashing neon signs. Cars and trucks of all species were parked in the gravel lot. A portable sign announced a hot deal on radials. A handwritten sign in one window proclaimed free popcorn on Fridays. Men, mostly in creased caps, were coming and going, carrying boxes or cumbersome grease-encrusted objects (carburetors, most likely).

I am always leery of men in caps, especially those with cigarettes dangling from their lower lips. They are indeed the salt of the earth, these men who construct houses and farm and raise livestock and repair things for those of us who are inept. Most of them are gentlemen, as chivalrous as any knight. Others of them spit, snarl, and brawl. I can rarely predict which are which.

Therefore, it was with some trepidation that I entered the store. Aisles stretched in both directions. Everybody seemed intent on his personal quest, be it a spark plug or a battery. It was clearly a male mileu. I wandered around, avoiding minor collisions, until I spotted a man in a khaki jumpsuit with an embroidered patch above his pocket. A tightly cinched belt did little to constrain his belly, which hung over his belt like an impending avalanche.

When he finished talking to a man with a drooping mustache, I approached him.

"Hi," I said, "I'm looking for Bud."

The man grinned affably at me. "Old Bud, Bud Junior, or Buddy, who's Bud junior's boy? Buddy works in the stockroom. Well, he's supposed to work, but he ain't got the balls to do more than push a broom. Most of the time he hides out on the dock, reading some fool comic book."

"Whoever's in charge of hiring," I said.

His grin dissolved. "I hate to break it to you, little lady, but we ain't looking for no one right now." He took his time studying me, letting his eyes wander down my chest to my admittedly attractive legs. "Damn shame, although I don't reckon this sort of place is what you're looking for. Lot of our customers want advice about transmissions or whatever they're working on."

"I'm interested in a previous employee."

"You from the government?"

I shook my head firmly. "No, I'm not. I'm trying to help the family of a woman who worked here a couple of months ago."

He did not look as though he believed me. He took a handkerchief from his back pocket and wiped his neck while he decided whether or not to throw me out onto the parking lot gravel on my derriere. "I reckon you can have a word with Bud Junior. He's in the office. Should be, that is. If you'll pardon me, I got a customer waiting."

"Thank you," I said to his back, then went down an aisle and eventually found the office in a far corner. I had no idea what to expect as I opened the door. File cabinets dominated the walls, all piled high with ledgers and catalogs. Framed certificates citing the employees of the month hung on the wall. The majority of them were slightly askew. The man seated behind the desk was wearing a pastel blue suit and a striped green tie. His hair was slicked down, his chin far from prominent, his eyes alarmed. "Yes?" he gurgled as if no one had ever dared to breach his sanctuary.

"Are you Bud Junior?" I asked.

"Who are you?"

I felt as if I'd shown up with an assault rifle. I quickly sat down and crossed my ankles. "I'm trying to help the family of Rosie Neely. I understand you gave her a job earlier in the summer?"

"Is there a problem?"

Good heavens, I thought, maybe there was some sort of blackmarket scene in progress, and I was suspected of being from the FBI or the IRS. "Not that I know of," I said. "I was hoping I could speak to some of her coworkers."

"About what?" he squeaked. "We didn't

fire her, you know. She just stopped coming to work. Has she filed some kind of claim or grievance against us? Surely not sexual harassment? Some of the fellows call women 'hon' and 'sweetpea,' but they don't mean anything by it. She and I worked late a few nights, but I swear I never laid a hand on her. It's her word against mine, you know, and I'm a family man and a deacon at my church. Are you a lawyer?"

I wished I'd changed into jeans and smeared oil on my face. "I am not a lawyer, Bud Junior. Rosie was killed in an accident. All I'd like to do is talk to any friends she might have made while she worked here."

"Oh," he exhaled, rocking back in his chair. "Why, I'm real sorry to hear about her passing away. She was a good worker, and polite. I was thinking after a year or two I might move her up to the accounts receivable department. All the time she was here, she never was late or took a sick day." He pressed his fingertips together as if preparing to pass judgment from the bench. "I suppose you might talk to Toffy Sue in the parts department. The two of them used to eat lunch together in the break room."

"Thank you very much." I stood up and headed for the office door.

"Any time you need auto parts, give me a

call. I can give you a ten percent discount," he called before I could close the door.

I found the counter of the parts department and waited while various men transacted business for unknown items that were designated solely by long numbers. Heads were scratched. Cigarettes were stabbed out in an overflowing ashtray. Receipts were studied. Thick spiral notebooks were consulted. I received a few looks, but apparently auto parts were more intriguing. I was about to disrupt the flow of activity to inquire about Toffy Sue when a short, rotund woman with fiercely bleached hair came out from the narrow metal aisles and slapped down a small box.

"This should do the trick," she said to an emaciated young man with a ponytail.

They examined it more closely, then he nodded and left with it. "Help you?" the woman said to me.

"I hope so. Are you Toffy Sue?"

"I reckon I am. And yourself?"

"A friend of Rosie Neely's family," I said in a low voice. "Is there somewhere we can talk for a few minutes?"

"Rudy, I'm taking five," she said, then came around the counter and motioned me to follow her. Once we were in a room with battered couches, vending machines, and a coffeepot with a thick layer of crust in the bottom, she said, "What's this about her family? Is some relative taking an interest in her after all these years? That brother up north somewhere?"

I told her what had happened and why the police believed they had identified the body. "It's not official yet, but there isn't really much doubt," I concluded gently.

Toffy Sue lowered her head for a long moment, then blotted her eyes with a tissue and met my gaze. "Yeah, she used to swear her jaw ached whenever it was about to rain. That's how she knew when to bring an umbrella when she came to work. Nice woman, never said a bad word about anybody. We used to have lunch in here when we had the chance. Poor, sweet Rosie. God bless her."

"I know she quit working here rather suddenly. Do you know why?"

"She told me that she'd been offered a better job. She was gonna get room and board, along with a decent salary, all for looking after some disabled woman. Not bathing or feeding her, just doing the housework and shopping. It sounded too good to be true, and I told her as much. Said she ought to check out this woman before she gave up her job here. But Rosie wouldn't listen."

That explained the finances — someone other than Rosie had paid the deposit and rent. "Did she say anything about this disabled woman? Did she mention how they met, or where?"

"Not much," said Toffy Sue, her brow crinkling. "Rosie was at a café, and this woman just sort of struck up a conversation. The woman insisted on treating her to lunch, and got around to offering the job. Rosie was so excited when she told me that I thought she was gonna pee in her pants. This boardinghouse where she lived was noisy and dirty, and she was afraid of a couple of the men who lived there. Rosie wasn't a looker, if you know what I mean, but she was pretty in her own way. I kept urging her to try some lipstick and mascara, but she wouldn't."

"Did Rosie say anything else about the woman? What she looked like? Where she was from? How she could afford the house and Rosie's salary?"

"Nothing that I recollect." Toffy Sue got to her feet. "I'd better get back. Rudy gets real pissy if I take off more than a few minutes. Of course, it doesn't matter when he takes the parts catalog and spends half an hour in the can. Men!"

"You mentioned that she was afraid of some men at the boardinghouse. Did she have a reason?"

Toffy Sue sighed. "No, she was too timid for her own good. One of them glanced at her in the hallway, and the other held open the front door one morning when she was going to work. That's all it was."

"You've been a great help, Toffy Sue," I said. "One last question, please. Did Rosie ever mention being interested in the Renaissance?"

"Say what?"

"There's a group that likes to dress up in medieval costumes, long gowns and armor, things like that. There was a Renaissance Fair this last weekend."

"I saw something on the news about that. No, Rosie liked to read romance novels and watch game shows. That's one of the reasons she was so pleased about her new job. Damn shame, just when things were looking up for her."

I returned to my car and considered what I'd learned. Rosie was not using the name Angie for some nefarious purpose. She had most likely not called Lanya, since she could scarcely carry on an intelligent conversation about ARSE. She was not the woman Edward had met in California four years earlier. Rosie was pretty much summed up by what was in her file at DHS.

So who was Angie and where was she?

Edward and the fairies were the only people who might have seen her. Tracking down Rhonda Maguire and her cohorts would require Caron's assistance, and I wasn't ready to go to the bookstore. I still didn't know Edward's address, but Lanya might.

I stayed on the bypass and turned down the highway to Anderson and Lanya's farm. The only vehicle parked in the yard was the mud-splattered station wagon. There were no shrieks or whoops, intimating the children were not yet home. I knocked on the front door, waited a few minutes, then knocked more loudly. The house remained silent. This meant that no one was home — or that Lanya was still locked in her bedroom. The latter seemed more likely. I went around the house and onto the screened porch. The kitchen was vacant. I opened the door and called Lanya's name. There was no response. A vague uneasiness kept me from going inside the house, although I realized I might have to do so sooner or later.

I went back across the porch and sat down on the top step. The sun was hot, but not unbearably so. Insects and butterflies fluttered over the vegetable garden, and bees were enjoying the hollyhocks alongside the house. Blue jays battled at a bird feeder. A deflated plastic wading pool was surrounded by oddments from the kitchen cabinets. In the pasture, all traces of the Renaissance Fair were gone, except for trampled paths and a few paper cups caught in the weeds.

It was past noon, and Caron would be taking out her frustration on unwary customers. I was not leaping from one brilliant deduction to the next with the grace and agility of a gazelle. I was confident that Rosie Neely had been living in the blue house on Willoughby Street at the time of the fire, but I couldn't come up with a reason why such a quiet woman with few friends and no enemies might have been the intended victim. Angie had disappeared. It seemed more logical to think the fire had been set to frighten her badly enough to convince her to leave town. It would have been nice to know what the police thought, but I doubted Lieutenant Rosen would fill me in on the details.

I decided to go in the house on the pretext of picking up the clothes I'd left there on Saturday. I would knock on Layna's door but not persist, and if I happened to see a box of ARSE material, I could have a quick look for Edward's address. If I came up empty-handed, I would slink back to the bookstore and spend the afternoon rearranging the window display with beach books. And, when I rallied the courage, call Peter and meekly invite him over for dinner. We would eat steaks, drink wine, and discuss potential honeymoon destinations.

The floors creaked as I walked through the kitchen. Dirty dishes were piled next to the sink, and bread crumbs were already attracting a thread of ants. Empty bottles and jars cluttered the counters. I continued into the living room. The door of the room in which I'd changed clothes was closed. I tapped softly. "Lanya?"

"What?" demanded a hoarse, snuffly voice.

"It's Claire Malloy. I came by to pick up my clothes. Shall I come back later in the week?"

"No, wait there." Footsteps thudded across the room and a key turned in the lock. Lanya opened the door and glared at me.

I tried not to grimace. Her unkempt hair hung down her back. Her bathrobe was haphazardly buttoned and badly stained. Her face was pasty, accenting her red, swollen eyelids. Her nose dribbled steadily, leaving her chin glistening with moisture. "Are you ill?" I managed to say. "Can I get something for you?"

"Are you alone?"

I nodded. "I don't want to intrude, Lanya. I should have called first. Why don't I come back —"

She caught my arm and yanked me inside the bedroom. After she'd locked the door, she turned around and said, "Did Anderson send you?"

"No, I was just driving out this way and —"

"Sit down," she said, pushing me toward a chair. "It would be like him to find someone else to spy on me. He's a coward. That's why he likes to put on his armor and bash people with his sword. He knows he looks manly and brave, but he won't get hurt. If he accidentally gets a bruise, he stays in bed the rest of the week, whining like a damn baby and making me bring him ice packs." She shoved her hair out of her face and began to pace around the room with such fury I was surprised the glass didn't rattle in the window frames "The noble Duke of Glenbarrens cries when I have to remove a thorn from his foot. He's afraid of the bees and won't go anywhere near the apiary.

When he saw a snake in the pond, he wouldn't go out in the yard for months."

"Was he like this when you married him?" I asked.

"I don't know." She flopped down on the bed. "Not as bad, anyway. As long as he can control things, he oozes confidence and charm. I wouldn't have married him if Benny hadn't . . ."

"Betrayed you?"

"Exactly! The very night before Benny and I were supposed to get married, he went after some tramp at the camp. They snuck into the woods, but they were making so much noise that all of us could hear them. I was humiliated. Anderson took me to his tent to calm me down, and — well, we decided to get married. Anderson admitted later that he'd only done it to get back at Benny."

"Would you have been happier with Benny?"

"No," she said, her shoulders sagging. "Neither of them is worth a puny pence. I should have finished my degree in agronomy and bought a vineyard. Salvador told me it wasn't too late. He promised he'd back me —" She fell back on the bed and covered her face with her hands. "It doesn't matter now, does it? He's dead, and so are my dreams. Anderson will walk out on me one of these days. He'll send child support payments and see the children once a year. I won't be able to afford to sell this sorry place. I'll just get older and fatter and lonelier."

I would have said something encouraging had anything come to mind. I sat for a long while, listening to her whine. "Maybe," I said hesitantly, "Edward might be persuaded to invest some money in a vineyard, especially if you tell him what Salvador promised."

"Why should he believe me?"

"Anderson did, didn't he? Wasn't that what you two were arguing about Saturday afternoon in the backyard?"

She sat up and looked at me. "How do you know about that?"

"Several people overheard you," I said, hoping she wouldn't demand a list or specifics. For all I knew, they'd been arguing about the laundry.

She smiled wryly. "Yeah, Anderson believed me. Salvador found a vineyard listed for sale on the Internet. He said that if I'd take a six-week course in viticulture and enology at a college in California, he'd go into partnership with me. I think he was smitten with the idea of having his own label. Something classy to mention ever so casually at cocktail parties. Anderson exploded when I told him I was leaving in September and that he could do the cooking and cleaning and help with homework."

"I suppose he was angry at Salvador, too."

"Of course he was, but that doesn't mean . . ." Her bloodshot eyes widened. "I didn't see him again until the final battle of the day. Someone would have seen him go down to the archery range — unless he changed clothes after our argument. He prefers to wear shorts and a T-shirt under the armor so he doesn't get his royal garb all sweaty. The dry cleaners don't take proper care with it."

"They don't get much practice," I said. "You know Anderson better than I, but I can't imagine he'd kill Salvador just to avoid six weeks of drudgery. Wouldn't he be more likely to hire a cleaning service and a nanny?"

Lanya shrugged. "He wasn't thinking that clearly when I told him. I thought for a moment that he was going to hit me. I turned my back on him and went to warn Salvador. I don't know what he did after that."

"And did you warn Salvador?"

She yanked a tissue out of a box and blew

her nose. "Yes, but he didn't take me seriously."

"Were you angry?" I asked, remembering what Incz had said.

"I wasn't so much angry as frustrated. I expected him to be proud of me for telling Anderson about the vineyard, but he just shrugged. He was acting so peculiar that I gave up and left."

It struck me that although the Renaissance Fair was all music and gaiety on the surface, it had been a bubbling cauldron of acrimony (as well as eye of newt and tongue of frog). "I need to ask you about Edward," I murmured.

"What a tragedy," she said automatically. "Spending all those years searching for his father, and then — well, to lose him. He must be heartbroken. Have you spoken to him?"

"He's distraught. I'm hoping you have his address. I'd like to find him and make sure he's okay."

She seemed much more cheerful now that she'd tacitly accused her husband of a brutal murder. "Yes, somewhere. Let's go in the kitchen. You can have a glass of mead while I look for my notebook. It's so hard to keep track of things because of the children. They're forever moving things and forgetting to put them back. One day I found Anderson's razor in the sandbox. They'd tried to shave one of the cats."

I spotted my clothes in a heap in the corner and scooped them up. Lanya sighed when she saw the disarray in the kitchen, but fussed around until she found a jelly jar and a gallon jug of what I presumed was mead.

"Now you sit here and enjoy this while I find my notebook," she said. "It should be in a drawer in my little office." She bustled away, humming like one of her bees.

I couldn't bring myself to sample the mead on an empty stomach. I was painfully aware that it was well into the afternoon. The last thing I needed to do was show up at the bookstore with alcohol on my breath. I poured a few drops in the jelly jar and swished it around. I heard Lanya chortle in triumph and was waiting in the living room when she came out of a hallway.

"Here's the address. He doesn't have a phone yet." She handed me a slip of paper. "Do tell Edward how sorry we all are for his loss. I think it would be a nice gesture for our fiefdom to get together for a little memorial potluck in honor of Salvador. Let's say Wednesday at six o'clock, shall we? Please tell Edward when you see him. I expect you to come, too, Lady Clarissa. You're one of us now."

"I'll have to check my calendar," I said, easing toward the front door. "My fiancé is back in town, and we have to make wedding plans."

"You must bring him with you. After all, he is your knight in shining armor."

"I'll mention it to him." I did not add that I would do so shortly after the next Ice Age receded.

"We look forward to meeting him," she called as I got in my car.

I turned around and drove as rapidly as I dared toward the highway. Peter was not apt to fancy himself my knight in any kind of armor, and the members might not be all that pleased if he showed up at the memorial potluck. He is not always the most pleasant of interrogators, particularly when he's tired. And miffed at me, which he surely had been — and would be, as long as I kept finding myself involved in his investigations. This would the last one, I swore. I had not intended to get snarled in this one, and had done my best to disregard it. In the future, all my energy would be directed at bookselling, gardening, and getting Caron through high school and safely packed off into the hands of some naïve college dean in a distant state. I would read travel magazines and gourmet recipes. I would memorize the phone numbers of every caterer in Farberville. In my spare time, I would write mystery novels and use my earnings to buy Peter a new sports car every year. I would be a wife, a wanton lover, a sympathetic ear, a friend in need.

As soon as I talked to Edward about Angie, anyway.

Edward lived in an old house that had been chopped into apartments. It was only a few blocks from my duplex, but lacked both the view and the charm. The gray paint was peeling and streaked; several cracked windowpanes were held together with duct tape. I went up a few creaky steps to the porch and read the names on eight rusty mailboxes. Edward lived in 2-C, which implied the second floor. I went into a foyer of sorts and up a staircase, ignoring the graffiti sprayed on the walls and the subtle stench of beer. I kept a watch for bats as I continued down a hallway. Edward's door was open, and discordant music pulsated from within the apartment.

I stuck my head in and shouted, "Edward?"

After a moment, he appeared from another room, wearing only a towel around his waist. "Claire? What are you doing here?"

"I came by to see how you're doing," I said glibly. "May I come in?"

"Yeah, sure, give me a minute." He retreated, closing the door behind him.

I found the source of the din and turned down the volume to a tolerable level. The room functioned as a living room and kitchen. The furniture had come from a thrift shop or a yard sale, and the walls were a dirty beige. Edward had made no effort to disguise its bleakness with so much as a poster. He had made at least one friend, I noted as I spotted a lacy bra under the coffee table.

I sat on the edge of the sofa and tried not to stare at the remains of a marijuana joint in a saucer. The pungent aroma lingered. It occurred to me that I might have come at an inauspicious time, but I was worried that I might make things more awkward later if I were to leave. All I needed was five minutes to show him the photo of Rosie Neely and ascertain if she was the person he'd spoken to on the porch.

Edward was dressed in jeans when he came back into the room. "Excuse the mess," he said. "This is temporary. I haven't even unpacked my suitcases. Do you want a beer or something?"

"No, thank you. I promise I won't stay long. I need to ask you something."

"How I'm doing? Okay, I guess. The detectives were mad at me because I left the Ren Fair, but they let me explain and seemed satisfied. They let me go after a couple of hours." He opened the refrigerator door. "You sure you don't want a beer?"

"I'm sure," I said. "I want to show you a photo."

He sat down next to me and peered at it. "Who's that?"

"It's the woman who died in the fire at Angie's house."

"It is?" He sounded bewildered. "What's her name?"

"That doesn't really matter. You went by the house after the potluck and talked to someone. If it wasn't this woman, then it was someone calling herself Angie. I want to know who and where she is."

"Hold on," he said. He bent over the photo and studied it more carefully. "The woman in California had longer hair, dangly earrings, and a lot of makeup. She was wearing a sort of beret with beads and flowers, too. I couldn't really see the face of the woman I talked to on the porch that night. She stayed in the doorway, with the light behind her. This might have been her." He held the photo at arm's length and squinted at it. "Yeah, it might have been. And she wouldn't have recognized me, since I was in garb when I met her the first time. Nobody remembers my face, just my pointed cap and purple tights."

"Maybe so," I said as I took the photo from him and put it in my briefcase. "My apologies for interrupting you this afternoon. Lanya said to tell you that the fiefdom is having a potluck in Salvador's honor on Wednesday at six."

"She would, wouldn't she? They can all sit around and talk about how much they loved and respected my father. Even the murderer will shed a few tears."

"It's not my idea, Edward, and I can promise you that I won't be there. You don't have to go, either."

"Oh, but I think he should," said Fiona as she strolled into the room, wearing only a T-shirt and panties. She smirked at my expression, which was less than composed. "Surprised to see me, Mrs. Malloy? I realized that Edward and I have many things to discuss, so I dropped by. Don't you think the two of us should plan the funeral? In a way, I'll be Edward's aunt, since I'll be the mother of his half brother. Does that make me an almost stepmother or a half aunt?"

CHAPTER FIFTEEN

"Ick," said Luanne as she refilled my cup in the beer garden. "It sounds incestuous, even if it's not. Technically, they're not related. Still . . ."

"I had the same reaction," I admitted. "All I could think to do was get out of there. I skittered down the stairs and out to my car in record time. I was calmer by the time I got to the Book Depot, but I was glad Caron and Inez had locked up and left. Fiona is carrying Edward's father's baby. It gives me the shivers."

"Yeah." Luanne leaned back and gazed at the wisteria. "It's not the age difference, although there's a big gap in maturity. From what you've said, she's a conniving seductress and he's an innocent kid."

"Or maybe he's not," I said. "He wasted no time consorting with the enemy, so to speak."

"Nor she with him."

"True. Fiona told me yesterday that she believed Edward was lying, but if he wasn't, she would be happy to split the estate. Maybe she decided it was wiser to consolidate it. Edward may feel the same way."

"Have you told Peter?"

I took a sip of beer. "No, but I'm going to tonight. I left a message inviting him for dinner. I think it's prudent to put a few glasses of wine into him before I admit I've been talking to his suspects. He gets testy about that. I'm sure that Jorgeson has already told him that I was at Salvador's house yesterday. I didn't intend to confront Serengeti, but there she was. And then Fiona showed up at my house later, and she looked so pathetic that I had to let her inside."

"You posed as a lawyer this morning at DHS, and subsequently talked to Rosie's friend at the auto parts store. You went to Lanya's, and then Edward's apartment, where you happened to run into Fiona. Yes, I think Peter may be irritated by all this activity."

"No kidding," I said, wondering if I'd finally gone too far. "I was just trying to help."

Luanne rolled her eyes. "Peter's always so appreciative, isn't he? You can bleat apologies over chianti, but he may not be buying this time. I hope you realize I've put down a nonrefundable deposit with the caterer."

"That's not funny."

"I didn't intend for it to be." She handed me a tissue from her purse. "Please do not snuffle in public. I have a reputation to maintain in this beer garden. These lowly college kids hold me in awe. All the guys wish they had the courage to ask me out, and all the girls secretly hope they'll be me in twenty years. Now buck up and figure out how to lie to Peter."

I took her advice and drove home. Caron was not there, which was fine with me. She no doubt assumed I had Ruined Her Life, as she would say, by making her spend most of the day in the bookstore. I wasn't sure I hadn't ruined mine, either. What was even more maddening was that my snooping had led me nowhere. All of the key players had been out of pocket for at least a few minutes Saturday afternoon. Most of them admitted they'd stopped by the archery range. I had no way to piece together the time frame. Their motives were thicker than molasses. Had Salvador received Edward with open arms, or had he denied paternity? I had only Edward's word. Fiona had visions of Vail and Bimini, but again, Salvador might have laughed at her. Julius would have been furious, in either case. The same problem arose with Lanya and Anderson, and as for Benny, his undeniable ego might have been struck a mortal blow if Lanya told him about her business venture with Salvador.

Only William and Glynnis Threet were without motive. As far as I knew anyway; I was still curious about Percy.

I was having trouble figuring out where Serengeti fit in to all this, beyond being a first-class wacko who envisioned herself as Queen Zanthra. I wasn't sure Peter would get anything more out of her than I had. He wouldn't tell me if he had, being a closed-mouth sort — and too busy to return my call.

I changed into more comfortable clothes and poured myself a drink. I was sitting on the balcony when Caron pounded up the stairs. "Sorry about today, dear," I called.

Her face was stony when she joined me. "Where's your wedding dress?"

"I didn't see anything I liked," I said truthfully. "Where have you been?"

"Inez and I took our costumes back to the college drama department. That man — Mr. Valens — had the audacity to bawl us out because we didn't take them back yesterday. It's not like the theater is putting on some dumb play by Shakespeare tonight. He would have had an Absolute Fit if Inez hadn't taken them to one of those one-hour dry cleaners while I was doodling at the Book Depot half the day. That hippie freak showed up and started raving about some comic book character. It was all I could do not to yawn in his face. Do I look like I care about comic books? He may have the mentality of a six-year-old, but I don't. He ought to be locked away."

"He's not that bad," I said.

"Vlad the Impaler adored kitties and puppies. Oh, Mr. Valens says he wants to talk to you. I told him you were at the mall."

"Why does he want to talk to me?"

She stared at me. "I should know?"

"No," I said. "I apologize for ruining your day. Do you have plans for tonight?"

"Yeah, Louis Wilderberry and I are eloping at midnight. He's going to lean a ladder against the balcony so I can scramble down into his arms. Other than that, no."

"What light through yonder window breaks?"

"Give me a break, Mother," she said, then went inside.

I was still on the balcony when Peter drove up and parked at the curb. As he came along the sidewalk, he glanced up but did not smile. It was unfortunate that Louis Wilder-berry had not shown up a few hours early with his ladder. Short of scrambling down a rickety trellis, I was trapped. I went inside just as Peter reached the landing. "Hello," I said cautiously.

"Do you have any beer?"

"I think so," I said, then scurried into the kitchen and rooted around the refrigerator until I found one. "Would you like some crackers?"

"What I would like is to be cast ashore on a deserted island with miles of white beaches and coconut trees. I'd like to lie in the sun in utter solitude, listening only to the waves breaking against the shore and the cries of distant seagulls. At night, I'd sleep in a hammock under the stars. Food and drink would appear mysteriously. I would bathe in a waterfall."

"Utter solitude? Does that mean I'm out of the picture?" I asked as I sat down near him.

"I'm afraid so. It seems that when I invited you to go for a sail, you were too busy bothering my suspects to come along."

"Oh." I considered taking offense, but I was a little shy on self-righteous indignation. I opted for a diversionary tactic. "I know how Salvador made his fortune."

"So do we. He wrote and illustrated graphic novels under a pseudonym. His series about some medieval warlord is tremendously popular, especially in Japan. There have been a couple of TV series based on his characters, as well as animated movies. His earliest novels are a hot commodity if they're in pristine condition."

"Graphic novels. I couldn't remember the trade term."

Peter glanced at me, still grim. "You should have gone ahead and broken into the file cabinets. Forget your hairpin?"

"I did not engage in criminal activity," I said. "The front door was unlocked."

"How convenient for you."

I didn't think it was worth the effort to offer my feeble excuse about my concern for Edward. Even Jorgeson had failed to buy it. "I suppose you heard that I was talking to Serengeti. I had no idea that she would be there. Did she admit she's been living there?"

"That's about the only thing she admitted at first," he said. "She wouldn't give us any information about herself — no name, previous address, anything. Finally, when I'd threatened to hold her indefinitely, she broke down and allowed an officer to escort her back to the house to fetch an identification card. Turned out to be an expired driver's license from Oregon. The photo matched and had an address for some little town. The police there said she was in some kind of commune. She had a couple of warnings for possession of marijuana, nothing they take very seriously out there, and a speeding ticket. She claimed that she left there three or four years ago and drifted around, living in seedy hotels or homeless shelters. Whenever she found a job, she was paid in cash."

"What's her real name?"

"Michelle Galway. She showed us a house key and said that she did light housekeeping and modeled for Salvador. After that, we had to let her go. The victim was killed fifteen miles away. If she has a car, we can't find it, so we can't place her at the scene."

I leaned back on the sofa and propped my feet on the coffee table. "I don't think she killed Salvador. She told me she wanted to humiliate him because of some slight in the past. One can slander the dead, I suppose, but it wouldn't be as entertaining."

"Anything else, Miss Marple?"

I dutifully related all my encounters in the past twenty-four hours, although I omitted the trip to the DHS office and implied the uniformed officer had mentioned the auto parts store. "As far as I can tell, any one of the key players could have gone by the archery range and waited until no one else but Salvador was there. All he or she would have to do is suggest a private conversation at the edge of the woods."

"While carrying a battle-ax."

"The murderer could have come up with some story about returning it to Benny, or how irresponsible it was to leave it in the Royal Pavilion with all the kids running around."

"Not bad," Peter conceded. He popped open the beer and sighed. "I've had about six hours of sleep since I arrived here Saturday. The amount of paperwork generated by two hundred thirty-two potential witnesses is unbelievable. The national media have picked it up because of the extraordinary circumstances. The captain won't come out from under his desk. The mayor has been calling every half hour to demand some new tidbit to offer at the next press conference. Even imperturbable Jorgeson is starting to mutter about retirement."

"Does the media know about Salvador's works?"

"Some hotdog reporter traced the copyright at the Library of Congress. We've been warned to expect the Japanese media to show up tomorrow. They'll probably declare a national day of mourning. I may take the FBI up on their offer."

"What offer?" I said, stiffening.

"I'll tell you about it later. Thanks for the dinner invitation, but all I want to do is go home, take a shower, and get some sleep." He stood up and pulled me to my feet. After a brief interlude of fooling around, he released me and tromped down the stairs.

"How embarrassing," Caron said as she emerged from the hall and went into the kitchen. "You two behave like you're in middle school. Why is there never anything to eat in this house? What's the point of having a refrigerator if it's always empty?"

I squelched my pubescent tingles. "You're absolutely right, dear. Take the cash in my purse and go to the grocery store."

"Now? I'm waiting for Carrie to call."

"Now," I said. "If Carrie calls, I'll tell her you've gone into the forest to shoot something for dinner."

"That is so not hilarious."

"If you want the car at some time in the next month, then go now. It's a long walk to the mall."

Caron appeared in the doorway. "How would you know that?"

"I have an impeccable sense of distance,"

I said, giving her the benefit of my steely maternal glare, perfected over the last decade. She spun around and flounced out the kitchen door. Once I heard the car start, I replenished my drink and sat down to watch the local news.

Ken and Barbie did not let me down. After their customary teasers and several commercials, Barbie settled down with her latest breaking news. It seemed that Salvador Davis, victim of a brutal murder, was the bestselling author of a series of comic books (Barbie hadn't done her homework) featuring Lord Zormurd and various wizards, dragons, and swamp denizens. His first, *Zormurd and the Castle of Fire,* written a year after he'd moved to Farberville from New York City, had been made into a movie starring actors known for their brawn rather than their brains. His pseudonymous persona, Stark Reality, was in demand as a speaker at fan conventions and trade shows. He'd recently won a prestigious international award.

Barbie fluttered her eyelashes earnestly. "As of this afternoon, the police have interviewed hundreds of those who attended the Renaissance Fair but have no leads. The mayor has promised to keep us informed as the mystery deepens." She went on to recap everything that had already been said, then tossed the ball to Ken, who filled us in on escalating prices at the pumps.

When the phone rang, I picked it up, expecting to hear Carrie's voice.

"Mrs. Malloy, this is Julius Valens. I need to speak to you."

"If it's about the condition of the costumes, you'll have to take it up with the girls. I had nothing to do with the transaction."

"No, not about that." He cleared his throat. "Can I come over to your apartment?"

That struck me as a very bad idea. The last thing I wanted was a distraught and despondent rejected suitor sobbing on my sofa half the night, while I wrung out handkerchiefs and poured endless cups of tea into him. Or, if he were enraged, putting a fist through my wall. My landlord was not only humorless, but also hoping for an excuse to throw me out so he could put an apartment building on the lot.

"You may not come here, Julius," I said. "Why don't you come by the bookstore tomorrow?"

"I can't wait. It's about Fiona. She's disappeared, and I'm afraid something has happened to her."

I bit my lip for a few seconds. "She's nearly thirty years old, and it's not even dark yet. Maybe she went shopping or to a movie. She could be taking a nap or simply not in the mood to answer the phone."

"She promised to meet me at four for coffee. I waited for an hour, then went to my office in case she called."

"It was a traumatic weekend for all of us. She may have forgotten about your date."

Julius sucked in a breath. "I realize it was traumatic, Mrs. Malloy," he said evenly, although the sarcasm was hard to miss. "It wasn't exactly a carefree day at the Renaissance Fair, was it? The detectives kept us at the farmhouse most of night. My parents watched the news and were hysterical when I was finally allowed to go home. I may have been testy with Fiona yesterday morning, but we were both exhausted. She planned to spend the day at school, and meet me at the health food café at four o'clock. It's almost eight."

"I can't help you, Julius."

"I drove by Salvador's house. It was locked and dark inside."

"Okay," I said. "Try the mall. I can guarantee it's crowded and brightly lit."

"Lanya told me you went to her house to get Edward's address. Why did you do that?"

I felt a chill. "I also went to Bud's Auto Emporium and the beer garden on Thurber Street. I went by Lanya's because Anderson was worried about her. I do not have to account for my actions, any more than you do. If you want to continue this conversation, come by the bookstore tomorrow."

"What about Fiona?" he asked coldly. "Does it have anything to do with Edward?"

"I've already told you that I can't help you." I hung up and stared at the campus lawn that undulated down the hill to my street. Shadows were longer, and it would be dark soon. Julius had alarmed me. I did not want to be in the apartment if he decided to come by, but I couldn't leave until Caron came home from the grocery store. Because I was, according to her, the cruelest and most miserly parent of any student at Farberville High School, she did not have a cell phone. For once, I wished she did. I also wished I had Edward's phone number so that I could warn him. Lanya might have given Julius the address as readily as she'd given it to me.

I made sure my front door was locked. I debated the wisdom of turning off the lights and arming myself with a dull knife, or behaving like a total ninny and calling Peter. To say what? Julius could be sitting down to macaroni and cheese with his parents. The SWAT team would be annoyed if he was watching a movie when they broke down the door. And he hadn't admitted anything beyond being worried about Fiona.

Now, of course, I was, too.

When Caron at last came up the back steps, I was waiting at the door. I grabbed a sack of groceries from her and said, "Are there more in the car?"

She gave me a wary look. "No, just these two. Is something wrong?"

"I don't know," I said. "I want you to go to Inez's and stay there until I call. I'll put everything away."

"What is going on?" she demanded.

I gave her a little shove. "I don't have time to explain now. Take the car and go."

"I am not going to leave you here by yourself. I have a right to know, so you might as well tell me."

I dug through the sacks and pulled out the frozen items. As I stuffed them in the freezer, I said, "Mr. Valens is upset and may decide to come over here. I don't want either of us to be here." I stashed milk, orange juice, and fruit in the refrigerator. "Please go, dear. I need to let . . . some other people know he's on the warpath."

Caron turned mulish. "Then I'll go with

you. You are babbling, Mother, and in no condition to go anywhere on your own. If we run into Mr. Valens, the two of us can handle him. He's a bully, that's all."

I was touched by her desire to defend me. It would not do, however, for her to see her AP history teacher frolicking with a college student. Caron, like many of her peers, adheres to a strict moral code when it comes to adults. "It's not a situation in which your presence would help," I said hastily. "It won't take long, and then I'll go to Luanne's and call you at Inez's house. Okay?"

"I don't like this one bit," she muttered, but allowed me to nudge her out the door. "If I don't hear from you within an hour, I'll call Peter. Maybe he can talk some sense into you."

"Fine, fine," I said, then waited until I heard her drive away. I turned off the lights and went down the back steps to the alley. Edward's apartment house was only a ten-minute walk. Once I'd delivered my warning, I could be at Luanne's in another fifteen minutes. I had plenty of time to prevent Caron from calling Peter, who would not be pleased to be disturbed. It might be prudent for Caron to stay with Inez and for me to sleep on Luanne's sofa,

I thought as I put my hands in my pockets and began to walk briskly. Julius Valens could pound on my door to his heart's content. There were no downstairs tenants to be annoyed. Eventually he'd figure it out and slink away to his parents' house for milk and cookies.

It was dark when I arrived at Edward's apartment house. I couldn't see his windows, since he lived in the back. I tried to remember if there was a fence, but I hadn't paid attention earlier. Shrubs, maybe, and trees. More dirt than grass. I decided to risk a foray to ascertain if Edward's lights were on. If they were not, I would assume he was out and I'd head for Luanne's. If they were on, I might be able to get a glimpse inside and decide how to proceed. I was not eager to knock on his door and explain that Fiona's would-be fiancé was apt to come calling. I am fearless when the situation calls for valor, but I prefer to avoid pointless confrontations. And, frankly, not to be cast in the role of a busybody.

I bit down on my lip as I ventured into the murky depths of the forest primeval. I was more concerned about rosebushes than beasts. I immediately tripped over a tricycle left by a small satanic creature. After rubbing my shin, I stood up and peered at what

I thought might be Edward's window. All I could see was a drab ceiling, which was likely to be the decor in all the apartments. Three tentative steps later I determined that there were indeed untamed rosebushes. Quietly vocalizing some Anglo-Saxon expletives, I untangled myself. My arms were sticky as blood oozed from the scratches.

The entire idea was increasingly ridiculous. Whatever altruistic ideals had propelled me here were rapidly evaporating. The only weapon Julius might have access to was a prop gun from the theater, and although it would make for a dramatic scene, no one would stagger back and collapse from the impact of a blank. However, I was there and the clock was ticking.

The side yard was a forest, but the backyard was a jungle. There had once been a patio, I determined as I stubbed my toe on a flagstone. A birdbath loomed like a mutant mushroom. Dry leaves crackled as I tried to move furtively. Some sort of shed had collapsed in the distant past, and small creatures scurried as I approached. I could see the windows of the back room of Edward's apartment. Lights were on, but no one obligingly moved into view. There was no way of telling whether anyone was inside.

I heard a cough behind me. Stifling a

screech, I spun around. The beam from a flashlight caught me in the face, blinding me. I shaded my eyes and said, "Who is it?"

"Mrs. Malloy?"

"Turn that blasted thing off!" I snapped.

The beam lowered. "It's Corporal McTeer, ma'am. We met earlier this summer."

I remembered the young black woman who'd done her best to keep me under house arrest. "What are you doing here?" I demanded.

"Following you. I was supposed to make sure you were safe at home, but then you came sneaking out the back and I figured I'd better stick with you."

"Is this Lieutenant Rosen's bright idea?"

"He was concerned. If you don't mind me asking, just what is it we're doing here? There are chiggers and ticks in these weeds, and I've already got two mosquito bites. I'm not what you'd call a nature lover."

"Any chance you'll go away, Corporal McTeer?"

"No way. Lieutenant Rosen can be mighty fierce when someone disobeys his orders. I don't want to be demoted and spend another two years filing papers at the PD. Sorry, ma'am, but I'm staying on your heels until you're back home."

I leaned against the birdbath and contemplated my next move. I'd already bruised my shin and suffered scratches, and I wasn't about to give up at this point. "Do you have a weapon?"

"I sure do." She hesitated, then added, "Do you?"

"Of course not," I said. "I prefer to use my cunning charm. Here's what we're going to do, Corporal."

Three minutes later we were on the front porch of the apartment house. Corporal McTeer stood under the feeble light, her arms crossed. She was looking nervously at the sidewalk, having been cautioned about Julius Valens. I went upstairs and along the hall to Edward's door. As before, it was ajar. I knocked, then went into the living room, determined to have my say and exit with all possible haste. To my astonishment, Edward and Benny were sprawled on the sofa. At least a dozen beer cans and several empty wine bottles were on the coffee table, along with bags of chips and pretzels.

"Good evening," I said lamely.

"Welcome, Lady Clarissa!" boomed Benny. "We're having a wake of sorts. We can't give Salvador a proper Viking funeral because of pesky laws, so this is the best we can do. You want a beer?"

Edward grinned at me. "Surprised?"

"Yes, I am," I said. "I didn't know the two of you were friends."

Benny slapped Edward's shoulder. "I was just telling the kid about his dear old dad. Salvador and I were buddies fifteen years ago. We met at a war in Kansas, got drunker than skunks, and chased after every damsel in the camp. Caught a few, too. Salvador was a helluva lot smarter than all the pretentious old farts dressed in royal garb lording it over their subjects. He was living in New York then, but we kept in touch and went to a lot of the same events. We shared a tent on occasion, as well as bourbon and beer. There was one time when we lured these two blondes to join us for the night, and —"

"I don't think I want to hear this one, Benny," I said. "Was Salvador writing graphic novels back then?"

"Before the Lord Zormurd series?" asked Edward, leaning forward.

Benny brushed crumbs off his beard. "Yeah, but he couldn't sell anything. He admitted it was all derivative drivel, to use his phrase. Mostly science fiction junk. The editors like his artwork, but not his stories. Every time he got a rejection in the mail, he'd call me and gripe. He was selling a few paintings, and scraping by when I suggested that he move someplace more affordable, namely Farberville. He lived in a crappy apartment like this until he had his first big sale. We stayed drunk for three days to celebrate."

I stared at Benny, who was getting teary. The previous day he'd spoken harshly about Salvador, and now he was overcome with maudlin memories. In the silence, Edward went to the refrigerator and returned with three beers.

"Shall we drink a toast to Lord Zormurd?" he said as he offered me a beer.

I shook my head. "No, I can't stay. I need to have a word in private with you."

"I shall tolerate no motley-minded secrets," said Benny. He took a beer from Edward and gulped down half of it. "As Sir Kenneth of Gweek, I demand you have your say, Lady Clarissa."

The clock was still ticking. "All right," I said. "Edward, I won't speculate about what's going on between you and Fiona, but you should know that Julius is upset. He may show up tonight, looking for her."

"The ferocious Squire Squarepockets?" Benny brayed with amusement. "I could grab him by his bow tie and toss him out the window without raising an eyebrow. You and Fiona, huh? Now that's a hoot. She put the make on me, but I don't care for prissy girls with pinched smiles. Anderson and Salvador were less picky. For all I know, the plume-plucked wench was getting it on with William Threet right there in front of Percival. If ever there was a classic cuckold, it was Julius." He whacked Edward again. "Find somebody your own age, lad. She's a python in panty hose."

"I have no idea what Claire is talking about," Edward said.

"Whatever." I nodded at them and left, making sure to close the door behind me. Apparently Benny had not yet noticed the bra under the coffee table. Fiona was probably hiding in the bedroom, desperately hoping Benny would either leave or pass out. Or she might have fled without her bra. I didn't care.

Corporal McTeer was sitting on a metal chair on the porch. We walked back to my duplex. She declined my offer to come upstairs for tea, and promised to watch for Julius. I called Inez's house and told Caron that all was well. She tried to hide her relief, but I could hear a tremble in her voice as she told me that they were watching movies and she'd be home in the morning.

Having done my good deed for the day

(as well as quite a few less laudatory ones),
I found my novel and retired for the night.

CHAPTER SIXTEEN

I was minding my own business (which required minimal attention) when Peter and Jorgeson came into the Book Depot late the next morning. They both looked grim, although if it were a competition, Peter would have won hands down.

"I didn't do it," I said.

"Do what?" Peter growled, in my opinion rather brusquely for one greeting his betrothed.

"I have no idea, but I'm innocent all the same. The only things I've done today are have a double latte, read the newspaper, and sell a book on dog grooming to a man with a nasty little poodle that piddled on the floor. He didn't apologize, nor did the dog."

"We have a problem," Jorgeson said.

"So do I," I said. "Can't you smell the urine?"

Peter crossed his arms. "A body, at Salvador Davis's house. Michelle Galway, also known as Serengeti. After the interview at the PD yesterday, she asked for a lift to a coffee shop near the campus. She must have walked the rest of the way. This morning I sent a couple of officers to the house to collect the boxes of comic books and graphic novels. They found her in the studio."

"Oh, dear." I sat down on the stool before my knees buckled. "What happened to her?"

"Her throat was slashed with a utility knife," Peter said. "There were several in a drawer. Artists use them to cut mat boards. Very sharp and nasty."

"When — when did it happen?" I asked.

Jorgeson's cell phone chirped. He glanced at Peter, then headed outside.

Peter waited until the door was closed, then said, "The medical examiner thought six to eight hours before her body was found. After midnight, at the earliest. She was wearing bizarre makeup, like a ghoul. One of the officers had to dash into the nearest bathroom."

"It must have been awful. I've seen her in the goth makeup. She told me that she wore it so that Salvador wouldn't recognize her, but he's beyond recognizing anybody. I guess it was a way to cover up her scar." A vague idea began to slither into a recess of my mind, but I couldn't quite verbalize it.

"Do you have any idea who did this?"

"It could have been a burgler who thought the house would be empty. He might have been looking for something of value in the studio when Serengeti surprised him. He panicked and grabbed the utility knife."

"She certainly could have had that effect on a nervous intruder," I said. "Do you want some coffee?"

"No, thanks." He ran his fingers through his adorably curly hair. "We've already had a word with each member of that Renaissance club. No one has much in the way of an alibi, except you, of course."

"I hope you didn't make Corporal McTeer sit in my yard all night."

"She was relieved at midnight by another officer, who said that unless you climbed out a back window and slid down a drainpipe, you were home." He consulted his notebook. "Benny Stallings, Edward Cobbinwood, and Fiona Thackery claimed they were in their own beds, alone. Anderson and Lanya Peru sleep in different bedrooms. Julius Valens lives with his parents, but he has an apartment in the basement with a door that leads outside. William and Glynnis Threet aren't likely suspects, but either of them could have slipped away. He takes out his hearing aid at night, and she finally admitted she sleeps in the guest room because he snores like a motorboat. An Evinrude, to be precise. As for motive, who knows? They're all peculiar."

"None of them ever mentioned Serengeti to me," I said. "Maybe it was random. There hasn't been an obit in the newspaper, but everybody in Farberville is aware of Salvador's murder. He had an expensive house and car. Someone might have assumed the rich leave cash and jewelry scattered around like bread crumbs. Was the house locked?"

"Jorgeson made sure it was locked when they left yesterday, but it was open when the officers went by this morning. We found the Galway woman's fingerprints all over the house, and a lot of others. From what I've heard, he entertained both downstairs and in his bedroom. There's no way we can identify the majority of the prints, unless he hosted meetings of Felons Anonymous."

"Not quite his social circle."

Peter's eyes narrowed. "Corporal McTeer told me about your outing last night, or as much as she knew. Why on earth did you go to Edward's apartment, and what does Julius Valens have to do with it?"

I related the sorry story and showed him my scratches. Sympathy was not forthcoming, although he did wince when I mentioned that the telltale bra was under the coffee table when I left. "I was home before ten o'clock. I have no idea what happened after I left," I added virtuously.

"Edward told us that Benny had been there," he said, "but he forgot to mention Fiona. I suppose I'd better hunt them down again. And you" — he jabbed his finger at me — "need to keep your nose out of it. Two people have been brutally killed in the last three days. Consider yourself grounded until I say otherwise. You'd better be here or at home. Don't go to the beer garden with Luanne or to her apartment. She can visit you."

"Grounded?" I said, miffed. "Don't be absurd. I shall go wherever I please."

"I can charge you with interfering with an investigation and keep you in custody for forty-eight hours."

"You wouldn't dare!" I sputtered, now outraged.

Peter glared at me. "Wouldn't I?"

"I am a card-carrying member of the ACLU. Do you want them to organize a protest at the PD? Better yet, at the mayor's office? As reluctant as I am to become a *cause célèbre,* I will accept the burden to fight back against a totalitarian police state."

"You're making absolutely no sense, but

you're quite sexy when your face turns pink and your eyes flash."

"My face is not pink."

"Is too."

"Is not!"

Regrettably, Jorgeson came back inside in time to hear my schoolyard retort. "Tut, tut, children, play nice. Lieutenant, the captain's waiting for you. From what I could hear, the office is packed with Japanese reporters and cameramen, all demanding a statement about their idol, Stark Reality. Because of their accents, it took the captain ten minutes to figure out who they meant. He tried to tell them that we didn't know about any stalkers. It's what you might call a madhouse."

"Don't blame that on me," I said, still sulking.

They left without further ado. I grabbed the feather duster and attacked the poetry rack. Dust was billowing (poetry is not among my bestsellers) and I was sneezing convulsively when my science fiction hippie ambled in. If he found my behavior curious, he did not feel the need to make any comments regarding it, but instead hunched down in front of the fantasy paperbacks.

I stowed my weapon under the counter and sat down, feeling somewhat calmer.

"What do you know about this guy called Stark Reality?"

He popped into view. "The guy who got killed at the Ren Fair? Man, that was gruesome. There was a scene in *Zormurd in the Tomb of the Wizards* where one of the zombie warriors attacked Zormurd with a battle-ax. Zormurd caught him in a death grip and ripped his head off. It exploded like a puff ball. Very cool."

"I'm sure it was. Did you know that Salvador Davis was the author?"

The hippie sank out of view. "Yeah, I heard it a few years ago at a con in Omaha. These computer whiz kids can find out most anything. All this business about privacy is a farce. If one of the little smart-asses cared, he could get your Social Security number, SAT scores, all your tax returns, the location of your family burial plot, and your dog's name. I had a dog, name of Rabelais. I don't remember what happened to him."

I refused to be sidetracked. "Weren't you curious about meeting the author?"

He reappeared at the end of the rack. "Why would I be?"

"Well," I said, floundering, "he wrote these graphic novels you seem to enjoy. He was a luminary in the genre."

"We are all luminaries in our own genres. You know, I think I'll go look for that dog. He could be around somewhere."

I cut him off at the door and held out my hand. He gave me a paperback, shrugged, and wandered out the door and up the street. He probably had another one tucked away somewhere, but I let it go. Instead, I called Luanne and explained that I was weak from hunger but not allowed to leave the premises under threat of incarceration. She agreed to show up with taco salads within the hour.

Between customers, I pondered the idea that had occurred to me. Serengeti had said something even more peculiar than usual. However, speculation without proof was pointless, as well as annoying. I went so far as to clean out the top desk drawer in my minute office, but I was too distracted to do more than toss out pens that had quit working years ago and gather up loose paper clips. I had several utility knives that I used to open boxes of books. They had modified razor blades that were wickedly sharp. It would require little effort to grab someone from behind and make a fatal incision. Weight or height would not be a factor — only surprise. I could not bring myself to envision the scene between Serengeti and the intruder.

A random act of unplanned violence — or a premeditated murder? I wondered if the ARSE members were aware of her occasional presence. She'd been in the living room the night of the cocktail party, but Luanne and I had not seen her when we arrived. Or hadn't noticed her, anyway. Black on black.

When the phone rang, I stared at it. If it proved to be Peter, checking on me, I might feel obliged to respond with justifiable hostility. If it was Luanne, wanting to know if I preferred hot or mild sauce, I didn't care. I finally picked up the receiver.

"Mother," Caron said, "can I keep the car for the rest of the day? Emily, Carrie, Inez, and I want to go to the lake, even though we'll have to sit on the rocky beach instead of going out on a party barge. It's so boring around here that Inez's mother offered to teach us how to knit, and I almost agreed."

"I suppose so," I said, then stopped to think. "Here's the deal, dear. In the briefcase in the living room is a photo of a woman. Before you go to the lake, I want you to get the photo and hunt down any one of the fairies who went to the dance class. It doesn't have to be Rhonda Maguire, who's likely to be too busy booking a Mediterranean cruise on a private yacht. Find out if the woman in the photo taught the dance class. If she'd didn't, get a description of the woman who did. Then call me."

"That could take hours," she groaned. "It's peak tanning time right now."

"Knit one, purl two."

"You are Totally Insufferable. Emily's mother is making us sandwiches and brownies. Inez is putting ice in a cooler."

"Then you need to hurry," I said. "And don't dare leave the city limits until you've called me, or I'll apprentice you to Sally Fromberger until you're eighteen."

"I cannot believe this!"

She hung up, as did I. I had the glimmer of another idea, hardly substantial but worthy of investigation. If Rosie Neely had taught the dance class, then I was wrong — but I would have bet a taco salad that I wasn't.

Luanne arrived with both hot and mild sauce. After we'd settled down to eat at my desk, I told her about Serengeti.

"That pitiful creature?" she said as she popped an olive in her mouth.

"I think she had less than benevolent reasons for posturing as she did. She told me she was an old girlfriend who was out for revenge. She wore the makeup so Salvador wouldn't recognize her."

"Okay," Luanne said, "but from what you've said, she was one of many."

"She's also the one who happened to show up just when Salvador's life was about to take a hit from a missile. Don't you think that's too much of a coincidence?"

"Coincidences happen. Read Jung if you don't believe me."

"I know they do, but this one's glaring. I don't know how to follow up on my idea, though. Do you know any computer hackers?"

Luanne wiped sauce off her chin. "Yeah, but it'll cost you. Remember that guy I was dating last year?"

"The rich man, the poor man, the beggar man, or the thief? How on earth could I keep track of all the men you date?"

"The one who stood me up on Valentine's because his fourteen-year-old son found a way to hack into the Department of Defense's top secret documents. They were having so much fun that he didn't call me for three weeks. I dumped him for an accountant who was indicted for tax fraud a month later. It was a bleak winter."

"How much will it cost me?"

Luanne giggled. "A six-pack of Mountain Dew and several bags of Doritos. Do you want me to call him?"

"Please do," I said. "Can you drive? Caron and her friends are going to the lake, so I won't have the car until at least seven."

She refused to agree until I told her what I had in mind, as improbable as it was. She called the kid, who agreed to see us at four o'clock. After we'd finished eating and she left, I pulled out the ledger and immersed myself in cash flow. Even Moses might not have been able to part my red sea, I thought glumly. When the phone rang, I lunged for the receiver. "Caron?"

"Yes, Mother," she said in the plaintive voice of a martyr. "I finally caught up with Martha Ellen at her hairdresser's. She goes to this guy named Riccardo, who was offended that I interrupted him in the midst of his delicate artistry. It was a haircut, for pity's sake, not the ceiling of the Sistine Chapel."

"Did you show Martha Ellen the photo?"

"Riccardo made me wait fifteen minutes while he trimmed her ends. I was ready to attack him with his hair dryer when he finally stepped back to admire his work. Martha Ellen said it wasn't the woman who taught the dance class. Her description of the woman who did was lame, but Martha Ellen can't tie her shoes in the dark. She had to spend her sophomore year abroad. She told everybody she went to boarding school in France, but nobody believed her. Can we go to the lake now?"

"What did Martha Ellen say?"

"That the woman looked like a transvestite clown. A dreadful yellow wig that swallowed her face, bright red lipstick, blotches of rouge. She wore a swirly robe with orange and pink flowers, and jabbed them with an umbrella whenever they missed a cue or tripped. Martha Ellen said when she got home, she had bruises on her butt. She and several others wanted to quit, but Rhonda convinced them not to because of that preposterous midterm paper. Now they're all worried that Miss Thackery will make them write it anyway. Martha Ellen doesn't know a footnote from a footprint."

"Remember to take sunscreen to the lake," I said, "and be home before dark."

I was relieved that none of the ARSE members dropped by the store to confide in me during the next three hours. At ten till four, I locked the store and sat by the back door to wait for Luanne. Neither Peter nor Corporal McTeer had peeked around the corner when Luanne drove up. Resisting the urge to dive into her backseat and throw a blanket over myself, I took the more decorous approach and got in next to her.

"I hope we aren't being followed," I said as I adjusted the rearview mirror so I could watch the traffic behind us.

"There's a purple wig in the backseat on the floor. I wore it for Mardi Gras. Shake the spiders out of it before you put it on."

"I do not need a disguise. I am not an escapee from detention."

Luanne moved the rearview mirror back into place. "Fine, then stop squirming around and staring over your shoulder. The kid's name is Max. I already picked up the chips and soda, and you owe me six dollars and change. And if I'm arrested for aiding and abetting a fugitive, I expect to be reimbursed for bail money. Every penny of it."

"Just drive," I muttered.

Luanne's ex-suitor lived in the historic district. As we walked to the front door, I glanced up the street for patrol cars. It seemed I had made good my escape, at least for the time being. The teenager who answered the door did not fit the stereotypic geek role, although he was short and wore wire-rimmed glasses. His hair was clean, his skin clear, and he was dressed in shorts and a T-shirt extolling the prowess of some band.

"Thank you so much, Max," Luanne said

as she handed over a sack from the grocery store. "I've been telling my friend how clever you are. She's very impressed. Anything new at the DOD?"

"You sure she's okay?" he asked nervously.

"She's a bleeding-heart liberal, a bookseller, and a stalwart defender of freedom of information."

"I can show you my ACLU card," I offered.

"No, that's all right," said Max. "Follow me."

We went into his bedroom, or what I supposed was his bedroom, since the bed was hidden under a mound of dirty clothes and magazines. He had more electronics equipment than a discount store. Some of it was vaguely familiar, but the majority could have been almost anything, including a communications center for an alien race.

"Sit anywhere," he said as he perched on a stool in front of a computer.

Luanne and I looked around, then I said, "We'll stand, if you don't mind. I'm interested in an adoption that took place about fifteen years ago or so. Since it involves a minor, the records may be sealed."

Max flipped some switches. "Details."

"The child's name is Edward, and he was adopted by a man named Cobbinwood. I don't know where, but my best guess is California. I'm sorry I don't know the year, but . . ."

Max was already attacking the keyboard, his fingers moving like those of a concert pianist. Screens flashed onto the monitor for nanoseconds, then were replaced by others. I thought I caught a glimpse of the word "California," but it vanished. After no more than a minute, he rolled back the stool and said, "You want to read it yourself?"

"Uh, yes," I said. "The records weren't sealed?"

"Does it matter?" he asked. "This was hardly worth the time. Now if you want to see the CIA reports on terrorist cells in Saudi Arabia, that'll take a little while. I'm going to get something to eat." He was opening a can of Mountain Dew as he left the room.

I sat down on the stool. "The adoption took place in Oakland sixteen years ago. The petitioner was Charles Stewart Cobbinwood. Edward's biological father was listed as unknown, and therefore without parental rights. His mother's name was Michelle Antoinette Galway."

"Who called herself Serengeti," said Luanne. "Good guess."

"It wasn't a guess. I just didn't know her

name until Peter told me yesterday. Coincidence, my foot. Edward told me that she moved away while he was at Berkeley, and that he hasn't had any contact with her since then. I think it's more likely that eventually she came to Farberville because Salvador Davis was living here. My science fiction hippie told me earlier today that Stark Reality's real name was practically common knowledge. If you knew one, you could find the other. Either Edward told her, or she found someone like Max who could produce the information between sips of soda."

"Did she come here to kill him?"

"I don't know," I admitted, "and I don't know that she did. She must have found out from one of her old friends that Edward had been accepted at the college. She got here first and managed to weasel her way into her ex-lover's life. Who knows what she planned to do when Salvador was forced to acknowledge paternity? Humiliate him, for one thing. Peddle her pathetic story to a tabloid. Better yet, demand twenty-one years of back child support. That could make for a nice sum, considering Salvador's financial situation."

"No kidding," Luanne murmured. "He was making scads of money from the Stark

Reality comic books."

"Graphic novels," I corrected her. "When I was talking to her yesterday before we were so rudely interrupted, she said something about how 'we' could sell his early work. That could only make sense if she expected to have influence over the estate."

Max came back in the room with a handful of chips and a jar of peanut butter. "Are you done? I need to get back to work."

Luanne gave him a suspicious look. "Work, Max?"

"Yeah, I intercept e-mails from brokerage firms, politicians, and celebrities, and sell them to interested parties. I'm saving up for a Carrera GT when I turn sixteen. I falsified my birth certificate, but my father still won't let me get a driver's license."

"Can you print this out?" I asked. "I don't want to get you in trouble, but I need a copy of it."

"No problem. I used my Turkish account, so no one can trace it back to me." He started the printer. "Hey, Luanne, you still mad at my father?"

"I'm afraid so, Max," she said. "I expected roses and jewelry on Valentine's Day. It may take me years to recover from the trauma."

He raised his eyebrows, but remained silent while he took a page from the printer and gave it to me. "You single?"

"Engaged, with a wedding date in two months. Thanks for your help, Max."

He was already back at the keyboard, typing at the speed of light. Luanne and I let ourselves out and retreated to her car. Neither of us spoke until we were on Thurber Street.

"What next?" Luanne asked.

"I don't suppose you want to take this to the PD, do you? Tell Peter that you had a brainstorm and —"

"Do I look like the village idiot?"

She dropped me off at my duplex and drove away before I could come up with a persuasive argument. I went upstairs and reread the document. Charles Stewart Cobbinwood and Michelle Antoinette Galway were legally wed at the time of the adoption. I had no idea how long their marital bliss had lasted. Maybe Charles Cobbinwood's death had refueled her fury at Salvador, who'd effectively prevented her from finishing her college degree.

Especially if she were a dance major. If there were roles for pregnant ballerinas, I was not aware of them. The dying swan did not waddle. The Sugarplum Fairy did not pause to practice Lamaze breathing techniques. Not even Nijinksy could heave a hundred and fifty pounds (or more) of perspiring flesh above his head. What's more, she could have decided to ignore the more pedestrian name of Michelle and call herself Antoinette. And when her career was cut short, more simply Ann. Ann Galway, ergo Angie.

I went into the kitchen and looked out the window at the charred remains of the blue house. Angie had hired Rosie Neely as a companion, or as a front. She'd blown it when she called Lanya. It was hard to figure out why she'd done so, although she might have seen it as a way to get in touch with Edward. It had worked well — Edward had been on her porch after the ARSE potluck. Had he been furious that she might sabotage his relationship with Salvador? Furious enough to burn down her house? And then to slash her throat when he found out that she hadn't died in the fire?

It was too horrible to consider. I started a kettle of water for tea and went into the living room to watch the news. Ken and Barbie had nothing new to report about Salvador's murder, but they were salivating over the scene with the Japanese media at the PD. It was, as Jorgeson had said, a madhouse. Rental vans blocked the street. Earnest Japanese reporters stood in front of their cameras, speaking excitedly and gesturing at the door of the PD, which was blocked by uniformed officers. The mayor, safely inside his office at city hall, insisted that he was doing everything possible to cooperate with the foreign press but could not comment on the investigation. More Japanese reporters were at the curb in front of Salvador's house. I wasn't sure how long the yellow tape would keep them from charging the front door.

Ken and Barbie were puzzled by the yellow tape, but they were too well coiffed to admit it. The chief of police had promised to hold a news conference in the morning. KFAR would be there, front and center, to keep us viewers informed of whatever startling new developments were announced. When the weatherman came on, I returned to the kitchen and made myself a cup of tea and a sandwich.

I touched neither as I tried to think how best to pass along my information to Peter without admitting I'd disobeyed his directive. Not, of course, that he had any right to tell me where I could and couldn't go. Had he been no more than an ordinary detective, I would have had no qualms about calling. I believe strongly in doing my civic duty, which includes informing the police of potential criminal activity. I never skip an election, be it a primary or a bond issue. I obey the speed limit in school zones. I do not litter, and I recycle newspapers and cardboard.

The tea was cold and the sandwich was beginning to curl when Caron returned. After dropping her wet towels on the kitchen floor, she went down the hall to the bathroom. Thirty minutes later she emerged in clean clothes, her hair dripping on her shoulders. Her nose was red, but she'd survived any perilous encounters with lake monsters.

"Did you have a nice time?" I asked.

She picked up the sandwich, examined it, and put it back on the plate. "Can I order a pizza?"

"I thought I'd make a stir-fry with all the lovely fresh vegetables you bought at the grocery store last night."

"You couldn't stir-fry your way out of a paper sack," she said as she flopped across a chair. "Why are you just sitting there like that? Shouldn't you be picking out napkins and candles for the wedding reception? Lining up a photographer? Rehearsing your vows? You've only got two months, you know."

"In theory," I said.

My darling daughter gaped at me. "What have you done, Mother?"

"I went to see a kid named Max. Go ahead and order a pizza if you want. I think I'll sit on the balcony."

"Max who?" she demanded.

I thought for a moment, then shook my head. "I don't know. Besides, it doesn't matter."

"What does this have to do with your wedding?"

I took the plate and cup into the kitchen and tossed the sandwich in the trash. I could hear Caron on the phone, whispering madly, and not about Italian sausage and mushrooms. Unwilling to intrude, I went out onto the little back porch and listened to the sounds of Thurber Street. This being a Monday, there was not a live band in the beer garden. On the weekend evenings, they could be heard as far away as Bud's Automotive Emporium.

Caron appeared in the kitchen and cleared her throat. "Inez and I are going over to Emily's house. She got new CDs in the mail today. You aren't going to do anything crazy if I leave you alone, are you? I'd hate to be stuck in a foster home for two years. I'd have to sleep on a bunkbed and do chores."

"Run along," I said. "Be home by midnight."

She grabbed the car keys off the kitchen table and skittered down the stairs. Once she'd driven away, I went through the living room to the balcony. The information I had about Angie and Edward gnawed at me like a live culture. I came up with a screwy plan to go to the copy shop and fax the adoption page to Peter. All I needed to avoid being identified was Luanne's purple wig (or Angie's yellow one) and sunglasses. And the means to get to the copy shop, which was at least two miles away. If Corporal McTeer was lurking in the shadows, I could ask her for a ride, but that would defeat my need for anonymity. Luanne had mentioned a date with yet another lawyer, so she was unavailable.

It was all too much. I was staring at the dark buildings on the campus, waiting for inspiration, when what to my wondering eyes should appear? CID Detective Peter Rosen, parking at the curb.

What I said at that point need not be recorded.

CHAPTER SEVENTEEN

"What are you doing?" he asked me as if I were poised on the edge of the roof.

"Waiting for Romeo. He must have stopped off to fight a duel with those pushy Capulet guys."

"I need to talk to you."

"Let me get my purse and we'll go out for sushi."

He came in through the downstairs door and up the stairs. I let him in and offered beer, but he did not seem to prefer idle conversation. "Tell me what's going on, Claire. Have you had another 'chance encounter' with the suspects? Are they huddled in your bedroom, waiting for me to leave so they can resume group therapy?"

I pointed at the paper on the coffee table. "Read it, Sherlock."

As he read, his brow wrinkled. "Where did you get this?"

"I can't tell you, but it's legitimate. The

woman who was killed in the early hours of the day was Edward's mother — and it happened in Edward's father's house. Pretty amazing, isn't it?"

"Where did you get this?" he repeated slowly.

"I think I'll have a drink," I said. "Are you sure you wouldn't like a beer and a sandwich?"

"How do you do it? We ran a standard background check on Michelle Galway, but nothing like this occurred to us. Sometimes you astound me — as well as exasperate me. Yes, I'd like a beer and something to eat. It's been a difficult day. I had Japanese film crews trying to follow me into the men's room. The captain finished off his private stash of bourbon and sent an officer out for another bottle. The mayor thinks we're stonewalling, when in fact we have no idea what to do next. There's no forensic evidence. The autopsies haven't told us anything we didn't already know."

I made a couple of sandwiches, gathered his beer and my drink, then sat down next to him on the sofa. "Did you find out when Fiona left Edward's apartment last night?"

Peter grimaced. "When I confronted Edward, he admitted that she didn't leave until early this morning. She confirmed it, although she wasn't pleased that we knew. She's worried that Julius will go ballistic if he finds out."

"So they both have alibis," I said. "How convenient."

"If they're telling the truth." He picked up a sandwich and took a few bites. "Do you think he knew that his mother was here?"

"It must have been a shock when her name came up at the potluck, his very first ARSE meeting. He told me that she disappeared two years ago." I explained how I'd arrived at the conclusion that Angie and Michelle (aka Serengeti) were the same person. "He must have known something was screwy when he learned the name of the woman who'd volunteered to teach the fairies. He didn't waste much time going by her house to talk to her." I took a sandwich and nibbled on a corner of it. "He might have been delighted to discover she hadn't died. He spoke about her with great affection and respect — but he could have been lying. He may have despised her for ruining his childhood. From what he told me, she chose to play the martyr instead of trying to make something of her life. Plenty of single mothers find a way to get vocational training or finish college with the help of loans,

grants, and part-time jobs. She chose substance abuse. He may have been appalled to
learn that she was in Farberville and could
sabotage his relationship with Salvador. He
had a lot at stake."

"So he set her house on fire? That's an
extreme solution."

"Perhaps," I said, "but unless there's a gas
can in his apartment, there's no evidence
that he did."

Peter finished the sandwich and leaned
back. "Or any chance of getting a warrant.
This woman who died in the fire had a history of mental illness."

"Rosie Neely did not set the fire," I said
adamantly. "She was a very nice woman
who was liked by her boss and coworker.
There was no suggestion in her file that she
ever had any obsession with fire. Most
arsonists start playing with matches and setting fires as children. She grew up in a
stable environment, got along well with her
brother, and did fairly well at school until
her father was injured at a job site —" I
stopped and took a sip of scotch. "Or so I
heard, anyway."

"You read her file? Her *confidential* file?"

"I must have seen it somewhere," I said,
struggling not to blush as he stared at me.
"No more than a glimpse. Nothing worth

mentioning. Or maybe I heard about it from one of your officers. Would you like another sandwich, or some fruit and cheese? Caron went to the grocery store yesterday. She wanted to order a pizza this evening, if you can imagine. She needs to work on her short-term memory, especially since she'll be taking the SAT this fall. She's avoided studying all summer, and will end up cramming the night before the test. It won't do any good if she can't remember the difference between a hypotenuse and — uh, a hippopotamus."

Peter held up his palms. "Okay, I won't ask, but if you get caught, you're on your own with the prosecutor. He'd like nothing better than to embarrass you in public. When he heard we were engaged, he had me go to his office so he could lecture me about how I was imperiling my career. He had a point."

"Would you like me to return your ring and tell Jorgeson's wife to yank up the chrysanthemums?"

"Don't be absurd," he said. "I'm going home to get some sleep. Corporal McTeer's outside, this time with orders not to allow you to leave without calling me."

"If you really want to know about the adoption paper and Rosie's file, I'll tell you as long as you promise not to hassle the innocent parties who were inadvertently duped."

"I don't want to know anything, okay?"

He left without so much as a friendly nuzzle. I tidied up and then went downstairs to the front porch. "Corporal McTeer?" I called quietly.

"Yes, ma'am?" came a voice from the shadows.

"Have you ever planned a wedding?"

"My sister's, although the jerk she married dumped her a year later and moved to Alabama with a slut. It was a real nice wedding, though."

"There's no reason to sit under a bush for the next few hours. Come upstairs and help me make a list. Is it cheating if I borrow something that's old and blue?"

The phone rang the next morning at seven o'clock. Aware that it would take a major earthquake to get Caron out of bed, I stumbled down the hall to answer it. "This better be good," I said by way of greeting.

"This is Anderson Peru. I'm sorry to call so early, but I'm worried sick about Lanya. About three hours ago, I heard her drive off, and she hasn't come home. I don't understand how she could do that. The children are home, and she always fixes breakfast for them. I'm supposed to be at work in an hour."

"Why are you calling me?"

"I don't know who else to call. She hasn't spoken to anybody except you and the police since Saturday night. She's kept the bedroom door locked, and only comes out to find something to eat after everybody has gone to bed. She's . . . not herself. She wouldn't even answer the children when they tried to persuade her to come out."

"Lanya's old enough to run away from home," I said, rubbing my grainy eyes. "It's been all of three hours, Anderson. Maybe she wanted to get away from the house for a while. It may just be a case of cabin fever."

"It's not like her," he insisted. "Should I call the police?"

I carried the receiver with me as I went into the kitchen to make coffee. "The police won't do anything without a reason to suspect some sort of crime. Adults are free to come and go as they wish, Anderson. Life, liberty, and the pursuit of happiness."

"Even if it includes driving off the side of a mountain? What am I supposed to do?"

"Put on your armor and make breakfast," I said. "Can't your daughter babysit the younger children while you go to work?"

"And they decide to find out which pieces of furniture float in the pond? What about your daughter? Does she babysit?"

"You couldn't afford her. Could Lanya have gone to Benny's?"

"I called and got his answering machine. Besides, he's likely to be in bed with his latest conquest. He doesn't waste any time when he's not working in one of those Arab countries. For some idiotic reason, the women all fall for his blustery barbarian routine. I've watched him in action for twenty years."

"He was telling Edward how he used to be close friends with Salvador and how the two of them chased barmaids at the Renaissance gatherings. Different techniques, I suppose."

"Yeah, I envied them from the shackles of my marital tent. They had quite a reputation. Benny'd make up outrageous scenarios with evil wizards and warlords, and then they'd get people to enact them. The campsite was more of a battlefield than the official arena. Swords would clang half the night, replete with screams, curses, and cloaked figures crashing into tents. They had a lot of complaints from the more puritanical campers." He took a breath. "But what am I supposed to do now? What if Lanya doesn't come back?"

"I suggest cereal and day care. That's the best I can do until I've had coffee, Anderson."

"Could you possibly drive by Benny's place and look for her station wagon?" he asked piteously. "That way I'll know that she's safe."

I would have felt more sympathy had I not been making such a mess with the coffee grounds and water. "Why don't you put your darlings in the car and drive by yourself? I don't know where Benny lives and I'm not sure I'd recognize Lanya's car."

"I've got to start calling around for a babysitter. I have a conference call at nine with our sales department and a nationwide clothing chain. I'll lose my job if I miss it. It will only take you fifteen minutes, and I'll be eternally grateful. Please do this for me, Claire."

There is nothing worse than a pathetic plea from a man, and although I'd only caught a glimpse of his children, what I'd heard about them was cause for concern. "All right," I said.

He gave me directions and I promised to report back as soon as I could. While the coffeepot gurgled, I threw on some clothes and detoured by the bathroom. Trying not to jiggle a mug of coffee, I went down to the garage and drove to Benny's house. It was on the fringe of the historic district, bland and unpretentious. The yard was neglected, but not to the point that it would raise the ire of his neighbors. There was no sign of Lanya's station wagon on the street. I didn't know what Benny drove, so I had no way of telling whether or not he was home. Ringing the doorbell was not an option.

Cabin fever, I thought as I drove past Max's house and down Thurber Street. She might be watching the sun rise by a lake, eating pancakes at an all-night café, or heading for California to learn how to stomp grapes. If I'd been a truly altruistic person, I would have driven to the Perus' farm and offered to watch the children while Anderson had his ever so important conference call. However, I wasn't, so I stopped to buy fresh doughnuts and then went home.

Caron was sitting at the kitchen table, glowering. "Where have you been? The phone kept ringing and ringing, so I finally got up and answered it. What kind of person calls at this Ungodly Hour? Is there no consideration in this world?"

"Was it Anderson Peru?"

"I have no idea. I picked up the receiver

and pointed out that it was seven-thirty, and therefore entirely too early to be calling anyone, and hung up. What business does he have calling here, anyway? Just because he's a make-believe duke doesn't give him the right to disturb people. Henry the Eighth may have beheaded some of his wives, but at least he waited until a civilized hour."

"Have a doughnut." I put the box on the table and went into the living room to call Anderson. When he answered, I said, "I didn't see her station wagon, but I didn't search the area. Benny's blinds were closed."

"I'm going to be late," he wailed.

"Take the children with you. I'm sure they'll be thrilled to see where their daddy works."

"The little bastards would burn down the main warehouse within an hour. I need your help, Claire."

"Why don't you call Fiona? If she can deal with teenagers at school all day, she can handle your children."

He sucked in a breath. "That would be . . . awkward, especially when Lanya comes home from wherever she is. She and Fiona don't get along very well."

"Tell her — Lady Olivia of whatever — that it's a ducal edict and she owes it to her sovereign. Surely that's one of the perks of your role. If Lanya shows up, the two of them can sort out their differences in the sandbox. Good luck, Anderson." I hung up and returned to the kitchen. The only sign of Caron was a half-eaten doughnut on the table.

After I'd showered and put on clean clothes, I took a second mug of coffee and a doughnut into the living room and turned on the TV to catch the morning news show. Ken and Barbie's clones were interviewing a sleek Japanese woman who was the editor of a pop culture magazine. She was explaining with great intensity the reasons for Stark Reality's popularity in her country. According to her, Lord Zormurd and his loyal warriors symbolized the sword-wielding Samurai caste until they were abolished in the late nineteenth century. Zormurd, of course, was the great shogun, master of martial arts, protecting the peasants from barbaric foreign armies. The clones feigned interest, although it was likely neither of them could find a Japan restaurant. To their relief, the interview ended and they resumed blathering about the weather (good) and the traffic congestion near the mall (bad).

I left the doughnuts for Caron and walked to the Book Depot. I was not surprised to find Edward in the parking lot, juggling grimy beer bottles that he'd found in the weeds beside the railroad tracks. "Hi," I said as I unlocked the door. "I would have brought you a doughnut if I'd known you'd be here."

He followed me inside and sat down at my desk. "Guess you heard about the second murder. That woman with the weird makeup. I caught a glimpse of her in the living room the night of the cocktail party."

"Your mother," I said.

"What?"

"Get off it, Edward," I said irritably. "The detectives know who she was, so there's no point in pretending. Michelle Galway, right? How could you act as if the name meant nothing to you?"

"I was too stunned to say anything. I didn't know what to say. Something like that — well, it freezes your brain. You have to let it melt slowly and try to figure out what it means."

I started the coffeemaker and shooed him out of my chair. "You talked to her after the potluck, remember? I saw you on the porch."

"That was Angie," he protested.

"You knew who she was before you went to her house. Yesterday you identified the photo of another woman as being that of your mother. Was that a diversionary tactic to throw me off the track?"

"Okay, so Angie was my mother. I just didn't want the police to start wondering about it. When I started searching for information about Salvador online, I read some back issues of the local newspaper. Your name came up several times, and I could tell you had some kind of affiliation with the police department. I figured if I told you that my mother vanished a couple of years back, you'd pass it along."

"You juggle lies as adeptly as you do beer bottles. Go away, Edward. I need to find a way to make a quarterly installment on my taxes. My accountant is too priggish to allow me to juggle figures."

He sat in sullen silence for a moment. "That night on the porch I told her to get the hell out of Farberville if she ever wanted to see a nickel from me in the future. All I wanted her to do was leave before she screwed things up. If she'd just gone back to Oregon, everything would have been fine. When she died in the fire, I felt awful. Then the police said that she was murdered at Salvador's house. I promise you that I wasn't lying when I said I was stunned. I was also terrified that the police would think

I'd done something to her. My mother was a mess, but she was my mother all the same. We survived together for all those years, and we were going to be okay once Salvador acknowledged me. He would have agreed to send her money, if only to keep her away from him. She wasn't supposed to come here." He sat forward and stared at me. "I swear that's the truth, Mrs. Malloy. You have to believe me."

"No, I don't have to believe one word you say. Let me ask you this: Were you aware that Salvador Davis and Stark Reality were one and the same?"

"Yes," he said in a small voice. "I mean, I wasn't until I started searching for Salvador on the Internet. I didn't realize he was such a big deal, though. He wrote comic books."

"Are you telling me you weren't curious enough to follow the lead and find out more — like how much money he made?"

Edward opened his mouth to refute my presumption, then shrugged. "So I knew he was rich. That was like a bonus. I would have wanted to meet him anyway. He was my father."

"An especially lucrative bonus, I should think. You and your mother must have been excited at the possibilities."

"I shouldn't have told her," he said with a

groan. "She was getting by in Oregon with her stoned hippie friends. They had a big house out in the country, grew pot in the national forest, and found jobs when they needed cash. Nobody paid much attention to them. All she had to do was stay there until I dealt with things here. It's not my fault."

"Ah yes, my daughter's motto. You'd better go to the PD and explain to Detective Rosen why you failed to mention a few details when you were questioned."

I sent him on his way and sat down at the counter to read the newspaper. There were pictures of the Japanese reporters attempting to storm the PD, and of the mayor sweating at a press conference. Farberville had been a busy place lately, I thought. Bikers, Renaissance impostors, and now foreign media. Peter and I might prefer a house in the country, although we would not grow pot or welcome castaways. Caron had never gone through the adolescent stage in which she imagined herself atop Black Beauty, clad in a trim gray jacket and spiffy little riding helmet. A swimming pool and a suite would appease her. I could read *Town & Country* instead of *Publishers Weekly*.

I was envisioning myself greeting guests for a weekend house party, which would

feature croquet, tennis, cucumber sandwiches, and martinis, when the phone rang.
"Ask not for whom the bell tolls," I muttered as I picked up the receiver.

"Claire, this is Anderson. Something terrible has happened!"

"Did your conference call get rerouted
through Siberia?"

"It's Lanya. The police just called. They
want me to go over there and talk to her,
but I don't know what to say. They think
she's armed."

"Lanya? What's going on? Where is she?"

"Fiona's house. From what the police officer said, she's taken Fiona hostage and is
threatening to kill her! I'm supposed to go
reason with her and convince her to come
out. I'm afraid that if she has a gun, she'll
shoot me first. You have to go there. She'll
listen to you."

"Where are you now?"

"In my car. A woman down the road offered to keep the kids until noon, so I made
it to the office in time for the call. In the
middle of it, my assistant told me I had an
urgent call from the police. My first thought
was that the boys had stolen the woman's
car again. It never crossed my mind that
Lanya could do something this crazy. Will
you go to Fiona's?"

"What's the address?"

He told me and I promised to meet him as soon as I could. There was no reason to call Peter, since he was probably already there, along with half the police force. I locked the store, hurried back to my duplex to get the car, and drove to a subdivision of distressingly similar brick houses. An officer flagged me down and ordered me to turn around and leave. I obliged, then found a place to park one street over and cut through the few backyards that weren't fenced. The street was crammed with official vehicles, tight-lipped uniformed officers, the omnipresent KFAR news van at a discreet distance, and Japanese reporters swarming like gnats behind the police barricade. I spotted Peter and Anderson in the yard of a vacant house across the street from Fiona's residence. A real estate broker's sign announced the house was for sale at a reduced price. I wiggled through the crowd, squirmed through a gap between the sawhorses, and joined them. Lanya's station wagon was parked in Fiona's driveway, and there was a second car in the carport. The curtains in the house were drawn as if it were vacant, too. Unfortunately, we all knew it wasn't.

"Have you tried to talk to her?" I asked

between pants, unaccustomed to sprinting.

Peter gave me a chilly look. "I'm amazed the media got here before you did."

"I walked to the bookstore this morning, so I had to go home to get the car. Well, Anderson?"

"No, she let Fiona speak a few words on the cell phone, then cut it off. Knowing Lanya, she might have put it down the garbage disposal or smashed it with a hammer. She doesn't like cell phones. I set mine to vibrate when I get home, and go outside if I need to take a call."

"Why do you think she's armed?" I asked Peter.

"We have to assume she is. You can't hold someone hostage with a nail file." He went over to a police van nearby and disappeared inside it. Anderson and I stared at the house until Peter returned with a tweedy little man with sad eyes. "This is Dr. King from the psychology department at the college," he said to Anderson. "He wants to ask you some questions about your wife's mental stability. You can sit in the car over there." After they'd moved away, he said, "Do you think she might listen to you? She did let you in her bedroom."

"I thought you questioned her yesterday about Serengeti's death."

"Through the door. She refused to unlock it."

"Oh," I murmured, gazing at the blank windows of the house. "What if she *is* armed? I don't fancy finding out the painful way — or the fatal way, for that matter. Why don't you take off your tie, tousle your hair, and woo her with your boyish charm?"

"I don't want to get shot, either. I can't make honeymoon plans from a hospital bed."

"What honeymoon plans are you making? Shouldn't I be consulted?"

"When we have time, I'll take you out for a romantic dinner and explain. Okay, here come Dr. King and the husband. Maybe they've come up with something."

Dr. King pulled Peter aside, but I could hear him as he said, "Mr. Peru won't do it. He says a great deal of her current anger is directed at him, and he has to take their children into consideration. I have to agree that they won't fare well if their mother ends up in prison for killing their father. That's more than traumatic."

We were all standing around helplessly when Sally Fromberger swept up in her cape, brushing aside officers as if they were pesky autograph seekers. She handed Anderson a plate covered with foil. "I know from watching TV shows that these hostage situations can drag on all day. I thought you all might like some freshly baked muffins to keep up your strength. Why, Claire, I haven't seen you since the Renaissance Fair. Wasn't it something? I do hope we'll have one every year."

I truly wished that I was armed. "Go back to your café, Sally. This is a dangerous situation."

"Lanya wouldn't shoot a prioress," Sally said with a chuckle.

"I would," said Peter. "Since that's not possible with the media watching, I'll settle for having you arrested. Officers, remove this woman and stick her in a cell at the PD until I get there and can file an arrest report."

Sputtering, Sally was hauled away. Peter and the psychologist went behind the van to continue their discussion. Although I hadn't seen a drape twitch across the street, I felt as though Lanya were watching us. Was Fiona tied to a kitchen chair, with a sock stuffed in her mouth? And more importantly, would Lanya actually shoot any of us if we approached?

For the next three hours, nothing much happened. Anderson and I sat down on the porch of the vacant house. He tasted a muffin, then put it back on the plate. The media remained behind the barricade, but they were clearly disappointed at the lack of drama. Those on camera knew they were losing their audience to game shows and soap operas. Dr. King was escorted to a police car and driven back to his ivy tower, where he could regale his colleagues and students with his intrepid attempt to assist the police in a life-and-death crisis. I hoped he might see the irony when he ate his tuna salad sandwich in the faculty lounge.

Anderson's cell phone rang. Peter, who'd been conferring with the officers, hurried over and told Anderson to answer it.

"What'll I say?" asked Anderson, his voice quivering.

Peter glared at him. "Why don't you find out what she says first, and we'll take it from there?"

Anderson punched a button as if it were a glowing ember. After listening for a moment, he looked up and said, "It's not from across the street. It's the woman who's babysitting my children. I told her I'd pick them up at noon."

"Tell her you're busy," I suggested.

"She said if I wasn't there in fifteen minutes, she would take them to the county line and dump them. She's, uh, kind of upset."

"She hasn't been watching TV?" I said.

Anderson licked his lips. "No, and that's one of the reasons why she's upset. I have to do something with them, Lieutenant Rosen. Is there any chance you can put them in a cell next to that crackpot in the cape?"

I had an idea. "Go fetch them, Anderson, and bring them back here. It's our best shot at ending this Mexican standoff. Trust me."

Peter seemed doubtful, but he told one of the officers to drive Anderson to the woman's house and return with the children. "Would you care to elucidate?" he asked me.

"Not now," I said. "Is there anything to drink in the van? Iced tea would be nice."

"It's not a concessions booth, but I can scrounge up a bottle of water." He stalked away, and when he returned, merely handed me the plastic bottle and went to stand in the shade under a tree.

I kept my fingers crossed as I unscrewed the top of the water bottle and took a sip. It occurred to me that Peter should have gotten the key to the for-sale house, where there would be facilities should the afternoon drag on. I made a note to remind him the next time we were involved in a hostage situation.

CHAPTER EIGHTEEN

"Oh, my gawd!" Luanne shrieked as I came into her store. "I saw it on TV! What an absolute hoot. The cops, the SWAT team, the reporters, the teary husband — and who saves the day? Some filthy little barefoot kids! What did you say to them?"

"I told them that their mommy was making chocolate chip cookies in the house across the street," I said. "I knew Lanya wouldn't shoot them, and they were howling so loudly that she had to open the door. After that, the situation defused. Fiona came outside and said it was all a terrible mistake, that she and Lanya were in the kitchen drinking coffee the entire time and hadn't even noticed the commotion outside. They appeared to be highly entertained by what they claimed was a misunderstanding."

Luanne grinned. "Was Peter highly entertained as well?"

"Far from it. When he demanded to know why Fiona had called 911, she swore she hadn't and that she'd lost her phone at the Renaissance Fair. She claimed it was one of her students, pulling a prank."

"And what did Lanya say?"

I perched on the edge of a display case of beaded purses. "She couldn't sleep so she went for a drive, and then thought she might stop by Fiona's house so the two of them could check the invoices and receipts from the fair. Since Fiona is a teacher, it seemed likely that she would be up and about early in the morning. Once they started, they lost all track of time."

"A tempest in a teapot."

"Prospero was blowing steam out of his ears. He and the others had been there since nine o'clock, concerned about the purported victim as well as the purported perp, who might have harmed herself, too. Hostage situations often end with murder and suicide. Fiona's lucky that the police didn't throw a tear gas canister through a window and break down the front door. That would diminish her goodwill in the neighborhood."

Luanne went into her back room and returned with a bottle of designer water. "You must be exhausted," she said as she gave it to me. "So what do you think was going on behind the drapes? Do you think the two of them . . . ?"

"I hadn't considered that," I admitted, "but I don't think they have an intimate relationship, if that's what you mean. They both have impressive track records for heterosexual activity. They were giggly and complacent when they came outside, but not at all guilty. Peter says he's going to file charges against at least one of them when he has more information about the call to 911. They'll have to send the tape and a recording of Fiona's voice to the state lab, and it may take a week to get the results. If they end up with proof that she made the call, she's going to have to come up with a better story."

"If she's telling the truth about her cell phone, any of her students could have pocketed it," Luanne said. "They seemed to resent being forced to participate. Well, not the pirates. They were having a jolly time."

"An adult would have turned it in at the Royal Pavilion or the ticket table at the entrance. The only reason I'm confident Caron isn't guilty is that she couldn't have known Lanya was at Fiona's house. I don't know why any of the other students would, either."

"Except the ones who live nearby or

deliver newspapers to that particular neighborhood."

I finished the water and took out my car key. "I need to open the bookstore on the off chance someone might want to buy a book in the next two hours. I'll talk to you later."

When I arrived at the store, I had to struggle to unlock the door. My adrenaline had ebbed, and I was indeed exhausted. Peter had conceded that my scheme worked, but he'd stalked off without saying anything further. Anderson had been sitting on the curb, moaning about the publicity and its impact on his job. He had not spoken to his wife, nor she to him. It was likely to be a wee bit tense at the Peru home for the next few days — or until she left in September for the course in California. And I had a feeling she would go. Salvador would not be around to see his name on a wine label, but his heirs would as they raked in their share of the profits. If I was right (as I tend to be most of the time), the details had been finalized at Fiona's kitchen table that morning. Whatever Lanya's intentions had been when she arrived at dawn, they had been defused by the promise of financial support. If I was right, I amended with a modest smile.

I was searching through my desk drawers

for a forgotten candy bar when the bell above the door jangled. "I'll be there in a minute," I called, secretly hoping whoever it was would creep away.

Caron and Inez came into the office. "We saw you on TV," the former said accusingly.

"How'd I look?" I asked as I gave up my search.

"Not too bad, considering," Inez said, blinking at me.

I didn't pursue it. "What are your plans for the rest of the day? Promise me you won't take anyone hostage. I've had my fill of that for the day."

"Mr. Valens called," Caron said. "He wants us to help out at another amateur production this weekend. Ten bucks an hour, each. I told him we'd think about it. I'm not sure I've fully recovered from the last one. At least it's not the same group. They're still trying to wiggle out of their lederhosen."

"The money's not bad," I commented.

"If I'm going to sell my soul, I'm not doing it for less than eternal youth and fabulous riches."

"Or a date with Louis Wilderberry?" Inez said slyly.

Caron made a face that would have frightened a gargoyle. "Did you see him Saturday?

He was repulsive. Emily and Carrie told me he went behind one of the tents and barfed all over his shoes. That is So Infantile. You know, he and Rhonda make a perfect couple. He'll go to a second-rate college on a football scholarship, and she'll join a sorority and major in elementary ed. She'll get pregnant, they'll get married, and then the two of them will spend the rest of their lives in some dumpy little house. I can hardly wait for our tenth class reunion. Would you like to ride with me in my limousine, Inez?"

Inez dismissed the offer with a flip of her hand. "No, the Secret Service won't allow it. They'll fly me into town in a helicopter and deliver me in a bulletproof car with tinted glass. I hope my bodyguards won't intimidate the little people."

"I'm glad to hear you're already worrying about it," I said. "When do you have to let Mr. Valens know?"

"He said you can tell him at the potluck tomorrow." Caron shook her head disapprovingly at me. "I never thought of you as a person who went to potlucks. Is this something married people have to do? Will you be wearing polyester pants before too long? Will I have to get braces even though I don't need them?"

"All of the above," I said.

"Let's go to Ashley's," Caron said to Inez. "Her brother gets off work in half an hour. Maybe he'll be wearing those tight jeans and no shirt. He is so hot."

Inez did not agree, and they were debating the matter as they left. I hung around the bookstore for another hour, then locked up and drove home. I'd forgotten about the potluck in Salvador's honor, or at least shoved it to a conveniently obscure corner of my mind. There was little chance that the state lab would analyze the tapes any time soon, so Fiona wouldn't be incarcerated like good-hearted but seriously misguided Sally Fromberger. I hoped Peter had let her toddle away when he returned to the PD.

I scarfed down an apple and a handful of chips, then made a drink and retreated to the balcony. Too much had happened too quickly. As Edward had claimed, I too felt as if my brain were frozen. In my case, he was the primary cause. Did I believe him? He was worse than an onion — every layer of lies could be peeled back to expose yet another layer. I couldn't imagine him killing his mother in such a cold-blooded fashion. Then again, he was a schemer of Machiavellian aptitude. Once he learned Salvador's name, he'd done extensive research — and had not stopped until he found out about his father's successful career and life in Farberville. His mother could have talked about ARSE activities when she was in college, leading him to look for articles in the local paper that mentioned the local fiefdom and its members. Joining it gave Edward a way to check out his father and decide how to approach him. And my name did pop up in the newspaper on occasion. Although I've always done my best to let Lieutenant Rosen and the CID take credit for solving cases, there had been times when the press found me more photogenic. One of the reporters had given me the dubious sobriquet of "Miss Marple." A brief biography was usually included. Edward knew I was widowed, and he knew that Carlton was not his father. Watching me sweat must have amused him.

He did have legitimate grievances. If Salvador had not walked away from Michelle (or Angie, or Serengeti, depending on the moment), Edward would have had a more normal childhood, although possibly not one of wealthy comforts. Salvador's initial success had not come until after he moved to Farberville. Maybe it was because of something in the water. I doubted that fluoridation could inspire genius, but I had been wrong once or twice in the past.

Benny's behavior was perplexing. If he'd had such venomous feelings about Salvador, why had he ended up reminiscing about him on Edward's couch? Other than his atrocious behavior at the cocktail party, I had seen no interaction between him and Salvador. Had their friendship soured to the point of violence? Vikings were not known for their laid-back approach to problem solving.

I shifted my attention to Julius Valens. I'd allowed myself to be alarmed by him, mostly because of the belligerent behavior that I'd only heard about. He must have been thrilled when someone as charming and attractive as Fiona Thackery had shown interest in him. He worshiped her, and she betrayed him. Had he been quivering with rage all along, and finally snapped? Salvador certainly wouldn't have worried if Julius suggested they go behind the archery target to talk privately.

Fiona had threatened someone at the farmhouse while I was trying on the gown. Salvador might have had a reason to believe that he was not the father of her baby. He was no longer in a position to protest. Fiona had wasted no time forming an alliance with Edward. It was possible that neither of them wanted paternity tests. With no one else having a claim on the estate, probate would proceed smoothly. Half of a fortune was preferable to years of litigation.

I realized I had only one course of action to resolve this mess before my relationship with Peter imploded. I would not, however, stoop to polyester.

"I cannot believe we're doing this," Peter said as I knocked on Lanya and Anderson's front door the following evening. "We could be having dinner at a quaint country inn, and gazing at each other in the warm glow of candlelight while the maître d' pours wine."

I batted my eyelashes at him. "That's the first romantic notion you've had for days. If we're lucky, we could be out of here in an hour. I shouldn't think that we need dinner reservations on a Wednesday night."

"I wasn't talking only about dinner. I have designs on your virtue."

"Did you and Leslie discuss her virtue?"

Peter stepped back. "I wish you'd get past that. She showed up at my mother's house the day before I left. She brought her new husband, Jean Pierre something, to show him off. He was bewildered but charming. My mother dragged him down to the wine cellar half an hour after they arrived to ask his opinion about the collection. Leslie and I congratulated each other. When I began to tell her about you, I realized I couldn't bear to be away from you one more day. That's why I came home early."

"Oh," I said.

"I'd like to get this over with as soon as possible. Do you have any idea what you're going to say to these people?"

"I'd like to think I've read enough mysteries with classic dénouement scenes to pull one off in my sleep. I will gladly step aside if you want to take over, Sherlock."

Lanya opened the door. She beamed at me, then recognized Peter and gulped. "Why, Claire, I didn't realize . . ."

"I believe you and Peter have already met," I said as I herded him inside.

"Several times . . . under different circumstances. I see you've brought some fruit and cheese. Everybody else is on the porch. Please help yourself to a beverage in the kitchen before you join us." She skittered away to warn the others.

"I feel like a piranha dropped into a goldfish bowl," Peter said.

"And that is what you are, darling. Would you like mead, wine, or a soda?"

"Maybe later."

I escorted him out to the screened porch. Everyone looked appalled by Peter's presence, as I knew they would be. "You've all met Peter Rosen, the head of the CID division," I said cheerfully. "He's been keen on the Renaissance since boyhood, and thought it might be fun to attend an ARSE meeting."

"How nice to see you again, Constable," Glynnis Threet said. "Why don't you come sit with William and me on the sofa? Percival had curly dark hair, too. Would you like to see a photo of him?"

"Not now," said her husband.

Glynnis began to dig through her purse. "But it's such a darling photo. It was taken after Percival won Best of Show at the county fair. The blue ribbon matched the mohair sweater I made for him as a birthday present."

William took her purse away from her and moved over to make room for Peter. "Were you a fan of the Arthurian legends when you were young? My friends and I used to make helmets out of cardboard and joust on our stick horses. My cousin Manfred lost an eye one summer in such a contest. What fun we had."

No one else was motivated to share memories. Edward was sitting in the same corner, mutely watching. Julius and Fiona sat next to each other on kitchen chairs, but the chill between them was palpable. Anderson was sprawled in a battered wicker throne, looking as bored as he had at the Royal Pavilion. Benny stood behind him like a museum guard.

Lanya added my plate to the others on the table, then cleared her throat. "Welcome, all. As you know, this is a tribute to Salvador, our brother in mock war and true peace, and an honored member of our fiefdom. How shall we proceed? Anderson, will you propose a toast to Lord Galsworth, Baron of Firthforth?"

I noticed Edward flinch at the word "Galsworth." I was pleased that everyone was on edge. I had a theory that explained almost everything, but I had no proof. What I needed were emotional outbursts and wild accusations in the next few minutes, if I was going to end up dining in a country inn. I couldn't stop myself from looking at the potluck offerings on the table. Lanya's mysterious casserole — or Chateaubriand, medium rare, with a rich béarnaise sauce. My resolve stiffened.

"What a splendid idea," I said to Anderson. "Let's have a toast to Salvador Davis, a man of many different titles and talents."

"Yeah," said Benny. "Make a toast, Duke."

"I'm too tired to play games," Anderson muttered.

"Then how about you, Benny?" I said. "You and Salvador were close friends for more than a decade, weren't you? Or Edward, what about you? He was your long-lost father, and he welcomed you into his arms as if you, rather than he, were the prodigal son." No one was leaping to his feet. I turned to Fiona. "You had an intimate relationship with him."

"What did you say?" said William. "That's an outrageous accusation, Lady Clarissa! Fiona is engaged to Julius."

Glynnis blinked moistly. "Such a sweet couple."

There was an awkward silence. Peter was staring at me, waiting, but he was the only one willing to make eye contact. I finally took a breath and said, "Well, then, if no one wants to offer a toast, we'll just have a cozy conversation about Salvador and all the people he loved so dearly. It's difficult to know where to start. The beginning is the logical place, I suppose. Twenty-two years ago Salvador impregnated a young woman named Michelle Galway. She had to give up on her dreams of becoming a dancer in order to support her child. The child was

Edward, who was later adopted by a man named Cobbinwood. Hence, the name. Is everybody with me thus far?"

"Michelle Galway?" said Lanya. "Why is that name familiar?"

I waited in case Peter wanted to jump in, but he did not so much as raise an eyebrow. "That," I replied, "is the name of the woman whose body was found at Salvador's house yesterday morning. It's reasonable to assume that none of you recognized the name except for Edward, of course. It was his mother."

"The woman with the crazy makeup?" said Benny. "I ran into her at Salvador's house a couple of times. She was damn impossible to talk to. She said her name was Serengeti, but her response to every other question was that she didn't like it when people asked her that. Spooky." He swiveled his head to look at Edward. "That was your mother? It's no wonder you like to run around in purple tights."

"You are a clever gal, Clarissa," said Glynnis. "Do tell us who killed her."

"In a few minutes. Michelle went by the nickname Angie. I presume it's because her middle name was Antoinette. Although she gave up her potential career, she remained interested in the Renaissance events. She must have taught fairies to dance over the years. Isn't that so, Edward?"

He shrugged. "Yeah, on and off. She couldn't afford the admission tickets, so she'd volunteer in exchange for free passes. She had me wearing garb when I was four years old. When she had a few extra dollars, she'd find clothes at a thrift shop and alter them."

"You must have been adorable," began Glynnis, then stopped as she realized everyone was glaring at her.

"I'm sure he was," I said politely. "Michelle went through some rough financial and emotional times, as did her son. I'll come back to that later. Let's move on to the very trite eternal triangle, consisting of Lanya, Anderson, and Benny. All in college together. Cheap wine, a little pot, weekends at Renaissance Fairs, where they could really let loose. Benny and Lanya decided to get married, but Benny gave way to his carnal urges and Lanya married Anderson. That meant that Anderson not only got the girl, he got the kids, the mortgage, the monthly bills, and the boring job in an office. Benny was stuck with the high-paying, exotic job and the freedom to bed every wench he could persuade."

"It's not exotic," Benny protested. "Arabs

don't let their daughters go out without a chaperone. I mostly play poker with the crew."

"Whatever," I said. "What's more intriguing is that you and Salvador became good friends years ago. Fifteen, did you say? Something like that. He was an unsuccessful young painter and graphic novelist back then. He lacked the imagination to break into the genre, but he kept trying. Eventually, after he'd moved here, he finally hit the big time with Lord Zormurd. Salvador moved from a shabby apartment to a very expensive house. He drove a Lamborghini and entertained lavishly. When he traveled, it was to conventions where he was the center of attention."

"What's the point of all this?" said Fiona. "Why are we listening to you ramble on as if you were in the front of a classroom? I think we should put a stop to this and have something to eat. What say you, milords and miladies?"

"I think it's interesting," said William. "And the point of it, Fiona, is to determine who killed Salvador and this woman. By the way, are you knocked up?"

"William!" Glynnis gasped.

Julius stood up. "No, she is not. We are

both saving ourselves for our wedding night."

The silence this time was profound. Not even Glynnis dared to sniffle. Teeth clamped down on lips. The rough floor seemed to fascinate everyone except Julius, who remained on his feet, his fists on his hips. He reminded me of a grumpy troll defending a flower bed (or a deflowered bed, anyway).

"Julius," Fiona said at last, "we need to talk. Why don't we go out to the front porch?"

"Everyone needs to stay in this room," Peter said. "It's . . . ah, safer."

"I wasn't suggesting we go into the woods to hunt for witches," she said in a voice that was likely to be effective with boisterous teenagers.

Peter was not cowed. "Please remain here."

Fiona looked as though she wanted to fling her wine at him, but regained enough composure to grab Julius's hand and pull him back onto his chair.

I tried to collect my thoughts. "Salvador was finally successful, although he was reticent to elaborate on his source of income. He went into seclusion to work on his latest project, and felt no need to discuss the true nature of it. You all tolerated his eccentricities. It was going smoothly when waves from two directions rocked his yacht, both superficially positive. The foremost was the arrival of Edward, the son he never knew he had. Salvador was stunned. He called me more than a week ago to talk about it, but changed his mind. He managed to resolve his feelings and decide how to deal with the news."

"I told you he was pleased," Edward said. "He felt guilty about deserting my mother and me, and never bothering to find out if we were okay. He was going to make it up to me. I didn't ask him for anything; he offered."

"And very generously, according to your version," I said. "Sadly, it's the only version we have. You lied when you told me that you didn't approach Salvador until the day before the Renaissance Fair; he called me almost a week before that. I have to admit I have some reservations about you, Edward. You manipulated me without a qualm, even though you knew I was frantic with worry. The only reason I can come up with is pure malice. It's intriguing that you chose to be a jester, a naïve fool whom no one takes seriously. Your mother hid her identity, too. You might want to take this up with a psychiatrist one of these days."

"Leave her out of this," he said. His eyes narrowed as he noticed Fiona staring over her shoulder at him. "It's a bunch of crap. If you were all that frantic, it was your own fault. All I ever did was confide in you because I was apprehensive and didn't have anyone else to talk to." His lip curled for a second, although I suspected I was the only one who caught it. It did not seem like the moment to mention that he needed to find a psychiatrist from the Freudian school of thought.

"Are we going to eat soon?" asked Glynnis.

William leaned across Peter to poke her. "Quiet, dear. I'm still waiting to hear if Fiona's really a virgin. Highly unlikely in this day and age, if you ask me."

"Nobody asked you," Julius said huffily.

I smiled at Glynnis. "I hope we'll all be eating soon, wherever we may be. After this conversation with Edward, Salvador knew he was going to have to deal with the situation. He may have felt unsure what a DNA comparison would produce, but he had to face the possibility that it might be conclusive evidence of his paternity. Did he talk to you about it, Benny?"

Benny was startled by my question. After a moment, he said, "Not the fatherhood thing. He asked for my advice about finances. I don't know anything about corporations and trusts, so I told him to call a financial advisor. He wanted to make sure all his money was inaccessible if he was sued down the road. All his millions tied up in neat little packages, wrapped in legal jargon."

"He asked me that stuff, too. I told him to consult a lawyer," Anderson said. "This is getting tedious. I agree with Glynnis that it would be nice to eat before midnight. Could you speed it up, Claire? Lanya's steak and kidney pie is bad enough when it's hot, but unpalatable when it's congealed."

I caught Lanya before she could swoop down on him and add his entrails to her dish. "I'm doing my best," I said. "Salvador intended to prepare himself for paternity by protecting his assets. He also felt like he needed to tell you, Fiona."

Fiona glanced at Julius, then said, "We had a discussion during the Renaissance Fair. I merely pointed out that he had an obligation to our child to provide for its upbringing and future welfare."

Julius's face mottled with angry splotches. "Then you are pregnant! Was I going to be the fallback if Salvador didn't believe you? Were you planning to hastily consummate our relationship and pretend the child was premature? I am not a fool, Fiona. I tried to be tolerant when you flirted with other men, and I never questioned you when you went home early because you said you had a headache. But what about the promise we made to each other?"

Fiona shrugged. "It was your idea, not mine. Since Claire is probably going to drag Edward into this, you might as well know that he and I reached an agreement in bed. We're getting married, and will sign a pre-nuptial so that when he inherits Salvador's estate, we can split it without additional taxes. The marriage may not last long, but it's much more convenient than contesting the division of the estate. Unlike Salvador, I went to the trouble of speaking with a lawyer. I hope you're not too upset."

Julius pulled back his arm to slap her. Anderson grabbed his wrist and growled, "Don't make me drag you outside and beat you to a bloody pulp, Squire Squarepockets."

"Don't be preposterous," Julius squeaked, relaxing his arm. "I was going to stand up and leave, that's all. Let go of me." After Anderson obliged, Julius cradled his wrist and whimpered, while the rest of us exhaled.

William waggled his finger at Julius. "We

do not tolerate that sort of thing here in Avalon. If you feel the need for violence, then train to become a knight. I understand it's very cathartic."

"Try it again and I'll arrest you for attempted assault," Peter said coldly.

Julius mumbled something, but it was just as well none of us could understand him. Fiona rose and joined Edward in the corner. Benny took her seat, managing to bump Julius's shoulder hard enough to leave a bruise.

Lanya went into the kitchen and returned with a bottle of wine in one hand and a jar of mead in the other. "Refills, anyone?"

Glynnis held out her cup. "How thoughtful of you. Lady Clarissa, you said earlier that two things had happened to Salvador. We know more than we wanted about Edward and his mother. What is the second? Would you like us to guess?"

"The second," I said, "was good news. Salvador was informed that he'd won an award, the Gryphon, for his most recent graphic novel. It comes with a hefty sum of money."

"Oh, yes," Lanya said. "That drunken man from Australia mentioned it, didn't he? A black-tie ceremony in Paris. Salvador was too modest to talk about it."

"Or embarrassed." Benny gulped down his wine and wiped his lips on the back of his hand. "An award that no one's heard of, presented by publishers of friggin' comic books! Not on the same level with the Nobel in literature. All he could have looked forward to was seeing Zormurd on lunch boxes and Lego boxes."

My stomach growled (in French, no less). "Then perhaps we should wind this up. First, I believe that Angie, or whatever we choose to call her, set fire to the house herself. She'd hired an innocent woman of a similar build and age as a housekeeper. That might have been a coincidence, but Angie must have used whatever savings she had to rent the house. She couldn't have paid a salary for very long. As much as I hate to even consider it, it suggests some degree of premeditation."

Fiona turned to Edward. "Your mother hired a woman in order to fake her own death? That's monstrous. Swear you didn't know anything about it."

He shook his head. "Of course I didn't. I mean, she was my mother. Sometimes she was kind of crazy, but I always thought it was because of the drugs and booze."

"Kind of crazy?" Benny snorted. "Kind of sociopathic is more like it."

"How ghastly." Lanya shivered as if a blast of cold air had blown through the screen. "Why would she want to . . . do that?"

"In case her son found out she was in Farberville," I said. "When she arrived, she was obsessed with Salvador. She'd done some research and come up with a scheme to get close to him without revealing her identity. He bought it and she began to model for him. She overheard remarks about the Renaissance Fair and wanted to find out more about it. What better way than to call and offer to help? She may not have known Edward was in town until then. At that point, she needed to avoid him, but he came to her house and threw a fit."

"I didn't throw a fit," Edward said. "I just told her to leave."

"I think you were more adamant than that. Did you threaten to tell Salvador if she didn't leave town immediately? She was fixated on revenge, and you could have ruined everything. She faked her death, although she chose a cruel, heartless way. That's when she moved into Salvador's house."

"Without asking his permission?" asked Glynnis, enthralled. "How delicious. Some of our friends in Connecticut had a hermit living in their garden shed. He was perfectly harmless, and it amused them to point him out to their guests when he prowled in the back of the garden. Percival was beside himself with excitement the first time we spotted him. Don't you remember, William?"

"Shush," he said. "You're interrupting this fascinating story. Please go on, Clarissa."

I glanced at Peter, who was doing his best to remain expressionless. The corners of his mouth were twitching, however. "Thank you, William," I said primly. "Now let's move on to the day of the Renaissance Fair. Salvador has been hit with the news that he is a father, and has reached some sort of decision. I don't think we'll ever know what he intended to do in the future, but that's not relevant. The beehive has been poked, and its inhabitants are irate. Salvador is at the archery range, located behind the row of booths and tents and therefore not visible from the main walkway. Visitors find him, some to shoot arrows at a bale of hay, others to speak privately to him. The various stages offer music, dancing, comedy, and skits. It's a sunny day, and the attendees are in a jovial mood. Food, drink, entertainment, and souvenirs are there for all. At five o'clock, when the ARSE members retire to the farmhouse, Salvador does not appear, nor does he appear at the banquet at six.

Edward sings the ballad, causing a certain amount of consternation. The announcement of Salvador's death overrides it."

"We were all there," Anderson said, yawning.

"Yes, we were, and so was Edward's mother."

I had their attention. Peter was the only one who wasn't gaping at me, but he was clearly surprised. I didn't know how to elaborate without tipping off my prime suspect. That, and the fact that I had not one iota of proof. I needed it to be true because it was the key to her murder, as well as Salvador's. I had no choice but to trust my instincts, if I wanted to get the matter resolved before the charming country inn flipped off its lights.

"Yes," I continued with an admirable display of confidence, "she dressed as a medieval bag lady. The allure of the Renaissance Fair was too strong for her to resist, and she knew she would never be recognized. I can't say for sure how she got there, but I think if the police want to interview their two hundred and something witnesses, they'll find someone who saw a perfectly normal woman walking along the road and gave her a ride. Once there, she dressed in garb. She was then free to stroll around the fair."

"That was my mother?" Edward said. "I saw her, and I guess everybody else did, too. A lot of people dress up in weird outfits for these things. I just assumed she was . . ."

I gave him a chance to complete his sentence, but he looked away. "We saw her, but more importantly, she saw the person who took the battle-ax to the archery range to murder Salvador."

"None of the witnesses saw anybody carrying a battle-ax," Peter said.

I tried not to sound condescending, although I may have not been entirely successful. "No one would if the guilty party took the ax from the Royal Pavilion and went behind the tents to the edge of the woods. The scrub pines and brush would provide cover until the person reached the bales of hay. Then it was just a matter of waiting until Salvador took a break to collect stray arrows. Angie was likely to have been lurking nearby, spying on Salvador."

"And just watched when . . . ?" said Fiona.

"Let's say she chose not to intervene. She may have been eavesdropping when Salvador asked some of you about burying his assets in trusts and corporations. She couldn't count on his generosity toward

Edward or even a lawsuit for back child support, but it was probable that Edward would inherit. Until the estate was put through probate, collecting blackmail from the murderer would provide a steady income. She met her victim in Salvador's studio on Sunday night around midnight. Her proposal was not well received, shall we say."

"This is speculation," Fiona said. "You don't know what she saw — or who. How long do we have to put up with this farce, Lieutenant Rosen? I've lost my appetite and would prefer to leave."

"No, no, no," said William. "I'm on the edge of my seat. This is quite as exciting as a mystery novel, although in this situation, the culprit is more likely to be a page than a butler. Do go on, Clarissa."

"Are you implicated, Fiona?" asked Glynnis, peering hopefully at her.

"Of course not!" she snapped.

Benny looked back at her. "It makes sense. You didn't know what you could count on from Salvador after you had the baby. Being the legal guardian of what you thought was his only issue would allow you to get your hands on his estate, once he was dead. Edward's announcement ruined that, but you didn't waste much time coming up with an alternative scheme."

"Shut your bloody trap!"

He wiggled his tongue at her. "Lady Olivia of Ravenmoor is violating the code of civility. Tsk, tsk."

"Can it, Benny," Anderson said.

"You gonna make me?" he taunted, wiggling his tongue at Anderson for good measure. "I should have whomped your butt in the final battle, but Lanya had told me what a jerk you were and I lost my temper. Why don't we have a rematch in the yard, this time without armor?"

"You say when, asshole," Anderson snarled.

Lanya elbowed me from behind. "Get on with it before this escalates further. They've both had too much to drink."

"I noticed," I said dryly. "Listen, please. I never accused Fiona of killing Salvador. Benny, would you like more wine before I continue?" I watched as he grabbed the bottle and took a drink. "You may be hoping that I'll accuse someone else, but I'm afraid that the metaphorical arrow is pointing right at you."

"Why me?" he said as wine dribbled onto his beard like drops of blood. He banged the bottle down on the coffee table. "Salvador and I were old buddies."

"You really shouldn't have mentioned

that. From what I've heard, you were the one who made up fantastic action scenarios with warlords and wizards. Salvador needed plots like yours, not his trite efforts that wouldn't sell. Did you come up with the name 'Zormurd' yourself, or was that Salvador's only contribution?"

"I don't know what you're talking about."

"He stole your stories, your characters, your entire fantasy macrocosm. He became rich and famous, albeit in a limited circle, while you played poker in a hut in the sand. And to top things off, he confided in you that he was going to take steps to protect his assets if he lost a lawsuit. You couldn't even sue him. You must have been seething."

"I started making up stories about Waldsenke when I was a kid. I was Zormurd, and Lady Maves was my girlfriend back in sixth grade. When she started sharing her lunch with a kid named Dwayne Pendark, I made him the villain. I could never draw them, so I just wrote about their adventures. Salvador loved the stories so much that I gave him all my old notebooks. He promised me that if he ever succeeded, he'd share the money with me. When the time came, he claimed that he'd merely used some of the names and settings, but the ideas were his own. Yeah, I was angry, but it was a long time ago. It doesn't prove I killed him."

I made a face. "No, it doesn't. Lieutenant Rosen has been complaining about the lack of forensic evidence, but this was a particularly messy way to kill someone. Some of the blood must have splattered on the murderer, yet not one witness noticed it. You can wash your hands and face, but it's very difficult to get bloodstains out of clothes. I think Lieutenant Rosen will find those stains on the street clothes you were wearing under your armor. You cleaned yourself up before you came to the banquet. Did you do the same earlier, before you put on the armor for the championship bout? If you didn't, there will be smears on the inside of the armor as well as on the clothes."

Lanya gave him a horrified look. "You did that to Salvador because of his silly comic books? Oh, Benny!"

"They weren't his," Benny said coldly, "and they weren't silly."

William cleared his throat. "Actually, they were. I leafed through one while I was picking up an order at the mall bookstore. The anachronisms were glaring. Several of the weapons were not developed until the sixteenth century. I fully expected to find one of the characters using a flashlight in the swamp."

I intervened before Benny could respond. "There was nothing anachronistic about the battle-ax. Did Angie materialize while you were putting on your armor, or did she wait until you went to Salvador's house the next day to hunt for your notebooks? You knew I was there, since my car was in the carport. If I'd come an hour later, would I have been the one to find her body?"

Benny poured the last of the wine down his throat and stood up. "I'm leaving. Everybody just sit there until I drive away, okay?" He staggered into the kitchen.

Peter went to the back door and motioned to an unseen figure. Jorgeson nodded at me as he stepped out of the darkness. After a brief whispered conversation, Peter let the door close and turned around. "Benny will be escorted home and asked to hand over the clothes and armor. If he does not comply, he'll be held until we get a warrant."

"Is that it?" demanded William, his eyes popping with eagerness. "Shouldn't you shoot him or something?"

"I'll look into a firing squad in the morning," Peter said. He held out his hand. "Your carriage awaits, Lady Clarissa."

I took his arm, as befitting my title, and we swept down the back steps as if we'd both been coronated.

"You were out awfully late," Caron said when I came into the kitchen the next morning. "You make such a big deal about me calling or leaving a note. Don't I deserve the same courtesy?"

"Yes, dear, you do." I started a pot of coffee and nibbled on the last stale doughnut while I waited. "I'll do better in the future."

"Yeah, right. Was Mr. Valens pleased that we're going to work on his stupid production?"

"I didn't have a chance to tell him, and if I were you, I'd let it go. He was in a nasty mood last night, and it may not improve for a long time. I do have some good news, though. Miss Thackery won't be teaching AP history in the fall, so you don't have to worry about the midterm paper."

"That means we'll get stuck with Mrs. Collins. She makes her upper-level classes memorize poetry and recite it in front of the class. One of the senior girls fainted in the middle of an Emily Dickinson sonnet. Too pathetic."

I tossed the remainder of the doughnut in the trash and poured a mug of coffee.

"You'll need to get the reading list as soon as possible and get busy before school starts. You're going to miss three weeks in October."

Her brow lowered. "Why?"

"You and Inez, if her parents agree, are coming along on the honeymoon. Peter brought it up last night and we talked about it for a long time. It will be a wonderful opportunity for us to see something more of the world, and very educational."

"Oh?" she said. "What if I don't want to go on *your* honeymoon? What am I supposed to do — sit in a hotel room and watch movies while you two . . . act like newlyweds? I'm old enough to stay home by myself for three weeks. You can call every couple of days and check on me. I'll call Sergeant Jorgeson if a serial killer tries to break down the door. Go on your own honeymoon with Peter, and leave me out of it. The idea's gross."

"We need passports," I said, "and tetanus boosters just to be safe. I don't think we have to worry about malaria or yellow fever."

"The only way I'm going some hideous place with mosquitoes is if you stuff me in a trunk and ship me there. I'll pound on the lid until someone hears me and lets me out, and then you'll be arrested for child abuse. I'll take my chances at a foster home."

"I'll have to find out how hot it will be," I continued. "We'll definitely need sunglasses and cameras. Sunscreen, too."

Caron crossed her arms. "You have totally lost your mind. You need to be medicated and locked up until these delusions go away. I promise I'll visit every Sunday afternoon with flowers and a copy of *The New York Times*. For a while, anyway. I may get bored with the whole thing."

"Several guidebooks, of course, and a phrase book, although I suspect most everybody will speak enough English for us to get along."

"Stop right now. You need a cold shower."

"I imagine we'll be taking lots of them in Egypt," I said serenely.

ABOUT THE AUTHOR

Joan Hess is the author of both the Claire Malloy and the Maggody mystery series. She is a winner of the American Mystery Award, a member of Sisters in Crime, and a former president of the American Crime Writers League. She lives in Fayetteville, Arkansas.